# JOIN IN THE ROMANCE OF A REGENCY CHRISTMAS

Let the beauty of the holiday season sweep you away to all the festivities of a traditional Christmas in Regency England. And enjoy the blossoming of romantic love in these six charming tales of holiday joy. Bedecking the halls with garlands, enjoying a moonlit sleigh ride, joining in a round of Christmas carols, watching the Yule log burn, and catching a few stolen kisses beneath the mistletoe — these are just a few of the enchanting moments you'll share with the characters in *A CHRISTMAS TO CHERISH*.

So treat yourself to a special Christmas gift and sit down wth Georgina Devon, Violet Hamilton, Valerie King, Mary Kingsley, Meg-Lynn Roberts, and Olivia Sumner for a Christmas you won't soon forget.

# A Memorable Collection of Regency Romances

## BY ANTHEA MALCOLM AND VALERIE KING

# A Christmas to Cherish

**GEORGINA DEVON**
**VIOLET HAMILTON**
**VALERIE KING**
**MARY KINGSLEY**
**MEG-LYNN ROBERTS**
**OLIVIA SUMNER**

**ZEBRA BOOKS**
**KENSINGTON PUBLISHING CORP.**

# CONTENTS

# A Gift of the Heart

## by Georgina Devon

"I want to make sure I understand your meaning perfectly, Miss Russell." The Marquis of Davenport's full, well-shaped mouth curved into a sardonic smile. "You want to become my next *chère amie.*"

Lavinia Ann Russell blanched, but she met Davenport's cold, black eyes without flinching. She couldn't afford to let him intimidate her into retracting her proposition. Others depended on her.

Her chin inched higher. "That is precisely what I meant, my lord."

The watery December sunlight coming through the library window glinted off his coffee-dark hair as Davenport took a step toward her. Small shivers skittered down Lavinia's spine, and she wished she could blame her reaction on the pervasive chill in the unheated London townhouse. But she could not.

Even now, his complexion unfashionably swarthy from years in the West Indies heat, and his skin marked with premature lines radiating from his eyes and bracketing a sensual mouth, he could make her pulse quicken. She didn't need the emotional upheaval this man had always been able to create in her heart. Her nerves were already stretched to the breaking point by the happenings of the last week.

Fortunately for her composure, he stopped his progress before reaching her. Lavinia relaxed, but only momentarily.

His gaze roved over her, lingering at her mouth, breasts, and hips. Red emblazoned her cheeks at his boldness, but

9

she held herself proudly under his intense scrutiny, returning as good as she got.

He was as slim today as he'd been at twenty-four, although, perhaps, less fashionable. His hair was worn a trifle too long, curling around his collar, and his jacket was just a shade too loose on his broad shoulders to be all the crack. But his powerful thighs were encased in formfitting inexpressibles of a buff color. Whipcord lean, he exuded an aura of power.

Lavinia knew she had made the right choice.

"So, Miss Russell," he propped his hip nonchalantly against the corner of the desk separating them, "you have decided to take up Harriette Wilson's calling. I wouldn't have thought it of you."

The color that had heated her cheeks fled, and she shivered in the cold room. "What you would have thought, my lord, is irrelevant."

For the first time since entering her library he smiled, a genuine showing of amusement that lit his dark eyes with an inner glow. It reminded her of the charm that had initially drawn her to him when she was only seventeen and enthralled by her first London season.

"Touché," he murmured, his eyes holding hers as a hawk holds its prey. "As you say, my opinion of your actions is not important. The only opinion of mine that matters is whether or not I will make you my next mistress."

Her fingers clenched in the folds of her black muslin morning dress. He was being more cruel than she'd anticipated, but then, he had reason. She'd once given him the cut direct in front of every stickler of the *ton*.

"However, Miss Russell, I want to know why you choose to follow this path and why you choose me to lead you down it."

She did not think her reasons were any of his business, but she could tell by the harsh line of his jaw that he wanted an answer and would persist until he got one. It would do her no good to say that she'd loved him since she was seventeen, and might very well do a great deal of harm. Davenport was in the market for a mistress, not a wife.

Still, she took a deep breath and decided to give as much of an explanation as she could without baring her heart to his contempt. "My lord—"

"Davenport."

"As you wish . . . Davenport. I have two younger siblings to care for: a brother in Eton and a sister in a finishing school." She paused to swallow the lump forming in her throat. "Emily was to have her come-out next year. Now all I hope for is enough funds to see her through this last year of school and then to settle her as a governess with a respectable family. I want John to finish at Eton and then, hopefully, get a position as secretary to some lord. Neither governesses nor companions, the only genteel forms of employment available to me, make the blunt necessary."

She studied his countenance for some reaction, any reaction, to her slang term for money, if not her reason for approaching him. There was none.

Instead he said, "I'd heard that Russell's suicide had left you strapped, but even the gossipmongers did not know to what extent. It must be great for you to take this drastic step."

Lavinia blinked rapidly to stop the moisture in her eyes from becoming tears. She did not hold Davenport's plain speaking about her father against him, he only repeated what every tongue in London was wagging. Nonetheless, it was impossible to keep the bitterness from her tone.

"The old tabbies lost no time in spreading the latest *on dit*." Smoothing at the fine weave of her black skirt, she met Davenport's look. "I loved my father, but he had many weaknesses, the greatest of which was gambling. The night he . . . he did away with himself, he wagered everything we had left. And that was not much since he'd been playing deeply for many years. When he lost it all on a single throw of the dice, he was unable to face the consequences."

She shrugged and closed her eyes to block out the memory, trying to let the pain of her loss flow into the acceptance she'd spent so many hours striving to reach. It had only been a month since her father's suicide, and in that time she'd met with the solicitor to learn the devastating condi-

11

tion of her father's finances and had written to tell John and then Emily why they could not come home for Christmas.

There was no home to come to. She was selling it to help pay their father's debts.

Despite her efforts, a lone tear coursed down her cheek, and she swiped at it with trembling fingers. She opened her eyes and took a deep, shuddering breath. "I've had to sell everything. There is nothing left for me to use to raise funds." On barely a whisper, she added, "And I've still ten thousand more pounds to find to pay off Father's gambling debts."

Davenport's eyes narrowed, but his voice was smooth and deep, not a hint of emotion marring its baritone depths. "You have great expectations from a protector."

At first she did not comprehend his meaning; then she realized that he was talking about the monies she needed. "No, I do not believe so. I intend to pay off Father's debts over time, not with a large sum gleaned from the man who decides to accept my proposition." Pausing to still the flutter of her vocal cords, she forced herself to speak clearly. "The solicitor says Father's largest creditor has agreed to give me five years to pay him back."

The marquis' mouth twisted into a sardonic grin. "Generous of him. What interest is he charging you for that gracious consideration?"

Had he always been this cynical? she wondered. The harsh angles of his cheek and jaw seemed even harder than she remembered.

Her eyes slid away from his piercing gaze as she answered. "No interest at all. While I have not met the gentleman, he has acted in a most humanitarian manner."

"Most generous, indeed," he murmured.

His long, blunt-tipped fingers picked up the quill she'd been using to write letters before he arrived. Fascinated by his deft, sure movements, she watched him finger the fine feathers in the shaft. The slow, provocative strokes were strangely exciting to her, and she allowed herself to imagine his fingers on her, perhaps sliding down her hair. Immediately, her skin flushed.

Grasping at any means to end her dangerous imaginings, Lavinia blurted, "Now that I've told you what you wish to know, do you accept my offer?"

Davenport's fingers stilled. Very carefully, he laid the quill down, not spilling a drop of the ink still visible on its point.

"You have not explained why I am the one with the dubious honor of deflowering you."

A small gasp escaped her at his crudity and it was on the tip of her tongue to upbraid him, but the mocking gleam in his eyes prevented her. He expected her to take umbrage. Well, she would not give him that satisfaction.

Composing her thoughts as best she could with his hooded gaze heavy on her, she replied, "Six years ago you seemed mildly interested in me, and I thought, if you still were, you might be willing to make me your . . . your *chère amie*."

Deceptively nonchalant, he brushed a speck of lint from his jacket sleeve, but she saw the tiny pulse that throbbed in the vein at his temple. She had upset him, and she was glad that she was not alone in her discomfort.

"So, you thought a rake of my stamp would be willing to debauch a decent woman simply because he took a liking to her. Well, you do have a point. At one time I might have agreed without a second thought, but I find that age has tempered my youthful exuberance."

Her eyes widened at his harsh criticism of himself, and the golden fire burning in the depths of his black gaze made her take a step back from him. "You mistake my reasons, milord. I considered you first because of all the men I know who could afford my offer, you are the one whom I thought most likely to find me acceptable for the position. It has nothing to do with the reputation you bear."

A laugh, harsh and derisive, issued from between his big, even teeth. "At least you don't mince words and are honest. I prefer my women to be honest."

With an abrupt shift of his weight, he pushed away from the desk and paced to the mantel where he propped one shining Hessian on the grate. Frowning into the empty fireplace, he stated, "No wonder it is damnably cold in here.

13

Haven't you money for coal?"

She bit her lip. Embarrassment at the straits to which she'd been reduced warmed her so that the lack of a fire hardly mattered to her. "None for coal or anything else."

His frown deepened until his brows were a midnight bar across his forehead. Even his mouth was thinned. A thrust of his powerful thighs and he surged away from the empty grate and bore down on her, stopping when he once more reached the desk.

"If you become my mistress, Miss Russell, the Polite World will never receive you again. Your brother and sister will be ostracized by the *ton* as well."

His words pounded into her, and she took a step back, as though that might shield her from the irritation she felt emanating from his tautly muscled body. Still worrying her lower lip, she answered, "At least we shall eat."

"True."

"And no one in the *ton* receives us now. Getting a respectable job as a governess or companion would not change matters. Father committed suicide only after losing everything he owned, including the settlements put aside for his children. Not only are we stigmatized by Father's desperate act, but we are poor. Two solecisms the *ton* won't forgive."

"What about relatives?" His voice was harsh.

If possible, he appeared to be increasingly angry with the situation. Was he going to refuse her? For some reason, she'd never considered that he might turn her down. It appeared that she should have.

Anxiety lent her voice stinging animation. "None living whom I would care to appeal to or who would help if I asked." A small smile curved her lips at memories of her parent ranting and raving about both his family and his wife's. "Father never endeared himself to his relations."

"A ne'er-do-well for a parent and now you want a rake for a protector."

Her spine stiffened, and she met his sardonic gaze with a strength born of her own beginning irritation. "Since my father is not here to defend himself, I ask that you refrain from further comment about his character. As for a rake as protector, I am under the impression that only rakes keep mistresses."

A bark of laughter relaxed the chiseled lines of his face and the taut set of his shoulders. "You have much to learn of men. Perhaps this arrangement is for the best. However, I've no intention of buying a pig in a poke. Come out from behind that desk so I can see you better."

His abrupt order took Lavinia by surprise, and before she even realized she was doing it, she stood in front of the desk. There was no barrier between them now, only empty space. For an instant, apprehension skittered along her nerves.

Only then did she comprehend what she'd done automatically. Davenport had not even agreed to make her his mistress, and she was doing his bidding.

She had no choice. He was the only man she could tolerate touching her in the intimate ways required by such a liaison.

And when he advanced on her, moving with a lithe grace that was at once both dangerous and enthralling, tingling excitement sparked along her skin. But when he circled her, as though she were a mare up for auction, her emotions nearly exploded.

"I am not a piece of horseflesh for sale at Tattersalls."

He finished his circumlocution before answering. "True, Miss Russell, but you are a woman in search of a protector. In many ways, the situation is similar."

Mortification stained her skin from the roots of her hair to the flushed tenderness of her bosom. He was right, and there was nothing she could say in refutation.

Before she had calmed herself as much as she could under the circumstances, his hand shot out and his forefinger lifted her chin. Heat licked along her flesh from where he touched her, but she kept her gaze firmly on his face, searching for any feeling he might expose.

Slowly, he moved her head from side to side as he studied her features. "I once thought you the most interesting chit on the marriage mart," he murmured as though thinking out loud. "Now I believe you are the most beautiful woman I've ever seen."

15

Lavinia's eyes widened. Her? With her freckled nose and pale complexion, she was no diamond of the first water. He must be quizzing her. But what she saw in the blackness of his pupils, the deep brown of his irises, put the lie to her assumption.

Fire and heat blazed at her. Even as untutored in the ways of Eros as she was, she could not mistake the message his eyes sent. Desire, as untrammeled as the man holding her captive with only a finger, stared at her from the depths of his disillusioned soul. Her stomach tightened and her breath came in rapid spurts. Almost, she was afraid.

But as suddenly as the flame had come upon him, it disappeared behind the heavily lashed barrier of his eyelids as they slid down to hide all but the lower portion of his irises. He looked bored beyond tolerance. But he did not release her.

With his other hand, he lightly touched a curl at her temple. "Hair the perfect shade of red that Titian made famous. You are everything a man could want, and I'd be a fool to refuse you."

Refuse her? That could not happen. Lavinia took her courage in hand. Through lips gone soft and pouting at his touch, she murmured, "Then do not."

For an instant, passion blazed again in his eyes, and she thought he would crush her to him. But he did not. Instead, without saying a word, he released her and stalked to the fireplace.

His desertion left her feeling bereft and cold, strangely defeated. She knew she was lost.

Casting modesty to the winds, she pursued him. Barely a foot from him, the faint tang of his sandalwood lotion in her nostrils, she finally stopped. "What is your verdict, mi-lord?"

"You, Miss Russell, are as bold as a silver-eyed fox. A vixen, in fact."

She nodded, knowing that now was not the time to retreat. A sixth sense told her that, allowed to escape now, the marquis would never make her his ladybird. She could not let that happen.

"And you, Davenport, are a dark-visaged brigand. We

16

should make a good pair."

His lips curved up at the right corner, emphasizing the creases around his mouth. "Come here."

Once more she did his bidding until only the sighs of their breathing separated them. Excitement coursed through her blood as she read his intent in the hard lines of his face.

Slowly, exquisitely slowly, his head lowered until his mouth hovered over hers. His dark eyes stared into her light ones, giving her the opportunity to refuse.

Lavinia's hands clenched into fists at her sides. Her heart pounded until she thought it would jump out of her bosom. But she did not step back. She would give him her kiss and take from him the passion lurking in the depths of his soul.

As she watched, his eyes closed and his lips took hers. They moved languidly over her mouth, tasting her and teasing her with the promise of something more . . . something deeper. Her breasts tightened, the nipples hardening.

When he at last broke the contact, it was all she could do not to follow him. Dazed, and yet more alive than she'd ever felt in her life, Lavinia saw him move away.

"A cold fish, indeed, Miss Russell." His mouth twisted into a cynical grin. "It does not bode well for our future enjoyment."

His voice, deep and frigid, came as a shock to her, so absorbed had she been in the effects of his kiss on her body and mind. Then the import of his words penetrated the pleasurable haze.

"How dare you," she sputtered, mortified by his denouncement of their first kiss. "I am not some opera dancer with years of practice at my disposal."

"That was abundantly clear."

He left her stranded near the empty fireplace as he collected his many-caped greatcoat, beaver, and walking stick from the leather chair on which he'd deposited them minutes earlier. Turning back to her, he said, "But we shall soon remedy that lack in your education, Vixen. Fear not."

The arrogant cad. Lavinia drew herself up, tempted to tell him to go to the devil, but knowing she would only regret the harsh words. She appeased her ire by saying regally,

17

"I trust you can find your way out without assistance."

Setting his beaver at a raffish angle on his black locks, Davenport raised his gold-handled cane to his forehead in salute. "I can find my way in hell, if needs be." Pausing at the library door, he added, "My secretary will be in touch, with instructions."

Her shoulders sagged with relief. He intended to make her his mistress. She knew he would honor her requirements as well. He had not said so, but she sensed that he would.

The sound of the front door closing made her jump. He was gone for now, but soon he would return.

*What had she done?*

Her trembling knees threatened to send her catapulting to the floor. Her palms turned clammy, and her breath came in ragged little gasps that barely kept her from fainting.

*She had propositioned a man—asked to become his mistress and then agreed when he accepted her offer.*

On legs that shook, she made her way to the desk and sank into the huge leather wingback chair positioned there. She sat not a moment too soon. All physical strength fled her.

The enormity of her actions flooded her. Her world would never be the same. No longer would she be the eldest daughter of an English baron, not in the eyes of the Polite World. Forever more, she would be labeled whore, prostitute. A woman who sold her body for her livelihood.

She closed her eyes and her head fell onto her folded arms. For moments only, she allowed herself to wallow in remorse and self-pity. Then she lifted her head and squared her shoulders. No matter what she did, she was still the same person inside that she had always been. Only she could make herself feel like dirt, and she would not do that. In her heart, she knew she was doing the right thing, the only thing open to her.

Davenport would no more offer marriage to her than any other man of the *ton*. She did not expect that of him, had not expected it six years before. It did not matter that her heart beat faster when she thought of him or that her breathing

18

had liked to stop when she saw him for the first time in six years.

Nothing mattered but the welfare of her family. And she would never regret her decision. It had been made for others as much as for herself.

She firmed her jaw. Not giving herself further time to think on it, she picked up the quill Davenport had so recently caressed and dipped it into the ink stand. Then with determined calm, she continued the letter to Emily that she had just begun when the marquis arrived.

To her chagrin, the first word she wrote was marred by a large blob of black ink. She tried to blot the stain, but her fingers shook so badly that she only succeeded in spreading the ink more. Lavinia knew it would be impossible to finish the letter that day.

Taking a deep breath to try to calm her tremors, she rose and went to the window. Outside a light snow was beginning to fall. In two weeks' time it would be Christmas. She hoped Davenport would send for her before then.

She'd never spent a Christmas away from her family, and she knew this one would be hard. Yet if she were unhappy, how would poor Emily and John be feeling, stuck at schools with no one around? At least she would have Davenport.

Just the thought of his name warmed her in spite of the chill emanating from the paned window. And the memory of his kiss was a heated brand on her lips. She was glad she'd chosen him. Her response to his kiss told her everything would be all right between them. Just as she'd instinctively known so many years before.

Oh, she would be embarrassed and awkward, but she would find pleasure with him. And if she wanted more than pleasure at his hands? In her current circumstances, anything more from him was beyond her reach. Once . . .

But she had given him the cut direct at her father's urgings. Davenport was a rake, her father had insisted, and rakes had only one use for green girls. It was not marriage. She would never know if her father had been right.

Now she would have to settle for the considerations due a man's mistress, and never look back. It would never be enough to content her, but she would make it do.

The sound of the knocker reverberating off the entrance door pulled her from these ruminations. Who could it be? Since her father's death, no one, not even *old friends* had called.

Curiosity got the better of her, inciting her to move quickly in answering the summons. Outside stood a very dignified young man, his greatcoat pulled up around his chin to ward off the cold wind beginning to whip through the trees. White flakes sparkled on his hat's brim.

"Ma'am." He bowed. "I am Lord Davenport's secretary, Mr. Jennings. I've come to make arrangements for your removal."

Surprise made Lavinia step backward. "I had not expected the marquis to act so quickly." Then she saw the young man's lips were blue around the edges. "Won't you please come in?"

"Thank you, but first I must fetch Mary and tell the coachman to walk the horses."

Confused by his words, Lavinia asked, "Who is Mary and why must she come in?"

He smiled. "Mary is to pack your bags. Lord Davenport surmised that you would need help."

Lavinia flushed. The marquis knew she had no servants, so he sent his own to do the work. It was a gesture of kindness she would not have attributed to him. Not that she thought him unkind, but she had never thought him to be concerned with the mundane.

As soon as Jennings and Mary returned from the carriage, Lavinia ushered them into the library, where she could explain just what needed doing. Shortly thereafter, everyone was at work and before Lavinia quite realized it, she was packed and seated in a spacious barouche with a loaded fourgon following.

After one last look at the townhouse in which she'd spent the past seven years of her life, she asked her companions, "Where to now?"

Mr. Jennings answered, "To Lord Davenport's hunting box on the Scottish border. His lordship will meet us there."

"His lordship is late arriving," Lavinia said to no one in particular, there being no other person in her bedroom. Mary had long since gone to sleep, it being past midnight and the small household keeping country hours.

She threw off the downy comforter and donned her robe and slippers. Walking to the window, she was glad the moss green carpet had a thick pile. This might be a hunting box with only a master suite and connecting room for the lady of the house, but Davenport had spared no expense in outfitting it.

At the window, she pulled back the heavily napped, cream velvet curtains to reveal a full moon riding high in the black sky. Stars glittered around it like a celestial crown. Not a cloud marred the pristine beauty.

Lavinia took a deep breath of the cool air emanating from the glass and told herself that Davenport would arrive soon. He had to. How else could she become his mistress and earn the wages she so desperately needed?

Before leaving to visit his parents, Jennings had informed her that the marquis had arranged to pay the next quarter's tuition for her brother and sister. She was grateful for that, but wished Davenport would arrive.

A heavy sigh weighted down her shoulders. She prepared to release the drapery, but a movement caught her eye.

Then she saw it again. Someone or something was in the copse of oaks less than a hundred yards from the house. Squinting, she thought she could make out the outlines of horse and rider. But who would be out there at this time of night?

Surely it was not Davenport. If it were, he would ride boldly to the door.

Could it be someone with a sinister purpose? The only people in the house were herself, Mary, and Mrs. Hatchet, who was the cook and housekeeper. Jaimie, a big strapping lad, was in the small stable, too far away for Lavinia to reach him before the horseman would be down on them.

She had to do something. But what?

Then she had it. The gun room. There was a musket in there, and she knew how to use one. Her grandfather had taught her when he was alive, wanting to take her with him when hunting. While she'd learned to use the weapon, she'd never been able to kill with it.

Nonetheless, she squared her shoulders, there was a first time for everything. She sped to the door and down the stairs, to skid on the highly polished parquet of the foyer. Catching herself, she rounded the corner and bolted into the gun room.

It took her several precious minutes to light a candle. A few minutes more and she had the musket out of its glass case and loaded. She hoped it was in good repair.

Just in time. The sound of the front door opening and then closing came to her straining ears. The air whooshed out of her lungs. Her hands became wet from fear.

Somehow the horseman had gotten in the front door. Perhaps it had not been locked. She had thought Mrs. Hatchet locked it every night, but she might have forgotten this evening. They'd been busy planning the Christmas decorations.

Boots on the flooring echoed like cannon shot to her sensitized ears. The hair on her nape stood up. She wanted to sink into the floor, or hide in the cubbyhole of the pedestal desk. It was impossible. She was the only one awake, and she was the only one with the wherewithal to protect them all. Mary's life, and Mrs. Hatchet's, depended on her.

Careful to make as little noise as possible, she made her way to the door. She was within five feet of it when it opened. Fear, sharp as a knife, stabbed through Lavinia, making her breathe in short, painful drags.

Because the light was almost nonexistent this far from the candle, she could barely see the intruder. The man was large and loomed above her. But she held her ground, bringing the musket up.

"Stop or I will shoot." Her voice sounded calm in her ringing ears, and she managed to keep the musket steady against her shoulder.

"That thing will leave a nasty bruise on your shoulder if

you do."

"Davenport!" His name was a catharsis, leaving her muscles as weak as fresh blancmange.

"In the frozen flesh." He took the weapon from her limp hands and strode to the desk where he laid it down. "Why aren't the fires lit? I have standing orders that fires be going in this room at all times pending my arrival."

Indignation at his arrogant demand followed fast on the relief Lavinia had felt. She jammed her fists akimbo on her hips. "If you want fires, milord, then you should notify someone of your imminent arrival. As it was, I instructed Mrs. Hatchet not to lay fires in rooms that were not being used. You may be as wealthy as Golden Ball, but there is no sense in wasting money."

"Frugality is not one of my vices," the marquis drawled, efficiently lighting two braces of candles so that the small room shone as though two bright suns were blazing within its walls. Only then did he look back at Lavinia.

His fingers stilled on the brass candelabra he was adjusting. His face, lean and expressionless, tightened into gaunt planes that contrasted starkly with the shadows over his heavy-lidded eyes. But his mouth, that wide, expressive instrument of pleasure seemed to beckon Lavinia closer.

A jolt of heat flashed straight to her stomach as she remembered the feel of his lips on hers and the delight they had given her. She wanted him to kiss her again.

When he spoke, his voice was deep and husky. "Vastly becoming attire and entirely appropriate. You are a fast learner, Vixen."

His unwelcome compliment broke the spell of anticipation that had held Lavinia dangerously in thrall. No longer did she want to feel his flesh on hers. Instead, she wanted to return his taunt.

She pulled the front of her velvet robe together across her breasts before retorting, "If I am a fast learner, it is not because I've been given instruction."

His mobile mouth widened into a wolfish grin. "Do not sharpen your fangs on me, for I will show you a better use of your skills than words."

So saying, he advanced on her with slow, measured tread that made her feel as though her stomach were trying to go through the small of her back. His eyes glowed in the radiance from the candles and his white teeth, showing between his parted lips, gleamed.

The moment Lavinia had been both dreading and anticipating was upon her. Davenport would take her, as their bargain gave him the right to do.

She licked dry lips. Her heart thumped until she thought it would jump from her throat. But, oh, the excitement was a delicious thrill that made her skin feel as though it were shimmering with electricity, like the sky just before a lightning storm.

When he was close enough that her robe swept his Hessians, he stopped and laid his hands on her upper arms. Sliding his palms along her shoulders, he smiled down at her.

Lavinia watched his eyes darken as his hands moved over her. The breath caught in her lungs when his warm skin met her exposed neck. He cupped his hands around her throat, like a magnificent choker, and his thumbs met in an inverted V at the tip of her chin. Resolutely, he urged her chin upward until all he had to do was bend his head downward and his lips would be on hers.

Lavinia's breasts tingled in suspense as she waited for his kiss. Of their own volition, her arms lifted and her fingers curled around Davenport's forearms, ensuring that he did not move away.

To her regret, instead of kissing her, he spoke, "Your eyes are the clear bright silver of the finest sterling. I spent many long hours in the West Indies wondering what color they would be when passion rides you."

Using the pad of one thumb, he rubbed her lower lip, sending sparks of desire streaking through her body. He increased the pressure of his strokes until her mouth parted and her breathing came in little ragged gasps.

Still, he did not kiss her. Yet, his gaze never wavered from her face and a slow, satisfied chuckle started deep in his chest. "I believe, Vixen, that when the time is right, your eyes will be like pewter; a smoky, satiny gray."

Would he never stop talking and kiss her, Lavinia began to wonder. She resisted the urge to rise on tiptoe and take what he'd been teasingly withholding. She was a lady—or had been raised one—and ladies did not press a man for his advances.

At last, his head lowered and Lavinia's eyelids slid down to cover the darkening of her irises as her blood heated with anticipation of his caress. After all these years of regretting the snubbing she'd dealt him, she was about to enjoy his lovemaking.

But it was not her mouth he was aiming for. His lips brushed against her temple, and then he pushed her away.

Lavinia's eyes snapped open, and her fingers clenched on his arms. "What game do you play with me, Davenport?"

Self-derision was rife in his reply. "I don't play with green chits, Miss Russell. What you and I share will be much more than parlor games. But not tonight."

If he'd slapped her, he could not have discommoded her more. How dare he make such a cake of her.

Her hands dropped away from his arms, and she drew herself up stiffly. "I see, milord. You have a headache."

Not waiting for his answer, she twirled on the ball of her foot and fled from the room. His rich, deep laughter followed her into the hall and up the stairs.

Slamming her bedroom door, Lavinia paced the room. She had worn her heart on her sleeve, had let him see the ardor she had sworn to herself not to reveal. And he had acted like an avuncular uncle toward her.

Not only was her heart bruised, her pride was pricked. And furthermore, unless he made her his mistress, she could not collect the monies she needed so desperately. Something had to be done and done quickly, for John and Emily's happiness if not for her own.

She advanced on the dressing table and stared into the oval mirror. The faint, yellow glow of a single candle showed her exactly what she was afraid it would. Freckles dotted her nose and cheekbones like those of some sunburnt waif. No wonder Davenport had only brushed her temples with his mouth. He was much too experienced a man to be interested in a woman who looked more child than seductress.

With a disgusted mutter, she slathered an extra amount of Roman Balsam into her skin. The mixture of barley flour, almonds, and honey was supposed to get rid of freckles. But in the ten years she'd been using it, she'd only managed to make them fade, not go away entirely.

Adding an extra dab, she told herself it was better than nothing. And nothing seemed to be all she was going to get from Davenport if she did not do something to turn the situation around.

Early the next morning, Lavinia was conferring with Mrs. Hatchet about the best places to find greenery for the Christmas bough and other decorations, when she heard Davenport's deep tones in the hall. He was talking with Jaimie. No doubt, about the care of his horses. Davenport had a reputation as a neck-and-neck rider, and his cattle were reportedly the finest in the realm.

Lavinia stepped outside the dining room in time to catch Davenport. "Milord?"

He turned at her question and his gaze traveled from her head to her toes, but no smile curved his mouth. "I am on my way out to the stable."

His curtness made her bristle, but Lavinia held tight rein on her temper. If she were to earn the monies she so desperately needed, then she must be in his proximity. Not to even consider the wishes of her heart.

She infused her voice with brisk matter-of-factness. "That is perfect, Davenport. Jaimie can hitch up the pony cart, and you may escort me to several of the places Mrs. Hatchet has recommended for gathering holly and yew."

One of his dark brows rose. "Yew?"

"To ward off witches, of course," she said briskly, almost laughing at the look of disbelief on his face. Not giving him the opportunity to refuse, she took her heavy wool pelisse from the side table on which she'd laid it earlier and allowed Jaimie to help her don it.

26

She smiled her thanks at Jaimie. "Besides, Davenport, while this may not be your principal seat and my brother and sister are not here, it is still only four days till Christmas. There is no reason why we should not enjoy the season. On Christmas Eve you will have to go with Jaimie and get a Yule log. I trust Mrs. Hatchet has a piece from last year's log put by to light this year's choice."

Davenport propped his left shoulder nonchalantly against the wall and crossed his arms over his broad chest. "You are a managing baggage, and I have not even installed you in my household on a permanent basis."

Her fingers paused infinitesimally in buttoning up her pelisse, but she refused to let his words hurt. "Do not be snide, Davenport. It does not become you."

"Neither does a ring through my nose."

But he pushed away from the wall and followed her to the stables where he helped Jaimie harness a complacent mare to the cart. After assisting Lavinia into the vehicle, he spread a warm blanket across her lap. That done, he got in the vehicle.

When he sat beside her on the narrow seat, his thigh was a hot brand against hers, Lavinia had to stifle the little gasp that rose in the back of her throat. As though he sensed her reaction, he slanted her a roguish glance that brought the heat to her cheeks.

"Comfortable?" he asked, flicking the reins to start the mare. "If not, we can ride horses."

"Perfectly." She forced her leg muscles to relax against the hard length of his. "I was just taken unawares by the way the cart swayed when you mounted."

He grinned down at her, and she was certain he knew she lied.

Try as she would, her body would not let her ignore his warmth so close to her. He beckoned to her like a blazing fire. His form even blocked out some of the bitingly cold wind that was coming from the north.

Davenport breathed deeply of the air. "There will be snow within forty-eight hours. I can smell it."

Shivering, Lavinia said, "It feels as though there could be

27

snow now."

He grinned at her. "Regretting your impetuosity in coming out in this weather?"

She lifted her chin and smiled at him. "No. I believe in seeing to what needs doing and not looking back. Life can not be lived looking over your shoulder."

He nodded. "A good philosophy, but not always easy to follow."

Lavinia studied his profile as he maneuvered the farm track. He was all angles and lines, harsh and unyielding. Only his mouth, the lips full and chiseled, spoke of passion that could burn a woman to cinders—or make a married woman leave her husband for the promise in his dark eyes.

Before she could stop herself, the words tumbled out. "Did you love her?"

She had thought the answer no longer mattered and had forced the question from her mind, not even allowing herself to contemplate it while she prepared to ask him to sponsor her. It appeared that she had not known her own feelings.

When she'd given him the cut direct at Almacks', so many years ago, she'd immediately regretted it and would have hastened to make whatever amends were necessary. But Davenport took that opportunity from her by running away the next day with another man's wife. The news had brought Lavinia to her knees, for—yes, she could admit it to herself—even then she had loved him.

Frowning, his lips a thin line, he turned on her. "What did you ask?"

Lavinia met his glare openly, but she had to clasp her hands together under cover of the blanket to stop their shaking. "I asked, 'Did you love her?' "

His voice as icy as the wind cutting through Lavinia's pelisse, he said, "Whom are we discussing?"

"Lady Hyde."

Without warning, he stopped the pony, sending Lavinia off balance so that she very nearly fell from the vehicle. She had not expected this reaction from him. She'd thought him a man of the world who, at worst, would tell her to mind her own affairs, not his.

In slow measured tones, Davenport said, "Lady Hyde is with her new husband in France. Madeline was a childhood friend of mine, nothing more."

Confused, but determined to learn all that he would reveal, Lavinia pursued the answers. "Then why did you run away with her?"

His eyes seemed to be staring into the past. "Madeline sent a note to my lodgings, which I found upon returning from Almacks'. She'd been married to an old man during her first Season, but she'd always been in love with Robert Matheson, a Scot who was a younger son with no future but the military. When she and I disappeared, I was escorting her to Matheson, who was badly wounded at Salamanca. Society chose to see the situation differently."

Relief at his disavowal of love for another woman washed over Lavinia, making her feel almost lightheaded. But she was still perplexed over the treatment his father had accorded him. "Since that was the way of it, why did your father denounce you? Why did he insist on disinheriting you?"

His gaze focused on her face, but instead of seeing bitterness in his eyes as she'd expected, she saw maturity and understanding.

"The duke was disappointed in his son and ashamed of his heir. To my father, the future Duke of Umberland should bear no moral taint. No matter that I had not seduced Madeline, he would not listen to me, and I had no way of proving that I did not make love to Madeline on the journey." His shoulders moved under the many layers of his greatcoat as though he were shrugging off a heavy burden. "When I returned two months later without Lady Hyde, it only made the situation more reprehensible in his eyes."

Impulsively, she put a gloved hand on his arm. Her voice trembled with indignation at his hurt. "So, he disowned you. The *ton* says he banished you to the West Indies, changed his will leaving every item not entailed to a distant cousin, and forbade anyone to speak your name in any of his residences. How can you be so accepting?"

He took her hand from his arm and raised it to his lips.

Even though he kissed her through a thick leather glove, his touch burned her flesh.

"You are young, Vixen, and your blood runs hot. My father is an old man who had his dreams ruined by my actions. It took many years, but finally the heat of the West Indies' sun burnt the anger from me. It is not always easy, but I can understand why he behaved as he did." A sardonic smile twisted his lips. "And it does not hurt that I am now a wealthy man in my own right because of my labors in those sweltering islands." Then, as abruptly as she'd begun the talk, he ended it. He released her hand and urged the pony onward. "But enough of my past."

Lavinia understood from his tone that the discussion was closed. Her heart was heavy for the rejection he had been through, and she longed to reach out and comfort him in any way he would allow. A look at his stern jaw told her more clearly than words that he did not want her compassion.

Neither did he want to talk with her, Lavinia decided several hours later as they trudged wearily into the hall of the hunting box, their arms laden with greenery. Since the revelations in the pony cart, Davenport had not spoken another word to her, nor had he allowed her to initiate any further conversation.

Well, two can play mum, Lavinia decided, taking off her soaked pelisse and handing it to Mary who was doing double duty in the wake of limited servants. "Thank you. I will take dinner in my room," she said.

Before Mary could answer, Davenport interjected, "Miss Russell will eat in the dining room with me. Please see that Hatchet prepares plenty. Gathering evergreens for Christmas has given me an appetite. And we missed lunch."

"I will—"

He stared at Lavinia, his lean body relaxed but his eyes hard. Softly, so that only she could hear, he said, "Remember our bargain."

"That would be hard not to do when I am a single female under your roof." *And when every fiber of her being tingled with the awareness of his blatant masculinity.*

30

He chuckled and his large hand descended on the small of her back. Warmth radiated from his caress until it encompassed her entire body. It was only a touch, the bare brushing of his hand.

The intensity of her reaction scared her. With a searing intake of breath, Lavinia jerked away from the contact and hurried up the stairs to change.

Behind the heavy oak of her door, and only then, she finally felt safe from the uncontrollable desire he evoked in her. She chided herself for being a fool. It would be better for her and more enjoyable for him that she did react so brazenly to his slightest stroke.

When she went down for dinner, Lavinia had composed herself sufficiently to watch with equanimity as Mary served them the simple, one-course meal and then withdrew to the kitchen where she would eat with Mrs. Hatchet and Jaimie. However, the maid was not long removed before Lavinia began to feel uneasy in the silence.

"For being so overbearing and insisting that we sup together, Davenport, the least you could do is engage me in conversation."

"Is it?" He cut a bite out of the succulent roast beef that was mounded on his plate and ate it with obvious enjoyment. "And I suppose that you also expect me to play the gallant."

"It would not go amiss."

"Very well, Vixen. As a gallant protector, I've provided your brother and sister with Christmas gifts. I was sure that you would wish it so."

His wording made it sound as though she expected him to do these things for her. Like . . . like a kept woman. Bile rose in her throat and she wanted to leave the table, but knew that if she ran from him and his hurtful words now, she would be running from him as long as their relationship lasted.

"That was very considerate of you, milord. May I ask what you gave them?"

His black eyes watched her like a hawk studying its prey. Almost, she felt as though he tested her. But it was a silly

31

idea and she shrugged it away.

He took another bite of the meat and chewed slowly. "I sent your sister a single strand of pearls, as befits a young lady. For your brother, I chose a prime-blooded stallion."

She had been wrong in London when she'd told herself she was the only person who could make her feel like a slut. "Those are too expensive. I cannot allow you to send them."

Davenport picked up his wineglass and swirled it so that the dark ruby liquid caught the candlelight and sparkled like blood. "They have already been delivered."

Humiliation squeezed her chest like a vise. "Emily and John will wonder where I got the means to purchase such extravagant items."

He took a sip of wine before replying. "And they will not wonder where the money comes from to keep them in school?"

Anger began to color her cheeks and to give her the strength to withstand his continued belittlement. "I told them there was just enough money left from the estate to pay their last tuition."

"Ah," he said, drawing the word out, his full lips thin, white lines. "You were very sure of your marketability."

He had done everything but call her a whore. She raised her chin. "I did what I had to. And not you or anyone else will make me feel cheap for doing so."

Fueled by pain and fury, she pushed up from the table and stormed from the room. Only later, huddled under the warmth of a thick down comforter, did she allow the tears to fall.


This is indeed a horrible Christmas season, Lavinia thought for the umpteenth time. Even decorating the parlor, with holly and yew on the mantel and over the doorways, did nothing to lift the pall of melancholy that Davenport's treatment at dinner the previous night had brought on.

Only two other times had she cried herself to sleep. The first had been after her mother's funeral, the second had been the night she had found her father's body.

Her despondent mood was interrupted by Mrs. Hatchet's voice coming from the doorway. "Very nice, miss. This may be his lordship's hunting box, but a woman's touch does not go amiss."

Lavinia smiled with delight at Mrs. Hatchet. The cook cum housekeeper was a stout woman with iron gray hair pulled back into a severe bun that did nothing to dampen the jolly contentment of her features.

"Thank you, Mrs. Hatchet. I thought that after the rooms are decorated we would make a Kissing Bough." She blushed to mention the old custom, but the holiday was already an unhappy one, she did not want to further darken it by leaving the Kissing Bough and its twelve candles out.

"A lovely idea, miss," Hatchet said, beaming like a brightly polished apple. "I will just fetch Mary to help. If you do not mind, that is. I daresay she would like to catch young Jaimie under the mistletoe."

Lavinia laughed, beginning to relish the fun of preparing the small house for the holidays. Davenport might treat her like a tramp, but the servants were all as respectful as though she were the marquis' wife, not his doxy.

And several hours later, mending one of Davenport's fine lawn shirts, Lavinia decided she did almost feel like his wife. To her left the fire burned brightly, warming the small parlor and casting an orange glow on the work in her hands.

She felt almost content. The small, neat stitches required to darn the cuffs forced her to concentrate on her task and not to dwell on thoughts of Davenport and the hopes she'd once entertained in regard to him.

She'd been a green girl that first season, but she was a naive chit no more. A man of Davenport's stamp did not want anything respectable to do with her—never had.

"So this is where you have gotten off to."

At the sound of his voice, running over her nerves like smooth honey, soothing and beckoning in one easy stroke, she looked up. He was leaning against the door jamb, his hair dipping rakishly over his left brow. He was not classically handsome, his features too irregular for that; nonetheless, she found him mesmerizing. Longing for what

33

he would never give her made her heart ache and her throat tighten.

He strode into the room, taking the chair opposite her and stretching out his long legs until his booted feet almost touched her slippered ones. His shirt was open at the neck and black, glossy hairs curled around the white lawn. Her awareness heightened at the sight.

"Still mad at me for last night?" When she did not answer, he shrugged. His eyes, hooded, roved over her with leisurely thoroughness. "You will have to grow a thicker skin, Vixen. What I did was nothing compared to the extravagance some fools lavish on their *chère amies*."

His continued derision bothered her more than she could admit, even to herself. Perhaps he was beginning to regret their arrangement and seeking to disgust her enough that she would leave. The thought turned her blood cold. But she had to know if he had tired of her before they had even begun their journey of desire.

"Davenport, do you have a particular reason for these continued insults? If so, pray tell me." She was proud of the way she kept her voice steady even though her hands were beginning to shake with mingled ire and dread.

His features gave nothing away, and his body remained loose limbed. "Should I?"

"You answer a question with a question. Evasion tactics ever mean there is something hidden." With slow deliberation, she folded the shirt she'd been mending and set it back into the wicker basket at her feet. "If you are trying to get me to renege on our agreement, then please say so and stop all of this petty sniping."

"I am merely testing your mettle." If possible he seemed to lounge more completely in the leather chair, but his eyes remained sharp. "Whose shirt are you mending?"

Irritated beyond measure, she spoke sharply. "Yours."

"I do not pay you to sew. Any woman can prick cloth with a needle, but only one can share my bed."

Lavinia flushed, and told herself that the roaring fire was too hot and too close for comfort. She was not a mouse to be toyed with at his leisure.

"Then why do you not take me to your bed?"

"Why do I not?" he mused, his long, blunt fingers templing under his chin as he studied her. "I have asked myself that very question since leaving your London townhouse."

"And?"

Abruptly, he rose until he towered above her, his shadow falling over her and darkening the room. "Come." His hand reached out to her.

Lavinia knew that once she put her hand in his there would be no turning back. Her heart as well as her body would be in his keeping for as long as he chose to hold them.

A knock sounded on the door. Torn between relief and chagrin, Lavinia turned from Davenport.

"Pardon me, miss," Mary said, drawing back even as she entered. "I . . . I didn't know. That is, I came for the mending."

Taking pity on the young woman, Lavinia stood up and took the basket to the maid. "Thank you for letting me do it, Mary. I enjoy sewing very much."

Mary bobbed a quick curtsy, twisting to include the marquis in the deference. Then she bolted.

But to Lavinia's way of thinking the damage was done. Davenport, his back to her, had one booted foot on the grate, and he was staring into the leaping flames with stark concentration. His complete posture rebuffed any overture she might make.

Doubting that he would even deign to be social, Lavinia held her head up and left. Tomorrow would be another day.


The next morning Lavinia stared out her bedroom window, her hair still hanging about her waist and her dressing gown pulled tight to ward off the December chill. Outside snow blanketed the ground and hung like a pure, velvet mantle from the barren trees and bushes. Davenport's prediction of snow had been correct.

Why didn't she feel as though it were Christmas? True her father's death was still fresh in her heart, and her brother and sister were not with her, but Davenport was here. That should have been enough.

Once it might have been, but no longer. He did not love her. If he did, she knew in her soul that his love would be enough for every Christmas of her life.

Her heart heavy, she turned from the window and made her way to the dresser where she took up a damp cloth and began to wipe away the Roman Balsam. At the first swipe, she heard the door open and whirled around.

Davenport stood in the doorway that connected her room to his. This was the first time the door had been opened since she'd arrived, and the knowledge of why that passage was there, combined with the dynamic presence of the man, caused her heart to skip a beat before racing like a thousand horses' hooves.

He was casually dressed in a navy hunting jacket, buff breeches, and Hessians. Consequently, she felt naked and tried with nerveless fingers to pull her robe even more tightly around her.

"Davenport! What are you doing here? I thought you would be at your morning ride."

He sauntered into the room, his arms swinging easily at his sides, his eyes traveling over the length of her. "Perhaps I shan't go. The view is much more enticing here, and, I warrant, the exercise as invigorating."

She blushed to the roots of her hair. "There is no need for crudity."

He grinned at her discomfiture. "What is this marring the perfection of your face?" He reached out and ran a finger down her cheek, coming away with a generous portion of Roman Balsam.

If possible, Lavinia blushed even more deeply. It felt as though the heat of her embarrassment penetrated to the very depths of her body, warming her in places she had never realized existed.

She turned her head away so that he could not easily touch her again and stepped backward, putting the chair between them. "That, milord, is a cream."

He sniffed. "Made of honey and almonds. I know that much, but why have you got the bloody stuff on?"

"There is no need to curse," she retorted, feeling pressed. Her vanity balked at telling the purpose of the concoction.

He raised one black brow. "Are you going to tell me, or must I use more drastic measures to get the information than a question?"

By the golden gleam in his black eyes she knew exactly what "drastic measures" would entail. Her treacherous body wanted his attentions, but her heart was developing a different desire. "It is for freckles," she blurted, her chin raising automatically.

"Freckles?" He moved a step nearer. "To make them?"

"Absolutely not."

Before she knew what he was about, he caught her jaw in his hand and lifted her face. His mouth curved in a wanton smile that made her insides flow like heated honey.

"Do not get rid of them, for they are one of your most attractive features. They keep you from perfection."

If he had not been holding her face in his hand, her mouth would have dropped open. "Perfection? Thank you for the compliment, but Spanish coin has never appealed to me."

He released her so quickly that she staggered and had to put a hand on the dressing table to steady herself. Where his touch had been, she felt branded.

His back to her, he took a deep breath as though he were fighting some strong compulsion to which he would not succumb. "As you wish, Vixen. However, I did not interrupt you to tell you how beautiful you are. I came to tell you that Jaimie and I are going for the Yule log you seem to feel is so necessary to our holiday happiness."

She blinked, trying to shift the image of him making love to her to the more prosaic one of him fetching the Yule log. It was not an easy transition, and it showed in the tremor she could not eradicate from her voice.

"That is wonderful, Davenport. Do not forget that it must be an ash."

"Not so. We are practically in Scotland, and we have always had a birch log here as the Scottish do. Ash is for the

37

English."

It was on the tip of her tongue to argue the tradition since the hunting box was in England, but it was not as though she were the mistress of the house and would desire good luck throughout the coming year. With a shrug, she turned away from his piercing gaze and taunting lips.

"As you wish. It is your home."

"So it is." Davenport's deep baritone mingled with the sharp click of his boots on the uncovered portions of floor as he went to the door.

Lavinia did not look around to see him leave.

When she was alone, she folded up on the chair and gazed at nothing, her heart beating slowly and painfully. He had merely stated fact when saying this was his home, and she was a ninny to have wanted him to say it was hers too.

She was still a ninny three hours later when her spirits soared just because she heard his voice in the hallway. Careful not to seem elated, she laid the beribboned Kissing Bough on a table.

Smoothing her black skirt down her hips and then her Titian locks back into the bun at her nape, she moved toward the door. It banged open before she got there, and Davenport backed into the room. With him came the clean, woodsy scent of outdoors and the cold dampness that smelled so fresh. He also brought a large log, Jaimie holding the opposite end.

The two men maneuvered the piece of wood into the fireplace and then, with grins splitting their faces, left the room. Before she could follow, they were back with another log.

Eyes wide with curiosity, Lavinia asked, "What is this, two logs?"

Jaimie, still grinning, left the room. Davenport, nonchalantly brushing dirt from his navy coat, smiled so that the lines around his mouth drew her gaze to his well-shaped lips. Against her better judgment, she wished that he would kiss her.

Davenport overturned her thought by saying, "You said we needed ash. I thought we needed birch. So, I com-

38

promised. We have both."

Warm contentment filled her at his unexpected concession. "Thank you. And tonight we must light them both with the sliver Mrs. Hatchet saved from last year's Yule log."

That evening, the two Yule logs blazed warmly in the grate as Lavinia looked around the cozy parlor. Everything was perfect. The tangy smell of evergreens teased her nostrils, and the mistletoe-laden Kissing Bough teased her fantasies. Combined with the roaring, crackling fire, they gave her a sense of the Christmas season.

Soon the servants and Davenport would join her for the Christmas Eve celebrations. At first, she had been surprised when Davenport invited the servants, but from Hatchet's response she'd quickly realized that it was a custom here.

A sound drew her attention, and she turned to see Davenport entering, a maroon velvet box in his hand. He was dressed in a black velvet coat and silk breeches. Silver lace sparkled at his throat and wrists. The elegant attire emphasized his saturnine features and dark complexion, making him appear the antithesis of the Christmas spirit.

Yet, he created in her a thrill of delight that was physical, for it made her shiver and her knees weaken. "You are early."

He strode into the room, seeming to fill it with his presence until all she could see was him, and all she could feel was her body reacting to his masculinity. She had to catch the back of a nearby chair for support.

"I have a present for you." He stopped when only a foot of space separated them.

The breath caught in her throat. "I . . . I do not have one for you. I'm sorry. . . ."

His hand shot out and his finger caught her chin, lifting it until her eyes met his. "Vixen, the gift you give me is yourself, and that is greater than anything I could possibly offer in return."

His words gave her hope. There might be a future for them beyond that of protector and ladybird. Just as she was

39

about to speak, the servants entered. The moment for shared insight was lost.

Mrs. Hatchet's sharp eyes took in the two of them. "Milord, Miss Russell. I hope we dinna be disturbing you."

Mary, excitement heightening her color, burbled, "Jaimie and Mrs. Hatchet said we was to come here."

The jumble of voices and the electricity of anticipation caught Lavinia up in the servants' Christmas spirit. Grinning, she said, "You've come at just the right time. The marquis was just preparing to fix the wassail punch." She slanted him a mischievous glance from under her lashes. "Weren't you, milord?"

He smiled good-naturedly. "Of course. What else would I be doing alone in the parlor with you, Miss Russell?"

Lavinia's skin turned fiery. "Nothing whatsoever."

With a low chuckle that set Lavinia's pulse pounding, Davenport began putting the wassail ingredients into a large silver bowl. In went hot ale, eggs, spices, and plenty of sugar.

"Oh dear me," Mrs. Hatcher exclaimed. "I've done forgot the apples." She rushed from the room, her ample skirts billowing in her wake.

Everyone laughed, and Lavinia glanced at Davenport, meeting his eyes. Together they shared their amusement at the housekeeper's chagrin. The sharing warmed Lavinia.

Mrs. Hatcher returned with a dozen withered apples that had been held back specially for this occasion. Davenport put them in the brew, gave it a good stir, and served generous portions to everyone.

Davenport lifted his drink and toasted. "May you all have a merry Christmas and a profitable New Year."

They all raised their silver cups in agreement. It was not long before Lavinia plunged into the spirit and began to sing the "Wassail Song":

> "Wassail, wassail, through the town,
>   If you've got any apples, throw them down;"

The others quickly joined in. Davenport's deep, melodious tones made Lavinia glad that she'd started the old song.

> "If you've got no apples, money will do;
> The jug is white and the ale is brown,
> This is the best house in town."

Flushed with merriment, the servants drank heartily and Jaimie exclaimed, "And the marquis is the best master of all."

"Thank you, Jaimie." Davenport's voice was serious.

To Lavinia's surprise, Davenport's complexion had darkened at the praise. She'd thought him impervious to what another person said of him, and particularly a servant. Every other member of the aristocracy whom she knew would have considered Jaimie's opinion irrelevant.

Jaimie, because of his toast, had moved forward so that he was standing under the Kissing Bough. The twelve lit candles on the decoration highlighted the green-silver enticement of the mistletoe threaded throughout the evergreen ornament.

"Jaimie, lad, you are surely caught now," Davenport said with a significant look up at the Kissing Bough.

"Aye, milord, that do be the way of it," Jaimie replied, his gaze going immediately to Mary.

The young woman, wringing her hands in the folds of her apron, met Jaimie's look shyly. Mrs. Hatchet pushed Mary forward and the two young people exchanged a chaste kiss.

Lavinia watched the byplay, marveling at the innocence of the exchange. She knew Jaimie and Mary cared for one another, but their lips met and then parted with nary a sign of overwhelming passion. Lavinia knew that had she and Davenport been under the mistletoe, it would have been impossible for her not to melt into his embrace.

When Mary broke away, she giggled nervously. Jaimie's eyes glowed, but he did not pursue her.

Before the moment could become awkward, Davenport stepped forward. "Well, now that you've met your obligation, Jaimie, I have small gifts for all three of you."

He reached up and from the interwoven branches of the

Kissing Bough drew three small packages. These he distributed to the servants with a smile and word of appreciation for each.

Lavinia's heart swelled with pride for this man who could be so considerate of those less fortunate than himself. But when his munificence led him back to her, he spoke so quietly that only she heard.

"I have a very special gift for you, Vixen."

His mouth curved, softening the hard line of his jaw, and his eyes sparkled with an emotion that made the breath catch in her throat.

"You owe me nothing," she murmured, her gaze dropping away from the intensity of his.

"Do I not? Then we must remedy that oversight."

Before she could reply, he turned his attention back to the servants, where it stayed for several hours. The fire was still burning merrily when Mrs. Hatchet announced that it was time for Mary and Jaimie to finish their last-minute chores for the night.

No sooner were the servants from the room than Davenport was at Lavinia's side, his hand lightly skimming her skin before coming to rest where her neck met her shoulder. The searching look he subjected her to singed her to her very toes. It was as though he questioned without words, but unable to fathom what he asked, she could only drown in the depths of his black eyes.

If the poets were right, and eyes are the windows on the soul, then she would gladly give herself into this man's keeping. Instinctively, she knew him to be honorable and secure. If only he loved her . . .

The wish brought poignant regret. She forced herself to look away, and at the same time moved her head so that his touch fell away. Taking a step backward, she made herself smile as though nothing mattered but the happy season.

She offered a pert curtsy. "The Christmas season becomes you, milord."

His mouth curved upward, but he did not smile. "And I think my gift will become you."

The fingers holding her skirt clenched, merriment deserting her. She knew that what he intended to give her would be too extravagant to be a proper gift. She also knew that she must accept it gracefully, for by Society's and Davenport's standards she was a lady no more. Later, when they were no longer together, she would return whatever outrageous gifts he gave her.

But her decision could not quell the disappointment that swamped her as he opened the box to display a parure of emeralds and diamonds that consisted of a necklace, two bracelets, ear bobs, and a tiara. It was a beautiful set and obviously old. Had it been given to her as his wife, she would have been proud to accept it.

"It is stunning," she murmured.

He set the box on the nearby table and lifted out the necklace. "Turn around."

She did as he ordered, knowing that it would be futile to argue. The touch of his fingers on her nape caused her to draw her breath in sharply. And when his thumb ran down her spine, then up till it reached the neckline of her bodice, shivers of pleasure radiated from the deepest part of her.

"Your skin is as fine and creamy as fresh milk," he murmured just before his lips alighted on her bare shoulder.

Her skin was now afire, and her breasts ached. All she had to do was twist on her heel, and his mouth would slide over her flesh, along her collarbone, and . . .

Before she could act on the temptation, he moved away. She sighed in relief, not wanting to be that vulnerable to him. Nor did she want to desire him this potently, especially when she was just another woman he would adorn with expensive jewels in recompense for using her to slake his lust. It did not matter that she had offered herself to him. She was beyond rational thought where he was concerned.

"Turn back around, Vixen. I want to see the earrings on you."

Resigning herself to wearing the beautiful gems that she wished could have meant more than payment for services not yet rendered, Lavinia pivoted. The hunger in his black eyes stopped her cold. His pupils were expanded so that only slivers of dark brown iris showed.

And when he reached out to put the jewelry on her ears, she noticed that his fingers shook. He wanted her as badly as she wanted him. The knowledge was balm to her battered heart.

As he attached the glittering emerald drops to her earlobes, his mouth curved into a smile so devastating it drew her like a moth to a flame. She knew that this flame would burn her very soul to cinders, yet, in this instant, it was a fate she would rush to meet if only to have his love — or even the parody of his love.

He studied her for long minutes while her pulse pounded and her stomach knotted. Would he never speak?

"They become you. I am glad."

After slipping both bracelets on one of her wrists, he reached for the remaining piece of jewelry, taking the tiara from its satin bed and setting it on Lavinia's hair. As it passed in front of her, she recognized the tiara as a beautiful piece of workmanship. But when it sat on her hair, she could not stop a feeling of tawdriness from assailing her. Still, she kept all emotions from showing.

Meeting Davenport's intense scrutiny, she said, "These are too expensive."

He smiled, a slow, lazy movement that set her pulse pounding and her ears ringing. In one lithe movement, he took her in his arms and his kiss hovered a moment away from her lips.

"You will soon earn their value many times over."

Before she could speak of the hurt caused by his equating her love with money, his mouth covered hers. He moved against her with a thoroughness that swallowed her protests. The heat from his flesh penetrated the layers of clothing between them and seeped into her, coiling like a serpent in her abdomen.

When he pulled away to take a breath, she heard someone whimper. Only when she saw the gleam of satisfaction in his black eyes did she realize the someone was her. Shame would have stained her skin, but she saw the hunger he could not hide, the taut line of his cheek, and the harsh angle of his jaw.

He craved her as badly as she did him.

A gasp escaped her swollen lips as he swung her up and bore her from the room. Twining her arms around his neck, she buried her face in the hollow between his shoulder and chest. She did not look up until she heard a door being kicked shut.

They were in his room, a place she had not once entered, even though she had lived in this house for almost two weeks. It reminded her of him: stark and spare, dark and haunted, yet strong. There was a minimum of furnishings, and it was of sturdy oak stained deep brown: a large wardrobe, a wash stand, and a massive bed.

The bed caught her attention. It was simply made with a plain headboard and no other ornamentation except the thick fur that spread completely over it, serving as a coverlet.

He deposited her on the luxuriant fur and followed her down, the length of his lean body flush with hers. His mouth caught hers and drank deeply of her ardor.

Tremors of awareness rippled through her limbs. She wanted more. Eagerly, she returned his kiss.

Chuckling deep in his chest, he drew away to gaze at her. Propped on one elbow, his free hand combed through her hair until her bun was a mass of curls on the pillow.

"Your hair is liquid gold." His features tightened. "And your eyes are like smoky, satiny pewter when you are aroused, as I knew they would be."

His deep voice rumbled over her nerves, turning her muscles to molten desire. All she had ever wanted, the greatest gift any Christmas could provide, was in her arms.

In a hushed voice, throaty with the passion heating her flesh, she asked, "Am I a wanton to enjoy this? To want you so?"

Her fingers caressed the clean line of his jaw and the full curve of his lower lip. His intake of breath was a harsh noise. He caught her roving hand and stilled it in the strength of his own.

His eyes burned into her. "Not wanton. Merely young and not yet jaded."

Without conscious thought, words tumbled from her. "I love you."

Before she realized what he intended, he released her and stood by the bed staring down at her. She lay in disheveled vulnerability, uncertain what to do.

Abruptly, he turned from her and strode to the door connecting their rooms. He opened it and motioned for her to leave.

Devastated by his desertion after her declaration, she scrambled from the bed, escape her only thought. All she wanted was to leave the painful reality of his rejection. But his harsh words followed her as she skirted around him and into the haven of her own room.

"Give it time, my dear, and you will begin to view what we just shared as a job, not love." His mouth twisted cruelly as she glanced back at him. "I find myself unwilling to bring about that natural fate on Christmas Eve. Perhaps tomorrow."

*Perhaps tomorrow.*
*A job, not love.*

The words rang in Lavinia's ears, just as they had for the past twenty-four hours. Tomorrow was today, and he had not come near her. She did not even know his whereabouts.

Now she sat alone at the dinner table, a piece of Christmas goose on her plate and plum pudding in the bowl set before her. It would be so easy to cry into the food, but she knew that the wound he'd dealt her was too deep for tears to cleanse.

Last night he had refused her passion. Even worse, he had mocked her love. Her heart felt as though it had stopped beating and become a cold stone in her tight chest.

She finally had to admit to herself that she'd done her best to make him love her and she had failed. Realizing that, she also realized that to let him make love to her would be to perform the act that would be the beginning of her emotional death. Not even for Emily and John could she do that.

Lavinia wanted nothing more than to flee the room, escape the hunting box, return to London and poverty. She wanted to pretend the last two weeks had never happened.

But she could not.

Somehow she managed to get down several mouthfuls of food before pushing away from the table. There was no sense waiting there in solitary splendor until Davenport returned from wherever he had gone on Christmas Day.

Restlessly, she entered the parlor which was cozy and smelled redolently of fresh holly and bay. The reminders of Christmas, the season to celebrate the birth of the baby Jesus and hope, did not lighten her despondency.

Her shoulders slumped as though all the strength had drained from her back. Just yesterday evening, her hopes had been so high. A sigh escaped her.

"Bored already, Vixen?"

"You." She spun around so fast that the book she'd just picked up flew from her nerveless fingers and landed with a loud thump just short of Davenport's feet.

With a casual grace that set Lavinia's heart pounding to painful life, he stooped and retrieved the book. "Byron? No wonder you are acting as though the world has come to an end. George is nothing if not melodramatic."

His indifferent remark put starch back into Lavinia's posture. Her heart might be broken and her future a dark shadow of unhappiness, but she would be damned if she'd let him know to what depths of despair his rejection of her love had plunged her.

Davenport sauntered farther into the room, setting the book on a table he passed and then propping one booted foot on the grate. Glancing down at the orange flames of the roaring fire, he said, "The Yule log burns brightly. I hope you put next year's piece where it belongs."

How could he mock her so cruelly? The splinter of Yule log saved for the next year always went under the mattress of the mistress of the house. His words implied that she would be with him next Christmas—in this very house. She knew very well from the gossipmongers that his mistresses never lasted past six months. And she no longer wanted to be his mistress, not even for Emily and John.

She clenched her shaking fingers into fists and took a deep breath. "Milor—"

"Charles. If you can profess to love me, it is only fitting that you call me by my Christian name."

Shame engulfed her at his mockery of her love, but she met his gaze without flinching. His black eyes were shadowed, masking his emotions from her scrutiny. Was he angry, or merely amused at her? It was impossible for her to gauge his feelings.

"After your pointed rejection of my sentiments, I prefer to call you Davenport." She lifted her chin. "While you were out, I have had considerable time to think. You seem to find me repulsive, since you have been unwilling to consummate our relationship. Therefore, I'm asking that you arrange for my return to London. I cannot . . . will not remain here in your debt. I did not offer myself to you for your pity. I did it as a business arrangement between two adults, and I fully expected to perform my end of the bargain."

Before she was finished, her shoulders ached with the effort to hold them proudly erect. It had not been easy to say those things to him, but he had given her no other recourse.

A seriousness and intensity settled on him, the likes of which she had seen only once before—when he'd carried her to the bed. "What if I tell you we will finish what we have started? Today. Right now."

He was toying with her, and it made her want to lash out at him. "It is too late. I have decided to return to London and seek another man who will not make game of me as you have done."

His brows shot together and his complexion darkened. In two short strides he was gripping her upper arms. "You will go to no other man."

Her breath came in ragged gasps that she strove to smooth. "You do not own me."

"Do I not?"

"No."

"Who better than I, Vixen, when I own your father's vowels?"

She gasped. "What? You?" The smile of satisfaction he

48

wore told her the truth. "Why did you not tell me?"

He released her and moved away, his back toward her. "There was no need to do so. You made my part easy by contacting me first." When he turned back to face her, his expression was unreadable. "I bought the vowels from your solicitor, not knowing exactly what I intended to do with them. Your proposition made them obsolete."

Lavinia strove for calm. Everything was happening so fast, she no longer knew what she needed to do.

"What do you plan to do with them now? Will you still give me time to repay them?"

"Perhaps."

Her insides began to churn. "Perhaps?"

"Do you still plan on returning to London?"

Her eyes widened as his meaning became apparent. "You are using them to keep me when I no longer wish to be kept."

He shrugged, his shoulders tense. "I do what I must."

"Must?" Her voice rose. "Must? Must I stay when you have mocked and belittled my love for you? Is that the price *I* must pay for those vowels?"

His words a whisper she barely heard over the anger causing her ears to ring, he said, "You have one other alternative, Vixen."

She clamped down hard on the words of rebuke she longed to throw at him. Instead, she stared stonily at him.

"You can marry me." His voice cracked and he took a deep breath.

If she did not know better, she would have thought the words cost him dearly. However, she knew he continued to toy with her for an end of his own which she could not even begin to imagine.

She forced her trembling lips to stillness. "What despicable May game are you playing?"

Under heavy lids, his eyes searched the very depths of her soul. "What game did you play with me six years ago? I thought you had a *tendre* for me and then, at the next moment, you cut me."

She took a deep breath, trying to still her screaming

nerves. "My father warned me against you. He said you would offer me a slip-on-the-shoulder if I encouraged you. Even then you had a reputation for fast women and high stakes."

"Did you love me then?"

She closed her eyes, unable to look into the disturbing depths of his. "I . . ."

He moved to her and grabbed her shoulders. "Look at me, damn it. Did you love me?"

Her lids fluttered open and she steeled herself to see fury and implacable determination in his. She whispered, "Yes."

"And you love me now?"

He was so cruel, his fingers biting into her flesh and his words beating at her. "Yes," she murmured.

"Then marry me."

"Marry you, knowing you do not love me? Make a hell on earth for myself?" She twisted from his grasp. "No, thank you."

He followed her, so closely that when he spoke his breath was a warm caress on the back of her neck. "What if I loved you?"

"Stop it," she ordered, head averted, tears forming in her eyes. "Stop this punishment. I was only seventeen when I snubbed you. Do not continue to make me pay for something I only did from fear."

"If anyone is being punished, it is I," he said. "To have you in my house, only a door separating us. Every night I suffered agonies of indecision. I wanted to make love to you until you glowed with desire. I wanted to feel you respond to me as completely as though you were made only for me. But I held back, knowing that once I touched you I could never settle for less than your complete devotion. Your complete . . . love."

She blinked away the threatening tears, now more confused than ever. What was he saying? Surely, it could not be what her eager heart was thinking.

Cautiously, she turned so that their gazes met. "What *do* you want from me?"

His mouth twisted into a bitter caricature of a smile. "The

same thing I wanted from you six years ago."

"Six years ago?" She repeated his words, all the time telling herself that he did not mean what she thought. He was not telling her that he loved her, had loved her for six long years.

He took a deep, shuddering breath and, with the fingers of one hand, smoothed back a stray curl at her temple. His eyes looked deeply into hers.

"I loved you then and wanted to marry you. I want the same now. I thought I could make you my mistress and be done with it. I was wrong."

Her heart swelled with love and hope. "If that is true . . ."

He caught her to him, crushing her against his chest. His mouth swooped down on hers, scouring her lips with the flames of his love. When he finally ended the kiss, she felt dizzy and bewildered.

He said, "It is true, as God is my witness. As true as I can make it without a minister to bind us."

She knew he spoke what his heart felt. His eyes, the windows on his soul, told her that his love for her was deep. His hands, which shook on her shoulders, told her how important her answer was to him.

"Then I will marry you, Davenport, for neither one of us will have any happiness otherwise."

Again he caught her to him. This time the kiss was slow and gentle, a melding of souls as well as bodies.

When at long last they parted, he carried her to a chair, on which he sat down with her across his lap. From his coat pocket he took a small maroon velvet box. Springing it open, he revealed a simple emerald and diamond ring, the mate to the parure of jewelry he'd showered her with the night before.

This time she felt no dread or embarrassment. This time, it felt right.

He took the ring from its satin bed and slipped it onto the third finger of her left hand. Raising her hand to his lips, he kissed the ring.

"This was my grandmother's engagement ring." He smiled tenderly down at her. "She gave it to me for my wife. I want

51

you to have it as a Christmas gift and a pledge of my love."

Now tears did fall from Lavinia's eyes, but they were tears of happiness. Everything would be all right.

With a soft cry of joy, she flung her arms around her love's neck. "I will wear it always, and always remember my love for you and our first Christmas together."

# The House Party

## by Violet Hamilton

Revenge, at first though sweet,
Bitter ere long back on itself recoils.

— John Milton

Her first glimpse of Winterbourne Manor did little to allay the uneasiness which had been her companion since leaving Bath. Arabella gave a rueful shrug as she thought of that cozy watering place and regretted, not for the first time, accepting this Christmas invitation. More of a summons, really, she decided. The gray stone facade of the manor, standing on a slight rise at the end of a long drive, matched the bleak bare wintry Dorset weather. Trim and well cared for, the house had a somber air with its narrow unshuttered windows, flat pediments, and massive nail-studded door. Whatever welcome awaited her, she must put on the best face possible. No good could come from antagonizing her guardian and perhaps the holiday spirit would lighten the atmosphere.

Stepping from the coach she noticed a spare middle-aged man of military manner had emerged and was stolidly watching her arrival.

"Good afternoon, Miss Stapleton. I am Baker. I was the general's batman and now serve as butler. The general's compliments and would you please attend him immediately." He hesitated and then added as a sop to politeness, "If that is convenient."

Of course it wasn't. Arabella longed to be conducted to her room, to have an interval to rest and collect herself before meeting her guardian after all these years. Courtesy demanded she accede to this order, however, and feeling rather like a junior officer expecting a reprimand, she nodded, but could not resist adding, "I am quite chilled and tired, so I hope the interview will be brief."

Then, chiding herself for being so disagreeable, she gave the man a smile and surrendered her cloak, hat, gloves, and muff. Indicating that she was at his service, she followed Baker's rigid figure, expressive of his disapproval, across the slate floor of the vast hall, repressing a wicked desire to stick her tongue out at the unbending back.

Baker threw open a door on the left and announced, "Miss Stapleton has arrived, General."

Arabella, who had not seen her guardian in some years since he had been serving abroad, was surprised at how little he had changed. General Roland Eustace Pettigrew stood to welcome her, a tall impressive figure of some forty odd years, with a tanned face, piercing blue eyes, and black hair worn in the fashionable mode, à la Titus. Altogether a handsome man with undoubted charisma, and quite aware of it, Arabella decided at first glance.

"Ah, my dear. How happy I am to see you. It has been much too long, but the exigencies of the army, alas, prevented me from visiting you. Now you are here we will become friends, I know, and share together this, my first English Christmas for too many seasons." He guided her to a chair, smiling down with a practiced address which Arabella thought must work havoc on susceptible ladies.

"It is kind of you and Mrs. Pettigrew to invite me, sir," she replied, and then waited, as if wondering where her hostess was hidden. Then, as he made no excuse, she continued, "I believe it has been at least six years since our meeting, and then, at thirteen, I was too distressed over the loss of my parents to think of much else." She remembered that tragic time all too well, if not the man who had assumed responsibility for her.

56

"Yes, indeed, a sad occasion. But soldiers must accept the fortunes of war. I regret exceedingly that your mother did not live long enough to see what a charming daughter she produced." The conventional compliment and brief careless reference to her parents, Arabella considered an impatient sop to the proprieties. Arabella wondered why her father had thought this man would make a commendable guardian for his child. She knew Pettigrew had no children of his own, however, so she absolved him of condescension. He probably was more accustomed to dealing with young officers and high-ranking military types, and had developed this rather pretentious style as a protection. It did not endear him to her, but she must not be critical. No doubt on more intimate acquaintance she would be influenced by the charm she thought he easily exerted when the occasion demanded it.

"Well, we must try to bridge the gap of years. I hope you will enjoy yourself this holiday. We will be a small party but a congenial one, I pray. Mrs. Gresham and her son, Austin, have already arrived, as has my aide, Captain Mark Rothfield. An old school friend, Sir William Ashford, whom I trust you will find amiable, will be joining us soon. And my wife's niece, Alice Overton, lives with us. So you see, not an overwhelming number of people, and I am sure you will fit in beautifully," he informed her, as if he could not countenance any other outcome.

Arabella wondered about her hostess. Did she allow her husband to manage all their domestic arrangements? Of course, the general had vast experience in issuing orders, and expected obedience, no matter what surface pleasantries he adopted.

No doubt he assumed this facade to overawe her with both arrogance and empty compliments. It behooved her, for the present, to pretend she was acquiescent, but the general had not made a favorable impression, a fact of which he was unaware. A conceited man and a demanding one, with little respect for women as individuals, she decided. He was convinced he could order his life and those of his dependents to his command. Why should his ward pose any problem?

As if more vital matters awaited, Pettigrew indicated their conversation was at an end. "Now I must not keep you. I know you need a rest after your journey, not used to campaigning, eh?" He smiled. "My wife will be along to escort you to your room, which I hope you will find comfortable. We will have a long chat later about your future," he promised.

We certainly will, Arabella vowed; but she was reluctant to embark on any questions at the moment.

Almost as if awaiting her cue, a slight woman scuttled through the door.

"So sorry. I meant to be on hand to welcome you, Miss Stapleton, but domestic duties . . ." Her voice trailed off, and she darted a placating look at her husband.

"I have welcomed Arabella, as I think we must call her, in your regrettable absence, my dear. We cannot stand on formality," the general insisted fulsomely, looking at his wife with a frown.

Mrs. Pettigrew was not quite what Arabella had expected. She had thought the general's wife would be a mature beauty of regal appearance and some sophistication. Dressed fussily in an unbecoming, frilled, yellow merino gown which did not compliment her sallow complexion, Mrs. Pettigrew was a small, faded woman, with pale blond hair untidily arranged. Her pale blue eyes darted about, as if unwilling to meet the gaze of any challenger. Vestiges of the delicate beauty which must once have attracted the general remained, but hers was a personality which would only have flowered in a happy atmosphere. Arabella decided that Mrs. Pettigrew had experienced rather little of that condition in her married life.

"Now, do not keep Arabella waiting, my dear," the general ordered impatiently, obviously eager to see the last of them both.

Unwilling to add to her hostess' problems, Arabella assented, turning her back on Pettigrew and saying in a soothing manner, "It is so kind of you to have me, ma'am. I am sure we will become fast friends." Certainly Mrs. Pettigrew needs a friend, Arabella thought, but she wondered if she would ever penetrate the woman's vague disordered mind.

Without waiting for any more of the general's condescension, she followed her mute hostess from the room. The general stood politely until they had left, then frowned into the fire. Miss Stapleton appeared to be an agreeable girl, perhaps a little too reserved. But there might be depths here not at first realized. He would have to walk carefully with her, although he did not anticipate any rebellion. Few women resisted his charm when he was pleased to exert it. He had handled far more mettlesome types.

But she was a real beauty with that creamy complexion, luxuriant chestnut hair, and wide green eyes. Some man would enjoy governing her. Too bad he stood as guardian to such a delectable piece. He wondered if he had been wise to invite her. She was happily situated in Bath, living on her modest competence, with an aged companion to lend propriety. He shrugged. Her inclusion in this party was just a kindly gesture on his part. He basked in the knowledge that he was behaving with forbearance. She would cause no trouble.

Arabella, chatting smoothly with Mrs. Pettigrew, would not have agreed with the general's summation of her character and intentions. She had several pressing questions to ask her guardian and would not be fobbed off with charm and vague assurances. Her uneasiness had not been stilled by his reception of her, but she had a guest's responsibility toward his wife and would bide her time.

"What a pleasant room," she said when they reached the allotted chamber. It was the merest politeness, for the bedroom's one cheerful note was the generous fire burning on the hearth. With its heavy, solid, old-fashioned mahogany furniture and somewhat musty velvet fittings, the room did not offer relaxation although it could claim a certain massive dignity.

"Do you think so? I thought a few light chintzes and more graceful modern furniture might be more appropriate, but the general dislikes change. The house belonged to his father. We have just come to live here since Waterloo, and it's so expensive decorating. . . ." After confiding in Arabella Mrs. Pettigrew let her voice trail off in a way Arabella was coming to accept.

"I am sure I will be most happy here," Arabella reassured her hostess.

"Well, I will just send along your maid to unpack and settle you in. I am sure you are longing for tea, and we'll be gathering shortly in the drawing room. Then you will meet the rest of the guests. Of course, if you would rather . . ." Again she seemed unsure of just what she should offer.

"I will join you after I have removed some of this travel dirt. Please do not concern yourself, Mrs. Pettigrew. We will get along famously, I know," Arabella promised, wanting to comfort the woman.

After a few false starts and some more vague suggestions, Mrs. Pettigrew removed herself, giving Arabella a much-needed respite to consider how best to approach her host.

Until now her experience with the general had been confined to a few duty letters. She had suggested upon leaving school that she remain in Bath in a small house once owned by her parents, and until recently leased to an elderly couple who died just as she was completing her schooling. The general, thoroughly occupied with chasing Napoleon from Europe, had agreed.

Her father, Major Richard Stapleton, had fallen at Salmanca, and her mother had died soon after of a virulent fever caught on the Peninsula where she had accompanied her husband. Arabella had happy memories of her bluff, cheerful father and her pretty loving mother who had left her orphaned at thirteen. General Pettigrew had been the major's commanding officer, and since neither of her parents had close relatives, the general had been named as her guardian. He shared his trustee's duties with a Bath solicitor, and it was that gentleman's puzzlement over the decline in Arabella's income which had inclined her to make this visit.

Elias Purvey, of Purvey, Hayward, and Purvey, had been a dear white-haired old man with a touching faith in his fellows. While he was alive he had never questioned General Pettigrew's handling of Arabella's affairs. Henry Purvey, his son, who had inherited his father's clients, but not his charitable view of human nature, did question them. Arabella's income had fallen lately, and although she managed to live within it, she wondered about the reason for its decline.

Henry Purvey was even more suspicious. He reported that sometime ago the general, well within his rights even if he had not seen fit to seek advice from Henry Purvey, had sold her investments, prudently lodged in the funds at three per cent, and had bought some Indian trading stock. Henry's letter querying this transaction had received a brusque reply. He had then explained matters to Arabella and, while not expecting a woman to understand the intricacies of finance, had been surprised at her quick grasp of the situation. She had assured him she would get some answers from the general on this Christmas visit. Until then he was to hold his peace. She did not like to think that her guardian was an embezzler, and she would not accuse him of any wrongdoing, but she deserved an explanation and meant to have one.

After dismissing her abigail, a pleasant Somerset girl who helped her change her traveling dress for a costume of heavy green cashmere accented with white linen collar and cuffs, she gave some thought as to how she would handle the general. He did not appear a man who would entertain allegations against his conduct with equanimity. As his guest and ward she must behave with courtesy, but she would not be dismissed. She took a mostly charitable view of humanity, but had learned to trust her own judgment. She would not play the meek ward and be stampeded by the general's suave tyranny. Turning the other cheek had availed his wife little, and moreover, she did not share Rachel's compliant nature. Having decided how to proceed, Arabella set her chin and with a determined cast to her eye, descended into the drawing room.

On her arrival she was immediately taken in charge by the general, who greeted her with flattering attention, and steered toward the guests gathered around the tea table at which Rachel presided.

"This is a long-deferred reunion for us. My ward has at last honored us with a visit. She lives quietly in Bath and unfortunately my duties have kept me occupied so that we have seen very little of her since she was so tragically orphaned," he explained, making Arabella feel like some poor waif who had been generously sheltered by his magnanimity.

Showing none of her distaste for this introduction, she nodded pleasantly to Rachel and then turned to meet the other guests. Mrs. Olivia Gresham, a statuesque brunette, stunningly dressed in a cerise gown which highlighted her figure, had all the style and sophistication Arabella had expected and not found in the general's wife. She glanced at Arabella appraisingly and then dismissed her.

"You are fortunate in your guardian, Miss Stapleton," she advised, giving the general a glowing smile which he received as his due. Then turning to the young man at her side, she said, "This is my son, Austin, Miss Stapleton. You young people will have much in common, I am sure," she insisted graciously.

"Delighted, Miss Stapleton," Austin Gresham said and bowed slightly. A tall, very thin young man, with receding blond hair and a weak chin, he was dressed in a dandyish fashion, with uncomfortably high shirt-points and a waistcoat which fitted him with excruciating tightness. He quite fancies himself, Arabella decided.

"I am sure you will make friends with our niece, Alice Overton. You girls can exchange confidences and will be quite comfortable, I know," the general continued, indicating a demure figure who stood by Rachel's chair. Although not a real beauty she had a certain distinctive air and a smooth closed face. Her deep brown eyes showed no emotion. Everything about her spoke of control and deference, traits Arabella thought she must need in this rather complicated household.

"How do you do, Miss Stapleton. General and Mrs. Pettigrew have been anticipating your arrival," Alice said softly. Her voice, beautifully modulated, was the most appealing aspect of her personality. Arabella acknowledged her greeting politely, although she could not quite fathom Miss Overton's position in the household. She did notice Miss Overton's avid interest in the guest who now awaited an introduction.

"And this is my aide, Captain Mark Rothfield, Arabella, a brave fellow who has proved invaluable to me."

"You will add a great deal to the festivities, Miss Stapleton," the young officer said graciously. As tall as Austin Gresham, but lacking that young man's fashionable air, Mark Rothfield had a shock of chestnut hair, a firm mouth, and steady blue eyes. He also had the air of an amused spectator and the undoubted presence of a military man.

"Thank you, Captain Rothfield. I am very happy to be included," she said, meeting his frank gaze of appreciation with a smile, though not unaware that Alice Overton was watching this meeting with a considering air. Could she be interested in the captain and not wish to entertain the thought of a rival? Well, Arabella had no intention of flirting with the captain. She had had some acquaintance with the military and had, in the past, found these men more often than not careless philanderers. Alice could relax.

The general indicated she must sit down by Rachel and receive a cup of tea, which Arabella was happy to do. The company, although few, appeared somewhat disparate, but she must observe the courtesies. Bath society had taught her the rules of casual conversation, and although inclined to a certain wariness, she was fully prepared to enter into the spirit of the holiday.

Rachel asked her yet again if she was comfortably established, and Arabella reassured her hostess that she was, while Austin and Mark resumed their discussion of the London theater. The company seemed a bit stiff, but Arabella conceded it might take some time for them to be at ease with each other. However the tea-table amenities were almost immediately interrupted by Baker, who announced, "Sir William Ashford."

Striding into the room was a gentleman of about the general's age, but of a very different type. Gray-haired, of middle height, with a tanned face that had a gentle cast to it, he looked both kind and worried. He ignored the general and hurried to greet his hostess.

"Ah, Rachel, how pleased I am to see you again. It must be at least three years since our last meeting," he said, bowing over her hand. Then, nodding to the general in a rather distrait way, he asked with insistence, "Are you happy living in this rather isolated countryside, my dear?"

Before Rachel could either agree or complain, her husband interrupted. "Now, William, don't upset Rachel. Delighted to see you, old man. And how are you getting on in that dessicated watering place you call home? Why you want to bury yourself in Sidmouth with all those old tabbies I cannot fathom."

Looking neither annoyed at this criticism of his home nor prepared to contest it, Sir William just smiled at the general. "It is very kind to include an old bachelor in your Christmas house party, Rachel. We must have a long chat about happier days," he insisted. The general ignored this allusion, if that was what Sir William had meant.

It was obvious to Arabella that Sir William was more than fond of Rachel Pettigrew, and she could not help but wonder, if they were old friends, why Rachel had not preferred this accommodating man to the general. Surely they were much more suited. The general himself might not notice that his wife had brightened considerably under Sir William's tender regard, but Arabella found it fascinating. She was not surprised that the general did not consider Sir William worthy of jealousy, having much too good an opinion of his own apparently superior assets. She was content to watch this byplay and was a little startled when Captain Rothfield approached her and made some untoward remark about Bath.

"Do you know the city well, sir?" she responded.

"I have an aged aunt who lives there and considers that the waters keep her alive," he informed her with a grave smile.

"Isn't that a good thing?" she asked. "Perhaps I know her. I have a wide acquaintance in Bath, having lived there through my school years and beyond."

"Lady Harriett Rothfield," he answered.

"Yes, of course, a formidable old woman." Arabella chuckled, then apologized. "But with a kind heart, I am sure." Lady Harriett, the daughter of an earl, was a mean avaricious old woman who had exhausted four companions and was the terror of society. But of course Arabella could not say that. Was Captain Rothfield establishing his position? How suspicious she was.

"Not at all. She is a difficult nasty old lady, but I acclaim your tact. I think she was thwarted in love, and that has made her turn her frustration on all whom she meets," he explained with an engaging smile. Arabella decided to acquit him of snobbery.

"Still, you like her. I can tell." Arabella was discovering that Captain Rothfield had a charm of his own, not the accomplished manner of his chief but a certain amused tolerance, which she appreciated, of the world's foibles. She might have to make an exception for this officer, although her experience of the type in Bath had not made her fond of the military. Nor had her brief exchanges with the general softened her attitude. Conscious of Alice Overton's interest in their conversation, she wondered just what the relationship between the two really was. Probably Mark Rothfield was well accustomed to the admiration of gullible girls, but she would acquit him of any intention of taking advantage of such admiration until she knew better. For the present she thought him the most sympathetic of the Pettigrew guests.

Before long, the company broke up. The general summoned Mark to the library, and the rest of the party wandered into the hall, where two footmen were decorating the walls with holiday greens. Arabella, about to ascend the stairs to her room, was approached by Alice Overton.

"Would you like a tour of the house, Miss Stapleton? Or may I call you Arabella. It's odd that we have not met before, but I am grateful for this opportunity to get on friendly terms."

Arabella, willing to cooperate and hoping to discover a bit more about Alice, agreed. They mounted the steps to the upper story, where Alice informed her the gallery was not only the most impressive room in the house, but it held the portraits of the Pettigrew ancestors. Arabella had to admit the long, parqueted gallery was a dignified, if trifle austere, sight. Lining the walls were portraits of the general's forebears, a great many of them military men in splendid uniforms. Not surprisingly the wives looked properly chastened, displaying a becoming docility. Alice explained the subjects' histories briefly as they strolled along. Obviously she was proud of her connection to such illustrious men and women.

Arabella responded politely, though privately she thought the somber room, darkly paneled with small leaded windows that allowed little light to penetrate, rather gloomy.

"The general's portrait will soon join the others. He looks quite splendid in his uniform. Wellington thinks a great deal of him, you know. He has had a brilliant career."

"I am sure of it," Arabella responded briefly. Then, her curiosity getting the better of her, she asked, "Have you lived with the Pettigrews for some time, Alice?"

"No. My parents have been gone for some years, but I lived with an uncle and aunt until Waterloo, Then when the general and Aunt Rachel moved here, I joined them. I try to help Aunt Rachel as much as I can as household duties are rather demanding and she is not strong."

Arabella had the impression that Alice rather despised her aunt for her inability to manage and preferred the general. Although she did not share this opinion she could understand it.

Alice seemed eager to confide. "When the Pettigrews move to Salisbury, where the regiment will be stationed in the spring, I will accompany them. Of course, Mark will be going too," she added carelessly, but Arabella sensed she was about to hear more about the general's aide.

"Has Captain Rothfield been on the general's staff for long?" she asked idly.

"He joined him just before Waterloo. Before that he was with the Coldstreams, in the Peninsula," Alice continued, almost simpering. "He was mentioned in dispatches. We are all so fond of him."

Arabella wondered if she was being warned off this eligible man. So this was the reason for Alice Overton's tendering of friendship, she concluded cynically, then reproved herself for such unkindness.

Feeling she must make some response, she decided that she would not mince words. "He seems a charming man, and I am sure you find him a very agreeable companion in this isolated household."

"Oh, yes. And, of course, I know I can trust you to keep our secret. We have an understanding of sorts, but Mark has not yet discussed this with his father, the earl, so there will be no announcement yet."

"My best wishes. I hope it all works out for you, Alice," Arabella replied, convinced that this young woman's purpose in escorting her on this tour of the house had been to let her know how matters stood between herself and the captain. Arabella, from her little acquaintance with them both, could not help but think that Alice might be a bit premature in her expectations, but she did not voice her doubts. If the two were affianced, Arabella had no intention of entering the lists, although she obviously could not reassure her companion of her disinterest in the captain. She could not blame the girl for trying to attach such an eligible *parti*. She assumed the match had the general's approval, and a formidable ally he would be. Arabella dismissed, a bit regretfully, any idea she might have had that Mark Rothfield could take any place in her own future, and as the two girls continued their stroll about the manor house, nothing more was said about the secret engagement, if there was, in fact, such an arrangement.

While Alice Overton was confiding her hopes to Arabella, the general was exercising his own persuasion in the library.

"Well, Mark, if you will just send off this dispatch to the War Office, I believe we can abandon work for the rest of the holiday. We deserve a respite, I think."

"Yes, sir. I am sure the house party will be an enjoyable change from military duties for you," he agreed.

"I must tell you how much I appreciate your assistance, and the tactful way you have fitted into our ménage here. I am glad you get along so well with Alice. You young people must find it rather boring so far from the gaieties of London. Even a barracks town is more exciting than the wilds of Dorset, but we will be off in the spring. Alice will accompany us, which I am sure you find agreeable." His tone was a bit questing. The general intended that his personable aide marry Alice. The girl needed a husband, and he himself would benefit from the connection to the Rothfield family. Whether the two would be suited did not interest him.

"A very nice girl," Mark offered noncommittally. He had a good idea of what the general wanted, but had no intention of offering for Miss Overton. That had not been his reason for attaching himself to General Pettigrew. If the general suspected what his real purpose was, he might be both incredulous and indignant, but Mark was not yet prepared to show his hand.

Rachel Pettigrew and Sir William had settled in the morning room for a comfortable cose. At least that had been Sir William's plan, but Rachel seemed reluctant to confide in her old friend. The morning room received the benefit of whatever sun might be shining, and its pale yellow walls and cheerful, green and yellow print draperies and chair coverings were a welcome relief from the more dismal furnishings of the rest of the manor.

But Sir William scarcely noticed the decor. He was intent on discovering what had been happening to Rachel during the past few years and why she looked so unhappy. The last time he had seen her in London she had been far more relaxed. Possibly that was because her demanding husband was then serving abroad and she was visiting an old school friend who allowed her far more license than her husband. Sir William, who had wanted to marry the young Rachel Overton himself, had humbly conceded that she found the dashing, young Roland Pettigrew a far more exciting beau. He only wanted Rachel's happiness, but he was not persuaded, in the twenty years which had passed since her wedding, that Pettigrew had offered her this. Rachel had simple tastes. Army life, with its foreign postings, hardships, and intrigue, had not suited her retiring nature. And Sir William had heard disturbing rumors, even in distant Devon, of the general's philandering. He thought it was rather insulting for Roland to have invited the luscious Mrs. Gresham, whose reputation as a promiscuous widow had reached even his ears, to be a guest over this family holiday. Why did Rachel permit such behavior? He would not be so crass as to ask, but he probed gently.

"Dear Rachel, I am sorry to see you looking so careworn. I really did not think this idea of living in remote Dorset would appeal to you. Roland should never brought you here," he protested.

"Well, it is his family home. And the expense of seeking

69

other accommodations when he will be posted to Salisbury in the spring seemed unnecessary. I must confess I would have preferred a nice comfortable watering spot — Bath, Tunbridge, even Sidmouth." She smiled at her old friend. They had many tastes in common, and the circumscribed friendly routine of these towns had an appeal for them both. But if Rachel remembered that she could have made a different choice of husband she hesitated to complain.

"What is that Gresham woman doing here? You should not have allowed it, Rachel." Sir William had abandoned his first intention to avoid the subject.

"Roland insisted. But surely, William, he would not invite his mistress to his home. I know you think he is selfish and unfaithful, but he is a great one for the proprieties, you know. And he is quite impressed with young Rothfield and his connections. He would do nothing to cause gossip which might endanger his career." She spoke with a certain bitter resignation that justified all of her old friend's fears.

"He should be horsewhipped. You should never have married him, my dear." Sir William's normal calm acceptance of life's troubles had vanished in the face of this evidence of Rachel's unhappiness.

"I believe he agrees with you. I could never give him a child, you know. He feels that deeply."

"Ridiculous. He should be grateful to have your devotion and love."

"Thank you, William. You are such a loyal friend, and your support is a tonic to me, but let us talk no more of this. Tell me about Sidmouth. It sounds charming."

Sir William would have liked to continue his questions about Rachel's marriage, but seeing that they only caused distress, and the situation could not be altered, with his gentle tact and kindness, he soon had her smiling at his stories. But although he hid his indignation he did not forget it, and vowed he would not let Rachel's unhappiness go unpunished.

Mrs. Gresham would have been amused rather than embarrassed to learn she was the object of Sir William and

Rachel Pettigrew's conversation. But she was not amused by the demands her son was making in the acrimonious interview held in her bedroom.

"Really, Austin, I just do not have the money to give you. I would if I could, you know," she said placatingly, eyeing her son with pity. "I do wish you would not gamble. You are so unlucky."

"I have had a bad run of cards lately. But what's a fellow to do? I must pay my debts of honor," he whined, striding about the room and not meeting his mother's gaze. Then, as she made no suggestion, he added slyly, "Perhaps you can get the money from our generous host. You might even pop that rather nice emerald bracelet he gave you, for favors received, no doubt."

"Really, Austin, must you be so sordid." But Mrs. Gresham did not look annoyed, only smug as she glanced at the bracelet on her wrist. "General Pettigrew is a good friend, but I cannot trespass on his kindness to rescue you from your folly."

"Oh, come, Mother. I know you are his mistress, and I must say Mrs. Pettigrew must be the veriest ninny not to know. If she does, surely she would object to entertaining her husband's *chère amie* at a family Christmas party." Austin was not above a bit of blackmail if it would help to solve his problem.

"If you are threatening to tell our hostess any salacious tale about Roland and me, I would advise against it. He can be quite formidable, you know, and I believe it would be foolish to kill the goose that lays the golden egg," she insisted a bit crudely. She made no effort to defend herself against her son's accusations, and seemed indifferent to the immorality of carrying on her liaison with the general under his wife's eye. She made no attempt to cultivate women, thinking they had little influence with their husbands or relatives, and her small knowledge of Rachel Pettigrew convinced her the woman was too weak-willed to make any trouble.

If Mrs. Gresham cared for anyone, it was Austin, and

she would help him if she could. "When we return to London, I might be able to sell some jewelry, but I warn you, Austin, this will be the last time. Roland is not particularly fond of you, and if he ever suspected that I was paying your debts with the jewelry he gave me, it would be all up with us." If she were shocked, either by Austin's transgressions or her own solution to his troubles, she gave little sign of it, peering with satisfaction in the long mirror and finding the reflection to her taste.

"You are a Trojan, Mother. And you know how much I love you," her son said, sighing happily and crossing the room to give her a careful hug. Then joining her in looking in the glass, he approved, "You are still a great beauty, and there are other gentlemen with deep pockets you can charm, if by any chance you fall out with the general. At any rate I find him a bit overwhelming, and certainly this dim manor house is not where I wanted to spend Christmas."

"Really, Austin, you are so unrealistic. I had to get away from London for a time, and Roland is more amenable in his family home, bleak as you find it. Perhaps the holiday spirit will make him more generous than usual. I expect a really splendid gift in honor of the season," she explained complacently.

"I wonder what he will give his wife. Not emeralds, I am sure, for she would not show them off as you do," he complimented.

"No, but please be careful, Austin. The general requires tactful handling, and I need his support right now," his mother insisted. Then, as if to signify the conversation was at an end, she added, "Now run along, dear boy, and try to behave with some address. You might pay some attention to his ward. She has a comfortable competence, I think, and might do for you."

"She is a pretty piece, and if it pleases you I will turn on the charm," he promised, not at all unwilling to play his part if it kept his mother in a sweet mood.

Despite Rachel's efforts to create a festive spirit suitable to the season, dinner that evening lacked the cordial and joyous mood which might have been expected. Arabella, having donned her best emerald silk gown for the occasion and wearing her mother's pearls, was not surprised to be eclipsed by the stunning Olivia Gresham, lavishly turned out for a country party, in a crimson and silver gauze creation. Olivia's jewels were eye catching, a brilliant necklace and matching earrings of diamonds and rubies. She cast Rachel Pettigrew, modestly dressed in a cream silk which emphasized her pallor, completely in the shade. But then, Arabella conceded, Mrs. Gresham probably always attracted attention. Pure jealousy, she conceded, for Olivia Gresham was a startlingly beautiful woman. Alice Overton, who studied to be unobtrusive, again wore gray, not a flattering color.

Conversation at the table consisted mainly of the general discussing his martial exploits. He received little assistance from Mark Rothfield, who had escorted Alice in to dinner and was seated directly across from Arabella. Arabella noticed that Rothfield's expression was closed and watchful, and she wondered what he really thought of his chief. Uncritical admiration was certainly not evident in his reaction, but the general did not appear to notice. Olivia Gresham gave Pettigrew all the encouragement and admiration he needed, and Arabella found herself disliking her guardian more and more as the evening progressed.

After a splendid meal of partridge, roast beef, and syllabub, she followed her hostess, Mrs. Gresham, and Alice into the drawing room, determined to quiz Rachel Pettigrew. This visit was not progressing as she had hoped, but she would not abandon her intention to solve the question of her missing funds.

Seating herself beside Rachel, Arabella made an effort to win that shy woman's confidence.

"I can see you have arranged for our comfort and enjoyment this Christmas. I do hope it has not been too much for you," Arabella said kindly. She was concerned about her hostess' wan expression and the nervous tremors which afflicted Rachel. Evidently Mrs. Pettigrew was very unhappy, and Arabella suspected she knew the reason.

"Not at all. The general was eager for you to join us and for old friends to gather here this Christmas."

"Is Mrs. Gresham an old friend?" Arabella asked boldly, wondering what Rachel's reaction to such an outrageous question would be.

"Well, of course, I do not know her so . . ." Rachel looked distractedly at Alice Overton as if wishing for some relief.

Taking pity on her, Arabella changed the subject. "But Sir William is a friend of long standing. What a nice man he seems to be."

"Oh yes, William is a dear, so easy and undemanding. I knew him as a girl, you know," Rachel explained, anxious to avoid any discussion of Olivia Gresham, which intensified Arabella's belief that Rachel knew exactly what that lady's relationship to her husband was.

"He seems very fond of you," Arabella probed.

"I almost married him," Rachel blurted out. Then recollecting where her loyalty lay, she added, "But then Roland came along, so dashing, so insistent, and my parents felt . . ." Her explanation trailed off.

No doubt a far better *parti,* and Rachel could not have prevailed against an ambitious mother, Arabella thought a bit caustically. But she showed none of her disgust. "And did you enjoy following the drum?"

"Well, I did little of that, you know. Roland felt campaigning was too arduous for me, especially after I lost the baby," Rachel explained.

"What a shame," Arabella's sympathy was engaged by this poor distracted woman, who had never realized that by giving in to her bully of a husband she had only earned his contempt. It was unfair to press her, but Arabella could not resist one further question. "Did you know my parents well, Mrs. Pettigrew?"

"Not as well as Roland, but your mother was a lovely woman. Such a tragedy for them both to die so young and leave you an orphan," Rachel's kind heart went out to this bereft girl, although she envied Arabella's poise and adaptability. "They left you well provided for, which must be a comfort," she added as if that somehow excused their deaths.

"And the general has proved such a conscientious guardian," Arabella offered, not at all sure she was convinced of that.

"Naturally, he regretted not seeing more of you, but now you are here, he hopes to make up for past neglect," Rachel said in defense of any criticism, which must mean she felt there was some reason to excuse him. Arabella altered her opinion of her hostess, deciding that Rachel was not as indifferent to events as she had first appeared. She would have liked to pursue the matter further, but just then the gentlemen joined them.

She noticed that Alice Overton tried to attract Mark Rothfield's attention, but he came over to his hostess instead. The general joined Mrs. Gresham, making no attempt to hide his interest. After a few words to her, he turned to the company, and said with a smile, "Olivia has kindly promised to sing for us. She has a charming voice. Alice, my dear, I know you will be pleased to accompany her."

Whether Alice was pleased seemed unimportant. She took her place at the pianoforte and looked expectantly at Mrs. Gresham, who glided over to the instrument, and then summoned the general archly. "You must turn the pages for me, Roland," she insisted coquettishly.

"Delighted," he agreed, looking at her possessively, and taking a stand near the pianoforte where he could continue to enjoy her languishing looks.

Arabella was not surprised to discover that the lady had a trained and clear contralto which did justice to the rather spirited rendition she gave of some old country tunes. Then Olivia insisted they all join in with the songs of the season, which they proceeded to do. Only Rachel Pettigrew remained by the coffee service and ignored the caroling group. The singing managed to dispel some of the awkwardness of the evening, and some vestige of Christmas spirit lightened the hearts of the assembly. But Arabella, joining in with enthusiasm, could not help but think they were a strange company, all with thoughts far from peace and good will.

As the last chords sounded Rachel slipped away, missed by no one with the exception of Sir William, whose gaze followed her wistfully as she left the room. Arabella noticed he watched General Pettigrew and Mrs. Gresham with a disapproving eye. Alice Overton, her duties finished, sidled up to Mark Rothfield and drew him to one side, which left Austin Gresham to make his approaches to Arabella. If she found his cloying compliments a trial she did not give any evidence of it.

Finally the evening wound to an end, the general reminding Sir William and Mark that they would be joining him on a ride about the estate in the morning. Austin refused the invitation, insisting he wanted to escort Arabella on a walk instead. She felt courtesy demanded she agree, but she was not anticipating another intimate conversation with this shallow man. As she was about to depart for her bedroom, Mark Rothfield approached her.

"I am so sorry we had so little chance to talk this evening, Miss Stapleton. Perhaps tomorrow you will have some time for me." He smiled winningly and with what Arabella thought was sincerity. Still, she was conscious of Alice's eye on them and did not rush into agreement.

"I am sure that can be arranged, Captain Rothfield, if your duties permit," she assented a bit sharply. He looked amused, as if he knew exactly what she was thinking, but bowed and said, "I will see that they do."

Arabella could not help but feel a small glow of excitement, which was quickly quenched when Alice, accompanying her to her room, said smugly, "Mark is so attractive, and I fear he has quite an eye for the ladies. Not to be taken seriously, of course, but it can cause misunderstanding."

"I am sure I understand Captain Rothfield, Miss Overton. I have had some experience with gallant young officers," Arabella replied. Then she added for good measure, "Bath is crowded with the military, you know."

"I meant no malice, Miss Stapleton. Now have you everything you need?" Alice retreated swiftly into her role of meek companion, not fooling Arabella for a moment. Alice Overton would not accept any rivalry in her aim to attach the captain.

Lying in bed, Arabella, although tired from her long day of traveling and meeting the Pettigrews and their guests, could not fall asleep. Overstimulated by the challenge of these various personalities, and the enigma of the general, she felt on the edge of some crisis. The clatter of the wind through the avenue of barren beeches beyond the windows of her room only added to her feeling of uneasiness. Why had the general invited this strange assortment of people for this holiday? She doubted he was filled with the spirit of peace and good will normally attributed to the season. How insensitive to make overtures to Mrs. Gresham under the eyes of his wife. Had he invited his former schoolmate, Sir William, to prove his own superiority and worldly success?

And Mark Rothfield. Surely such a personable and well-connected young man would have preferred to spend Christmas with friends and family in a more intimate and relaxed manner. Wouldn't the general have granted him leave if he had asked for it? Did that mean Rothfield really cared for Alice Overton, as the general hinted? Would this Christmas see an announcement of their engagement? Arabella did not believe that Mark cared two pins for Alice Overton. He had some other, mysterious reason for remaining at Winterbourne Manor this holiday.

And why had the general insisted on her own presence? He had been content to ignore her for six years, using the excuse of his military duties, a pretext Arabella believed spurious. Surely, if Pettigrew had cared enough he could have spared the time to visit one lonely orphaned girl.

Arabella wanted to be fair, but her instinctive distrust and dislike for her guardian could not be denied. Had he asked her only to allay her fears about her dwindling income, spurred to such a pass by her solicitor's uncomfortable questions? She would tax him about this alteration in her affairs in the morning, for she could not settle until she learned whether her suspicions were unfounded or unhappily deserved. She would insist on an accounting as soon as the general returned from his morning ride. Having made her decision, Arabella slowly drifted into sleep, her last thoughts not of her guardian's guilt or innocence but of his enigmatic and attractive aide, Mark Rothfield.

Toward dawn Arabella fell into a deep slumber after several hours of tossing and turning, and was surprised to be awakened by her abigail when the morning was more advanced than she wanted.

Drawing wide the curtains, Betsy told her mistress that the day was quite fine but with little hope of snow if she were wishing for a white Christmas.

"Very warm for the season, they was telling me in the hall," Betsy confided in her soft Somerset drawl, meanwhile setting the rooms to right and placing a tea tray across Arabella's knees.

"I hope you are not unhappy, missing your family at Christmas, Betsy. I am so grateful that you consented to come with me." Arabella further expressed her gratitude with a smile.

"Land's sakes, miss, why wouldn't I rather be here than in that crowded cottage with my sister Jane's brats creating a ruckus and Ma making me do all the work? And you have always been so good to me, taking me untrained an' all. There is not much I wouldn't do for you, Miss Arabella."

Touched by this testimony of affection from the usually taciturn Betsy, Arabella felt immensely cheered. "Well, I must dress and join the other guests. I should not have slept so late. What will Mrs. Pettigrew think?"

"She won't care. And that hoighty-toity Mrs. Gresham

hasn't stirred yet. The niece is up. Fair gives me the shivers the way she sidles around, spying on everyone. And she was quite sharp with one of the housemaids this morning, though what call she has to criticize, I don't know," Betsy sniffed. Like most of her kind she did not respect dependents of the quality, and she had taken Alice Overton's measure immediately.

"Well, I think she tries to help her aunt. Mrs. Pettigrew seems quite frail, and perhaps depends on her niece to take over some of the household management," Arabella explained, not wanting to pay heed to Betsy's gossip, but not entirely disagreeing with it.

"Miss Prim-and-Goodly she is now, but once she catches that handsome captain, you see how her tune changes. I know her kind," Betsy insisted uncharitably.

Unable to resist, Arabella asked, "And do the servants think he will offer for her?"

"Not for a minute, for all the general keeps nudging him. The captain, a real handsome gentleman, can do a great deal better for himself. It's a mystery why he stays here," Betsy said shrewdly.

Arabella, in thorough agreement, realized she must restore some decorum to the conversation. She had no business querying her abigail about her fellow guests. "Well, Betsy, enough of this gossiping, not at all the thing. I believe my blue merino for this morning. This house appears very drafty, and in it I would be comfortable."

Betsy soon had Arabella dressed and ready to descend to the hall to discover what her hostess had planned for the guests. With several days remaining before Christmas, Rachel must be at her wits end for entertainment, Arabella decided. Accustomed as she was to the sociable and busy routine of Bath, she wondered if there were any exchanges between the Pettigrews and their neighbors. If not, the Pettigrews must find Winterbourne Manor rather tedious. As she walked into the dining room, she saw that only Austin was still at the dining table. Oh, dear, she really was not in the mood for his flirtatious ways.

"Ah, good morning, Miss Stapleton. Lovely day. I do hope I can hold you to that walk later this morning. Dashed fine weather," he exclaimed with rather forced jollity.

Arabella, now being served some ham and baked eggs by the silent Baker, nodded cheerfully at Austin but made no promises. In a few moments they were joined by Alice Overton. Mrs. Pettigrew evidently did not breakfast with her guests. Alice made her excuses.

"Aunt Rachel rarely breakfasts downstairs, preferring the privacy of her room, and of course, she often does not really feel well. I try to spare her as much anxiety as possible," she explained with what Arabella thought rather prim complacence.

"Yes, of course, most kind I am sure," Austin answered inanely. He seemed to find Alice Overton intimidating and turned from her to seek Arabella's more comfortable conversation.

"The general and Sir William have a nice morning for their ride," Alice offered. "And Mark went with them. He is such a splendid horseman, and likes the exercise whenever he can be spared from his duties." Her insistence on bringing Mark's name into the conversation whenever possible seemed rather pathetic to Arabella. Although she could not warm to Alice, she felt sorry for her due to her anomalous position in this household.

"Do you ride yourself, Miss Overton?" Austin asked in a bored tone. He really must take his mother to task for dragging him along on this odious house party. Too wearying for words.

"No, no. I wish I did. I have asked Mark to teach me, but he is so busy with the general's affairs, we haven't been able to set a time."

Arabella cast about a bit frantically for some other topic of conversation. "What time will the gentlemen return? I really would like a private talk with my guardian," she said to Alice.

As long as the private talk would not be with Mark, it

was evident that Alice would do all in her power to fall in with Arabella's wishes. "Well, usually the general is gone about two hours. He likes to ride about the estate to see that all is marching well, repairs, you know, and visits with the tenants. Not that there are too many, just the Home Farm and two outlying smaller farms which have been leased by the same families for years."

"How far are you from the nearest village?" Arabella asked, more to be amiable than from any real desire to know.

"Well, Badminster is about ten miles. Really, we are quite isolated here."

"Still, in the summer months, I suspect it is delightful," Arabella contributed. And I understand you will be off to Salisbury in the spring. That will be pleasant."

"Yes, indeed. Both Mark and I are looking forward to it," Alice agreed. And what did she mean by that? Arabella wondered.

Austin, annoyed at being ignored, turned to Arabella. "And now, how about our walk, Miss Stapleton?" Since politeness demanded it, he added, "Will you join us, Miss Overton?"

"Thank you, but no. I have several chores I must attend to, as well as consulting the cook and checking with Baker, you see, about tonight's arrangements."

Alice's refusal provoked relief in both Austin and Arabella. Seeing no way out of the stroll, Arabella said she would meet Austin in the hall after donning cloak, hat, and gloves. Then she left the dining room, wondering with some amusement how Austin would persevere with Alice.

A few moments later Arabella and Austin left by the terrace doors leading from the dining room into the barren garden. As she suspected, Austin was a stroller rather than a walker, and preferred conversation to a brisk pace. They proceeded slowly through the formal garden, where a few late roses still bloomed, and wandered toward the heath. Turning to examine an unusual bit of shrubbery, Arabella caught sight of their hostess strolling in the distance. Indicating the figure to her companion, she said idly, "There is Mrs. Pettigrew. I thought Alice suggested she remained in her bedroom for most of the morning."

"She is probably taking advantage of this amazingly clement weather," Austin suggested languidly.

Not wishing to be rude, and eager to break up their tête-à-tête, Arabella hailed her hostess, who looked toward them in confusion, as if wondering who they were. Then, seeing there was no chance of avoiding them, she waited until they caught up with her. She wore only a shawl over her brown morning dress, but she carried a basket over her arm in which lay a bunch of Michaelmas daisies.

"Just looking for a few late-blooming flowers, to brighten the Christmas greens," she explained as they drew near. "How lax of me to absent myself. I should be asking you what you wish to do this morning. I am afraid it is rather dull for you."

"Miss Overton told us you would be resting," Arabella explained, seeing that Austin would be of no help in reassuring Rachel.

"Yes, well, I was restless. And since we have invited some neighbors for dinner this evening, I thought some flowers for the table . . ." Rachel's voice trailed off as though these explanations were too tiring.

"We are just admiring the gardens," Austin said tepidly.

"Not at their best just now, I fear, although some flowers are still blooming. But I will not interrupt your walk. The men should be in soon from their ride, I suppose," Rachel suggested vaguely.

As if on cue, Sir William appeared, almost running from the direction of the stables. Seeing Rachel, he hesitated, then, trying for composure stopped, steadied himself and announced, "Roland has had an accident, fell off his horse. I left the captain with him and have sent one of the grooms for a doctor, but we must get him back to the house. I am sorry, Rachel, to give you such news."

"How could such a thing have happened? Roland is such a splendid rider. Is he badly hurt?" Rachel asked anxiously.

Sir William hesitated, and Arabella thought he was not prepared to tell Rachel just how badly the general had been injured. "I don't know, but we must get him home. The doctor is ten miles away and will be a time getting here. We cannot leave him out there on the heath."

"No, of course not. We must send some men out. . . ." Rachel's normal indecisiveness seemed to take over, and she looked distractedly at Arabella as if her guest might solve the problem. Seeing that Rachel was rapidly losing control, Arabella responded crisply. "Austin, why don't you and Sir William organize some of the footmen or grooms and secure a wagon. I think it's dangerous to move injured people, but we surely cannot leave him there, as you say, especially since it looks as if the weather is lowering. I will take Mrs. Pettigrew to her room. She should not be left alone now."

"Quite right, Miss Stapleton. What a sensible girl you are. Come along, Graham. We will get the men off in the wagon."

Austin had contributed little to these plans, and looked as if the whole affair was not his concern, but he could hardly ignore this plea for his help so he trailed off after Sir William.

Arabella, gently nudging Rachel toward the house, was rather surprised at Mrs. Pettigrew's lack of reaction, but attributed it to shock. After hurriedly escorting Rachel to her bedroom, she called her maid, instructing the woman to give her mistress sal volatile and some hot sweet tea. Leaving Rachel in the maid's competent hands, she went to alert the rest of the household. She met Baker in the hall and asked the butler where Alice Overton could be found, thinking Rachel Pettigrew would prefer the company of her niece to a relative stranger.

"I am afraid, Baker, that the general has met with an accident. The men will be bringing him home soon, and we have sent for the doctor. But where is Miss Overton?"

"I believe she went for a walk on the grounds, miss,"

83

Baker informed her. If he was distressed or surprised by the news of the general's accident, he did not show it. Arabella wondered fleetingly what he really thought of his master. But she had little time to worry about Baker's feelings. She must find Alice. How peculiar that she had gone for a walk on the grounds after refusing Austin's invitation to accompany them on their morning stroll. Before she could pursue this thought Alice ran into the hall and, seeing Arabella, cried out, "I understand there has been an accident. Where is Captain Rothfield?"

Taking pity on the distraught girl, Arabella explained, "The general took a toss from his horse. Captain Rothfield remained with him while Sir William came back with the news and to get help. He has sent a groom for the doctor. That is all I know, Miss Overton. Mrs. Pettigrew is naturally upset, and I took her to her room. I think she needs you."

For a moment Arabella glimpsed an ugly expression in Alice's eyes, quickly masked by a show of compassion. "Poor lady. I do hope it is not serious. Aunt Rachel is so prone to vapors. I will go right up."

Arabella watched as Alice calmly took off her shawl, which was all the covering she had worn on this mild day. Where had the girl been? Surely she had not gone to the stables to accost Captain Rothfield when he returned from his ride, hoping for a private conversation. And that nasty look. What had that meant? Was it just animosity toward Arabella, or had it some deeper meaning? Really, the inmates of this house were an enigma, all having private thoughts they were reluctant to reveal, none of them exactly what they seemed.

Arabella, not knowing quite what to do while awaiting the arrival of the injured man, walked restlessly toward the morning room. Here she tried to settle into a chair near the fire, hoping to get her thoughts in order. Sir William had been rather incoherent, understandably, but Arabella wondered just how serious the general's injuries were. She suspected it would take the doctor some time to arrive, and hoped he would not be too late, for somehow she sensed that this accident had been a serious one. Obviously the general was unconscious, unable to remount his horse, and perhaps he was losing blood from his fall. How had the accident happened? The general was an experienced horseman, accustomed to riding over these familiar acres. Had his horse shied unexpectedly, or stumbled? A miserable outcome to what might have been a pleasant holiday, Arabella decided, but then she caught herself up. The holiday, even before this had shown no signs of being a happy occasion. There were too many inchoate emotions, too many complicated motives among the various guests. She wished she had never entered Winterbourne Manor, and she suspected several of the other guests shared her feelings.

Her musings were interrupted by a disturbance in the hall, and she hurried to the door of the morning room to see two burly men carrying the general's inert form into the library, followed by an anxious Sir William and a cool, if a trifle muddied Captain Rothfield. He did not accompany the others into the library, but noticed Arabella hesitating in the doorway of the morning room and walked across to her.

"I suppose you have heard that the general has fallen from his horse," he said abruptly. "Come in here. I must talk to somebody, and you seem a sensible girl." A bit taken aback by this announcement, Arabella was too curious to take offense, and stepped aside so that the captain could join her. He walked over to the fireplace, where he stood for a moment warming his hands.

"It's damnable. I don't know what to do. After Sir William left to get help, the general's horse returned and began to move toward his master, who was lying on the ground. I noticed that the saddle was askew, and when I led the horse away and tied him to a nearby tree, I examined the saddle carefully. The girth had been cut through. Someone had sliced it, probably only partially, and when the general rode at his usual headlong pace, the girth fell apart, causing the general to lose his seat. It was a malicious act if not worse. I know the doctor has been sent for, but the man is dead, a broken neck. The accident was deliberate," Mark Rothfield explained.

"But that is horrible. Who could have played such a trick?" Arabella gasped.

"Not a trick, I believe. The general was not universally beloved, you know. I suppose there are several of us in this house party who will not mourn him," he said with a ferocious frown, eyeing Arabella sardonically.

If she were shocked, she did not show it. "Even you, Captain Rothfield?"

"Especially me. I disliked him heartily. I only took this post to discover some evidence that he sent my brother to his death. Then I intended to lay the story before a court-martial board. The man was a menace," he blurted out.

"Well, I admit to having wondered why you were here. You did not appear inordinately attached to General Pettigrew. But, then, I did not find him an agreeable man myself," Arabella said calmly.

If the general's accident had been contrived she did not find it either surprising or a matter for grief, and she made no attempt to dissemble. "He was my guardian, but we had very little to do with one another. I came on this visit very reluctantly, in order to discover what he had been doing with my income. My solicitor thought he was manipulating my funds. Although I will not accuse him of embezzlement, I wanted some answers," she explained frankly, responding to Mark Rothfield's own disclosure of an ulterior motive for his attendance at this house party.

"Thank goodness you have been honest with me. I thought you were a sensible girl, and I was right. I expect there will be a great deal of false regret and sham sentiment expressed when the general's fate is made known, but we at least can be truthful with one another. I quite agree with you that he was a disagreeable man, and several of the guests here besides myself will shed no tears for him."

While Arabella applauded Mark Rothfield's forthright

manner, she did not wholly enjoy being thought of as a sensible girl, a suitable person for confidences and little more. In that she was underestimating the officer.

"Listen, Arabella, if I may call you that. I believe I can trust you, and I hope you return the compliment. This household is a very uneasy one. Sir William dislikes the way the general has treated his wife. I suspect Mrs. Gresham's only interest in the general was to wheedle money from him. She has a notorious reputation, and that son of hers is always under the hatches. We each have our own reasons for detesting Pettigrew, and I cannot think Miss Overton liked him overmuch either, plaguey female that she is. He kept trying to foist her on me because he fancied the Rothfield connection." Mark Rothfield's scorn was evident, and Arabella felt a small glow of reassurance. Obviously he did not care at all for Alice Overton.

"But if you think someone in this household arranged for the general's death, whom do you suspect?"

"Well, neither you nor me," he insisted with a small smile. "But that still leaves several suspects. That man Baker for one. He was the general's batman, but I don't think he is especially devoted to him. I wonder what hold the general had on the brute."

"Oh, dear. It's all so hateful, and at Christmas time, when we should be hoping for peace and goodwill," Arabella protested. "How will you discover who is responsible, and if you do, what then?" she asked, going straight to the heart of the problem.

"I don't know. It would be my duty to drag the culprit before the parish constable or magistrate and see that he paid for his crime. But I am not sure I would do that. I just have to know, to satisfy my conscience, I guess," he said in a troubled tone. "Will you help me?"

"Of course. But what can I do?" Arabella felt pleased that the captain wanted her assistance, but she had several questions of her own. Not for a moment did she think him capable of such a despicable act. If he disliked the general, as he had admitted, and wanted to bring him to justice for the death of his brother, she sensed he would not have taken his revenge in such a paltry underhanded manner. He would challenge the man outright, after finding some evidence of his villainy. Why she had such confidence in Mark Rothfield she did not know, but from the beginning she had felt sympathy with him, and he must feel equally confident of her or he would not have been so open.

"We will have to put our heads together and see what we can learn about motive and opportunity. But first I will change from these mud-stained clothes, and I must be on hand when the doctor arrives. Then I'll see about notifying the magistrate. Thank you for your trust, Arabella."

"You're welcome, and I thank you for your faith in me," she responded simply.

"I meant what I said about your being a sensible girl, but you are also a very attractive one. I think I will enjoy our collaboration, and perhaps we will both find what we are seeking." He crossed to her side and took her hand. "If there is a murderer in this house, take care. I would not want anything to happen to you. About the only decent outcome of this house party is my meeting you. I wonder if you feel the same." He looked down at her with a warmth that was unmistakable.

A bit breathless in the face of this plunge into emotion, Arabella found herself at a loss. Could he mean what she hoped he meant? All thoughts of the general and his mysterious accident receded under the impact of a rush of feeling she could not describe. But Arabella was as honest as she was sensible, and she could not disguise her reactions. "I do, Mark, but this is hardly the time to pursue our own emotions. As you do, I want to find out what happened."

"Yes, that must be our first priority. But, Arabella, don't be misled by Alice Overton. I care nothing for the girl, and I owe her no allegiance. Until now I have been quite heart free," he insisted, but behind those fervent words was an implication she could not ignore.

A certain confusion prevented Arabella from quizzing him further. She absolved him of being a flirt, but what was happening to them was too sudden for her to comprehend. She retreated into practicality.

"Do go change, and while you are gone, I will give some hard thought to how we should proceed. There are some questions we must discuss—about where the members of this household were this morning."

"I will be quick. Wait for me," he requested. Then, taking her hand, he raised it to his lips. "Till later." And he walked from the room, leaving Arabella prey to some expectations which had little to do with the puzzle of the general's accident. Before she could gather her thoughts, she was interrupted by Sir William, who entered almost on Mark's heels.

"Ah, Miss Stapleton, this is a sad affair. General Pettigrew is dead," Sir William informed her in sorrowing tones. "Frightful. He was such a fine rider. Always was a hard goer, but I never thought he would come to such an end. Took a header at the five-barred gate, a tricky jump, but I still can't understand it."

Arabella, not wanting to break Mark's confidence and explain that the general's death had been caused by a cut girth, murmured something soothing. "I know it is a shock. He was such a vital man."

"I always believed he'd outlive me. I'm the old prosy one, never wanted excitement nor adventure. He might have been killed in battle, but to die this way . . ." Sir William sank into a chair by the fire, looking completely befuddled. "Poor Rachel. I wonder how she is." He turned to Arabella, as if she might provide him with some comfort, but she felt he was barely seeing her, had no real idea of who she was.

"I believe Miss Overton is with her. Has the doctor come? Perhaps he might see Mrs. Pettigrew, give her a sleeping draught," Arabella suggested, not quite knowing how to go on.

"Yes, the doctor is with her now, I think. He looked at Roland, said he had broken his neck. It's horrible, and with Christmas almost upon us, that makes it even more tragic," Sir William shook his head as if the whole affair was too much for him to accept.

Arabella, wanting to question him about the accident, hesitated. It seemed so heartless, for Sir William appeared to genuinely mourn his friend, and she thought the better of him for it, although she could not share his reaction. She barely knew the general, and what she had learned from coming to this troubled household had not evoked any affection for her erstwhile guardian. If what Mark had told her was true, and she wanted to believe him, General Pettigrew was responsible for his brother's death. And certainly Rachel Pettigrew had no reason to feel anything but relief at her husband's sudden end. She might be misjudging the woman. Perhaps, despite his treatment of her, Rachel still cared for Pettigrew, but Arabella could not quite accept that. And Sir William himself must have resented his former schoolmate for marrying the girl he himself loved and then causing her unhappiness. Could this just be a clever act, designed to lull any suspicions? Arabella's curiosity was aroused.

"Did the general seem in good health and spirits when you started on your ride, Sir William? If he had been feeling ill, faint perhaps, or was worried or distracted, that might account for the accident."

"No, no, he was in fine fettle, enjoying this holiday, and quite looking forward to the party tonight. Oh, dear, we must do something about these people. We can't have them here now," Sir William fussed, but obviously he was unable to assume any authoritative role in sorting out the household. Arabella, realizing that Sir William was overcome by the tragedy, or perhaps by remorse, decided this was a task she could assume.

"I will see Baker, cancel the dinner if this has not already been done. I am sure notes can be sent around to the neighbors, and the magistrate will have to be notified, in any case."

"Yes, yes. Good of you, my dear."

Arabella waited a moment, wanting to ask Sir William

if he had noticed anything at all that might throw light on the accident, but somehow she could not bring herself to question him. "If you will excuse me, then, sir. Unless there is anything I can do for you."

"No, I think not. I just can't quite take it all in. Shock, I expect. You might ask that Baker fellow to send in some brandy," Sir William suggested. Then he stared vacantly at his boots, at a complete loss on how to proceed.

Arabella, eager to be gone, left him to his musings. She could not believe that Sir William was enough of a dissembler to behave thus if he had had any hand in the general's death. But, she reminded herself that someone had cut the girth. And Sir William had had as much opportunity as any member of the household. He must have noticed Rachel's unhappiness. In a fit of anger or sorrow, could he have taken such a drastic step to rid himself of a rival? Arabella doubted Sir William had the decisive and ruthless character which would impel him to murder his onetime friend, but what did she know of festering jealousy and envy?

Crossing the hall on the way upstairs she met Baker emerging from the library. Calling to him, she told him of Sir William's request for brandy, then said a bit tentatively, "I know the Pettigrews had invited some friends for dinner this evening. I suppose the affair had best be canceled, and the proper authorities notified. Could you arrange that? I don't want to interfere, but I doubt Mrs. Pettigrew would want to entertain this evening."

The man's stolid face and hard eyes reflected no sentiment. He appeared unaffected by the tragedy. Had he no fondness for his late master?

"Yes, miss. I will attend to it. Captain Rothfield has already asked me. The doctor has just gone up to the mistress, and he said he would attend to the formalities. I imagine he will consult with Captain Rothfield," the butler informed her tersely.

"Thank you, Baker," Arabella was happy to escape the man for the safety of her room. Something in his manner repelled her. Normally she had friendly relations with servants, but she knew she could never warm to Baker. He had a secretive, almost insolent air, and now seemed almost smug. Could he be another who was relieved at the general's death? What a tortuous household this was, with so many hidden emotions and false faces.

Arabella suddenly felt overwhelmed by the fact that Winterbourne Manor, decorated for the Christmas holidays, had now become a house of death. Who among the guests hated the general enough to plan his death? Surely not Mrs. Gresham or her inadequate son, Austin. Neither of them could possibly benefit. On the contrary, Mrs. Gresham would lose both a lover and a source of income. Somehow Arabella could not imagine that sophisticated lady cutting the girth of the general's horse. And certainly her son, unless he had some reason for hating his mother's liaison, would not have made an attempt to murder his host. Of course, Arabella admitted, as she paced back and forth in her bedroom, she really knew little about the Greshams. Blackmail, scandal, resentment—all could be motives for either Austin or Mrs. Gresham.

There was the enigmatic and untruthful Alice Overton. But what could she gain from the general's death? Perhaps behind that meek facade lay another woman altogether. She needed the general's help in securing a suitable marriage, if not to Mark Rothfield then to some other eligible young man, but she must resent her equivocal position in this house.

Or could some groom or servant have decided to remove his master? Baker came to mind, but there might be others. How would they ever unmask the murderer? Arabella, beginning to feel the weight of suspicion and confusion dogging her, could no longer stay isolated in her room. She needed to take some action.

She walked down the hall and knocked softly on Rachel Pettigrew's door. The least she could do would be to inquire as to that poor woman's state of mind. After a few moments, Alice stuck her head out, keeping a firm hand on the door and not allowing Arabella entrance.

"How is Mrs. Pettigrew? Is there anything I can do?"

"She is sleeping. The doctor gave her a draught. It's all so ghastly, and somehow it seems worse that tomorrow night is Christmas Eve," Alice said, and for the first time Arabella felt some compassion toward the girl. It was dreadful for her and she appeared genuinely upset.

"Yes, it is a most regrettable accident. I wonder if we should leave. Surely Mrs. Pettigrew cannot want a houseful of people now."

"Perhaps that will be best. I will consult Mark. He will know what to do," Alice said, as usual wanting assurances from Mark, and again giving Arabella the suggestion that Rothfield was her ally in this trouble.

"I am prepared to do whatever Mrs. Pettigrew wants. If there is nothing to be done for her now, I will leave you unless you want me to sit with her for a while," Arabella offered.

"No, I think I had better stay. If she wakes she will not want a strange face in her bedroom. But will you ask Mark to come up? No doubt he is conferring with the doctor or magistrate. I understand Sir Joseph Hartley has been sent for."

"Certainly. I will attend to it right away." Arabella left, feeling even more disturbed. Was she wrong to trust Mark? Could Alice and Mark have conspired together. She wandered down toward the stairs, feeling useless and unhappy. Oh, why had she ever accepted this invitation?

As she reached the hall Mark was bidding farewell to a tall portly man. This must be the magistrate. She waited until the door closed on Sir Joseph, if that was the man, and then called to Mark.

"Alice wants to talk to you. She is sitting with Mrs. Pettigrew and needs some advice as to how to proceed, I think."

"Drat the girl. She is a menace. Any pity I feel for her is swamped by annoyance. I do wish she would realize that I am not prepared to be her protector and counsel. Come let us repair to the morning room and discuss this. Alice can wait," Mark insisted, almost pushing Arabella along the hall.

"But shouldn't you . . ." Arabella's protests were stifled after one look at his grim face.

In the morning room, he went directly to the fireplace and dropped some logs on the dying embers. Suddenly Arabella felt a chill foreboding. What was he going to ask her?

"Listen, Arabella. Sir Joseph, the magistrate, has stated that the general's death was an accident. I did not tell him of the cut girth, for what use would be served by raising all sorts of suspicion and trouble. I must admit I believe the man deserved his fate."

"But you can't condone murder?" Arabella gasped, sitting down suddenly as if the breath were knocked out of her.

"Perhaps not, although I am convinced the general did not jibe at my brother's death. But I can see no way to bring the murderer to justice. We have no proof that someone tampered with the saddle. Atkins, the groom, brought the horses around to the door, where the general and I were waiting. Sir William joined us almost immediately. There was no opportunity to do the job then. The girth must have been cut before the horses left the stable. Do you know where any of the household was at the crucial time?"

"Well, Alice, Austin, and I were in the dining room finishing breakfast. Then Austin asked me to go for a walk and I agreed. I had to go upstairs for my cloak, but I was only away for a few moments. We left almost immediately by the terrace doors to the garden."

"What about Alice?" Mark asked tersely.

"We asked her to accompany us, but she pleaded household duties. It was strange, because when we came in, she was just returning from outside. I have no idea what she was doing? But surely . . ." Arabella's voice trailed off. She was appalled at the thought of Alice as a ruthless killer.

94

"Perhaps. Well, you can give Austin an alibi, unless he arose early and sneaked out to the stable, which seems unlikely. And why would he want to kill the general? Unless he disliked his mother's arrangement with him." Mark frowned, entertaining that idea and then rejecting it. "No, I can't believe Austin is our murderer. Not that he would have scruples, rather he is lazy, indecisive, and cowardly," he judged with scorn.

"But it was a cowardly trick," Arabella objected, thinking she would not be disappointed if Austin had behaved thus.

"True. But then there is Alice. Did you see her during your walk, coming from the stables perhaps?"

"No, the only person we met was Mrs. Pettigrew who had been picking flowers. She had her basket on her arm."

"A basket," Mark exclaimed, his eyes brightening. Then he shrugged. "No, it's not possible."

Whatever Arabella expected, it was not an interruption by Alice Overton, although she should have known better. Alice sidled into the room, looking reproachfully at Mark, and turning to Arabella with a sad little smile. "You must have forgotten to give my message to Mark, Arabella, but I know how distracted you probably are."

"I had several claims on my time, Alice. What is it you wish to see me about?" Mark asked so abruptly that Arabella was almost embarrassed for Alice. But evidently Alice chose not to take offense. Moving closer to him, she said suggestively, "If we could be alone for a moment."

Arabella almost laughed at the look on Mark's face, but controlled herself. Couldn't the foolish girl realize he did not want to be alone with her? How could she ignore his indifference?

Mark, although perfectly polite, was not to be maneuvered.

"I am sure Arabella can help you with whatever seems to be troubling you. I have found her most resourceful," he explained with a wicked look at his co-conspirator.

Not easily rebuffed, Alice again smiled sadly as if deploring his lack of understanding. "Well, really, I wanted your advice about this house party. Surely Aunt Rachel cannot be expected to entertain guests after this tragedy. She is prostrate."

"You can hardly turf out people a few days before Christmas. And there might be a need for witnesses before the magistrates' court. I think they must stay at least until the funeral."

If Alice was disappointed, she hid it well. "Of course, we will be guided by you, Mark. I know Aunt Rachel is depending on you, as I am, to help us through this ordeal. She really is not well enough to cope with all the arrangements, and guests, too." Obviously Alice wanted to get Mark to herself and thought the death of General Pettigrew offered a fine pretext.

"I think you will find she will rally round quite quickly," Mark said wryly, reminding Arabella of his last words before Alice had interrupted them. Then, brusquely, Mark returned to the problem Alice posed. "I am perfectly willing to help both you and Mrs. Pettigrew through the next few days until the funeral. But then I will be leaving, as will the rest of the guests." He determined to make his position clear. In Alice's place, Arabella believed she would prefer it that way, but she doubted if Alice did. And she was right.

"Oh, Mark, how can you be so cruel, to abandon me, us, at a time like this. I was hoping . . ." She seemed to have lost all propriety, appeared to be ready to throw herself on his mercy even if watched by an embarrassed stranger. But Mark was equal to her appeal.

"Come now, Alice, you mustn't give way. Rachel will be relying on you for comfort. You must understand that with the general's death there is no longer a need for me here. I must return to my regiment," he explained reasonably.

But Alice was not to be consoled. Turning to Arabella, she gave her a look compounded of malice and frustration, and blurted out her disappointment. "It's your fault. I will never forgive you for casting out lures . . . you had no right . . . I explained. . . ." Then searching Mark's stony face for any sign of reprieve and finding none, she burst into tears and, gasping "Oh, I hate you, hate you both," ran sobbing from the room.

Arabella, feeling for the wretched girl, was inclined to go after her and started to do so, but Mark grasped her shoulders firmly. "Oh, no you don't. I will not be forced by that miserable girl into a compromising position, then forced into a sudden engagement. She has been working toward that end since I arrived here, and no matter how I ignored her she would not be discouraged. She had the general as an ally. I strongly object to being chivied into a misalliance. I am perfectly capable of choosing my own wife, and let me tell you, it won't be Alice Overton." His look into Arabella's eyes was full of meaning, and she hoped she understood what he intended. But with Alice's example before her she did not intend to make a fool of herself, no matter how much she wanted to believe him.

She gave him a stern look, and removed herself from his grasp before her feelings could betray her. "When we were interrupted, you looked as though you had made a startling discovery."

Amused, Mark merely grinned unrepentantly, and said, "Quite right. We must settle this business before we turn to our own affairs. But I warn you, Arabella, I will not be deterred from improving our relationship. I will follow you to Bath and camp on your doorstep, if need be."

Reassured, Arabella was still hesitant to let him have his way. "We will see. I rather suspect you of having the military's penchant for flirtation, Captain." Then she turned to the matter which concerned them both. "What did I say about meeting Mrs. Pettigrew that caught your attention?"

"The flower basket, Arabella. Don't you see that anyone who meant to cut that girth had to have a tool handy. You can't wander around carrying a knife without exciting comment, but she could have hidden it in the bottom of her flower basket."

"Rachel Pettigrew plan the death of her husband! Nonsense. She would never attempt it, no matter how badly he treated her. She does not have the character, the ruthless strength to carry out such a scheme. Although, I grant you, he sorely tried her patience and, through the years, destroyed any love she may once have felt for him."

"Nothing is more dangerous than a weak person driven against the wall. Mrs. Gresham's presence, the general's obvious relationship with her, and finally the sympathy and concern of Rachel's old beau, Sir William, might have driven her at last to rebellion."

"But how can we prove it, and do we want to incriminate this poor woman?"

"I must know, for my own satisfaction. And the first thing to do is to examine that basket. Where would it be?"

"I believe there is a garden room off this one. I think either Baker or Alice must have placed it there when Mrs. Pettigrew came in and heard the news."

"Yes, of course. Well, we must look immediately, because once she remembers and can get away without Alice noticing, she will try to retrieve it."

Acting on his words, Mark hurried to a small door near the windows and opened it. It led to a glassed-in patio, no doubt pleasant in summer, but quite chilly and bleak at this time of year. A shelf, lined with baskets, pots, and other paraphernalia of gardening lined one wall. Arabella spied the basket immediately, as it contained the remains of some wilting Christmas roses.

"Yes, here is the knife. But really it proves nothing. It could have been used for the roses, you know." Arabella had carefully parted the flowers and found the knife in the bottom of the basket. She did not pick it up, just indicated it to Mark. He glanced at it, and then at the shelf which held a pair of secuteurs and some scissors as well as vases, more baskets, and some greenery left over from the holiday decorating.

"If she only intended to snip flowers I doubt she would have taken such a large sharp knife, but she would have needed it to cut through leather." He stood lost in thought.

"She must have sneaked down to the stables and cut through the girth before the groom brought the horses around. She would not have cut it all the way, just enough so that it would sever when extra strain was put upon it, like jumping the five-barred gate."

"You are quite right, Captain Rothfield," Rachel Pettigrew said. Arabella and Mark, completely engrossed in his explanation, had not heard her quiet approach. "I did not mean to kill him you know, just give him a scare and lay him up for some time, so he could not chase after Mrs. Gresham in my house."

Arabella looked at Rachel Pettigrew with astonishment. She seemed quite different, determined, assured, braced for whatever crisis lay ahead. Neither surprised nor condemning, Mark was evidently prepared to listen to whatever Rachel had to say.

"I suppose I knew I could not avoid discovery, although I felt quite clever, deceiving both my maid and Alice and scurrying to the stable. I knew Roland would be riding his gray. I would not have endangered you or William for any reason. I will not try to excuse my action and am perfectly ready to pay the penalty. I wanted to punish Roland not kill him, although I am not unhappy that he is gone. He was a bad husband, and not a nice man," she explained simply, as if they would understand, but it was clear that she was not hoping for any sympathy. Then, with a grasp of essentials Arabella had not dreamt she possessed, Rachel turned to Mark as she asked, "What will you do, Captain Rothfield?"

"Nothing, dear lady. I agree that the general was not a nice man. I can't condone murder, but I accept that you only wanted to injure him, put him out of commission over this holiday, so he could not carry on with Mrs. Gresham. The magistrate has already determined that he had an accident, and I told no one of the cut girth besides Arabella here. I am sure she will keep silent." Mark spoke with calm assurance, as if he had no doubt of the outcome, and he was right in his belief that Arabella would keep silent. What would be served by talking? It would only bring more unhappiness to Rachel.

"Thank you, Mark." Rachel smiled at him and, raising herself on tiptoe, placed a quick kiss on his cheek. Then she took Arabella's hand in both of hers and said knowingly, "I am so happy for you both. I expected little from this Christmas, but your meeting has been the one fortunate outcome. Bless you both."

And before either Mark or Arabella could demur, she had slipped from the room as silently as she had appeared.

Despite the tragedy of General Pettigrew's death, Christmas at Winterbourne Manor was not the somber occasion that might be expected. Perhaps the removal of his devious and ruthless presence lightened the hearts of some of the guests. Rachel Pettigrew, although properly quiet and reserved, appeared to have shed her fragility and indecisiveness. Sir William offered her comfort and the promise of future happiness. Arabella and Mark, enjoying their new understanding, could only anticipate happier days. If Olivia Gresham mourned her erstwhile lover, she did it in private, and her son, Austin, still concerned about his debts, was on his best behavior. Only Alice sulked, but that could be laid at the door of her lost hopes.

Christmas Eve, after a traditional dinner, the lighting of the Yule log, and a visit from the carolers, passed quite tolerably. On Christmas morning gifts were exchanged. Arabella had brought a delicate Norwich shawl for her hostess which was received with pleasure, and copies of Jane Austen's new novel, *Emma*, for Alice and Mrs. Gresham. She had hand-embroidered fine lawn handkerchiefs for the gentlemen. Mark, cleverly not singling out any of the women, had given them silver nosegay holders. He explained to Arabella, with a wealth of meaning, that he intended to give her a more valuable token of his regard in the New Year.

The funeral the next day was a quiet affair, since none of the general's officers in arms had time to make the journey and pay their respects, but Sir Joseph Hartley represented the community, and conveyed his regrets to Rachel, which she received graciously.

The house party would disperse on the following day, and that evening Mark drew Arabella aside after dinner to tell her of his plans.

"I must report to my regiment, since my duties here are done, and then pay a visit to my parents in Wiltshire, but in the New Year I intend to come to Bath," he said with a rather anxious look in his eyes.

"I will be happy to see you. And of course, you will be visiting your aunt, Lady Harriett," she agreed with an engaging twinkle, feeling secure enough to tease him a bit.

"Not at all. I will put up at the York, and have little time for more than a courtesy call at my aunt's. I intend to be very occupied," he threatened.

"In taking the waters at the Pump Room, no doubt," Arabella agreed dulcetly.

"Don't try to gammon me, my girl. You know I am coming to Bath to court you," he objected. Then, taking her by the shoulders, he looked deeply into her eyes. "And I mean to succeed." Before she could protest, he took her in his arms and gave her a passionate kiss which stilled all her questions. She could not resist him as a betraying warmth spread through her body, and she returned his caresses with enthusiasm.

"So it has turned out to be a happy Christmas, after all," she murmured, bemused.

"But it will be a much happier New Year," Mark insisted, determined to have the last word. And so it was.

# The Sounds of Christmas

## by Valerie King

# One

"And where is the drawing room located?" Susan Elstow queried of the aging butler, Mr. Bellows.

"On the first floor across from the landing, miss," he responded politely, turning to lead the way toward the stairs.

"No!" Susan cried, her heart singing as she stayed Bellows with a gentle touch upon his arm. "I beg you will not announce me."

"But, miss!" Bellows returned, greatly shocked. "Whatever do you mean?"

"Oh, I know it is most improper, particularly when I am unknown to much of the family, but I beg you will indulge me. You see, I wish to catch the inmates of Lord Stagsden's home completely unawares and startle them with a greeting of *merry Christmas!*"

"But 'tisn't done! The master is like to bite my head off for such a disregard of decorum! Now if you will wait one moment—"

"But I cannot!" she insisted in her lively, arch manner, rushing past the aged retainer before he could so much as set his creaking knees in motion. Picking up the skirts of her gown of white figured muslin, she began racing lightly up the stairs. With each step, flakes of fresh-fallen snow fell from her hooded cloak of cherry red velvet. Her spirits fairly danced with excitement.

When she had reached the second landing of the square staircase, she looked down into the butler's frowning, anxious face and winked at him. In resignation, he cast up his white, liver-marked hands, and gave his tufted, graying head a disapproving shake. "His wrath be upon your head, miss!"

"Nonsense!" she remonstrated with a smile.

As she began ascending the second set of stairs, she paused suddenly mid-flight.

Something had caught her attention. Something was amiss, but what?

She gasped and whirled around, taking in the state of the ancient, wainscoted hall at a quick glance. She was completely overset by what she saw. For though there could be no argument that Lord Stagsden's home was under the care of a fastidious housekeeper—the gleam of beeswax was everywhere—and though it was obvious his lordship had taken great pains to preserve the integrity of four hundred years of history—no hideous architectural solecism smote her eye—and though the furnishings were impeccable in design and placement—a simple elegance had clearly ruled the master's hand—still the house appeared positively barren.

Staring at Bellows in complete astonishment, she extended her arms and gestured to the entrance hall below. "Where are the Christmas greens?" she cried out in a strong whisper. Not one sprig of holly or trail of ivy, no fresh branch of box or yew was present to proclaim the advent of the most joyous season of them all.

Bellows' pale, wrinkled face seemed to collapse a trifle as he responded, "Since Lady Stagsden—so young and so dignified, poor thing—was laid to rest in the family vault, nought but a mite of greenery has been set out, and only then just before Christmas." He sighed. "The sounds of Christmas were buried with the young mistress. Except for the pealing of the church bells, the season passes by as though a blanket of snow rests over the house just as it buries the blackthorn and holly in the yard."

"I see," Susan responded quietly. The warm feelings of anticipation which had heretofore characterized her spirits underwent an abrupt change.

When her dear friend Ianthe, who was sister to Lord Stagsden, had invited her to the Lodge for Christmas, Susan had been a little surprised, greatly pleased, and terribly grateful. She felt she had been granted one last opportunity to win the heart of the man she loved. And a last chance it most certainly was, since just following Christmas she was to travel directly to an unknown house in Kent, where she had been engaged as governess to six young girls.

Susan still did not entirely comprehend the origin of Ianthe Lovell's invitation, for though she considered Ianthe to be an excellent friend, she had never been one of her true intimates. If anything, she was better acquainted with Robert Lovell, Lord Stagsden's younger brother, than with the flighty gregarious sister with whom she had not once shared an intelligent conversation. Yet, all she knew of Robert was that he was a younger son, without many expectations, who longed for a life in the military which had, oddly, been forbidden him.

Really, the invitation was extraordinary when she considered the matter. Whatever Ianthe's reasonings might have been, however, Susan was sensible enough to simply be grateful. At the same time, she had expected Lord Stagsden's home to be as welcoming as any other she might have graced during Christmas. But the butler's grave countenance as he spoke of his lordship's deceased wife and the absence of any sign of celebration altered her preconceived notions entirely. She had a prescience of pervasive unhappiness, and rarely was she mistaken in her initial impressions of either people or places.

"Oh, dear," she murmured as she ascended the stairs, with her soft white skirts in hand, her feet moving much slower than before. The problems which loomed before her had multiplied considerably during the past minute.

However was she to succeed in piquing Lord Stagsden's interest—not to mention winning his heart—when his house still belonged to a woman who had been buried for five years and more.

Susan Elstow was all of twenty and nearly on the shelf, since most of her friends by the end of their second season were well married and in a fair way to setting up their nurseries. She had not been bereft of proposals, not by half. She had received no fewer than eight, in spite of her penurious circumstances.

Still, she had refused them all because of the state of her heart, choosing an occupation which had never quite been the object of her girlish hopes—she still could not credit she would soon become a governess!—rather than betray what she believed was a true and honest love.

Several flakes of snow, sitting upon her thickly fringed black lashes, melted and seeped into her crystal blue eyes. She blinked the droplets away, the door to the drawing room looming closer and closer, then gave her head a gentle toss, invoking her habitual confidence. She approached the carved wood door, commanding her heart to a quiet stillness as she carefully opened it just a trifle that she might listen in wanton stealth to the conversation of the room's inmates.

A puff of warm air, redolent with the smell of a crackling log fire, struck her cheek. The first voice to greet her ear brought such a crushing sensation to her chest that she could hardly breathe. How familiar, how exquisite were the rich tones of Lord Stagsden's voice. How much she had longed for this moment. How completely had her love for the viscount possessed her heart. His words, however, offered little hope or comfort.

"I told you in the beginning Miss Elstow should not have been invited to the Lodge, Mama, but it is hardly possible to turn her away from our door at this eleventh hour as you are suggesting."

"But it is only seven o'clock, Geoffrey," the dowager returned in faint accents. Lady Stagsden was known to be invalidish. "Surely you could see her settled at The Swan, or perhaps—"

"You mistook my meaning entirely," his lordship returned with a sigh. "I won't have my house disobliging in its hospitality, so you had best sustain yourself with hartshorn and lavender water and accustom yourself to the notion of having a guest through Boxing Day."

"Mama!" Ianthe cried. "Promise me you will make her feel welcome! Promise!"

"I will promise nothing," the failing voice whimpered.

"Well, I wish I had been consulted!" a gruff, heavy male voice interjected. Susan was not certain, but she believed the voice belonged to Ianthe's uncle, Horace. "Had someone bothered to inquire of me just how a stranger in our midst would affect the serenity of Christmastide, I could have told you at once how it would be. Poor Miriam cannot possibly bear the burden of a guest at such a time. You know quite well, Stagsden, that the exigencies of the season never fail to catapult her into a decline. Really, your selfishness toward your mother is quite to be wondered at!"

Susan had never met this addition to what was amounting to a rather sad chorus of complainers. She did know that Horace had been a resident of Stagsden Lodge since the death of the viscount's father some eleven years ago.

Ianthe's disappointment rang through the chamber on a small, theatrical sob, "Not you, as well, Uncle Horace!" she cried. Susan could just see Ianthe, with her large hazel eyes widening and filling suddenly with tears as she continued, "And what of your selfishness, hanging upon my brother's coatsleeves from time out of mind and never giving a fig if—"

"Ianthe!" Lord Stagsden cried. "Pray don't take a pelter and begin saying things you will wish unsaid later. Miss Elstow is welcome in my house, as your guest, and we shall all make her as comfortable as though she were one of our family."

"I would not wish that on her for the world," Ianthe rounded thoughtlessly.

A tense silence ensued until the viscount queried, "Whatever do you mean by saying such an unhandsome thing?"

"Nothing to the purpose," was Ianthe's unhappy response.

"I shan't dignify your pouting lips further, but I would like you to tell me a little of Miss Elstow? Do I know her? Have I met her?"

"Oh, Geoff!" Ianthe cried. "You have danced with her at least a hundred times. Well, perhaps not a hundred. I have even seen you laughing when in her company. How could you not know who she is? But then I am not in the least surprised. Only, when will you forget your darling Emily and begin living again?"

Another dreadful silence followed. The solemnity in Stagsden's voice as he responded was not lost to Susan. "You have no cause to speak so unkindly about my love for Emily."

"Really, Ianthe!" her mother cried. "How very cruel you can be."

"I'm sorry, Geoff," Ianthe breathed. "Truly I am. But she has been dead for five years, and I do so wish to see you happy again."

The chamber fell completely into silence this time.

Susan leaned her head against the smooth oaken door. The coolness of the wood was a balm against her suddenly feverish cheeks. These then were the difficulties which stretched before her—a houseful of what she could already perceive was a collection of rather difficult people, a beau who was not a beau and who did not even for the moment remember who she was, and but three weeks to infuse a Christmas spirit into a lodge where thus far she had not found even one sprig of holly to celebrate what should be the most joyous season of the year.

Giving the door a shove, she walked quickly into the room, offered a cheerful smile all round, and began her assault on the unsuspecting inmates of Stagsden Lodge.

## Two

Susan could barely restrain a laugh at the varied expressions of surprise which afflicted the faces of the people about her as she cried out, "Merry Christmas to all!"

"Good heavens!" Horace muttered.

"Goodness gracious!" Lady Stagsden murmured, a frail hand pressed to her bosom.

"Oh, it is just like you!" Ianthe cried with spirit.

"Where is Bellows?" Stagsden queried, his face a mask of astonishment.

Susan directed her first remark to Lord Stagsden. "You mustn't fault your good butler," she began, dipping a curtsy and smiling at the object of her heart's desire. "He was quite overset by my insistence that I ascend the stairs and pounce upon you all without warning. I hope you will forgive me!"

"There is nothing to forgive!" Ianthe exclaimed, moving forward with hands outstretched to greet her friend.

"Such manners," Lady Stagsden uttered in failing accents, her lashes fluttering ominously. "Ianthe, I knew it was a mistake from the beginning. Now here she is, destined to tear my nerves to pieces! I have never been so shocked in all my existence! Never! She should be committed to Bedlam or . . . or transported to New South Wales or, at the very least, The Swan, where she may take a coach back to—"

"Mama." Lord Stagsden politely intervened. "You forget yourself. Miss Elstow entered a room unannounced, that is all. To my knowledge she broke none of His Majesty's laws."

Lady Stagsden scowled reproachfully at her son.

Ianthe gave Susan's hands a squeeze. "Well, I think it marvelous, Sukey, that you would be so audacious. What a start you gave us, but it was precisely what was needed to shake the megrims from my wretched family!" She was by now smiling warmly as she planted a kiss on each of Susan's cheeks. "I, for one, welcome you wholeheartedly."

Glancing toward Lady Stagsden, Susan could see that the poor woman was growing more agitated by the second. She sat in her Bath chair, nervously twisting a lace kerchief through her fingers, moaning faintly and taking shallow breaths.

She will fall into a swoon if she does not take care! Susan thought.

When Ianthe had relinquished her hold on her friend, Susan immediately approached the ailing dowager. "My dear Lady Stagsden," she cried, flipping back the edges of her cloak and kneeling before her. "Have I offended you so terribly?" She took the dowager's hand in her own and pressed it gently. "When your daughter begged me to attend her family for Christmas, I, who lost my parents so many years ago, was impatient to join your circle. If my impetuosity has offended you, I beg your forgiveness. Indeed, if you wish for it, I will gladly begin again. I shall quit the room directly, descend the stairs, and have Bellows announce me properly. You have but to speak the word and I shall oblige you."

"Really, my child, what nonsense you speak. Announce you? After you have completely disturbed our quiet family evening and shattered my delicate nerves? I am sure the damage has already been accomplished!" Lady Stagsden took in a deep breath and leaned her head slowly against the tall back of the wood chair. She sighed and murmured that no one had considered her feelings for

113

years; she might as well be dead for all the attentiveness and consideration she received from those who purported to love her.

Susan bit her lip. She thought Sarah Siddons herself could not have delivered so keen a performance. She was not surprised when the dowager peeked from beneath her lashes to see how she had been affected by her speech.

"Ianthe has told me how sickly you are, ma'am," Susan said coaxingly to the feeble woman. "I was not thinking of you, but only of my own pleasure in being here. But now that I am here, I wonder if you would do me the honor of receiving a gift I brought you from London. It is a mere trifle, but when I saw it in a shop in New Bond Street I was convinced it was made for you."

"A gift? For me?" Lady Stagsden queried, her acquired lethargy beginning to dissipate. She leaned forward from her resting position and her blue eyes, in quick stages, grew bright and alive.

"Well, it is Christmas, you know. My aunt was used to give me presents each day for weeks before the actual holiday. I have been in the habit of thinking gift-giving and the holiday inseparable."

From the deep pocket of her cherry velvet cloak, which to her dismay she noted was dripping melted snow upon the floor, she withdrew a present wrapped with silver paper and bound with a silk black ribbon.

Lady Stagsden seemed to Susan to be inordinately pleased with her gesture. So much so, that her soft heart was struck with a deep compassion for the woman before her. She had been told in bitter accents by Ianthe that her mother was an absurd invalid who had confined herself to a Bath chair so that she would not be obliged to go about in society. "She is the most willful, stubborn female I have ever known and positively delights in pretending she is ill that we all must fawn over her and do her bidding. I am sick to death of living under the weight of all her supposed diseases, nonetheless her im-

114

pending demise. I begin to think you would be foolish to come, but pray do not change your mind or I shall be utterly despondent."

Lady Stagsden unwrapped the silver paper, her fingers trembling slightly. She was smiling, her eyes clouded with emotion. Susan thought of how the smallest mite of kindness often stretched into miles of happiness. When the ribbon had been laced through her fingers that she might not lose it and the silver paper was spread away from the gift like a rose opening fully to the sun, the dowager drew in her breath. "My dear, it is charming. And just what I have been wishing for these many weeks and more, for you must know that my maid broke the last little house I had for burning my pastilles. And do look at the lovely pink roses climbing up beside the front door, the chimney covered with ivy! Geoffrey, look!" She cradled the little china house in the palms of her hands, her expression appreciative and childlike. "Horace! What do you think? Is it not perfection?"

Horace grunted and moved to stand by the fireplace, where he spent the next few minutes absently opening and shutting his ceramic snuffbox and staring down into the fire.

Susan watched him for a moment and then decided he must be her next object. But how was she to win the approbation of a man whose gray brows, when drawn together in so severe a frown, gave him the appearance of an ogre?

When she had received Lady Stagsden's third offering of thanks, she removed her cloak and was surprised to find Lord Stagsden ready to receive it from her. She turned to smile at him, by way of expressing her appreciation, and felt her heart turn over. He was one of the handsomest gentlemen of her acquaintance and even more so in the soft glow of candlelight which caught the sleek line of his jaw in relief. His nose was straight, his brows a firm arch over gray eyes, eyes which had from

115

the first been able to cut through her thoughts, spin them about, and, when they reached the tip of her tongue, jumble them up so that conversation did not flow easily from her lips. Did he know the affect he had upon her?

He was dressed immaculately in evening wear, sporting a black coat molded to perfection across broad shoulders and black pantaloons which fit snugly about strong, athletic legs. Modest shirt-points rested against the sides of his face, held in place by an exquisitely tied neckcloth, his black hair was cut fashionably *à la Brutus* and a single, elegant seal hung at his waist. From the first he had followed Brummell's lead in all matters of fashion, dressing exclusively in blacks and whites, and was now, himself, copied by many of his youthful admirers.

He smiled at her and mouthed the words *Thank you.* Susan felt a blush bloom on her cheeks and a regiment of butterflies begin marching about her stomach. How very much she loved him!

She watched him cross the chamber and disappear into the hallway, her red cloak across his arm. For the first time since entering the drawing room, she was able to glance about her. The draperies, wall coverings, and furniture were decorated entirely *en suite* in a beautiful red silk damask. Just as the expansive entrance hall had been furnished with taste, so was the drawing room. Glistening mahogany occasional tables were placed conveniently near the sofas and chairs, and a rosewood pianoforte sat regally in a corner opposite the fireplace. Still, the absence of Christmas greens shouted at her again dimming the initial impression of quiet elegance.

Ianthe, intrigued by Susan's gift, knelt beside her mother and examined the small, China house. Susan took the opportunity to make her way to the fireplace, where she begged to know of Uncle Horace whether or not he attended the races at Newmarket. Horace's eyes brightened and her well-placed question led to an easy

116

discussion of gaming in all forms, ending with a challenge to a game of cribbage which Susan accepted with alacrity.

# Three

On the following morning, Lord Stagsden sat beside his five-year-old son, Christopher, in the breakfast parlor where a fulsome meal was being served in an array of resplendent silver dishes scattered across the sideboard. A log fire crackled on the hearth, the morning sky was rich with snow clouds and several times Kit's oversized linen table napkin slipped from his lap onto the floor. Each time, Lord Stagsden patiently retrieved the offending article.

Betwixt these times, his lordship stared unseeing at the unlit candles stationed on the middle of the table. An odd duo of emotions strove within him. The more familiar of the two was the terrible blankness which had covered his soul since the early and untimely death of his most beloved wife during her confinement five Christmases ago. It was as though death had cloaked his ability to feel just as surely as the snow had descended upon the countryside and silenced even the sound of the leaves in the wind.

Strangely enough, the sensation was quite peaceful. He felt safe and serene when possessed by the void his bereavement had caused.

At the same moment, however, an inexplicable force was at work in his heart, and he was extraordinarily uncomfortable because of it. He felt as though someone had taken a cup of water and thrown it upon his snow-covered soul. The water melted the snow just enough to turn it to ice which seemed to crack and grate against his nerves. He could not account for the sensation. He did not know from whence it had come nor, more precisely, who had provoked it. He suspected, however, that its origins had something to do with Miss Elstow's arrival, but why, he could not say.

At the mere thought of Susan Elstow, Lord Stagsden again experienced the sensation of water splashing on his snowy heart, and he shifted his gaze to stare out the window.

The parlor, situated at the east end of the house had a lovely view of the chalk hills some four miles distant. The hills were presently molded with snow, but in the summer were a vast expanse of green that seemed to roll on endlessly.

At the border of his property, just before the hills eased toward the cloudy sky, red berries from several rows of holly shrubs winked through a heavy dusting of white powder. The weighted branches of the snow-laden yew trees, standing like sentinels on the white lawn, hung heavily toward the ground.

*Susan Elstow.*

She had stunned his family by bursting open the door last night and, in a frightfully cheerful manner, crying out a bright, *merry Christmas to all*. She had still been wearing her cloak, which dripped a trail of wet snow across the carpets and onto his mother's lap rug as she impertinently leaned over his afflicted parent and took one thin hand within the shelter of her own. His mother had seemed quite taken aback and displeased at first, but Stagsden had noted with surprise that the dowager's countenance altered so much with the first mention of the gift, he would not have believed she was the same woman who, moments earlier, had been complaining of Miss Elstow's presence in her home.

Miss Elstow's affect upon Horace had been equally astonishing. If he had not known better, he would have believed that the young woman, whom he had immediately recognized as a charming dancing partner of his upon numerous occasions during the course of the past two seasons, had made it the object of her evening to see the cantankerous leech well entertained. Which he had been—by God!—enjoying two rounds of cribbage, one of backgammon, and a full hour of piquet. The latter he had won, but not without Miss Elstow playing quite stupidly and quite beneath her abilities. Geoffrey had become extremely curious about her in that moment. He could not respect that she had pandered to the old man's vanity; at the same time, he had never seen Horace pinch the cheek of one of Ianthe's friends before, and that with a silly smile on his lined, pudgy face. "If I were but a decade or two younger," he had begun, only to have Miss Elstow silence his flattery with a singularly uncalled-for, yet oddly acceptable, hug.

Perhaps that was what he disliked most about her. She was always kissing and hugging someone or other. He was grateful Robert had not been present. He was of Miss Elstow's age and would clearly have been bowled over by such scandalously affectionate treatment.

Thoughts of Robert served to cause him to wince as he picked up his cup and took a tasteless sip of lukewarm coffee. He had come the crab over Robert when the boy had arrived past midnight and the house had already fallen deep into its slumbers. Robert had insisted the mail coach, upon which he had been traveling, had lost a wheel somewhere near Turvey, but the glitter in his bleary eyes had told its own tale. Robert was in his cups and had probably spent several hours at The Swan rather than face his brother. Geoffrey wondered how much his gaming debts had amounted to this quarter alone and how long it would take for the young cub to confess his misdeeds and beg for an advance upon next quarter's allowance.

"Papa," Christopher said, interrupting his reveries.

"What is it?" Stagsden responded, turning with a smile toward his son.

The boy merely looked down at the floor, where his napkin had again taken up residence.

"Oh, for heaven's sake," his lordship murmured, slightly irritated. He leaned over the armrest of his own chair and swiped the napkin swiftly from the polished wood floor.

Just as he handed it back to Christopher, a familiar, exuberant voice called from the doorway. "Good morning." Susan was greeting father and son.

Lord Stagsden found himself staring at a vision of Christmas. His sister's guest was wearing an emerald green velvet gown made high to the waist and with long sleeves, the latter gathered in three successive tiers and trimmed with red satin ribbons. Her skin was a beautiful milky white against the dark green of the gown, an exquisite contrast to the coal black of hair which had been pulled up into a delightful knot atop her head and which sported at least one sprig of fresh holly leaves. Her eyes appeared as blue as a summer sky glinting with sunlight. Laughter resided there, if not in full force then simply waiting for amusement. He liked this about Susan, that she loved to laugh, a quality he now remembered from having partnered her so frequently. He found himself bemused suddenly as to why he had failed to recall her name when he knew her face so well.

"Good morning, Miss Elstow," he responded politely, rising from his seat and offering her a bow.

A footman seated her and began offering her a variety of dishes. To Stagsden's surprise, she did not refuse anything but took a minuscule portion of each dish so that by the time the servant was finished, her plate appeared like a colorful counterpane.

"Who are you?" Christopher asked, when his father failed to introduce him.

"I'm sorry, Kit," Lord Stagsden apologized. "May I

121

present you to Miss Elstow. She will be staying with us over the holidays."

"How do you do?" Christopher responded, rising as his father had done and making a small bow. His napkin, of course, slipped to the floor, and Lord Stagsden gave a murmur of disgruntlement.

He would have performed his duty again, but Susan was before him. Moving swiftly to retrieve the napkin from the floor, she held up the large, linen square and pretended to give careful judgment as to its size. Afterward, she stepped behind Kit and, with a deft movement, tied it quickly about his neck.

"Do you know what I saw yesterday while traveling here to your home? I saw a mail coach carrying plucked Christmas turkeys to London. There were at least two dozen of them hanging all over the coach, and every time the coach hit a bump in the road, the turkeys would bounce and give the vehicle the appearance of flight. I laughed until my sides ached. I wish you could have seen it. There! How does that feel? Now you won't have to worry about your napkin anymore."

"Look, Papa, Miss *Elbow* has fixed my napkin just the way Nurse does."

Lord Stagsden scowled. "Then I can only say that I blame Nurse for your inability to keep your napkin on your lap. And though I appreciate Miss *Elstow's* efforts to help you, I cannot approve of them. You may wear your napkin in that manner only this once, little man."

To Susan, he said, "I wish you would have asked me if I felt it was appropriate, Miss Elstow. I hardly consider this proper conduct for the breakfast parlor. I expect my son to behave as I do."

"Nonsense!" Susan responded, not in the least dismayed by this reproach. She returned to her seat and countered with, "I'm sure when his feet touch the floor as yours do, and he is able to sit as tall and in as dignified a manner as you do, his napkin will no longer slide from his lap, or then again, perhaps it might." She smiled at him in a mischievous manner and said, "May I suggest you retrieve your own?"

Stagsden felt for his napkin and found to his dismay that it lay in a pretty, white drift beside his chair. Christopher let out a howl of laughter when he caught sight of his august papa's napkin on the floor, and Susan could not restrain giving vent to a trill of her own. Stagsden stared at the traitorous piece of linen for a moment. He did not at first respond, save for muttering a disgusted *"What the deuce!"* This only caused Susan and Kit to laugh all over again.

Caught by the absurdity of the moment, there was only one thing Stagsden felt he could do. Picking up his napkin, he tied it about his neck.

Christopher laughed and laughed, a childlike rumble that came straight from his stomach and seemed to cause even the flames in the fireplace to shoot a little higher, so delightful was its sound.

Susan looked thoughtfully at the child for the first time since entering the room. Ianthe had said little more of him than that he was sickly. She thought he had an air of sadness about him, and except for his pale coloring, she believed he appeared as sturdy as any young boy she had ever known.

He was remarkably good-looking, quite like his formidable papa. His hair was black and curly, his features a replica of his parent's the way he carried himself was an obvious imitation of an admired father. He lacks only one thing, she thought, to be truly pleasing in appearance — a rosy glow to his face, which a little exercise would certainly provide. She had learned from the maid assigned to her that Christopher was not permitted to exert himself. His grandmama was in a constant state of fear for his health.

Stagsden, appearing boyish above the not-so-intricate folds of his table napkin, apologized with a smile for his manners and for the acerbity of his tongue.

"You are forgiven, Lord Stagsden," Susan said, smiling kindly upon him. "If you will forgive me for my impertinence. It is my flaw, if you must know. I confess it wholly."

Stagsden looked into sparkling blue eyes, eyes that were both amused yet admonishing. He knew he had been corrected, yet did not resent it in the least. Instead a bizarre thought flew through his mind: When did I become so high in the instep? Kit is but a child, a young one at that.

He inclined his head to Miss Elstow and watched as a faint pink of pleasure touched her cheeks. She looked enormously pretty in that moment, as she dipped her fork into the scatterings of her singular repast. She is quite lovely, he concluded as he again examined her face. Why was it he hadn't noticed before? Her hair gleamed in the morning light, bluish glints reflecting off her black locks. Her lips were a deep rose, and her mouth was generous, never more so than when she was smiling as now, her teeth in a perfect, pretty row. Her eyes were large and of the clearest blue he had ever seen, cool water in an ever-flowing stream. Her brows were nicely arched and over all, her expression of teasing gentleness brought a light of beauty to her every delicate feature.

Stagsden took in a deep breath and felt as though a cup of water, quite warm this time, had just thoroughly doused his heart. Who was this Christmas angel who had come to Stagsden Lodge bringing with her more warmth to his abode than even the largest Yule log had ever done?

"Miss Elbow, I was wondering—" Kit began, interrupting his reveries.

"Her name is Miss Elstow." Stagsden corrected his son gently.

"I thought *Elbow* sounded awful funny," Kit said, undaunted by his father's reproof. "But I rather liked it."

"You may call me Miss Elbow, if you like, then," Susan responded, spreading a thin slice of bread with apricot jam. "But if your father has no objection, I wish you would call me Susan instead, or better yet, Sukey, for that is what my dearest friends call me. And I hope we shall be friends."

Both Susan and Kit turned to determine his lordship's pronouncement upon just what Christopher should call her. "If Miss Elstow wishes it, I'm certain Susan or Sukey would be perfectly acceptable."

"And will you call me the same, Lord Stagsden?" Susan asked. "I would like it above all things."

Lord Stagsden blinked at his sister's friend. How had it come about that in the few minutes Miss Elstow had actually been in the breakfast parlor, he would have arrived at the extremely odd condition of wishing to address her with such informality. He was not in the habit of doing so, and particularly not with Ianthe's giddy friends. But then Susan was not like most of Ianthe's intimates. "If you've no objection," he responded. "*Susan* suits you quite well."

"It does, doesn't it, brother."

## Four

Susan shifted her gaze to the figure of Robert Lovell, who stood lounging in the doorway and regarding her with a warm smile.

"Hallo, Robert," she called to him. "How do you go on? I did not expect to see you since you told me not three weeks past that you intended to spend Christmas in Italy."

"You can't bamboozle me," he responded with a glimmer in his eye. "As though you ever believed a single whisker I told you."

"And you've told enough in your time. I ought to be inured by now."

He entered the room in his loose-limbed manner, which to Susan's eye seemed nothing short of a swagger. He was an extremely handsome young man with compelling brown eyes, not unlike Lord Byron's, and never said a word to a young woman that was not a caress. For this reason she had never completely trusted him, even though his attentions to her had seemed quite marked in the past few weeks, even months. It flitted through her mind that Robert might have been the one to have prompted Ianthe's invitation for her to spend Christmas at Stagsden Lodge. At the same time she could not credit him with a serious intention, primarily because they were both impoverished. Whatever the case, she thought of Robert as a friend, and nothing more.

"So you know each other," Lord Stagsden said, the coolness of his tone surprising Susan.

Lifting a finely arched brow, Robert directed a frosty gaze upon his elder brother. As he took his seat, he said, "Yes, we do. Susan and I have perfected the art of the quadrille, and had you come to London for the Little Season you would have witnessed the prowess of our skills, wouldn't he?" Here, he turned his gaze, now more warmly lit, upon Susan.

She blinked several times. The constraint between the brothers was almost a tangible thing, and she found it difficult at first to concentrate on his question. "I suppose you could say we have, though I believe your skill leads us both," she answered at last, with a quick glance toward Lord Stagsden. *What is he thinking?* she wondered. His eyes were cloaked and guarded as he watched his brother.

"You are too generous with your compliments, Susan; I have said so often and often. As for who possesses the greater skill, there can be no doubt that you are an angel on your feet and a delight to partner. Isn't she, brother?" Robert seemed to challenge Geoffrey at every turn.

Though Susan was concerned about the evident disharmony between the siblings, she could not help but wonder just how Stagsden would respond to Robert's query and felt her chest constrict with anticipation.

To her immense pleasure Lord Stagsden smiled at her, all the while ignoring the provocation in Robert's tone, and replied, "I can say with all honesty that few excel in the art as well as Susan Elstow."

Her heart beat in a deafening cadence against her ribs, so much so that Susan could do little more than blush and murmur her thanks for his compliment. When an awkward silence seemed likely to ensue, she tore her gaze from his face, turning the conversation entirely as she addressed Robert. "And when will you be joining your cavalry regiment? I recall that you spoke most enthusiastically of a career with the Horse Guards. Have you any news on that score? I do think you are well suited to the army."

"I'll take that as a compliment, fair Susan, but I'm sorry to say that I won't be joining a regiment as I had hoped. Geoffrey forbids it."

"Nonsense!" Susan said with a smile, taking a sip of chocolate. "Whyever would he do that? You are teasing me again!"

Lord Stagsden, who had raised his cup to his lips, returned it untouched to the saucer on the table. With an indifferent glance out the window at the snow-laden countryside, then back to Susan, he said, "No, I'm afraid she's not teasing you in the least. I have indeed forbidden his pursuit of a career in the army these three years and more." Turning to Robert, he added, "And I consider the subject closed."

"What utter nonsense!" Susan cried, without thinking. "When anyone with a particle of sense can see that your brother was practically bred for military service. He is athletic and skilled with pistols—if tales of his success at Manton's are to be believed. But beyond this, he follows the mold of every scarlet-coated officer I have ever met. He is a trifle surly, a bit arrogant, and unendingly friendly. I am persuaded he would make a magnificent addition to His Majesty's Royal Army."

Lord Stagsden knew he ought to be deeply offended by Susan's interference, but since his own views were not far different from her own, and indeed his truculence was born of a sense of duty to his mother rather than willfulness, he found himself warming toward the beauty seated opposite him. He admired the fact that she would defend his brother from the sincerity of her heart. "I believe you are correct in your observations, yet my decision remains."

Robert set his elbow down heavily on the table and let his chin droop sadly onto the palm of his hand. "I ought to have warned you how useless it would be for you to attempt to champion my cause. My brother is as mulish

128

as he is autocratic." He then smiled at Susan in appreciation for her efforts.

Lord Stagsden wished to defend himself, but when he caught sight of the softened, warm expression on Robert's face as his brother regarded Susan, an entirely different view of her visit presented itself to him.

Was Robert in love with the chit?

More to the point, as he shifted his gaze back to Susan. Was she attached to his brother? And why did his heart suddenly freeze within his breast at the thought of it?

## Five

The first sennight of Susan's visit at Stagsden Lodge had passed, with only two remaining. The morning was again dull with clouds as it had been every day since her arrival, yet Susan's heart was merry with sunshine.

For some time now, she had been concocting a scheme which needed only Lady Stagsden's approval to implement and which would brighten even further the growing happy Christmas spirit of the Lodge.

So much had changed since she had first crossed the portals of the drawing room that to a large degree the Lodge was not the same place at all. Lady Stagsden, for instance, had progressively been leaving her Bath chair to take brief walks with Susan, to the incredulity of the entire household. The dowager's spirits had improved so greatly that she had even been able to set aside her constant fear for Kit's health and permit him to enjoy learning to ice-skate on a snow-banked, handmade pond which the gardener had created just for the purpose. Kit's cheeks were now blooming with health, and even Lady Stagsden had ruefully remarked at dinner on the evening before that perhaps she had been a trifle over-protective of her beloved grandson. Lord Stagsden had spilled a goblet of wine at that remark and had then turned to stare in astonishment at the change Susan had wrought with her simple ministrations to the widow.

Lady Stagsden was not the only one to benefit from Susan's enthusiasm and high spirits. Ianthe's peevishness

130

had all but disappeared. Every day, she and Susan practiced duets of traditional Christmas carols, while taking turns playing the accompaniments on the pianoforte. During the evenings, Robert naturally commanded the duets to be performed, and two nights prior Ianthe had actually played a full hour of *contredanses* while Susan danced, alternating with much pleasure as partner to both Robert and Stagsden.

The last entertainment of each evening, however, was saved for Uncle Horace, who claimed Susan as an opponent for whichever game of chance took his fancy. Since the entire family — save Kit, who would long since have seen his bed — gathered about the players; each victory and defeat was met with assorted cries and groans depending upon who had made what side bets. In addition, upon two or three separate occasions, Stagsden and his mother had challenged Susan and Uncle Horace to a spirited game of whist.

When even the servants had begun singing and humming carols, Susan knew she had effectively brought at least some of the sweet sounds of Christmas, as Bellows had once phrased it, home to Stagsden Lodge.

As for the sights of the joyous season, every day when Susan descended the stairs to join the family party, she winced at the utterly barren appearance of the house. She knew it was an impertinence and that she was more likely to incur his lordship's wrath rather than win his approval, but she had made up her mind — particularly when Bellows hinted that the entrance hall was used to be lavishly adorned with greens before *the unfortunate event* occurred — the lodge must be dressed properly for Christmas.

As for her own unspoken, modest campaign to attach Stagsden to her side, Susan felt she had made only a trifling progress. Though the viscount frequently sought out her company and appeared to enjoy conversing with her on all manner of subjects, his demeanor never altered from that of a host attempting to gratify his guest. He particularly seemed intrigued by her chosen occupation of governess—was she looking forward to taking six small girls beneath her wing?—and appeared not in the least distressed by the thought that their paths would likely never cross again, once she had taken up her first post.

No. He did not seem even mildly interested in her.

Perhaps it was for this reason, having little to lose, that she did not hesitate to lay her scheme before Lady Stagsden and beg the dowager to give her permission to dress the lodge with Christmas greens. "I could take several of the servants into the gardens and the home woods, and bring home enough greenery to accomplish the task in one day. I'm sure of it. I don't doubt that your son will be displeased, but I do so believe that Kit—and the rest of your family—would benefit enormously."

"Oh, my dear," Lady Stagsden said with a soft smile on her lined features. "What an enchanting notion. I had not considered it before, but my son's wish that the season be celebrated modestly has always cast a pall on my spirits. I oughtn't to give you permission, but since he is gone for the day visiting his mama-in-law, I will allow it, if for no other reason than to give pleasure to Kit—just as you've said. He at least ought to experience a *real* Christmas. Emily wouldn't have liked it, precisely, but then she is not here to complain! Oh, dear! Pray forget I spoke such unhandsome words! How thoughtless of me! Emily was a dear child, an excellent wife, but a trifle too . . . too spiritless to please generally." She squeezed Susan's hand and whispered, "Never tell my son I said as much. He doted on her, you know!"

"Yes, I know he did. And, of course, I would never breathe a word to him. Never!"

"Good girl!" Lady Stagsden responded. "Now, off with you! Geoffrey will undoubtedly return before night has fallen. Lord and Lady Astley live not twelve miles distant. He calls upon them every Christmas—like the good son he is. I only wish they were as attentive to him or to Kit. Oh, dear! I am beginning to gossip again! Now, off with you!"


"No," Susan responded forthrightly to Robert's question, as she set yet another white candle into the festive garland of holly adorning the mantel over the fireplace. "Your brother left quite early to visit Emily's parents. Ianthe and I have been happily employed since, attempting to bring a measure of Christmas cheer to your home."

"He will not like it," Robert returned with a smug smile as he leaned his frame easily against the mantel, crossing his arms over his chest. "Do not expect him to be pleased, if that is your object."

With the tips of her fingers, Susan pulled forward a bunch of red berries and snuggled them close to the base of a silver candle holder. "I am very certain he will not be pleased," she responded with a sigh, her task nearly accomplished.

"Then you are very brave," Robert said. "I should not like to have the roof collapsing upon me once he begins raising his voice to the rafters. I shouldn't wonder if he demanded that the servants remove every last bit of greenery. He has not allowed it, you know, for years."

"Yes, I do know."

For the first time since initiating her scheme, Susan felt a queasy sensation of anxiety attack her stomach, particularly since Lord Stagsden was due to arrive home at any moment. The sun's light, hidden throughout the day behind snow clouds, was fading rapidly, turning the sky to a dark gray. She could not keep from glancing toward the window which overlooked the drive. Lady

Stagsden had been seated there for the past hour awaiting her son's return.

Whatever her fears might be, however, Susan did not
regret her impetuous decision. The moment Bellows had
made it known that Susan was to transform the Lodge,
the servants had rallied instantly to her cause. The entire
household, mobilized like one of Wellington's vast armies,
searched through the attics for additional candle holders
and any silver trinkets to tuck into the garlands so they
might wink in the candlelight. Voices, footsteps, and even
shouts of laughter could be heard down every hallway as
the servants, Ianthe, Kit, and Susan herself scurried
about to transform Stagsden Lodge. Kit was beside himself with excitement, exclaiming every few minutes that
his papa would be so pleased!

Susan could only wait, wonder, and occasionally wring
her hands.

"I do not see him," Lady Stagsden called from her
Bath chair. "The light is nearly gone, and I am become
excessively worried that he is not yet returned. Robert,
do take the carriage and see if you are able to find him.
Perhaps he has met with some accident or been set upon
by footpads."

"What?" Robert laughed. "Footpads in Bedfordshire?"

"Highwaymen, then," his mother returned with a scowl.
"Just go. The sky is quite leaden, and I fear if it begins
to snow again, he shall lose his way."

"I wish he might," Robert muttered.

"You don't mean that," Susan said, shaking her head at
Robert.

"I most certainly do," he responded with a mocking lift
of an eyebrow. "For when he begins to rail at you for the
changes you have wrought in his house, I won't be able
to restrain myself from planting him a facer."

"Robert!" Lady Stagsden remonstrated. "Such an expression. I wish you would not —"

"Mama, I take my leave of you," he interrupted, crossing the room on his long stride. "I shall go in search of your beloved Geoffrey."

"Good boy," she murmured, as he crossed the portal and disappeared down the hall.

When his footsteps resounded on the stairs in a quick succession of thuds, Susan finally blinked. "Does he mean to do as you bid?" she queried of Lady Stagsden.

"Yes. He was always the most tiresome child, saying nay when he meant yea. But at heart he is good and, in the end, will do my bidding."

"I only wish Lord Stagsden would relent and permit him to go into the army."

"Stagsden does not please himself in this."

Susan turned to stare at the frail woman reclining her head upon the high back of the wood chair. Her face was outlined by the dull, fading winter light. "You mean you have forbidden it?" she queried, stunned. Until this moment she had supposed the viscount to have been the sole hindrance to Robert's future.

"My dear child," her ladyship responded, "when you have sustained the losses I have, you begin to value the lives about you as they ought to be valued. I buried three of my children early in their poor little lives, and another when he was a stout lad of nine. When dear Emily perished in childbed leaving behind little Christopher, Robert requested to join a cavalry regiment. I couldn't bear the thought of his going, and I knew I could not have withstood his entreaties. Geoffrey has borne the brunt of Robert's discontent himself these three years and more, solely for my sake.

Susan feat her heart go out to the sad woman in the Bath chair. She could see now how death had taken a toll on her willingness to embrace life. At the same time, of what use was it to keep Robert bound to Stagsden Lodge? She crossed the chamber and placed a hand gently upon Lady Stagsden's shoulder. The dowager responded by laying her own hand upon Susan's and patting it gently. "Dear ma'am," Susan began softly, "I know you will consider it a grievous impertinence, but—"

"But you think I should let him go into the army."

Susan paused for a moment, then whispered, "Yes, ma'am. He is terribly unhappy kicking his heels at Stagsden Lodge. He would make an exemplary officer, you know he would!"

There was no response from Lady Stagsden save a deep sigh and a second patting of Susan's hand. Afterward, Susan crossed the chamber, now redolent with the pungent smells of box, holly, and yew branches, and gave a tug on the bell pull. All was readied, she realized with a sense of satisfaction as she glanced about her and then at her fingers which were pricked and scraped from the handling of the holly. She would retire to her bedchamber and dress for dinner. In the meantime, the servants had but to tidy the drawing room and light the candles in order to turn the unhappy house into a festival of lights, soft greens, and the magic of Christmastide.

## Six

Lord Stagsden saw the dark figure pressing toward him in the growing gloom. He could not discern the identity of the rider, yet something seemed familiar about him, even at such a distance. He wondered if perhaps it was Robert, but then dismissed the notion as absurd. Robert had no reason to be traveling about in such inclement weather, particularly when the object of his gallantry was ensconced in Stagsden Lodge. The more he witnessed Robert's easy flirtations with Susan and the manner in which his brother's brown eyes lit up when she but entered a room, the more he was convinced that Robert was in a fair way to tumbling in love.

These thoughts filled him with disquiet for reasons he only partially understood. The match was wholly ineligible, on every score, but he knew this was not why the thought of Robert being in love with Susan distressed him so. He was, however, unwilling to acknowledge the true reason.

His thoughts drifted to his recent visit to the Astley estate in the neighboring village of Turvey. He had paid a visit to his late wife's family and as usual, Emily's mama had been draped in black crepe from head to toe, her demeanor solemn, tears rising as easily to her eyes today as they had five years ago.

Ordinarily, he had been comforted by her soft-spoken words of condolence, by her tour of the portrait gallery which held no fewer than seven paintings of her beloved daughter, and by their shared love for poor Emily. But on this day he had found himself unaccountably irritated, particularly when he had mentioned that Christopher had been wondering when he might receive another visit from his Grandmama Astley. The truth was Kit had not seen either of Emily's parents since Christmas past. And then, so many tears had been shed over Emily's absence that Kit had become greatly agitated and had suffered nightmares for a fortnight afterward.

Lady Astley had been profusely apologetic for this lapse in time—a year! She had exclaimed over her love for Christopher, had pronounced that it could not have been a twelvemonth since she had last laid eyes on the child, and had promised that soon after the New Year, when the snows began to melt in the lanes, or even later—perhaps in April or May—she would pay a visit. Until then, could Stagsden bring the boy around, say, in late January? "For, my dear son, you cannot know how I suffer during these cold months. You are blest with such a stout constitution that I'm persuaded you cannot comprehend what those of us not granted as much are forced to endure. Your mama would certainly sympathize with my ailments."

Several unhandsome thoughts regarding his mama-in-law rose sharply to the surface of his mind and fairly caused him to bite off the end of his tongue. He had longed to point out that a distance of twelve miles, in a closed carriage with bricks at one's feet and wrapped in a multitude of furs and thick carriage rugs, could surely not endanger one's health, Still, he kept his peace.

But he had had more to endure. The social call was in the end obliterated by the lazy appearance of Emily's father, who merely raised a surprised brow at seeing his son-in-law, and greeted him with, "What? You here? Deuced weather to be traveling about in. Hope you are able to find the Lodge in all this snow."

"It has not snowed since early this morning."

"Hmph," was the indifferent reply. "Looks like it will though. I daresay you ought to head home straight away."

And he had done so, with his temper in shreds and his heart aching in a manner he did not fully comprehend until he thought of Kit and of how he was unlikely ever to know his mother's parents.

As the figure before him neared, he was dumbfounded to discover that it was, indeed, Robert.

"Hallo," his brother called to him.

Stagsden was by this time only a mile from the Lodge, yet he found it oddly comforting to have Robert nearby. Eleven years separated the brothers, and for one of the first times in his life Stagsden realized that Bobby was no longer a child. "Whatever brings you away from the fireside, Robert? Or did you imagine I was set upon by highwaymen?"

"No, not by half," was Robert's smiling answer as he pulled his caped riding coat more firmly about his shoulders and turned his horse to ride beside Stagsden's. "Mama was worried for your safety, as you might well expect. As for myself, to own the truth there was something I felt I ought to mention to you before you turned up the drive."

"Indeed?" Geoffrey queried. "You intrigue me, especially with that rueful smile on your lips."

Immediately, Stagsden thought of Susan. He knew, without comprehending precisely why, that Robert's mission involved her. The thought again flitted through his mind: Is he in love with her? And again, as before, he felt the ice about his heart crackle and grate.

"You have all the appearance," he began, as Robert maneuvered the bay horse closer to his own mount, "of one who is about to relay dreadful tidings and pretend all the while that nothing extraordinary is amiss."

"Precisely so," Robert responded with a chuckle. "I will only say that you will not like what has happened one whit, but I beg of you, for my sake, that you will not be angry with Susan. She is wonderfully well intentioned, and because of her employments—regarding which I refuse to say a word—she was able to persuade Mama to actually remain in the drawing room for the better part of the day and in addition to that to stroll through the conservatory upon Susan's arm!"

"What?"

"Yes, you may well be astonished. Mama has been seated—albeit in her Bath chair—since one o'clock, by the window in the drawing room."

"You amaze me!" Stagsden cried, perplexed. "She has not done so since—I cannot remember when? But whatever has transpired? Do not tell me that Miss Elstow, among her other talents is also a physician?"

"She is marvelous, isn't she?"

Stagsden nodded, his brows drawn together. What did he think of her, really? "She has a habit of interfering, which I cannot like, and an impudence, which I find remarkable in that no one else seems bothered by it."

"*Your* reaction is easily explained. You do not like your will crossed, and she is not afraid of you. I admire her prodigiously."

Again, Stagsden set to contemplating the strange marvel that was Susan Elstow. His thoughts flew instantly to recalling how deucedly pretty she had appeared the evening of her arrival, with her cherry cloak framing her lovely face and her eyes alight with warmth as she bid everyone a merry Christmas. He recalled the sight of her the next morning in a green velvet gown and how readily she took him to task over Kit's table napkin.

His thoughts were interrupted when Robert suddenly burst into song. " 'We wish you a merry Christmas! We wish you a merry Christmas! . . .'"

His brother's voice pulled at the snowy silence all about Stagsden's chest. For some reason Stagsden felt another flood of warm water melting away the ice encrusting his heart. He could not remember a time

140

when Robert had been so happy.

The manor house was settled a half-mile from the King's highway, down a curved lane lined by shrubs and trees. Yews had been planted as a partial screen to the occasional traffic that made use of the highway, and snow lay in drifts on the ground, shrouding the trees and shrubs. Through the varied pattern of mounded bushes and dark tree trunks, like a lamp flickering behind the leaves of a tree, the manor was suddenly visible.

"What the deuce?" Stagsden exclaimed.

Robert stopped singing and laughed outright.

"It must be the darkness of the night which makes the house appear closer than it is," Stagsden commented, regarding the pretty twinkling of the lights as they passed by black tree trunks. "Or is it? Good God! Every window appears to have a candle burning brightly! No! Several candles! What is the meaning of this?"

"Remember, I forewarned you, brother!"

# Seven

Susan sat to the right of the fire in a winged chair of red silk damask. Kit was on her lap, and together they were noisily singing bits and pieces of every Christmas melody she could recall. At the moment they were humming the verses to "Deck the Halls with Boughs of Holly" and bringing down the rafters with " 'fa-la-la-la-la-la-la-la-la.' "

She was dressed in a white gown embroidered with red cherries and green leaves. Through her black hair, knotted atop her head, she had woven a red satin ribbon.

Uncle Horace sat opposite her, dipping into his snuff-box frequently and smiling at the merriment across from him. Lady Stagsden reclined on a chaise longue, her legs and shoulders covered with soft cashmere shawls of a delicate blue. She, too, was smiling as she watched her grandson and sipped a glass of sherry.

Ianthe, not completely satisfied with their efforts of the day, was opposite the archway leading to an adjoining music room, looping reams of red satin ribbon across a high shelf adorned with candles and sprays of yew branches.

Susan and Kit had just finished their final, loud " 'la-la-la-la-la-la-la-la,' " and she was presently in the midst of tickling him when the door opened and Robert and Stagsden strode in.

"Papa!" Kit cried, sliding and leaping from Susan's lap. "Look! Look! Christmas has come to our house?"

"I see that it has," the viscount returned easily, a smile reaching to his eyes as he caught up his son in his arms and held him in a surprisingly tight hug for a long moment.

Susan watched him, her heart beating so strongly it sounded in her ears. She feared he would be angry at all she had done in his absence; at the same time she knew a rush of affection so strong for the man now cuddling his child that she felt breathless and happy all at once. He caught her gaze and held it. What was in his eyes? Was he angry? His expression was surely one of astonishment, but would he give her a dressing-down and then insist the decorations be removed? He wouldn't be so cruel! Kit's heart would break.

She swallowed hard as he greeted in turn his sister, his uncle, and his mother. The latter pressed his hand and whispered something which to Susan's insistent eye looked very much like, "Be kind, my dear."

What he said in response, she would never know since his back was to her.

At last he turned, with Kit still held easily in his strong arms, and crossed the remainder of the room to stand over her. He looked down at her for a few seconds, giving his head a small shake and laughing ruefully. The smile which adorned his lips and warmed her heart, disappeared slowly, as he continued to look at her, his expression questioning and elusive.

What were his thoughts? She searched his gaze, which seemed to bore straight through her. For the first time since she had arrived at Stagsden Lodge she felt he was seeing her as a woman. Her heart swelled within her breast! For now she felt hope, especially when he took her hand in his and, raising it to his lips, placed a kiss upon it. Kit giggled and began exclaiming at his father's odd behavior, but Geoffrey kindly bid his son to be silent and afterward addressed Susan. "I have you to thank for such a warm homecoming. I am in your debt. I would not have believed this morning that I could have welcomed such an outrageous display of holiday merrymaking, but I do and I am deeply grateful for the joyous sound of Kit's voice as he sang with you. I have been listening for some time just outside the door."

Susan's eyes filled with tears. Never had she expected such generous appreciation! "You are most welcome." She breathed out the words, her throat constricted. "I was so afraid you would be outraged, and indeed, I could not have blamed you one whit if you had been! If the truth be known, I fully expected you to eject me from your house!"

"Never," he whispered. "And if I had been angry, I should have been the sorriest creature on earth. I'm glad you've come for these few days, Susan. I only wish—" Here he broke off suddenly, a faint color appearing on his cheeks above the clean lines of his starched shirt-points.

Susan felt her heart leap within her breast. What had he meant to say? What was it he *wished?*

When an uncomfortable silence ensued, Susan immediately remarked that she and Kit had been practicing one carol in particular, just for him, and if he wished, they would favor him with their hopeless but spirited rendition of "Oh, Come All Ye Faithful." "Though I think you ought to know," Susan added, "Kit believes it is a song about one of your hunting dogs, since the dogkeeper has been forever exclaiming that a good hound is the most faithful creature on earth."

Stagsden laughed and afterward took up a place by the mantel and watched Susan and Kit perform their song. His eyes were full of contentment and love as he glanced from his son's face to Susan's and then back again at least a dozen times.

No one noticed that Robert remained for a brief minute, then quietly quit the room.

* * *

Robert leaned against the paneled walls of the hallway outside the drawing room, feeling as though his chest had been crushed. He found it difficult to breathe and harder yet to swallow. He had suffered a severe shock when he had first entered the room on his brother's coattails. Susan had not once shifted her gaze from Stagden's face, *not once,* even to acknowledge his presence. No. Her eyes, her heart, her thoughts were all for his brother. Though he might have been able to explain her initial absorption by the fact that everyone was awaiting Stagsden's response to her decorations, he could not ignore the tender affection which cloaked her eyes from the moment Geoffrey had placed a kiss upon her hand, nor could he forget the soft tears which glimmered in her eyes afterward.

Thinking about that wretched kiss caused him at last to take in a gulp of air as a fury, like none he had ever known, engulfed him. Susan was in love with his brother!

She loved him! Why hadn't he seen it before or suspected it? Good God, whenever they had been together she had always asked a discreet question or two about Geoff. Now he knew why.

Well, he wouldn't have it! Stagsden had everything: the manor, the title, the wealth, even the right to order his future. While, he, Robert, had nothing. But damn if he would permit Stagsden to have Susan, whether she loved him or not!

# *Eight*

Susan watched the days fly quickly past as Stagsden Lodge became enveloped in the spirit of Christmas. Every tradition which had been suspended by Emily's unhappy demise was reinstated, the long wait somehow making each event poignant and special as it was enjoyed anew. Carolers were encouraged to entertain the lodge inmates, a delightful Christmas grog was shared round, Christmas cakes were received in abundance from grateful tenants, and Lord Stagsden pleased everyone by taking Kit out early one morning to go in search of a massive Yule log.

When the two arrived home, a team of horses dragging an enormous fallen log up the drive, nothing was more pleasing to Susan than the sight of Kit, all bundled up and red cheeked, riding astride the twisted log. He appeared happier and healthier than ever before.

Sunday services before Christmas, heralded by the sweet peal of church bells, brought the entire family together in tender fellowship. Lady Stagsden even surprised her family by walking from the coach into the church, leaving her Bath chair firmly behind, all the while holding tightly onto Kit's mittened hand. She took her seat in the family pew, amidst the audible gasps and proffered congratulations on her improved health.

Susan sat one remove from Lord Stagsden, with Kit squished happily between them. Twice during the sermon, she felt Stagsden's gaze upon her. Unable to resist the temptation of glancing at him, she was gratified by the warm light in his eye. Both times he smiled in response to her own smile, but the second time, he held her gaze for an unconscionably long moment until Uncle Horace, seated behind them, cleared his throat in a meaningful manner.

A blush immediately rose to Susan's cheeks, and though she believed once more Stagsden stole a glance at her, she could not chance meeting his gaze again. Uncle Horace would undoubtedly decide one or the other needed a flick at the back of the neck to keep their attention properly focused, and besides, she feared that Stagsden would begin to think her brazen and unladylike. Still, her heart beat powerfully within her. Was it her imagination, or had Stagsden warmed toward her? If she had not been scheduled to leave the day following Christmas, she would have been terribly pleased by the progress she had made. For during the evenings, when she would snare Uncle Horace into a game or two of backgammon, Stagsden would sit nearby, prompting her to play her best and not to let Horace's ill humor encourage her to rash or purposely careless play. Afterward, Stagsden invariably spent a half-hour merely conversing with her, all the while poking at the Yule log which everyone was trying to keep burning day in and day out just as in former times.

Susan valued these minutes more than any others. She had come to know a great deal about his lordship, about the loss he had sustained when Emily had perished in childbed, the love he had for his estate, and his peculiar interest in attempting to push for reform in the House of Lords. He was pleasant to talk with, particularly since he always begged to know her opinions, and from the night he had come home to find his house ablaze with candles, he had not ceased asking about her life, her interests, and her beloved aunt who had raised her since childhood.

The only circumstances that marred her joy, other than the persistent pressure of escaping time, were Robert's tendency to interrupt Stagsden when he spoke and to frequently laugh outright at his brother's opinions.

Susan was startled by Robert's behavior; at the same time she was convinced that the younger sibling suffered from a profound jealousy of Stagsden coupled with the lack of a proper pursuit. If only Lady Stagsden would relent and permit him to enjoy the occupation of his choice.

Beyond Robert's uneasy attempts to join in their conversation, nothing disturbed the sweetness of these small hours shared with the man she loved.

A week before Christmas, when nearly the entire family had retired to bed, Susan sat at the table in the morning room figuring a large, rustic sphere made entirely of bent willow twigs and small branches. With some difficulty, she had been fashioning the recalcitrant Kissing Bough nearly the entire day, but at half past eleven, her efforts were finally being rewarded; the twigs were sturdily in place; three large, glistening apples hung from the red ribbon in the center of the bough; and secured carefully to the sturdier branches were several small candle holders in which tapers would be placed and then lit once the bough was suspended from an appropriate beam. She had only to attach a sprig of mistletoe to the bottom of the bough and it would be ready to display and enjoy.

With a piece of embroidery floss she attached the mistletoe to the base of the sphere, and because of her intense concentration, she jumped when Stagsden's voice intruded.

"Whatever have you done?" he queried. "What is this?"

"Oh, you gave me a start! Now don't tell me you've never heard of a Kissing Bough."

"How intriguing," he said, approaching the table upon which the bough had been settled into a globe stand. "I have heard of them but they are not traditional in our little hamlet."

"My aunt was used to have one made up every Christmas Eve. I wasn't certain I could accomplish it myself, not being especially skilled in the art, but I do think I have achieved a passable result."

"You have used box and—what is this?" he fingered the evergreens laced through the frame.

"Rosemary. I do apologize. I believe I have stripped nearly every small shrub along your garden wall of its leaves."

"You will hear no censure from me. My home has never smelled so sweet or resounded so happily with so much old-fashioned cheerfulness as now."

Susan looked up at him and smiled. "It is rather nice, isn't it?"

"Very."

He remained standing over her, touching the rosemary and box evergreens, looking down at her with a smile of his own. She let him hold her gaze for a time until she felt a blush begin creeping up her cheeks. It was very disconcerting to have him look at her when her heart beat so strongly for him. Unable to bear more, she shifted her gaze to the mistletoe which dangled daintily from the sphere. When she had tied the final knot, she leaned away from the globe stand, the muscles of her back sore from her labors, and pronounced her task complete.

"What do you do with it now?"

"If you'll help me, it is to be suspended from the high arch over the doorway which leads from the drawing room into the music room. I had one of the servants, with your mama's permission, of course, place a hook there."

He lifted the sphere gingerly, and in a stately procession they removed to the drawing room. A servant was in attendance in the red and green chamber, replacing candles and lighting them as was his assigned duty until everyone was abed. He finished lighting the final candle, and with a glance of pleasure at the dazzling sight of the drawing room lit up like a display of fireworks, he quit the room, smiling all the while.

Lord Stagsden turned in a full circle about the room and gave his head a wondering shake. "I can scarcely credit that this is my house, my home. Have I thanked you, Susan?"

"At least a hundred times, my lord," she returned with a laugh as she moved to stand in the archway. "And now, if you please, I shall climb upon this chair and you may hand the Kissing Bough to me. After which I shall light the candles and you shall observe for yourself the charm of my aunt's tradition."

He obeyed her, handing up a chair that she might secure the Kissing Bough and light the candles. When she was done and the chair was returned to its place against a nearby wall, Stagsden moved to stand directly beneath the glowing object, looked up into it, and frowned. "Susan, I'm sorry to tell you this, but there's something dreadfully wrong with your handiwork. Come and see!"

Susan had the most horrifying picture of the sphere breaking apart and crashing to the floor—perhaps even starting a fire. She rushed to stand next to him and looked up, searching frantically for some telling weakness which might herald a disaster.

"Now it is perfect," Stagsden breathed out.

Susan looked at him, wondering what he could possibly mean, particularly if the Kissing Bough was about to disintegrate, but when his arms were suddenly slipped about her, one holding her waist tightly, the other drawn fast round her shoulders, his words and intention were made perfectly clear.

"Oh," she murmured as he leaned toward her. "And I thought the whole thing was going to crash down on top of you."

"We have a tradition here at Stagsden, if not of Kissing Boughs, then of mistletoe. Do you object to my kissing you?"

"I suppose I would be a poor guest to refuse you one small favor," she said, blushing in spite of her efforts to remain calm and dignified.

"Indeed, you would," he responded teasingly, after which he gently placed his lips on hers.

Susan did not precisely remember upon which occasion she had first dared to hope that one day Lord Stagsden would assault her in this wondrously tender fashion, but she rather thought it was the first day she laid eyes on him. It was one thing, however, to imagine and to hope, quite another to feel the exquisite sensation of having Lord Stagsden actually kiss her.

The experience was of short duration, and when he had done, he leaned back slightly and stared down at her, his eyes questioning. He did not utter the words, but she felt certain he wanted to know the state of her heart. Brazenly slipping an arm about his neck, she responded on a choked whisper, "Geoff, I had so hoped—"

But that was as far as she got, for he drew her into a crushing embrace, his mouth descending possessively upon hers. A warmth of tenderness and passion ignited between them as he kissed first her lips, then her cheeks, and spoke her name a dozen times. She clung to him, her heart overflowing with every soft sentiment. Returning embrace for embrace, tender word for gently spoken affection, she did not hesitate to caress each feature of his face as freely as he caressed hers.

The moment ended upon a crashing sound from the hallway and a muttered oath.

Robert had arrived and was undoubtedly in his cups!

# Nine

By the time Robert made his way to the doorway of the drawing room, Susan had separated herself completely from Lord Stagsden's embrace. Her color was high, her mind befuddled and her senses overwhelmed. She was deeply embarrassed by what had transpired, particularly since there had been no proper exchange of sentiment prior to such an extraordinarily passionate kiss! At the same time, she knew in her heart of hearts that everything was as good as settled between them.

Robert entered the chamber, rubbing his elbow and complaining loudly that the walls were harder than they ought to be for a poor fellow trying to make his way to a comfortable chair by the fire. His speech was slightly slurred, his eyes were red rimmed, and his shirt-points were sadly wilted. "What? You still ranging about the house, brother? Susan! By God, I thought you would have long since seen your pillow?"

This last greeting was one of mingled surprise and pleasure. Stagsden was forgotten as Robert cried, "I was hoping you had not yet retired, and here you are! Good God! What the deuce is that?" He was staring in astonishment at the Kissing Bough.

Susan explained her creation.

"A Kissing Bough! But how delightful!" he cried, his affectionate gaze landing upon Susan's face. "And I see a sprig of mistletoe. If you do not take care, Sukey, I shall catch you unawares and take advantage of you."

Susan swallowed hard, not knowing precisely what to say to Robert's gallantry. She knew him well enough, however, to realize that because he was in his cups what restraint he had previously shown her might disappear. She did not, therefore, hesitate to respond, "Did you enjoy your game of billiards? Oh, goodness gracious, is that the hour? No wonder I am fatigued past bearing. I bid you good night."

She crossed the room, heading on a brisk step toward the door when Robert stopped her with a gentle, "Susan, I beg you will not leave just yet. I . . . I had something most particular I wished to say to you. I know it must seem I am in my altitudes, but I promise you I am not so foxed that I do not know what I am about." He turned toward his brother and said, "That is, if Geoff has no objection to my speaking with you privately for a few minutes."

"Robert, it is rather late and—"

"Five minutes, only. Please."

Susan could not imagine what it was Robert wished to say to her, but she thought perhaps he meant to beg her assistance in speaking with Stagsden about a pair of colors. "Very well, if you wish it."

"Indeed, I do."

They both glanced at Stagsden to see what his reaction might be. Susan was a little surprised by the contemplative frown between the viscount's brows. "Perhaps tomorrow, Robert."

"I shan't importune her, brother, if that is what you fear. I esteem Miss Elstow far too much for that."

"Then if Susan does not object . . ."

"No, of course not," she responded, crossing the room to take up a seat by the fire.

Stagsden inclined his head and quit the room. Susan knew an enormous sense of disappointment that he was gone. She feared somehow that all which had transpired just a few moments earlier might vanish somehow. She

154

wanted to call him back, but knew it was impossible. She folded her hands politely on her lap and diverted her cluttered mind from disquieting thoughts, directing her attention entirely toward Robert.

It was well she did, for had she not been focused exclusively upon him, she would have been startled by the manner in which he quickly crossed the room and fell upon his knees before her. So swift were his motions that he was in full possession of her hands before she had even blinked.

"My darling Susan, my love!" he cried, placing a kiss on each of her hands. "I am a coward, I know, that I must fortify myself with brandy before being able to lay my cause before you, but you must forgive me for I am entirely untried in matters of the heart. Dalliance, yes, but not a love which I can no longer contain within my breast. You appear stunned? Have I not made the secret of my love for you clearer than this? My darling Susan, you must know that I have tumbled violently in love with you and wish you to become my wife. You must know it!"

He regarded her beseechingly from stricken eyes, waiting for words of reassurance.

"Robert!" she began, stupefied. "I . . . I don't know what to say to you. I hadn't the least notion! Truly! I mean, I always thought you were fond of me, but I never suspected it was in any serious way—that you were wishful of marrying me."

"You are teasing me," he responded, horrified. "When I have been dangling at your shoestrings this year and more? Who do you think prompted Ianthe to invite you to Stagsden Lodge for the holidays? Yes, you may stare, but it was I. You have but to ask her. Oh, tell me you knew of my love for you!"

"But I didn't. I didn't."

"Why do you think I—_I!_—should choose to do the pretty amongst the Tabbies the entire season and the

155

Little Season as well!"

"I confess I thought it a trifle odd, but I suppose I thought you were attempting to reform your character!"

"My God! Only in part, only because of you, because of your goodness and because I wished to be worthy of you! Susan, I love you! Please tell me you will do me the honor of becoming my wife."

If it had not occurred to Robert that two penniless people could scarcely marry without suffering the worst forms of penury and hardship, it most certainly occurred to Susan at this moment. "How could I become your wife? We should be forced to live in a gardener's cottage and take up a trade like spinning cloth or—or making needles, or some such thing."

"I know I will give you a shock, but I have considered our future. I intend to enlist! We shan't be comfortable for a time, but I plan to rise quickly and in a few years—"

"I could never follow the drum," she said, squeezing his hands. "Don't ask it of me. Don't even think of it!"

He seemed a little daunted by her announcement, but after a moment, he nodded seriously and said, "Then I shall think of something else. Perhaps I shall take holy orders as Mama wishes me to."

At this, Susan could not keep from laughing outright. "You, Robert? Don't be offended, but you are by far so ill suited to the church that I vow you would go as mad as Bedlam within a fortnight of taking over parish duties."

He smiled ruefully, his shoulders slumping unhappily. "Then perhaps I shall study law and become a solicitor. Can you not hear my heart in what I am saying to you? I shall do whatever I must to care for you and to make you proud of me. Besides, I'll be damned before I permit you to become a governess. You deserve a far better fate!"

Susan ignored this last comment and referred to the

previous one. "But I am proud of you. You're a strong, determined man who lacks only the right profession with which to secure your future and your happiness. Have I not said so often, and—"

"There! You see what an excellent wife you would make me. Only, consider following the drum with me. It would not be as hard as you think!"

"Even if I were of a temperament to do so, I still could not marry you."

"Whyever not?" he queried, his eyes filling with anxiety. "I know you are fond of me."

"Yes, very much."

"Then what is your reason?"

"I . . . I don't believe your brother would wish for the match."

"Is this your strongest objection?"

"There is another," she said, unwilling to confess her love for Lord Stagsden. "But because I don't believe you would be permitted to marry me, I shan't divulge the rest."

Robert smiled. "He will not disallow our marriage," he cried. "I will speak with him tomorrow. You will see. I know Geoff is . . . is fond of you."

Susan was unwilling to say more. She could not bring herself to speak the very simple words that she could not marry him because she did not love him and because she was convinced Stagsden would forbid the match; she merely gave his hands a squeeze, told him by all means to speak with his brother on the morrow, and after placing a sisterly kiss upon his cheek, bade him good night.

# Ten

Perhaps it was a fit of dementia, or perhaps it was a curious form of shock and disorientation which prompted Susan—on the day following Stagsden's most devastating kiss—to accept Robert's proposal.

Surely it was a form of madness, she thought, as she regarded Stagsden's back. He was standing at the window, a wintery light spilling over him from the east. He had been so cool and indifferent as he had spelled out in its entirety the fortune which he meant to bestow upon her should she choose to wed his brother. Robert, happier than she had ever seen him, had clutched at her hand, had kissed her fingers, and had called her his "darling," his "love" at least a thousand times.

She had experienced a complete breakdown of her will, due primarily to her dislike of hurting anyone—and Robert would be devastated if she refused him—coupled with the overwhelming sense of desolation which had descended upon her when Stagsden had cheerfully recommended she accept his brother's hand. The only words she had been able to utter expressed concern that she had a commitment to a governess post. He had blinked at her, a stricken look coming into his eyes; then the look had disappeared, to be replaced by his habitual stoicism. "You will be far better situated now," was his softly spoken reply. "Though I know you are extremely fond of children—Kit is devoted to you, and you have been acquainted with him for only a fortnight!—I am persuaded you will want children of your own."

"Yes." She had nodded dumbly. "I have always wished for a nurseryful, but, indeed, I can't—"

"Then I will say to you what you are forever saying to everyone else. *Nonsense!*" he had said with a smile. "*Nonsense!*" He had then risen from his chair and taken up his place by the window, from which he had explained the settlements he would have his solicitor draw up at once.

Susan should have spoken then. She should have ended either brother's belief that she could be happy as Robert's wife. But she was numb with shock.

Robert went to his brother and shook his hand warmly, begged forgiveness for all the grief he had caused him during recent years, and promised that Stagsden would be proud of him one day.

The remainder of the day was a polite blur until dinner that evening and the moment when Robert announced their engagement. Only then did Susan seem able to pull herself from her distraction and despair to rise to the occasion as a bride ought to do, smiling until her face would crack. She was nearly undone, however, when both mother and daughter—at the precise moment when Robert begged for everyone to congratulate him—cried out in unison, "But I thought—"

In the same manner, each woman clipped her words short, the faces of both paling as they exchanged a meaningful glance. Robert seemed a little taken aback, but pressed forward anyway, demanding the proper enthusiasm from each, which he considered his due.

Ianthe rose abruptly from her chair and came round the table to hug Susan. "Whatever have you done?" her sister-to-be whispered in her ear. "I know you are in love with Geoff!"

Susan could bear it no longer. Somehow she managed to gain her feet, though her knees were watery and useless. "I am overcome," she said, tears starting to her eyes.

As she ran from the room, she thought she heard

Stagsden call her name, but she wasn't sure.

The days following the announcement languished. A pall of gloom had somehow descended over the once-cheerful manor. Uncle Horace exclaimed that he was determined to quit the manor, since every time a light was lit in the Lodge, something happened to blow it out. He couldn't for the life of him explain what was amiss, but damme, the place should be jumping in preparation for Robert's wedding. Instead, he swore everyone was as miserable — save Robert — as if a funeral were about to take place.

Ianthe's peevishness returned, Lady Stagsden took to her Bath chair, Kit was no longer permitted to go out in the snow, and Susan had no strength whatsoever to enliven anyone's spirits since her own were lower than they had ever been in her entire existence.

The light had certainly gone out.

And worse for Susan. Since the wondrous evening in which she had shared a kiss with Stagsden, he had not once approached her to explain how it had come about, especially after he had kissed her so passionately beneath the Kissing Bough — that he had agreed to Robert's proposals. She felt betrayed. But how long she could sustain such a farce she did not know; yet the means to break an engagement that was wholly wrong, she could not imagine. Robert appeared delirious with happiness, scarcely ever leaving her side and confessing his love at every turn.

She tried as hard as she could to enter into his plans with enthusiasm, but her heart was breaking. Trying to joyously agree to a honeymoon in Italy was like drinking a bitter medicinal draught and exclaiming that it tasted like a sweet, honeyed lemonade! The words simply got stuck in her throat. She could do nothing more than burst into tears and again run from the room.

Matters were made even more worse by the fact that Susan had no relatives upon whom she could rely for advice. She was alone in the disastrous error she had made and knew not how to reverse it.

Robert had initially believed that he had achieved a stunning victory over his elder, autocratic brother when Susan had accepted his proposal and Geoff had offered him the moon to take her to wife. Though ecstatic with his success, he knew Susan's heart wasn't fully engaged—probably she did have a *tendre* for his brother; well, yes, he could admit to himself she loved him—but he knew Geoff. Geoff had married a well-dowered female, the daughter of an earl, well connected, extremely well bred. Susan was none of these things, and he would have in the end rejected her. Emily's manner had been cool and proper while Susan was . . . well, for all her spiritedness and industry, she could never please Geoff. Had she hoped to? He believed she had, poor thing!

Nonetheless, in time she would forget Geoff, and as for himself, he would do everything he could to make her happy.

But as he looked at her, seeing the dark circles beneath her eyes become more pronounced as the days marched slowly toward Christmas, the nagging doubts which had beset him from the moment his mother and Ianthe had exclaimed, "But I thought—" so spontaneously at the dinner table, had by now taken strong root in his heart. Susan didn't love him. He suspected she never would.

Still, she must prefer marrying him to becoming a governess! Surely!

A frost had settled over Stagsden's heart, freezing his emotions once again. He was far happier this way. Surely. He realized, of course, that Susan's acceptance of

Robert's offer had effectively killed the Christmas spirit in his house, but everyone would eventually come round to the betrothal.

Surely.

When Kit spent less time with his family, and more with Nurse in the schoolroom, Geoffrey told himself he was glad his home was returning to normal. Now he could be comfortable again.

When Ianthe told him he was a cold, unfeeling, impoverished excuse for a man and that she had never liked Emily, he lifted an indifferent shoulder, happy that the old, petulant Ianthe had returned.

When his mother remained in her room for two days straight, he merely sent a note, by way of the butler, to see if she wished for a visit from her favorite doctor.

But when Uncle Horace actually packed his bags and said he would rather live in bachelor quarters in Half Moon Street for the rest of his life than endure one more minute at "Stagsden Tomb," a crack occurred in the ice round Geoffrey's heart. He felt from that moment he had begun bleeding inside.

Horace had been leeching off his sister for more years than he could number, yet the man actually chose to leave this house, *his house,* because he did not care for the ambience?

He touched his chest, wondering if he would find an open wound there.

What was Susan Elstow to him? They had shared an extraordinary, surprising kiss—but that was all. Later, he had been grateful Robert had interrupted their embrace. For all her excellent qualities, Susan was not what he wanted in a wife. Emily was what he had wanted, and she had died. Susan was far too *alive* for him. She smelled of sunshine, and he wanted a cloudy sky for the rest of his life. She could turn his household upside down with a mere smile. He couldn't love her. If he did, he would risk losing her to death, and he couldn't do that.

He would never do that again! He had promised himself he would never do that again!

Horace told Robert that he would return for the wedding, of course, but he added that if his nephew was stupid enough to marry a woman who didn't love him, then he would come to the festivities for the joy of seeing someone besides himself, make a damned cake of himself.

On the morning of Christmas Eve, Lady Stagsden shocked the entire household by rising from her sickbed. She ordered her maid to crop her hair in a fashionable style. When this task was accomplished she stunned Bellows by ordering him to have two footmen take her Bath chair out into the snow and set it ablaze that she might watch it burn from her bedchamber window. She then rocked the remainder of any as yet unbruised sensibilities by announcing that she meant to quit Stagsden Lodge immediately, that very day, on Christmas Eve. She had decided to travel to Bath — and to take Ianthe with her — in order to partake of the nasty waters much celebrated at the *tonish* watering hole. She intended to recover her health. Horace had shown her the way — Susan, too, with her jubilant spirits! — and she meant never again to forfeit her life *before* she had actually paid her debt to nature.

Robert was angry that in the midst of preparations for his nuptials, his own mother and sister would leave, but Lady Stagsden told him she would be back in time to see him walk down the aisle in February, though she would not be moved from her present course. She no longer chose to live as an invalid, and once he was married, she meant to begin a tour of the Continent, which her husband had never wished her to do. "I have learned a great deal from your future wife. I am only sorry that in this final hour she chose to ignore her heart. I shan't ignore mine any longer, and so I bid you good-bye, my love. Write to me about your plans. And by the way, if you wish for it, I shall purchase you a pair of colors. It was never Geoff who had forbidden you to enter the army.

163

He did it for me, and I was wrong. I was selfish enough to try to keep you near me all these years. It would seem your brother and I suffer from a similar malady. We neither of us have the courage to live in the face of death. I know you do."

"*You*, Mama?" he queried, shaking his head in disbelief. "But all these years I blamed Geoff. How could you?"

"I confess I was wrong. So very wrong. But I mean to do better and will offer you again a pair of colors if you wish for it."

"But Susan says she cannot follow the drum."

"Then you have chosen the wrong wife for you. I am sorry. I blame myself. But I no longer intend to interfere in your affairs. I only hope one day you will find it in your heart to forgive me."

When Lady Stagsden and Ianthe actually rolled away in the ancient family traveling chariot, Robert confronted Stagsden. The viscount admitted it was true. "How very much it pained me to watch you kicking your heels all these years. You would have made an exemplary officer! I told Mama as much a hundred times, but she would not hear of it, and now you say she has changed her mind."

"Completely. She even offered to buy me a pair of colors."

"I am astonished!" Geoffrey cried, sitting down heavily upon a wing chair by the fire. The Yule log was still glowing with coals, but a cold layer of ash surrounded the now-diminished log.

Stagsden shook his head, feeling vaguely that he'd made a mull of it, but not precisely certain in what way. "It is too late, though," he murmured. "Susan cannot follow the drum. I know her. For all her vivacity, she hasn't the stamina or the strength of will to succeed as an officer's wife." He looked up at Robert, pleading, "You do know that, don't you?"

Robert was stunned by the strained expression in his brother's eyes. Geoffrey's concern was all for Susan. A deep, caring concern that transcended brotherly affection.

"Yes, I know," he responded slowly. "Don't worry. I will take excellent care of her."

"But you will not be happy."

"No, not entirely. But you know what she is! Susan works miracles with her kind, good heart. I shall certainly be far happier than I deserve."

# Eleven

"The banns have not been posted. There can be no scandal attached to you," Robert said quietly, pressing each of Susan's hands in turn. "I intend to join a cavalry regiment, just as you suggested times out of mind. Mama has offered to purchase a pair of colors for me. You are released, Susan. With all my heart, I release you."

Susan could do little more than stare at her former betrothed with her mouth agape and her eyes blinking rapidly. She felt so profound a relief that she did not hesitate to pull her hands from his grasp and to subsequently cast herself into his arms. "Thank you, Robert," she breathed tearfully. "I ought not to have—I am so sorry—but I am so grateful!"

He held her close, and Susan now realized how thoughtless it was of her to have hugged him, especially when he whispered, "I loved you so much, Susan, at least, I think I did. You were the first person to comprehend me, to fully understand my unhappiness." He drew back from her slightly and, searching her eyes, queried, "I did love you . . . I mean, I do love you, don't I?"

Susan, whose eyes were filled with tears, clung to his arms and said, "I haven't the least notion."

"I know what it is, then," he continued. "You have these wondrous qualities of compassion and vigor that draw all to you like moths to flame. You seem to have the spirit to enable those about you to finally change and

166

become animated where despair once ruled. I shall never forget you, and when I do marry. I shall name my first daughter after you."

"You will make a splendid officer."

"There, you see," was all he said, before he left her to tend to the packing of his own bags. It was Christmas Eve, but he meant to leave at once, lest the wondrous dream which had enveloped him—of actually being able to join the army—vanish before his eyes.

When Robert had gone and she had recovered from the stunning realization that she would not be marrying him after all, Susan realized that never in her entire existence had she experienced anything so ridiculous as coming to a house in which she was to pass the Christmas holidays only to have four of its permanent residents depart before she did—and by Christmas Eve!

How singular, she thought, as she sat in the drawing room reading Kit a story. The child's spirits were greatly dampened by all that had transpired. He missed his grandmama already, as well as Aunt Ianthe, and he was terribly saddened to learn that his new friend was not to wed Uncle Bobby, after all. "But what will I do without you, Sukey?" he asked, suddenly throwing his arms about her and holding her tight. "I won't ever have any fun anymore, not for as long as I live."

"Nonsense!" she whispered, hugging him close to her. "Besides, don't you know that I shall write you a letter every sennight, and if I am able I will travel all the way from Kent to visit you?"

"I don't want you to go!" he wailed and burst into tears.

Lord Stagsden entered the drawing room at that moment, and she glanced up at him, her cheeks rosy with embarrassment. What must he think? she wondered.

Fortunately, he smiled kindly upon her, his expression compassionate as he drew Kit into his arms and cuddled him. Susan watched father and son, both of whom she loved very much, and knew a sensation of loss so acute that the breath felt crushed from her. She wanted to leave now, that she might not be tormented further, but for Kit's sake, she remained. Once he had stopped crying, she challenged him to a game of spillikins. The remainder of the evening progressed peacefully until Kit's bedtime, at which early hour, Susan begged to be excused, complaining of the headache.

But it was not her head which ached, not by half, merely her heart as she pulled her portmanteau from the wardrobe and began the task of packing. She had already determined to leave the house at dawn and return to the village, where she intended to catch the London Mail. She could not pass Christmas Day at the Lodge with even a semblance of her habitually high spirits.

From the moment Robert had ended their brief engagement, Susan had realized that Stagsden's reasons for being aloof with her were very complicated. She had shed a great many tears over this realization, but once they had been spent and had doused her pillow, she felt able to set her feet on her former path, one that led to Kent and to a houseful of young girls. She began wondering about them and whether or not they were lively or dull, intelligent or stupid, silly or refined. She hoped for one of each, just for the pleasure of seeing what qualities she could pique in each young mind and heart.

There was now no reason for her to remain at Stagsden Lodge, certainly not with Lady Stagsden and Ianthe gone, as well as Uncle Horace and Robert. If it seemed odd to any of the neighbors that the young visitor had been abandoned by her hostess, it seemed to Susan the very best and happiest of circumstances. She had come to a house which had been somehow trapped in its carriage ruts so long that everyone had become mired about the ankles, their lives stayed to no purpose.

If she was credited with having given each stuck coach a push, she could be content. If her own hope of finding her love returned had ended unhappily, then so be it. She was made of stern stuff. She knew the value of shedding tears that she might move on, and she would not hesitate to fill her bandboxes and her portmanteau and silently steal away at the break of dawn.

The next morning Lord Stagsden sat in the nursery watching his son play at spillikins—a game Kit enjoyed tirelessly with Susan. His clumsy, small hands were a poor match for the heap of straws from which he was to remove one without disturbing the rest, but Nurse had a rule that until he reached the advanced age of six, he had three tries before she took a turn.

Geoffrey watched Kit with pleasure and remembered the delights the young boy had experienced over the past three weeks, singing carols with Susan, riding on the Yule log, emptying his Christmas stocking after breakfast, eating sugar plums until he had become almost ill, letting the wax from the Kissing Bough drip on his nankeens so that he could pick it off when it dried. He had become a different child since Susan's arrival.

And now Susan would soon leave. He was surprised when she did not descend the stairs for breakfast, but then, she had complained of a headache the night before. It occurred to him as well that since she would be leaving on the morrow, she might be involved in packing her belongings. Whatever the case, Kit had missed her sorely, especially since it was she who always tied his table napkin about his neck.

Thoughts of Susan brought a disquiet to his spirits he was loath to explain. The truth was he was greatly fatigued by all the upheavals her presence had inspired. His entire house had been transformed into nothing short of a candlelit conservatory, his family had all left, and now Kit was in despondency at the thought of losing Susan.

169

He ought to be angry that she had wrought so much uncomfortable change; instead he felt irritable, ready to fly into the boughs if his will was crossed. The truth was, he knew he ought to speak with her, to explain about the kiss they had shared beneath the Kissing Bough. But to what purpose? Did she expect him to offer for her as everyone else seemed to?

He rose from his chair and began pacing the room. Nurse and Kit only glanced at his odd behavior, then returned to the far greater amusement of spillikins.

He would be damned before he would offer for Susan because his staff or his family expected him to. Only the night before Bellows had expressed his delight that there would soon be a mistress in the house. And when Geoffrey had snapped at the aged retainer, the poor old man had blanched and said that Master Robert, before he left, had said that congratulations were in order and Stagsden was expecting the staff's well wishes.

He was furious with Robert for forcing his hand in this truly obnoxious manner. Bellows had quit his presence with strict instructions to relay the truth to the staff. But Bellows had had such a twinkle in his eye as he had turned on his heel to return to the nether regions, it had been all Geoffrey could do to keep his temper in check.

The morning was dark and cloudy, a perfect reflection of his mood. Didn't anyone understand that he could not lose another wife? He had done his duty: he had produced an heir, and if he kept Kit safe, he needn't worry about the future. He thought now how foolish it had been to have taken the lad out to hunt for a Yule log. He promised himself he wouldn't be that foolish again.

But these thoughts, rather than comforting him, became like a flood of boiling water over his frozen heart. Pain—cutting, burning, aching—tore through his heart. This was not the life he had envisioned for himself or for Christopher or for any of his offspring. My God, what had he done! He was no different from Emily's mother, locking up his affections, imprisoning his own *joie de vivre* within a tomb of fear.

He listened to his son's laughter as Kit exclaimed over a success, and suddenly, inexplicably, the last vestige of ice melted away. His heart felt free, like a river finally divested of grating, crashing ice floes. He knew his mind, his heart, his desires fully. He loved Susan, he needed her, he wanted her to become his wife.

"What have I done?" he murmured.

When Kit queried him as to what was amiss, he said, "Would you like it if Susan were to live here and become your mother?"

Kit stared at him for a long moment, then asked, "Can she do that?"

Lord Stagsden, unprepared for the simplicity of this question, laughed aloud. "I don't know," he responded. "I suppose I must ask her, but first, would it make you happy if she could?"

"Yes, I like her. She makes me laugh. She tickles me, and she lets me eat lots of sugar plums." He then cast a reproachful glance toward his nurse who merely adjured him that if Miss Elstow were to become his mother she sincerely doubted Miss would continue in such a manner.

Kit defended his friend. "Yes she would. You don't know her like I do. She's a right 'un, huh, Papa?"

"Yes, Kit, she's a right 'un."

His heart settled at last, Lord Stagsden went in search of his quarry. He did not find her in the library or the drawing room or the morning room, and when he finally asked Bellows where she had gone, the butler informed him that Miss had gone to the village some time past, and it was his belief she meant to take the Mail to Kent where she had a post awaiting her as governess to several children.

Since this was said with a disapproving austerity, Lord Stagsden did not hesitate to say, "Do not fret, Bellows. I

171

mean to bring her home. Have my curricle sent round, two hot bricks placed upon the floorboards—no, make that five. And have Nurse bundle up my son."

"You mean to take Master Kit with you?" Bellows asked, the impertinence in his question overshadowed by the astonishment on his face.

"Yes, it is high time he began going about in society. I haven't done right by him all these years, but I mean to redress my wrongs beginning now. Only see to it at once! And send my valet to my chambers. I'll need traveling gear and—oh, yes—your wife, I believe, was mending my greatcoat?"

"I'll see to everything!" Bellows cried, hurrying away to complete his tasks.

A full hour passed before the men were readied for their journey. Kit was beyond ecstasy, his cheeks red with pleasure, his nurse severe and frowning. "It'll be the death of him," she prophesied harshly.

As one, both father and son turned to her and exclaimed, "Nonsense!" Which caused them both to laugh as Stagsden tied a thick woolen scarf about Kit's neck and settled a proper beaver hat low over his ears. Within two minutes, they were bowling down the lane, a light snow catching the brims of their hats, their spirits high and unquenchable.


Susan was cramped between a large, portly man who was in the habit of taking a pinch of snuff every few minutes, then sneezing, and a lady who simply could not stop talking. The other occupants alternately coughed, wheezed, snored, or begged the chatterbox to stubble it. So it was to the accompaniment of a fair cacophony of human ills and failings that she endured the first six hours of her journey.

The sky began to darken as daylight pushed ever westward, to illuminate the great Atlantic Ocean. The Royal

Mail had just left a posting inn with fresh horses pulling the coach onward at lightning speed. Away the wheels carried her, away from Stagsden and Kit and the dozen or so servants who had expressed their sorrow that she was leaving. "For we had such hopes," the tall, thin housekeeper had pronounced tearfully.

Away she flew. Away from love.

Susan had wanted to say, and I had such hopes, too, but of course that was impossible. Instead, she had bid her farewells with a smile and had waved to all as the creaking barouche carried her to the village, to the mail coach, toward London, toward Kent.

The fatigue of traveling began taking its toll on her. When night fell, even with the sneezing and the chatter, she fell asleep. Where she was when she awoke, she couldn't say. But something was amiss! Someone was shouting, in fact several people were, and the coach was still. She glanced about her and saw that three of the occupants of the coach were leaning out the window. She thought at first a highwayman had held up the mail, but the eagerness of the travelers to stick their heads out the windows told its own tale and she knew she had nothing to fear.

Then she heard a familiar voice. "No, *Elstow,* you simpleton, not *Elbow.* I am searching for Miss Susan Elstow. Do you have such a woman aboard your coach?"

"Here now, 'ow should I know?"

"Will you at least check with your passengers. I must speak with her! At once! It is of the utmost importance!"

"I'm here," Susan said, her voice rough from sleep.

"Susan?" Lord Stagsden called out.

How was it possible he was here? Perhaps she was in a dream and had not yet awakened. By the odd chance, however, that she was indeed awake and was not dreaming, she called out more loudly, "Stagsden? I am here! I am here!" Her heart began racing madly, threatening to explode in her chest.

She pried herself from between the sneezing portly man and the chatterbox with some difficulty and not without a series of rumbled complaints about her hapless movements. She stepped on at least three separate feet and wounded one shin bone in her efforts to extricate herself from the coach. "Here!" she again cried, loud enough this time for Stagsden to recognize her.

"Susan! Susan! Have we found you at last?"

She wondered who the *we* could possibly be and at last reached the door to the coach. As it flew open, she could not mistake Stagsden's eyes above the muffler. She fell into his arms, and felt she was hugging a bear, a snow-covered one at that. She knew he was trying to kiss her, but the woolen scarf about his neck was preventing him from doing his duty properly so he set her down and unwound "the curst thing," then, pushing her bonnet away from her face, kissed her hard on the mouth.

She melted into him, all sense of decorum and propriety forgotten. Amongst the cheers which resounded shockingly both from within and without the coach, she returned his kiss.

"I've been such a fool," he whispered, kissing away her tears. "My darling, come back to Stagsden and be mistress of my home. Marry me, I pray. Kit needs a mother, and I want desperately to take you to wife. Will you come?"

Susan could not quite credit her ears. A sob escaped her throat as she replied, "Of course I will. Yes, of course. Geoff, I had hoped! I had dared to hope. I have loved you forever!"

Again he caught her to him and kissed her, wildly and thoroughly, until the coachman begged to know if Miss wished for her baggage. "I beg yer pardon, but we've a schedule to keep."

"Yes, if you please," she returned, glancing back at him shyly. When she saw all the passengers watching her with eyes agog, a terrible embarrassment overcame her and

174

her cheeks flooded with color.

Stagsden slipped his arm about her waist and drew her away from gawking eyes toward the back of the coach.

When she was in sight of his curricle, Susan heard a voice call out, "Sukey! Look! I am keeping Papa's horses in check!"

"Kit?" Susan cried. "Whatever are you doing out in the chill night air? Oh, Geoff, you shouldn't have. How could you have brought him with you on such an errand?"

"Well, it may have been a trifle ill advised, but he is well clothed and we have put warm bricks at his feet at every inn we passed. That is why it took us so long to overtake you."

"You must be exhausted! Both of you!"

Father and son looked at each other and chimed, "Nonsense!" Then they burst into the sweet laughter of shared amusement.

When the portmanteau and bandboxes were packed and bound somewhat erratically to the boot, Susan climbed aboard the curricle and was soon bowling up the highway back to Bedfordshire. Kit begged to know if they might sing carols since it was still Christmas Day.

"We can sing them all year long if you like," she replied.

"No, we can't," he responded, apparently shocked that she would suggest such a notion.

"Whyever not?" she queried.

Kit stared at her in amazement, the glow of the carriage lamp casting his surprised features into an odd mass of light and shadows. "Well, I don't know." He turned to his father. "Can we sing carols all year?"

"If Susan says so, then I suppose we can. I begin to think she knows more of Christmas than any of us."

"More than even you?" Kit asked, startled.

"Oh, yes," he said, gathering the reins into one hand for a moment and reaching over to give Susan's hand a

175

squeeze. "Especially more than me. But I intend to learn at her knee. I hope you will do the same."

"Yes, Papa," Kit responded earnestly.

"What utter nonsense!" Susan cried. "You are both being absurd. I refuse to hear any more of this nonsense."

Kit smiled a secretive smile. "See, Papa! I told you she says it all the time."

The curricle continued in a soft swish across the dark snow. In the distance a village glowed in candlelight softness, beckoning the travelers forward. Susan listened to Kit's innocent chatter as he began conversing with his father about the matched pair of black horses which pranced to the delicate tinkle of the small silver bells adorning their respective leather harnesses.

These are the sounds of Christmas, she thought, as Lord Stagsden and Kit, both muffled behind woolen scarves, spoke of how to judge the difference between a prime bit of blood and a glue-pot.

Yes, these were most definitely the real sounds of Christmas, the ones she would take to heart and remember all her life.

# MORE PASSION AND ADVENTURE AWAIT... YOUR TRIP TO A BIG ADVENTUROUS WORLD BEGINS WHEN YOU ACCEPT YOUR FIRST 4 NOVELS ABSOLUTELY *FREE* (AN $18.00 VALUE)

Accept your Free gift and start to experience more of the passion and adventure you like in a historical romance novel. Each Zebra novel is filled with proud men, spirited women and tempestuous love that you'll remember long after you turn the last page.

Zebra Historical Romances are the finest novels of their kind. They are written by authors who really know how to weave tales of romance and adventure in the historical settings you love. You'll feel like you've actually gone back in time with the thrilling stories that each Zebra novel offers.

## GET YOUR FREE GIFT WITH THE START OF YOUR HOME SUBSCRIPTION

Our readers tell us that these books sell out very fast in book stores and often they miss the newest titles. So Zebra has made arrangements for you to receive the four newest novels published each month.

You'll be guaranteed that you'll never miss a title, and home delivery is so convenient. And to show you just how easy it is to get Zebra Historical Romances, we'll send you your first 4 books absolutely FREE! Our gift to you just for trying our home subscription service.

## BIG SAVINGS AND FREE HOME DELIVERY

Each month, you'll receive the four newest titles as soon as they are published. You'll probably receive them even before the bookstores do. What's more, you may preview these exciting novels free for 10 days. If you like them as much as we think you will, just pay the low preferred subscriber's price of just $3.75 each. *You'll save $3.00 each month off the publisher's price.* AND, your savings are even greater because there are never any shipping, handling or other hidden charges—FREE Home Delivery. Of course you can return any shipment within 10 days for full credit, no questions asked. There is no minimum number of books you must buy.

# 4 FREE BOOKS

FREE BOOKS

## TO GET YOUR 4 FREE BOOKS WORTH $18.00 — MAIL IN THE FREE BOOK CERTIFICATE T O D A Y

Fill in the Free Book Certificate below, and we'll send your FREE BOOKS to you as soon as we receive it.

If the certificate is missing below, write to: Zebra Home Subscription Service, Inc., P.O. Box 5214, 120 Brighton Road, Clifton, New Jersey 07015-5214.

## FREE BOOK CERTIFICATE

# 4 FREE BOOKS

### ZEBRA HOME SUBSCRIPTION SERVICE, INC.

**YES!** Please start my subscription to Zebra Historical Romances and send me my first 4 books absolutely FREE. I understand that each month I may preview four new Zebra Historical Romances free for 10 days. If I'm not satisfied with them, I may return the four books within 10 days and owe nothing. Otherwise, I will pay the low preferred subscriber's price of just $3.75 each; a total of $15.00, *a savings off the publisher's price of $3.00.* I may return any shipment and I may cancel this subscription at any time. There is no obligation to buy any shipment and there are no shipping, handling or other hidden charges. Regardless of what I decide, the four free books are mine to keep.

NAME

ADDRESS _____ APT

CITY _____ STATE _____ ZIP

TELEPHONE ( )

SIGNATURE _____ (if under 18, parent or guardian must sign)

Terms, offer and prices subject to change without notice. Subscription subject to acceptance by Zebra Books. Zebra Books reserves the right to reject any order or cancel any subscription.

GET
FOUR
FREE
BOOKS
(AN $18.00 VALUE)

ZEBRA HOME SUBSCRIPTION
SERVICE, INC.
P.O. Box 5214
120 BRIGHTON ROAD
CLIFTON, NEW JERSEY 07015-5214

# Under The
# Kissing Bough

by Mary Kingsley

# One

The snow was falling harder now. It had been only a light flurry when Rebecca Ware had left the Widow Pollock's cottage out near Great Hill, but it had since deepened, blanketing even the wooded road Rebecca had to travel to reach home. Above her the sky was the color of burnished pewter, with no breaks to the clouds, and the wind was picking up. It was no day to be outside; it was a day to stay close to home and hearth. Yet Rebecca felt no urge to hurry. Days like this, when her tasks were done and little more was expected of her, were rare. When she reached home there'd be enough to do, but this time was for her alone. What, after all, was a little snow?

Spreading her arms wide, Rebecca turned in a slow circle, her face upturned, eyes closed, and mouth opened to catch a snowflake on her tongue. It was wonderful, it was glorious! She knew whose woods these were; they belonged to the Earl of Westover. He was far away, though, in London, and he would neither know nor care that she stood here, watching his trees fill up with snow. There were no other houses, no other people. No sound, except for the wind, and even that was muffled by the softly falling snow. No one to bother her, to make demands upon her; no one to ask her to do this or that. Just herself, to glory in the peace and freedom, if only for a little while. If she received no other Christmas gift, she would be satisfied.

Ordinarily Rebecca adored Christmas, with its old customs and the feelings of goodwill everyone seemed to feel. She loved the decorations of holly and ivy, the placing of fat white candles in the window to guide the Christ child on his way, the aromas of turkey roasting, and the excitement of stirring the Christmas pudding, for luck. She loved gathering with people and being social, in a relaxed, almost informal way that was absent the remainder of the year. Mostly, she loved the feeling of closeness with her family: the excitement of her brother Benjamin's return from school for the holidays; the twinkle in her father's eye as he adjured his children to remember the reason for Christmas but then reached into his pocket and pulled out a treat, an orange, perhaps; the way her mother, sturdy and no-nonsense, glowed like a girl, when Papa caught her under the Kissing Bough. Christmas was a special time, or, rather, it had been. Now everything had changed. This year, Christmas just meant more things to do, more duties. The snow, however, seemed to be returning to her some of her lost Christmas spirit, and so it was a gift, indeed.

"'Here we come a-wassailing, a-wassailing to you. Here we come a-wassailing, and Merry Christmas, too. Love and joy come to you, and to you your wassail too,'" she sang, aware that the words weren't quite right, aware that she hadn't hit the highest note, and not caring, "'and God bless you and send you a happy'—eek!"

Her words ended on a shriek as her feet suddenly slipped out from under her. Helpless to save herself, she windmilled her arms, to no avail, and went down in an ignominious heap in the snow, her skirts rucked up and her feet spread out. "Whoosh!" she gasped, trying to catch her breath, and then let out a laugh. If anyone had seen her, the proper daughter of the late Reverend Ware, her reputation would be in tatters for certain. Thank heavens there was no one about, she thought, getting to her feet and dusting herself off. Nothing was hurt but her pride. Where was she? The snow, beautiful though it was, coated every tree, giving each a uniformity it didn't ordinarily have. But there, there was the fallen oak that had gone down in a storm two years ago. Two miles to Westbridge. An easy walk on a sunny summer's day, but a daunting distance today, with the snow coming down as it was, thick and so heavy she could only see a few feet ahead. She had no choice, though. She had miles to go, and promises to keep.

No singing now. Rebecca pulled her hood tighter around her and thanked God for her stout boots and sturdy clothing, the country clothes she had despised when she had dreamed of wearing filmy muslins and fine silks. Life hadn't turned out exactly as she'd once hoped, but this was hardly the time to dwell on that. It was growing colder, and her fingers inside her mittens, wet from her fall, were growing stiff and numb. All she wanted now was to be home, in front of a warm fire, no matter what her duties and responsibilities there were. She would even make herself enjoy Christmas, if only she could get back safely.

Rebecca skidded again, this time going down hard on one knee and letting out a little cry. Clasping her knee, she struggled to stand, frightened for the first time. The solitude that had been so blessed before now was a danger. Already the snow was nearly to her knees, and she could barely feel her toes, so cold were they. Not a cottage in sight. She had to be near Bridgewater Manor, the earl's estate, and if so she could take shelter in the gatehouse.

Cold, so cold. Head bent against the wind, her knee throbbing, Rebecca struggled on, wincing at every step. She was growing sleepy. Snow, driving at her face, was soothing, lulling. She stopped, blankly staring at it, dazed, and then shook herself. This was no time to sleep, tired though she was. And, oh, her knee, how it hurt. If she could just reach the gatehouse to Bridgewater Manor, she would take shelter there, and try to get home once she was warm again.

This time when she fell she didn't get up right away. Strange, it didn't seem so cold anymore. Maybe that was because she was down so low, below the wind. The snow against her face was cold, but a delicious warmth was stealing over her limbs, bringing languor with it. Deep inside a little voice called a warning, too quiet to be heard. She was so sleepy. Surely there was no harm in resting just a bit, was there? She would close her eyes, just for a moment, and then get up again. Pulling her cloak more tightly around her, she snuggled up into a little ball, and fell asleep.

And, just a few feet away, the snow cleared for just a moment, revealing the posts that marked the drive to Bridgewater Manor.


The snow was falling harder now. Every now and then one of the fine bay horses in the team slipped, while the wheels of the curricle lost purchase and skidded. Yet the man driving the curricle held the ribbons lightly, even negligently, and not a trace of strain showed on his face. Simon Westbridge, the earl of Westover, had grown accustomed to showing a cool face to Society, even if that "society" consisted at the moment only of his valet, Manley, sitting beside him in tense, tight-lipped silence. He was almost home, close enough to brave what promised to become the worst storm in living memory. Bridgewater Manor was just a few miles distant, close, so close, and yet in the snow, so far. They would, he admitted to himself, be lucky to make it, and yet he was determined that they would.

It had been a long time since Simon had been home, and though for the most part he hadn't missed it, in the last weeks the urge, the need, to return had grown upon him. It was Christmas. A man shouldn't be from home at Christmas, even if everything that had once made it home was gone. And so he had made plans, sending his servants ahead to ready the Manor for a fine Christmas, the best Christmas, with all the customs and decorations he remembered from his youth. It was true he no longer had much of a family with whom to celebrate, not with his sister married and living in America, of all places, and his uncle off on one of his adventures, God knew where. The Westbridges had always had wanderlust; what had once been a big, noisy family had dwindled to himself and a few, attenuated relatives. That hadn't stopped his plans, however. There were others like him in his set who either had no family, or had no wish to spend time with the family they had. All had been eager to accept an invitation for a house party at Bridgewater Manor, to include a Boxing Day hunt and a Twelfth Night ball. What no one had bargained on was the snow.

The team slipped again, and this time Simon swore out loud, making Manley look at him in surprise. The earl apparently was not as at ease as he appeared. "Mayhap we should have stayed at the Star and Garter, my lord," he ventured, knowing he might very well earn one of Westover's famous black looks.

"Mayhap we should." Simon's voice was grim. "However, we did not, Manley, and if we turn back we would be in worse case. Bridgewater cannot be so very far ahead now."

"No, my lord," Manley said, but he sounded doubtful. The things he went through as valet to this man! True, Westover was a leader of fashion, and being his valet could only bring him consequence. The earl was, however, occasionally given to mad starts. This trip to the country, for one, when every right-thinking man would want to stay in town. Perhaps that wouldn't have been so bad, however, were it not for this storm. Manley detested snow. It was apt to stain the good leather of boots, and to ruin the nap of a velvet coat. Not that his lordship would ever wear velvet, though he could; with his broad shoulders, no one would ever mistake him for an effete dandy, no matter what he wore. Really, he quite did Manley proud.

Simon, beside him, leaned forward, his face set. As the wind picked up, blowing the snow against them with increasing force, he was beginning to entertain serious doubts that they would ever reach home. Damn, and there was no place else about where they could take shelter; they had crossed onto his land some time back, and now were driving through woods. There'd be no Christmas for him this year, after all; he would be very surprised if any of his guests could get through. Nor, he thought with the brutal honesty of which he was sometimes capable, would they care enough to try. No one really cared. There was no self-pity in that thought; it was, quite simply, a fact of his life.

Through the snow he suddenly spied the tall stone pillars that marked the drive to Bridgewater Manor, the stone globes on top capped with a pyramid of white. Home. Instinctively he relaxed, easing his grip on the ribbons, and the team shied. Cursing, Simon fought for control as the curricle slipped and slid across the road, to no avail. The team could not find purchase on the ice, and the curricle came up against a tree with a crash that jolted its passengers, then stopped and canted backward into a ditch. How ironic, Simon thought with surprising detachment, that he had come all this way, only to come to grief so close to home.

"My lord!" Manley exclaimed, sounding more disapproving than shaken.

"Take the ribbons," Simon said curtly, shoving them at him. "I'll have to lead the team."

"But, my lord, it's dangerous—"

"This is not the time to be fainthearted, Manley." With surprising ease the earl jumped out of the curricle, even though it was angled high above the ground.

184

"I knew I should have taken the position with Lord Burnell," Manley muttered, leaning forward with a worried frown as he took the reins. Burnell might not be quite so dashing as Westover, perhaps, but at least he led a settled life. Really, this was quite wearing on one's nerves.

Simon's mouth set in a grim line as he went to his team's heads, soothing them with his voice and his touch. The snow was nearly up to his knees; underneath was a coating of ice. Still, the horses hadn't slipped; he wondered what had made them shy like that. Thank God they were near home, he thought as he took hold of the harness. By dint of much tugging and urging, he set the horses in motion, and they strained to pull the curricle out of the ditch. Manley was holding on, he noticed; he only hoped the man knew enough not to saw at the reins, thus damaging the horses' tender mouths. Another tug, a slap on the flank of the off leader, and, there. They were on the road again. He wouldn't chance driving, though. With conditions as they were, it would be best to lead the team so that there would be no more mishaps.

He had turned to lead them toward the drive, his head set against the blizzard, when he noticed a lump lying by the side of the road. A drift of snow, most likely, he thought, but something about it caught his eye. It was too rounded, almost like a rock, though he could not remember any such obstacle being there. Almost he dismissed it from his mind, convinced that the urge to investigate it came only from the strain of the drive, but instinct told him to stop. Instinct, that had warned him of danger in the past. "Hold them," he said abruptly to Manley, and let go of the harness. Floundering through the snow, he struggled toward the lump, cursing himself for a fool all the time. He could be headed toward safety and warmth by now, he thought, bending over and laying a hand on the lump. And then he quite literally froze.

This was no rock. There was cloth underneath a light dusting of snow, and faint warmth. A person, who had been here for some time by the look of things. Frantically Simon brushed away the snow and rolled the figure over, staring down with undisguised astonishment at a face he'd not expected to see again. "Good God," he said, not realizing he'd spoken aloud. "Good God, Rebecca!"

# Two

Rebecca awoke to a white world: a lacy white canopy above her, white all around her. Snow, she thought drowsily, coating the branches of the trees, drifting around her body. And yet it was so blissfully warm. Too warm. *Move,* that tiny voice in her head commanded, and this time she heeded it. With a gasp she sat up, and her vision cleared. What she had thought were branches above her resolved into the netted canopy of a bed; the drifts around her were softly scented linen sheets, and a billowy eiderdown. She was safe. But where?

"So," an amused masculine voice said. "I see you're back with us."

"What?" Dazed, Rebecca looked up, and then suddenly clutched the sheets to her breast. "Simon! I mean, excuse me, my lord. Westover." Good heavens. Devil Westover.

The earl executed a mock bow. "The same, madam."

"What—" She glanced at the earl and then her gaze skittered away, touching on a mahogany wash stand with a porcelain bowl, velvet drapes at the tall windows, a huge dresser and wardrobe. Anything, to keep from looking at him again. For some strange reason, looking at him did funny things to her breathing. Of course. She was scared. She knew his reputation, everyone in Westbridge did, and to wake up in a bed with him near could mean only one thing. Though she didn't recognize this room, she knew where she had to be. Bridgewater Manor. But surely even he hadn't sunk so low in depravity that he would seduce her in his own home. "Why am I here?" she asked.

"Do you not remember, Becky?"

That brought her eyes quickly around to him, though she managed to hide how rattled she was. "My name is Rebecca, sir," she said, coolly, "and I don't recall giving you leave to use it."

"No?" He grinned and, to her rising annoyance, sat on the edge of the bed. Really, the man had no sense of propriety! But then, he never had. Always it had been like this between them, his teasing her, her growing flustered and unable to respond. And the more flustered she grew, the more he teased. At least, that had been so when they were young. She was older now and no longer quite so susceptible to a handsome face, particularly if that was all a man had to recommend him. They had changed so much, she, the daughter of a vicar; he, a man renowned for his dissolution.

"No," she answered, very firmly. Let him see that she was no light-minded miss to be trifled with. "Why did you bring me here, my lord?"

"Because you would have frozen to death, else," he said, suddenly serious. "Do you not remember?"

She did then, and with a clarity that was frightening: the cold, her wrenched knee, and, worst of all, her conviction that she would never reach shelter. "The snow."

"Exactly. The snow."

"I remember falling, and being sleepy—you carried me!" She stared at him in chagrin. She should be thanking him for saving her life, as surely he had, and yet gratitude was the last thing she felt at the moment. "Over your shoulder."

"Had to," he replied, so cheerfully that she wanted to box his ears. "You're no lightweight, you know." He grinned. "You've grown quite nicely, Becky. How is it I never noticed before?"

"I've—!" She stared at him indignantly. "I beg to inform you, my lord, that I am not one of your doxies that you can talk to me in such a way."

Simon let out a laugh. "Such language, Becky. And you the daughter of a minister."

"A minister sees much depravity, sir."

He laughed again, and Rebecca's fingers tightened on the eiderdown. "Becky, you wouldn't know depravity if it tapped you on the shoulder."

"No?" Her gaze was cool. "I believe I'm looking at it, sir."

That got him to his feet, making him cross the room to the window, his shoulders stiff and his face set. Oh, good gracious, why had she said that? Rebecca wondered, staring after him in dismay. Teasing was one thing; an outright insult quite something else. "My lord, I'm—"

"A remarkable thing to say, Becky," he said, mildly, cutting off her apology. "And here I thought I was behaving quite well."

He was, actually, all things considered. Rebecca looked down at her fingers twisting in the sheets. "We hear stories, my lord," she said, finally.

"I'll wager you do." His voice was dry. "Just what have you heard, Becky?"

"I'll thank you to address me properly, sir. And as for what we've heard . . . I'd rather not say."

"Rebecca, Rebecca. I don't recall your being such a prude." He turned to face her. "Shall I tell you what you've heard, then?"

"No, thank you, I already know."

"You've heard that I'm a rake," he went on, as if she hadn't spoken. "You've heard that I've fought several duels—three, I believe it was—and that I gamble excessively. Am I right?"

Rebecca's head was lowered. "Yes."

"Ah, I thought so. And women. You've heard about my women."

"You really shouldn't be talking about this to me, my lord."

"Come, Becky, as I recall you've always preferred plain speaking."

"Plain speaking, my lord?" She looked up at him, then, her eyes flashing blue fire. "Very well, then. Yes, we have heard all that, and more. None of it to your credit, sir. Oh, yes, we've heard about your gambling and your wenching and your wine, but I think no one holds that against you. What none of us can forgive is what you did to that poor Miss Phillips."

Simon's mouth tightened, so briefly that Rebecca almost didn't notice. "I see," he said, casually. "Heard about that, have you?"

"Yes. So don't go trying any of your charm on me, sir. I'm quite immune!"

"How fortunate for you."

"Yes. Now if you would please leave, my lord, I would like to get dressed and go home. My family must be wondering where I am."

Simon turned from the window, his hand clenching a velvet drape. "Sorry, Becky. I'm afraid that for the time being you're my prisoner," he said, and grinned.

"What! You wouldn't dare keep me here against my will!"

"When you've so clearly shown how distasteful I am to you? Of course I wouldn't. But the snow would."

"The snow . . ." Rebecca stared at him and then, forgetting where she was and how she was dressed, bounded out of bed to stand beside him, the floorboards cold under her feet. Snow. Good heavens, it was still snowing! Outside the world was a blur of white, the stately oaks and elms of the park lacy silhouettes against the leaden sky, barely visible through the swirls of white. "Has it been snowing all night?"

"Yes, and it shows no signs of letting up." He turned toward her, grinning. "It looks like we'll be snowbound together, Becky."

"Snowbound! But I can't be. I can't stay here."

"I realize the prospect of being in my company is re-
pugnant to you—"

"No, it isn't that—"

"—but I cannot see that you have a choice. No one
could get through this." Sympathy appeared briefly in his
eyes. "I'm sorry, Rebecca. I really didn't plan this, you
know."

"You could have brought me home when you found
me. Oh, no, now what am I going to do?"

"Make the best of it, Becky." He grinned, and his voice
dropped. "We could make the best of it together."

"We!"

"I usually plan my seductions much better than this,"
he went on, in that low, intimate voice, "but we could
manage, I think."

"There'll be no seduction, my lord," she said, frigidly.
"I am appalled you'd even think such a thing."

He shrugged, and in spite of her chagrin Rebecca had
to admit it was an appealing gesture. "It seems to be
what you expect."

"I—!" Yet again she stared at him, speechless. How
was it this man always contrived to put her in the
wrong? "My father used to say that you weren't beyond
redemption, my lord, but I wonder what he would say
were he to see you now."

That went home. She saw it in the sudden change of
expression in his eyes, which made her feel vaguely
guilty. "Your father was a good man," he said, quietly. "I
was sorry to hear of his death."

Rebecca looked away, unable to bear what appeared to
be suspiciously like sympathy. Sympathy, or any other
tender emotion, from this man was dangerous. "Thank
you, sir. It was a loss to everyone."

"It was. But I doubt that he'd see any harm in this situation, Rebecca, since I merely brought you in from the

191

storm. Even if," his eyes twinkled, "you're attired so fetch-ingly."

Rebecca, looking down, realized belatedly that she wore nothing but a nightgown. A voluminous one, to be sure, of heavy flannel and therefore not in the least re-vealing, but only a nightgown. Oh, dear. Whatever must he think of her? If he expected her to be discomfited, though, he would be disappointed. "Your tastes must be sadly deteriorated, my lord," she said, coolly. "Now, if you'll excuse me, perhaps I could change into something more suitable."

"A shame." He put his finger to the tip of her nose, and she drew back, startled. "You're a very attractive woman, you know, Rebecca. Or you would be, if you would stop being so prim."

Rebecca drew herself up to her full height which, to her secret sorrow, was considerable. Even he had noticed what a strapping girl she was. "I thank you for the com-pliment sir, and so nicely phrased as well. Now if you'll please leave, I'd much rather be alone."

He grinned at her, not one whit abashed. "Certainly. But don't think you can escape me so easily, Becky." He stopped at the door. "After all, we're snowbound together. Who knows what might happen?"

Rebecca held onto her composure by a mighty effort, in spite of the way he was smiling at her with that crooked, endearing grin. Oh, the man had charm, and he knew how to use it. She would not let herself fall prey to it, though. "What, indeed, my lord?" Her smile was sweet. "Perhaps you might even profit by my experience and reform your ways."

He looked startled, and then bowed. "A good answer, ma'am. I hope you won't be attired so seductively when you do try to reform me," he said, and went out, leaving Rebecca staring at the door, fuming with impotent rage. The nerve of him! It was bad to imply that she might actually flirt with him, but to tease her about her appearance was cruel. She couldn't help how she looked; she knew well she was the plain one in the Ware family, with her straight black hair and her great height. Ordinarily that didn't bother her. Papa had taught her that outward appearances didn't really matter, and usually she found that to be true. With a man like the earl, though, things were different. He was used to beauties throwing themselves at him, from all she'd heard, and he evidently expected the same from her. Well, he would have to wait a long time for that to happen. In all these years she hadn't tossed him so much as a look, and she wasn't about to start now. Even if they were snowbound together.

Snowbound! Rebecca sank down onto the chair and stared into the fire, appalled. How would she ever endure?

Simon's grin lasted exactly as long as it took to close the bedroom door behind him. There, he'd got out of that tolerably well, even though there had been moments when he had wanted to take that woman by the shoulders and give her a good shake. Truth to tell, he'd gone to her room out of concern for her, not from any desire for debauchery, no matter what she might think. He'd had a bad few minutes yesterday after finding her, knowing he had to get her out of the storm and yet struggling with it himself. Thank God his housekeeper, capable Mrs. Pope, had known what to do; he had carried Rebecca in, and Mrs. Pope had taken over, sending the maids scurrying for hot water and blankets and ordering him about, just as she had when he was young. In spite of his anxiety, that had given him an oddly warm feeling, a feeling of being home. It had lasted until the moment when Rebecca had opened her huge blue eyes and looked at him with distaste and apprehension, awakening the devil inside him.

Rebecca had always had that effect on him, though; always so prim and proper, with an air of being above everyone else, simply because her father was the vicar. He'd loved teasing her in the past, had enjoyed seeing the color come up into her face and knowing that she was at a loss as to how to handle him; he still did. It was different now, though. Damn, but she was pretty! Much prettier than he had ever expected. When he had found her out in the storm his first, quite irrational thought had been that he'd found a snow queen. An ice maiden, more like, he thought ruefully, stepping away from the door and heading toward his library. Still unmarried, no matter how pretty she was, and no wonder. Her tongue was sharp. She hadn't seemed to think twice about castigating him, the words she had used falling primly from her lips. Luscious-looking lips, full and red, the kind any man would want to kiss. He doubted that she had allowed any man to do so, and so what could she really know of his life? Her accusations hurt, though, more than he cared to show. Why that should be he didn't know; others had said much the same thing in the past. The opinion of an insignificant country mouse shouldn't matter, but it did. It always had.

Simon pushed himself away from the wall and started down the marble stairs. Snowbound, with a prim, prudish spinster, and his friends all far away. It was not going to be a very merry Christmas at all.

## Three

Sometime later, having been told by Mrs. Pope that
the earl wished to take luncheon with her, Rebecca left
her room. There was no need for him to call her en-
semble fetching now, she thought, with just a trace of
regret. Her round gown of blue merino had seen better
days, and her thick black hair was difficult to style in
anything but a heavy knot at her neck. Quite the best
she could expect, but not what he was used to, she was
certain. And that, she told herself firmly, was just as
well.

It had been an age since she had been inside Bridgewater Manor, though she'd seen it often enough from
the outside. A Jacobean mansion of rosy red brick, it
was imposing and impressive, as befit an earl. From her
perch on the marble stairs with their brass and iron
railings, Rebecca looked down into the great hall. Tiled
in black and white marble, it had a fireplace large
enough to hold an entire oxen and, on the walls, standards and battle implements that proclaimed the
Westbridge family history. Here and there were marble
statues, some quite fine, she noted, as she continued on
down. A splendid house, but one that inspired awe,
rather than comfort. For a moment she felt a pang of
homesickness so strong she had to shut her eyes against
it.

A footman opened the door of the drawing room for
her, and she walked in, relaxing a bit. It couldn't ex-

actly be called a cozy room, with its yellow silk wall coverings and blue brocaded sofas, but it wasn't quite so intimidating as the hall. Gratefully she held her hands out to the flames that leaped in the enormous fireplace, glad for the warmth. It had been drafty and cold in the hall.

"There you are," a voice said, warming her almost as much as the fire, and she whirled to see Simon. Her heart started acting erratically, beating in an odd way as he came near. "I thought you might cry craven and refuse to come down."

"Oh, no, my lord. It wouldn't be polite." She refused to cry craven now, either, as he came closer, closer, until he was standing only a few inches away. This close she could see so much in his face: the way his hair waved back from a high widow's peak; the flecks of gold deep in his brown eyes; the full, firm, well-shaped lips. No wonder he had such success with women, she thought. She, however, was not so silly.

"And by all means, we must be polite, must we not?" He smiled down at her. Just as he had expected, she was dressed primly, in a gown with high neck and long sleeves. It was not in the least revealing, and yet somehow it flattered her. It brought out the blue in her eyes, made the highlights in her midnight-dark hair shine brighter, brought a soft glow to her soft, pale skin. Good God, she was a beauty. Why had he never seen it before? He'd always thought her tall and gawky, but, with her slender figure dressed properly and her hair coiffed, she would be a sensation in London. He had the sudden urge to see her there, enjoying her success; at the same time, he was glad to have her to himself. "You look lovely, you know."

Rebecca turned abruptly away. "You needn't tease me, sir. As I reminded you, I am not one of your flirts."

"I never said that," he said, genuinely surprised, and

intrigued. No, she was not at all like any of his flirts, but she might be a more interesting diversion than he had expected. "But I'm glad you're here."

She turned her head slightly as he came up behind her. "Why?"

"Because I need your help."

His breath was warm on her neck. In spite of herself Rebecca shivered. What could Westover possibly want with her? She turned to him, her eyes wide with alarm. "For what?"

"Why, to celebrate Christmas, of course."

Rebecca stared at him, her unsettling feelings at his closeness temporarily forgotten, and let out a laugh. "Christmas!"

"Yes." He frowned. "What is so amusing about that?"

"I cannot picture you wishing to celebrate Christmas. Not Devil Westover!" she exclaimed, without thinking.

Simon's finely shaped lips thinned. "You have heard things, haven't you?"

Rebecca looked at him in surprise; there was an odd note in his voice. "My apologies, my lord. I did not mean to offend you." She offered him a tentative smile. "Mrs. Pope tells me you saved my life. I must thank you for that."

Simon shrugged. "Couldn't leave you lying in the snow, could I?"

"No, I suppose not. Though I did have every intention of getting up again."

"I'm sure you did," he said, and his eyes twinkled again. "What were you doing out in the storm, anyway?"

"I brought a basket of food to Mrs. Pollock."

"Of course. Doing good works." Rebecca opened her mouth to retort, and he went on. "That's not your job anymore."

"Of course it is. Just because my father is gone

197

doesn't mean I have to stop caring about people. Reverend Tillinghast and his wife are both busy. It's been hard here, you know," she said, looking directly at him. "But then, you've been in London, so I wouldn't expect you to be aware of such things."

"I know about conditions here, Rebecca, so spare me your sanctimonious looks. Is anyone actually going hungry?"

"Well, no, but the harvest was poor, and—"

"And I've had grain brought in. I assure you, Rebecca, I've no intention of letting anyone starve."

Rebecca looked down. "I know that, my lord," she said, finally. "Forgive me. I simply think that your tenants would like to see you here more often."

"They'd be seeing me now were it not for the snow." He glanced out the window. "We haven't had a storm like this in years. Makes it quite feel like Christmas."

"I am surprised you didn't stay in town, sir."

Simon turned. "Why?"

"Because you rarely come here anymore."

"It is still my home." He crossed the room to her, sitting beside her on the sofa. "I was serious, you know. Since we're snowbound, we might as well make the best of it."

"If you're suggesting what I think you are—"

"Damn it, Rebecca, I am not totally without morals," he said, losing his temper for the first time.

"I do wish you would not swear," she said, and for a moment there was silence. Then he chuckled.

"Very well, Becky, I shall try to refrain. And I shall also refrain from seducing you, difficult though it will be.".

"Simon!"

"There, that's better. No need for us to be so formal with each other, is there?" With his head tilted a bit to the side and that crooked smile on his face, he looked

198

endearing, irresistible. Everything within Rebecca urged her to lean toward him. "Why do you not use my name?"

"I can't, sir."

"You used to."

"Yes. But I can't anymore."

Simon gave her a long look. "I see," he said finally, and silence fell between them.

Rebecca stared into the fire. It was dangerous, being close to him like this; even more dangerous if she let down her guard and used his name. The only way she would get through these next days with her dignity intact would be to keep the distance between them. How she was to do that when they were alone in the house, save for the servants, she didn't know. Funny, though. It wasn't him she distrusted. It was herself.

"You really wish to celebrate Christmas?" she said, after the silence had gone on quite long enough.

"Yes, Becky. I really do. In fact, I had invited some guests. I doubt they'll be able to make it through the snow."

"Yes, Mrs. Pope told me."

"So there'll be no dissolution or dissipation here this year, Becky."

"I wasn't thinking that," she protested.

"No?" He arched an eyebrow at her, another unfair trick of his. "You sounded rather disapproving."

"Not of your friends." In fact, she thought it would be good for the manor to have some life again, and good for the village, as well. "I was thinking of Christmas."

"Christmas." He frowned. "Don't tell me you've turned Puritan on me and you now disapprove of Christmas, too?"

"Not disapprove, exactly, but don't you think it's a little bit of a humbug?"

Simon stared at her for a moment and then let out a

199

shout of laughter. "You, a minister's daughter, think Christmas is a humbug?"

"Yes, well—I fail to see what is so funny about it."

"Don't you, Becky?" His smile was filled with mirth, and something else. "You and I have rather changed places, I think. Am I not the one who is supposed to find Christmas boring, and are you not the one who loves it?"

"I don't think Christmas itself is a humbug," she said, suddenly earnest in her attempt to make him understand, though she didn't know why that should matter so. "I honor the spirit of the holiday. I simply do not like the way we choose to celebrate it. There's no meaning to it." She rose suddenly and paced to the fireplace, as restless as he had been earlier. " 'Tis a time of peace and goodwill, is it not? Then, if we can be so kind to others at this time of year, why not the rest of the time? Why must it be only at Christmas?"

"I don't know, Becky," he said, as serious as she. "People have asked that question for a long time, and I suspect they'll continue to ask it."

"But what is the answer?"

"There is none. I think we are meant to enjoy this special time, and be grateful that there are times when we can put hostilities and resentments aside." He paused. "Shall we call a cease-fire between us?"

Rebecca looked surprised. "I have nothing against you, sir."

"No?" Simon's smile was wry. "Very well, then, Becky. Even if you think Christmas is a humbug, will you help me to celebrate it?"

"I don't see why not," she said slowly, coming to sit on the sofa near him again. "There isn't much else for us to do, is there?"

"I'm sure I could think of something—Becky, 'twas a jest!" he called, as she rose and stalked out of the room.

"Good God, that woman is prickly." He was grinning, though, as he leaned back on the sofa, staring into the flames. This time at his home was not going to be at all what he'd planned, but he didn't mind. He was, in fact, rather looking forward to it.

## Four

The snow continued without letup, with gusty winds that blew it into drifts and biting cold that turned one's nose red if one dared to step outside. The staff worked diligently to keep paths open to the stables and to the other outbuildings, so that both humans and animals could have what they needed, but they had long ago given up on the drive. There was no real need for Bridgewater Manor to be connected to the outside world; like most estates, it was almost a town unto itself, with storerooms and pantries that would keep the house supplied until the weather abated. Nor would the world outside want to come to the Manor, not even in the ordinary way of things. With the snow isolating them, the people within might as well have been the only ones left in the world.

In the drawing room, Rebecca worked halfheartedly at a piece of netting she had found abandoned in a workbag in her room. No telling how old it was, or to whom it had belonged; it was something to do to keep herself busy. She was, quite simply, bored. From having too much to do she had gone to having too little, and the change was unnerving. At least at home she could be doing something useful. Not for the first time she thought of her family, her fingers clenching momentarily on the netting. There was nothing she could do for them, stuck as she was at the Manor, but she couldn't help worrying. For so long she had been their mainstay, the one they depended upon. How could they possibly get along without her?

A light touch between her eyes made her jerk her head back, and she stared up at Simon. "I beg your pardon?"

"You were frowning." He threw himself down into the chair facing her. "It seems to me you do entirely too much of that these days, Becky."

"And it seems to me you take things much too lightly," she retorted.

"There. We've got that out of the way."

She looked up at him in surprise. "What?"

"Our insults for the day. Perhaps we can go on to something more enjoyable."

"I don't know what." It was Christmas Eve. A day had passed since she had awakened to find herself snowbound with the earl, passed with excruciating slowness as she had tried to find things to do that would keep her out of his way. The relationship between them had not improved with time. He teased her as much as ever; she disapproved of him as much as ever. She had to admit, though, looking covertly up at him, that he looked rather well in close-fitting buckskin breeches and that superb coat of midnight blue superfine. And there she was, clad in her blue merino again. Without quite realizing it, she sighed.

"Is it that difficult, being here with me?" Simon asked, and Rebecca came out of her reverie.

"No," she said, though the truth was she was finding it more difficult by the moment. Of all people for her to be snowbound with! Still, she had no choice. She might as well make the best of it. "I suppose I'm bored."

"Good."

"Good?"

"Yes." He crossed the room with startling vigor and, grasping her arm, pulled her to her feet. "You can help me decorate the house."

"What?" she exclaimed as he pulled her out into the

203

hall. Normally neat, even austere, today it was cluttered, with boxes stacked near the stairway and enough ever-greens to build a miniature forest. "Simon, what in the world?"

" 'Tis Christmas Eve, Becky." He turned her toward him and smiled down at her, in his excitement looking almost like a boy. "Time to hang the greenery. In our case, the olive branch."

"I have no quarrel with you."

"No? Good." He gestured toward the greens. "These have been keeping outside. Bad luck to bring them into the house before Christmas Eve, you know."

"Yes, I know."

"We have holly and ivy—what else do we have, Mrs. Pope?"

Mrs. Pope bustled into the hall, her petticoats rustling about her stout figure. "Laurel, to put around the banister, and ribbons from when the countess was alive, God rest her soul. They look quite as good now as they did then. And the Kissing Bough, of course."

"Of course," Simon said, looking at Rebecca in such a way that she could feel herself growing red. "Excellent, Mrs. Pope. Miss Ware will help me put everything up."

Mrs. Pope beamed at them. " 'Twill be a proper Christmas after all, then. Like those we've not had since you were a lad, sir."

"Precisely. Well, Rebecca?"

Rebecca stared up at him. Oh, dear. Decorating for Christmas was really the last thing in the world she wanted to do, but Simon was looking at her so eagerly that, for the life of her, she could not disappoint him. "Where do we start?" she asked, resigned to her fate.

"You'll want an apron, miss, to keep your dress clean. I'll just get you one," Mrs. Pope said, and went out.

"Let's get the laurel around the banisters first," Simon said. "That's the worst job. I remember," he went on, as he went to the top of the stairs with a rope of laurel and began threading it through the banisters, "the butler we had before Hooper doing this. His name was Peacock—"

"I remember him," Rebecca interrupted. "Poor man, he didn't quite live up to his name, did he?"

"No, not quite." Simon grinned down at her, and they basked together in the shared memory of childhood. "Here, take the other end, Becky, and fasten it to the newel post with ribbon."

"This is lovely." Rebecca picked up a length of red velvet ribbon, plush and luxurious. What would a gown of this be like? she wondered, and then dismissed the thought immediately. Quite unsuitable for her, the daughter of a poverty-stricken minister's widow.

"Why did you never have a season, Becky?" Simon asked suddenly, as if reading her thoughts.

Rebecca started, and then tied the ribbon into a big bow around the newel post, studiously avoiding looking at him. "My father died."

"Of course. I'm sorry. But what about after?"

"Oh, I was needed at home," she said, lightly. "I'm sure I wasn't missed in London."

"I wouldn't be too certain of that," he mumbled, and Rebecca stared at him, not sure she'd heard aright. "There, that's that." He came down the stairs toward her, dusting his hands together and stripping off his coat. "Let's get the rest of the greens up."

Hooper and a footman came in, carrying a ladder, which they set up at the door to the drawing room. Somewhat to Rebecca's surprise, Simon climbed it himself, reaching down for the branch of holly Hooper handed to him. "Hand me the hammer, please, Becky," he said, almost absently, and she, just as automatically, did as he asked, gazing at him as he nailed the branch into place. Goodness, he was handsome! And it wasn't just his face. There was nothing foppish or weak about him, even though he was a man accustomed to living in town. His shoulders were broad, his arms under his fine

205

shirt of white lawn strong, his hands, holding the hammer, square and well made. Hands that were, surprisingly, used to working, she thought, as she watched him wield the hammer efficiently. Capable hands that would likely be just as proficient in whatever he used them to do, whether working or touching a woman.

Rebecca shook herself slightly and stepped back, just as Simon climbed down the ladder, giving her a quizzical look. "What?"

"What? Oh. Nothing," she said, forcing herself to smile. " 'Tis warm in here, isn't it?"

Simon gave her another look. "I thought it was rather chilly."

"Oh." Perhaps that was why she felt as she did, all shivery and strange. It was not unpleasant.

Simon grinned at her, a knowing grin that she wanted to wipe off his face. "There's still the drawing room to do," he said, and held the door open for her. After a moment, Rebecca passed through. Aggravating man. When she expected him to say something ordinary he was outrageous, but when she was braced for outrageousness, he turned polite! It really wasn't fair.

Simon helped the footman maneuver the ladder into place, and climbed atop it again. "So you never married," he went on, as if there had been no break in their conversation.

"No." Rebecca shut her mouth against saying anything else. Her life was her concern, not his.

Simon wielded the hammer. "Is there a bow for this, Becky? So do you plan to marry Lucas Woodward, then?"

Rebecca stepped back, startled, as she reached up the bow, and he quickly drew in his arm, to keep from falling. "Careful, Becky."

"How do you know about Mr. Woodward?"

"He is one of my tenants," he said, mildly. "The bow, Becky."

Rebecca handed up the bow, drawing her fingers quickly back as they brushed against his. "I can't see where it is any of your concern."

"The bow?"

"No, Mr. — you know quite well!"

"Why him, Becky?" Simon looked down at her, his face suddenly serious. "Surely you could do better for yourself."

"He's a good man."

"Good God, Becky, the man grows turnips! He's also coming onto forty, is losing his hair, and is stout."

"Looks don't matter."

"No?" He arched his eyebrow at her again, and again she had the impulse to smack that smirking look off his face. "If you say so. Of course, you realize he's been looking for a wife for years to take care of those unruly brats of his."

"I like children," she said, stoutly.

"Good, because you'll end by mothering Woodward, as well."

"Simon!"

He grinned down at her. "Do you know why I like teasing you?"

"Because you have a perverse sense of humor," she said through gritted teeth.

"That, too." He stood before her as he reached the floor, and she took an involuntary step back. "You rise to the bait so well, Becky."

"Humph." She turned away, her head held high. "As if I'm some sort of fish." Behind her Simon let out a shout of laughter, and her hands balled into fists. Whatever had she done to deserve this?

Stepping away from him, Rebecca picked up a pine branch and walked over to the mantel with it. She fully expected Simon to go on with his comments, but to her surprise, he worked as quietly and efficiently as she. Soon the drawing room was decorated and festive, with

207

holly over all the doors, ribbons on the cornices, and fat white candles in the windows and on the mantel. "It really does look quite nice," Rebecca said, stepping back to admire their handiwork.

"It does." Simon came to stand beside her. "Almost the way it did when I was young. You sound rather surprised, though. Do you not like decorating for Christmas?"

"I did, once. Now 'tis just another chore."

Simon looked down at her, for once serious. "Why? Surely you have help. I know your mother's been ill—"

"You do?" she said, startled. Obviously he knew everything that went on in the village. "Yes, she's better now, but we feared for her life for a time."

"I'm glad to hear she's recovering. But what of your brother? Surely he's home from Oxford for the holiday?"

Rebecca flushed. So here was something he didn't know. "Yes, Benjamin's home. Rather unexpectedly, though. I'm afraid he was sent down for playing pranks."

Simon grinned. "It happens to all of us."

"Yes, well, you could afford such nonsense, Westover! Benjamin knows quite well we cannot. And then to say that he played the prank only because it was one you played—"

"Did he, by Jove!"

"It's not funny!"

"No, I suppose not," Simon said, ruefully. "So it all falls on you, Becky?"

The sympathy in his voice surprised and unnerved her. "I don't mind. Are we done in here?"

Simon gave her a look, and then turned away. "All but the Kissing Bough."

"Oh. Then you don't need me any longer. If you'll excuse me, I'll—"

"Of course I need you, to make certain it hangs straight. Don't tell me you're scared, Becky."

Rebecca raised her chin. "Of what?"

His smile was knowing. "If you're caught under the Kissing Bough, you cannot refuse to be kissed, can you?"

Rebecca's look was innocent. "What is that to me?"

"We shall see. Let's get the ladder positioned—there. Hand me up the bough, Hooper."

"Do you need help with it, my lord?" Hooper asked anxiously. "It's quite big."

"I'll manage," Simon said, supporting the bough on the ladder while reaching for the ribbons that already hung from the ceiling. The bough was quite large, made of pine garland in a double loop and decorated with ribbons, candles, and a ring of red apples. From it, suspended by another ribbon, hung a ball of mistletoe. "Is that high enough, Hooper?"

"Yes, my lord, you should be able to walk beneath it without hitting your head, and you're the tallest one here."

"Good." Simon climbed down from the ladder, giving his handiwork a critical look. "You may go, Hooper. Thank you for your help. Well, Becky? What do you think?"

Rebecca, across the room near the fireplace, smiled. "I'm not standing under it, as you may have noticed."

"No, but I am."

"Simon."

" 'Tis a harmless Christmas custom, Becky."

" 'Tis a heathen Christmas custom," she retorted. "Papa told me the Druids used mistletoe in their celebrations."

"Smart of them. Come here, Becky."

"I don't think so, Simon."

"No?" He smiled at her, that charming, artless smile that did such funny things to her. "Well, at least you are using my name. That is some progress."

"My lord." Hooper stuck his head through the door. "Cook is ready to stir the Christmas pudding. She would have had it made earlier, sir," he said, as Simon crossed the room, "but what with the storm . . ."

"I understand. Of course we'll come. Be bad luck if everyone in the house didn't stir it. Rebecca?" He turned to see her crossing the room, and that lazy grin crossed his face again. "Well."

"What?" Rebecca said, and followed his gaze upward. The breath went out of her, in dismay, or something else. Without meaning to, she was standing under the Kissing Bough.

# *Five*

"Well." Simon walked across the room toward her. "And you said you wouldn't be caught under it."

"A mistake." Rebecca backed off, suddenly able to move. For a moment the sight of him stalking her had held her still, very much like prey who knew running was futile. But that was ridiculous.

"Come, Rebecca. We have already discussed this. You cannot refuse to be kissed."

"And if I don't want to be?"

He stopped directly in front of her. "Would you prefer it if I were Lucas Woodward?"

"No!"

That knowing smile crossed his face again. "I thought not. Give it up, Becky." His breath was warm on her cheek as he leaned toward her. "You're well and truly caught this time."

"Simon," she protested. She caught the sharp, crisp scent of pine and the sweeter one of sandalwood, just as his head bent and his kiss caught her parted lips. A brief kiss, a kiss that should have meant nothing. A kiss of friendship and teasing, and yet, when Simon stepped back, there was nothing of mockery in his face. Instead his eyes searched hers, and she, helpless, could only return the look. Time stretched, grew, and in that eternal moment she felt joined to him as she had never felt joined to anyone. Then Simon stepped back.

"I'll wager your Mr. Woodward couldn't do as well," he

said, grinning, and Rebecca's wonder fled.

"Simon!"

"Or don't you know that yet?"

"Simon!" she protested again, somehow unable to say anything more.

"Hasn't he kissed you yet, Becky?" he asked, still looking at her with that annoying smile.

"That is none of your concern," she said, her voice frosty, and sailed past him through the door. Behind her she heard a distinct chuckle. Annoying man! And yet . . . And yet, her lips still tingled, so much so that she longed to touch them with her fingers. Somehow she couldn't imagine Lucas Woodward, were he ever to kiss her, having such an effect on her. But that was only because Westover was more experienced, she told herself firmly. He knew just what would affect a woman most. It was too bad that that was all it was, that the kiss hadn't meant more, she thought, and then quickly banished such foolishness from her mind. He was only toying with her. She would do well to remember that.

"Aren't you coming to stir the Christmas pudding?" Simon asked, as Rebecca started up the stairs, and she stopped, looking down at him. The look of deviltry was still there, in his smile, and yet there was something in his eyes, something that disturbed her far more than his teasing ever could.

"I—Tell Cook I'll be down directly," she stammered, and fled to the safety of her room. She wished the blasted snowstorm would end so that she could go home. What had she ever done to deserve such a wretched fate as to be thrown into Devil Westover's company? Her life was never going to be the same after this. Never.


Everyone gathered in the drawing room that evening to see the Yule log lighted: Simon, who as head of the house would do the lighting; Rebecca; and the staff.

Since helping Simon decorate that afternoon Rebecca had kept a distance from him, staying in her room and trying to read. Now she hung back, not really wishing to see him, yet excited in spite of herself. For some reason she was enjoying Christmas this year. She would just be very careful to stay away from the Kissing Bough.

As if reading her thoughts, Simon looked up at that moment, and his eyes, filled with mischief, flicked up to the ball of mistletoe. Rebecca felt her face go red. Aggravating man! No gentleman would remind her of what had happened that afternoon. But then, Simon was definitely not a gentleman. At least, not so far as she was concerned.

The door to the drawing room opened, and several footmen came in, dragging behind them a log of enormous proportions, decorated with ribbons and greenery. A wordless sound of admiration went up in the room, with even Rebecca smiling. It had been a long time since she had lived in a house with a fireplace large enough for such a huge piece of wood. "A good log," Simon said, smiling for once without any mockery. "Ash?"

"Yes, my lord." The footmen, struggling with their heavy burden, maneuvered the log into the fireplace and then stepped back. Hooper handed Simon a charred length of wood.

"From the last Yule log that was burnt here, my lord," he said. "When the old earl was alive."

"That long ago?" Simon said, looking at him in surprise. His father had been dead for several years. Had it really been so long since he had celebrated Christmas at home? He looked up, serious now, and caught Rebecca's eyes, though she quickly looked away. He had planned to re-create Christmas with a party of people, with noise and laughter and fun, the way he remembered the holiday from his childhood. Strange, though. Somehow it felt more real, more meaningful, with just Rebecca.

Shaking himself a little, he lit the brand from a taper

and then set it to the log. The room was absolutely silent as everyone waited, and then a small flame spurted up. The people in the room released the breath they had been holding, and began to chatter. A fine log, already burning brightly, the sweet smell of wood smoke filling the room; large enough to burn now, and through the twelve days of Christmas. Good luck would be upon this house this year.

Flame spurted in Simon's heart, too, a feeling he hadn't had since he was a boy, of carefree joy so wide it encompassed everyone. "I'd say we need some music," he said, grinning broadly. "What say you to some carols before we drink a toast to the log?"

A chorus of voices answered him, but he had eyes only for Rebecca. Though he said nothing, she came toward him, as if in answer to some unspoken command. "Do you sing, Rebecca?" he asked.

"I love to sing, my lord," she said, her eyes shining. " 'Tis a splendid log."

"So it is. Are we back to being so formal again?"

Rebecca looked down. "It seems fitting." Indeed, it seemed more fitting than it had since she had awakened in this house—was it only yesterday? Watching him now, the head of the house, performing the ceremonial lighting of the Yule log, she suddenly had a vision of the old earl, and of all the others that had come before. Simon Westbridge, roisterer though he might be, was part of that tradition. He was very much the earl, and his servants knew it. And loved him. There had to be some good in the man, to inspire such feelings. She had best be careful, though, and not let the spirit of Christmas lull her into letting down her guard. Whatever else he might be, Simon was too charming for his own, and her, good.

"Come over to the spinet." He caught at her hand and, like a boy, pulled her across the room. "Do you play?"

"No, my lord, I fear I don't have that accomplishment.

214

But I do love to sing."

"Then I shall play for us," he said, and, sitting down, launched into a boisterous rendition of "I Saw Three Ships." Soon everyone had gathered around the spinet, with Rebecca just to Simon's right, and was singing lustily.

"Do play the 'Coventry Carol,'" Rebecca urged when they had finished. "That is my favorite."

"Will you sing it for us, then?" Simon asked, sorting through the music on the spinet.

"Of course," Rebecca said, looking pleased, and assumed singing posture, her hands clasped before her. Soon the strains of the old, old song came from the spinet. "'Lullay lullay, thou little tiny child,'" Rebecca sang, and everyone quieted. "'By, by, lullay, lullay. . . .'"

The last note was flat. Simon glanced up at her quickly, but went on with the playing as if nothing had happened. When she missed another note, though, he looked up at her again. She seemed unaware that anything was amiss, her face sweetly serious, her eyes gazing ahead as if she could see the child of the song. Simon suddenly bit the inside of his mouth to hold in a shout of laughter. She loved to sing, she had told him. What she had neglected to add was that she couldn't.

"Very nice, Rebecca," he said gravely when she was done, and before she could request another song, he began to play. Everyone joined in. "'Deck the halls . . .'"

"With balls of ivy," Rebecca sang, and Simon threw her another astonished look. "'Tis the season to be lively."

That was too much for Mrs. Pope. Throwing her apron over her face she ran from the room, and even over the singing Simon could hear her whooping from the hall. Hooper's eyes were suspiciously bright, and more than one servant had stopped singing, their faces red and their eyes watering. But Rebecca, sublimely unaware that anything was amiss, sang on. He wanted to jump up and hug her.

"Hooper," he said when the song was done, his voice not quite steady, "I believe it is time to drink the toast."

"Yes, my lord," Hooper said, and fled. The other servants followed with alacrity, and the sounds of their merriment filled the hall. Only Rebecca, still standing beside him, looked disappointed.

"But we were just starting to sing," she protested, as he rose and took her hand again.

"We can sing more later." He led her across the room to the fireplace, and kept hold of her hand. To his surprise, she didn't pull away. "Ah, the punch. Lamb's-wool, Hooper?"

"Indeed, sir." Hooper pushed a table into the room, bearing a huge silver bowl filled with a steaming liquid.

"Lamb's-wool! Why, I haven't had that in years," Rebecca said, her nose wrinkling.

Simon took the cup Hooper gave him and handed it to Rebecca. "Do you not like it?"

"I'm not very fond of ale, my lord." She sniffed delicately at the cup. "Though I must admit, this smells good."

"Cook makes the best I've tasted. A toast," he said, raising his cup. "To the Christmases that have been celebrated in this house, and those yet to be. And," he looked at Rebecca, "to our guest, who has helped make Christmas special this year."

"Gracious," Rebecca murmured and, to avoid returning his gaze, sipped at the punch. It really was rather good, she thought with surprise. Lamb's-wool had always seemed like a strange concoction to her, warmed ale with spices, eggs, and cream, but this was quite good, warm and soothing. It was a lovely custom, just as this had been a lovely Christmas Eve. The Yule log, the carols, and now this; standing beside Simon at the fireplace, as if she belonged there, the lady of the manor. A foolish dream, but she would indulge it for now.

"A merry Christmas to you, sir," Hooper said, raising

216

his own cup, and Simon smiled in return. It was a merry Christmas. He was home, and beside him was a beautiful woman, her hand still tucked in his. For one mad moment, it was as if he had married and his countess stood beside him. He wondered if she realized that he still held her hand, and decided not to point it out.

"And to all of you, too," he said. "Let us hope this year is better than the last."

A chorus of agreement went up at that, and then, chattering and laughing, the servants straggled out of the room, until only Rebecca and Simon were left. Rebecca could feel herself beaming. Had Christmas ever been so enjoyable before? Not even when her father was alive, she thought, and felt a little spurt of guilt. She had dearly loved her father, but she was finding unexpected pleasure in sharing this holiday with Westover. He wasn't quite the rake she'd thought him. Glancing up at him, she realized, for the first time, that he held her hand.

Her eyes went up to his in a startled sweep of lashes, and he met her gaze, his own eyes serious, holding an emotion she couldn't identify. "My hand, sir," she said, shakily.

"Yes." He raised her hand and examined it, slender and delicate and yet strong, though she struggled to free herself. "You're a hard worker, Becky."

"I cannot help it if my hands are calloused. I am not like the pampered beauties you have known."

"No. Not at all."

"You needn't mock me, Simon."

"Oh, I'm not. I honor you for it, Becky." And then, to her immense surprise, he bent his head and dropped a gentle kiss on her hand. At the feel of his lips, warm and firm, Rebecca drew her hand back as if it had been scalded. "Well." Simon smiled to himself as Becky turned away. "Shall we sit by the fire for a time?"

" 'Tis late. I should be abed."

"Not so very late. Would you leave me alone on

Christmas Eve?"

"Trying to make me feel sorry for you, sir? It won't work, I assure you," she said, but she sat in the chair facing him, before the fire. For a little while, there was silence. Rebecca gazed into the flames, but then, as if against her will, her eyes were drawn to him. He, too, faced the fire, the flames playing upon his face. Devil Westover, they called him, and with the flames playing upon his face he very nearly looked it. Yet the fire was in his eyes, too, touching upon emotions she wouldn't have thought he even knew about, let alone felt. There were lines beginning at the sides of his eyes, though he was still young, and a look almost of sadness in their depths. He really hadn't wanted to be alone on Christmas, she thought with sudden insight, and at that moment, he looked up to find her staring at him.

"What?" he said.

"Was this past year so bad?" she asked, before she could stop herself.

With a sigh, Simon settled back, stretching out his long legs to the fire. "I've had better. I lost my grandmother, you know."

"No, I didn't. I am sorry."

"So am I. She was a grand lady. It doesn't seem quite the same without her." He glanced around the room. "I had this thought of celebrating Christmas here as it was celebrated when I was a boy. Do you remember, Becky? My parents were always here, and relatives, and always a great many guests. But the snow put an end to that."

"I am sorry." Her memory of Christmases celebrated here differed vastly from his. She remembered tales of wild parties and of gaming that lasted well into the night; she remembered her father shaking his head over the way the earl and countess ignored their son . . . and her own smug feeling of content that at least she had a family who cared. If Simon wished to believe differently, who was she to correct him?

"I'm not." He smiled at her. "It's been different from what I expected, but somehow it feels as it should. People one cares about, and the various customs." His smile broadened into a grin. "Singing carols."

"Oh, yes, I did like that. I've always wanted to sing with the Christmas waits when they go from house to house, but they've never let me." Her brow furrowed. "I don't know why."

"They won't be out in this weather, at any rate."

"No, I suppose not."

"It was different when we were young, wasn't it? Things were easier."

"Surely things aren't so very difficult for you, sir."

"Sometimes, they are. When my grandmother died, I had no one left."

"But, your family—"

"Is gone, or has left England. And my parents never paid me much attention in any event. Grandmother was the one who really raised me, and she's gone." He paused. "Do you know, I'm quite alone in the world."

That made her look at him, and what she saw startled her. He was different than she had thought. He was not Devil Westover, nor was he only the man who teased her, something she now saw as rather flattering. He was simply a man, and a lonely one at that; a man who needed a wife, to stand by him. A man who needed her. Looking at him, Rebecca gave in to the inevitability of it. She was, and always had been, in love with Simon.

## Six

"But this is not the night to talk of such things," Simon said, and Rebecca came out of her daze. Oh, mercy! Had she given herself away? She must have, staring at him with her mouth agape, like a fish. He must be laughing at her right now, to think that someone so plain and ordinary could ever aspire to him. But no, he still gazed into the fire, though he smiled now. Perhaps he hadn't noticed.

"It's strange, Rebecca." He turned to her, and she quickly composed herself. It meant nothing that he was looking at her in such a way, his eyes alight, his smile warm and real. Nothing. "Tonight I feel as if anything could happen. As if the past doesn't matter. Do you feel that way?"

Rebecca didn't answer right away. In her experience, the surprises life held were often unpleasant. And yet, she understood what he meant. She did feel as if there were limitless possibilities ahead of her. Anything could happen. Who would have thought, just last week, that she would spend Christmas with a handsome nobleman at his estate? She, plain Rebecca Ware. Even more astonishing, he appeared to enjoy her company. " 'Tis Christmas. The magic of Christmas," she said, and, as she did so, felt her heart swell. Her Christmas spirit, long lost, had returned. She could not have received a better gift. "Everything seems possible at Christmas. My father would have said 'tis because the world is born again, and we have another chance."

"You miss him, don't you, Becky?"

"Very much. Papa was special. I could talk to him about all manner of things, and he wouldn't laugh at me. He'd try to understand, and he always helped me find new ways of seeing things. How I've missed him, these past years." She sighed, unaware that her face had grown wistful, giving it a sweetness that held Simon in thrall. "Mama is wonderful, but she's very down to earth and sensible. Sometimes she doesn't know what to do with me. She calls me her changeling child, I'm so different from my brothers and sisters." She paused. "She thinks I should marry Mr. Woodward."

"Is that what you want, Becky?"

"I'd like to marry. I'd like my own life."

"Somehow you don't sound very enthusiastic about it."

"Well, Mr. Woodward isn't exactly love's young dream, is he?" She shot him a smile. "But he's a good man."

"What would you do, Becky, if you really had your choice?"

"My real, honest choice?"

"Yes."

"Well." She gave him a look. "I would sing opera."

Simon quickly averted his head, biting the insides of his cheeks, hard, and squeezing his eyes shut. He had to say something. Even he couldn't be so insensitive as to laugh at what was evidently a long-held dream, but for the life of him, all he could manage was a strangled sound that he hoped she took as assent.

" 'Twas always a dream of mine," she went on, as if unaware of his reaction. "There is only one problem."

Simon had himself under better control now, though his voice when he spoke shook. "What is that?"

"I cannot sing." Her smile was impish. "I saw you look at me during the singing. It was kind of you not to point out that I missed notes on the 'Coventry Carol.' "

"And you didn't know the words to 'Deck the Halls . . .' "

"Didn't I?" She looked surprised. "Well, I don't know why that surprises me, I never know the words. So, you see, being an opera singer is quite beyond possibility. If I cannot even sing in English, how could I possibly manage Italian?"

It was too much. Simon put back his head and shouted with laughter. "Oh, lord. I dread to think," he said, when he could talk again. "You would, however, have a great many admirers."

"Oh, pish. I'm too plain."

"Who says that?"

"Everyone," she said, matter-of-factly. "Deborah is the beauty of the family. I am determined that she will have a season this year, even if we have to pinch pennies. She deserves her chance. We have an aunt in London, you know. She has offered to sponsor Deborah, if we can but come up with the money. And I have no doubt that she will take. She's so pretty, all pink and gold, and she has huge blue eyes."

"Like yours?"

Rebecca blinked. "My eyes are quite ordinary, sir."

"Mmm, no. In fact, I could write a sonnet to your eyes."

"Now you are bamming me," she said, good-naturedly. "You should be writing sonnets to someone who deserves them."

"I outgrew that stage long ago, thank you."

"Did you? Still, I'll wager you have women falling at your feet."

"Rebecca." He looked at her, smiling. "Why is it I suspect that you are not used to drinking?"

"I don't know. Why?"

"Nothing." He shook his head. It had to be the ale. Yesterday he would never have guessed that the oh-so-proper Miss Ware would be talking to him in such a way. "Still, I think you'd best go easy on the lamb's-wool."

Rebecca sipped from her cup. " 'Tis quite good." Another sip. "What are your dreams, Simon?" she asked, a bit surprised at her boldness. Perhaps he was right. Perhaps it was the ale.

Simon looked into the fire. "I have no dreams. Only responsibilities."

"What? Devil Westover? I'd not believe it."

He made a gesture with his hand. "I hate that name."

"Why? Did you not earn it?"

"No, I did not." He reached over and took her cup from her hand. "I think that's quite enough lamb's-wool for you tonight."

"Oh, 'tis not the ale. I usually speak plainly." Her smile was wry. "It's got me in a deal of trouble."

"I can imagine." Her question had rankled, and yet, looking at her, Simon couldn't find it in his heart to be angry with her. There was no malice in her face, only sweet honesty. She deserved better than he, he thought, suddenly humble. For, if he hadn't really earned his nickname, he hadn't been a saint, either.

"My lord." Hooper burst into the room, clearly excited. "Excuse me, but I thought you would wish to know. The snow has stopped."

"It has?"

"Yes, my lord. Come and see."

"Not a bad idea." He rose and held his hand out to Rebecca. "I think you could use some fresh air."

"Are you implying I'm foxed, sir?"

"I wouldn't dream of such a thing, Becky. After all, I am a gentleman."

"Of course." For a moment neither moved, but instead gazed at each other. Soon the road from the village would be cleared, and this interlude would come to an end. The snow had stopped.

"Come," Simon said, his voice suddenly brisk. "Let us see how much we have."

At the front door of the manor, Hooper and a few other servants were already assembled, gazing out in wonder at the icy world outside. Simon and Rebecca joined them, she wrapping her arms around herself against the chill air. It was a fairyland, magical. Trees drooped under the weight of the snow, stark black and white, and as they watched, the moon broke through the scudding clouds above. It touched on icicles that had formed on the portico, sending crystal shafts of light into the hall; it sparkled like diamonds on the smooth, fresh drifts of snow. The beauty of it was so great that Rebecca's heart ached with it. She couldn't think of anything more perfect for Christmas.

"Well," Simon said, and turned to come in. At that moment, startlingly clear upon the crystal air came the sound of bells.

"Oh, listen!" Rebecca exclaimed, stepping forward. " 'Tis the church in the village. They must be having midnight mass. Oh, how lovely."

They stood silent for a few moments as the bells continued to peal, joyous at this most joyous time of year. "You must wish you were there," Simon said.

"No," Rebecca said, looking up at him, and their gazes caught. And, as the last notes died away, as their eyes continued to hold, each knew that there was no one they would rather share Christmas with.

"Merry Christmas, miss." The maid opened the curtains to the white glare of sun on snow. " 'Tis a beautiful day. Cold, like, but isn't it good to see the sun again?"

Rebecca pushed herself up onto her elbows, blinking the sleep from her eyes. "Merry Christmas," she answered. She might not be at her best on this, or any other, morning, but that was no reason for her to take her bad temper out on the maid. "Have they reached us from the village yet?"

"Goodness, no, miss, and I'm thinking it will be an age before they do. His lordship's already up," she went

224

on cheerfully, lifting a tray and carrying it across the room to the bed. "Your breakfast, miss."

"Thank you." Rebecca sat up, pushing her hair back, and looked down at the tray without any pleasure. So the road from the village had not yet been cleared. It was only a matter of time, though. She should be glad, but she wasn't.

It was the best thing, she told herself stoutly, reaching for a freshly buttered muffin and biting into it without noticing the taste. All her life she had had foolish dreams, as her mother had pointed out to her, but this was the most foolhardy of all. To love the earl! Oh, of course she'd been attracted to him, even if she hadn't wanted to admit it; who wouldn't be? But to allow herself to fall in love with him was sheer folly. She had no doubt he'd earned his nickname, no matter his protestations of the night before. He could have any woman he wanted, and so what would he want with her? She had indeed had too much of the lamb's-wool last night. It had made the impossible seem real, and that caused a heartache she suspected might never leave.

She couldn't let him know, of course. She might be only the daughter of an impoverished widow, but she had her pride. When the snow was finally cleared away, Simon would return to London, no wiser as to her feelings, and she would resign herself to a life of spinsterhood. Marriage to anyone else, most especially the unprepossessing Mr. Woodward, seemed utterly beyond question now.

The maid came in again, carrying something draped carefully over her arm. Rebecca, just finishing her chocolate, looked up in surprise as the maid laid out a gown on the bed. Red velvet and lace. Rebecca's heart stopped for just a moment. "What is that?" she asked, in a surprisingly normal voice.

"It's a gown, miss."

"Yes, I know that. Why did you bring it to me?"

"His lordship had Mrs. Pope look it up. It belonged to the countess. He thought you might want to wear it."

Want to? Oh, yes, she wished to wear the gown, as she had rarely wished for anything in her life. In the past few days she had been acutely aware of how she must appear in her crumpled blue merino, and equally as aware that she could do nothing about it. But this. This was something she would never have dreamed of, not for herself. Rich, sumptuous velvet, with lace mellowed with age. She wanted to wear it. Oh, she wanted to. But she couldn't.

"Yes, I'd like that," she heard herself saying in a cool voice, as if velvet gowns were a fact of her everyday life.

"Very well, miss. I'll get water for you so you can wash, shall I?"

"Yes," Rebecca said, dazed. Still dazed, she rose when the maid returned, and washed; she stood still and allowed the gown to be draped over her with a whisper of silk, substantial and heavy and yet absolutely right. She let the maid dress her hair, refusing only the use of curling tongs, as Rebecca's straight hair rarely held a curl; and, finally, she let herself be turned to face her reflection in the pier glass.

For a moment, a stranger stared back at her, a stranger in a gown of wine-red, high in the waist, low at the bosom. A stranger with hair styled in a regal coronet of braids, with only a few tendrils allowed to escape and frame her face, softening the austere effect. A beautiful stranger, she thought, until she met her eyes and realized with a little jolt that she knew this person very well. Or, she thought she had. For this was no plain minister's daughter she saw. This was a beauty, one who looked a quite suitable match for an earl. An illusion, true, but then, this was Christmas. Anything might happen this day; anything might come true. Just for today she would forget about the reality of her life. She wouldn't let herself remember that Simon would soon return to London, leaving her behind, or that she had responsibilities that sometimes were heavy to bear. For today she would wear the velvet gown and believe that she was beautiful. Pretend that Simon returned her love.

In the hall Simon paced restlessly, unsure why he waited there but unable to settle anywhere else. Last night's magic remained with him. Last night had felt more like Christmas than any day ever had, and the Manor had felt more like home. The old customs were responsible for that, he supposed, even as he knew, somewhere deep inside, that he was lying to himself. It was Rebecca's presence that had made the night what it was. Though he had wanted to celebrate with friends, somehow he could no longer imagine Christmas with a noisy party of guests. He couldn't imagine it without Rebecca. He would miss this when he returned to London; he would feel a certain regret when at last the road into the village had been cleared. For today, though, he would enjoy what he had. He would enjoy Christmas.

A noise on the stairs made him look up, to see folds of heavy red velvet paired, incongruously, with aged, sturdy walking boots. Of course. She had nothing else to wear. The combination was so typical of her, though, that he had to bite his cheek to keep from grinning. He had been right in thinking that even she had vanity enough to succumb to the lure of a beautiful gown. He was surprisingly eager to see her in it.

And then, as she came into view, he stopped, and simply stared.

# Seven

"Well," Simon said, a slow smile spreading over his face as Rebecca stepped down into the hall. "I thought that gown would suit you."

Rebecca bent her head, blushing. "Thank you for it," she said, aware that her voice was breathless. "It was thoughtful of you to send it to me."

"Mmm, I think it was, too. You look quite recovered from your debaucheries of last evening."

Rebecca threw him a smile. For once, his raillery didn't bother her. It was simply part of him, the way he was, and for today, she would enjoy that. "When in Rome," she said, lightly, and had the satisfaction of seeing him look taken aback. "I'm quite looking forward to dinner."

"Indeed." Simon had himself under control again, though his lips twitched, as if with amusement. "Cook has outdone herself this year. Or so she promises me." Taking her arm, he escorted her into the drawing room, going to stand by the mantel while she sat on a sofa. "That color becomes you."

"Thank you. I must say, it makes it feel like Christmas, does it not?"

"Yes." A sound outside distracted him, and he went to stand by the window. For a moment he was very still, and then he turned back.

"What is it?" Rebecca asked.

"The drive is nearly cleared." For a moment, their eyes

met. Then Rebecca looked away.

"Well, 'tis about time the snow stopped."

"Yes. Becky."

"What was Christmas like here when you were a child?" she chattered, cutting him off. Something in his eyes, a certain look, disturbed her, made her uneasy. She was here for Christmas, only. When the road into the village was cleared, she would be gone.

Simon gave her a look, as if he knew quite well what she was doing, but he didn't challenge her. Instead, sitting in a chair across from her, he told her tales of past Christmases, until Rebecca was laughing merrily. He told of the time Hooper had dropped the turkey when he was bringing it into the dining room; of the game of blindman's buff in which an estranged couple had found themselves under the mistletoe, with the wife shrieking "It's not fair!"; of the sleigh rides that had ended up with everyone spilled into a snowbank. And he told of the first time he had been caught under the Kissing Bough, a boy between childhood and adolescence, by a giggling gaggle of girls, and how he had decided that girls might be silly, but that they had their attractions.

That last was intended to provoke her, and he could see by the flash of her eyes that it had. Before she could answer, however, the door to the hall opened and Hooper came in. "My lord, Miss Ware," he said, bowing. "Dinner is served."

"Well." Simon rose and held his arm out to Rebecca. "Shall we go in?"

Rebecca hesitated. His stories had been outrageous. What stayed in her mind, though, was not the image of him as a young boy surrounded by girls; but one of the two of them under the Kissing Bough, with no one else around. She wished she had that moment to live over. "Of course," she said lightly, and laid her hand on his arm.

The dining room, pale green with plaster medallions

229

on the wall, looked even more festive today. Laurel adorned the heavy velvet draperies, while pine boughs were laid upon the mantel. In the center of the long mahogany table more boughs had been arranged to form a circle, and from it rose several candles, their light faint against the brightness from outside. The table itself was set with the best china and sparkling crystal and snowy linen napkins, one setting at the head, one at the foot. They might as well be dining alone. Simon took one look at this arrangement and shook his head. "This will not do," he said, turning to Hooper. "I would like Miss Ware to be seated next to me."

"Of course, my lord," Hooper murmured, and gestured sharply toward a footman. Rebecca was aware of the tension in Simon's arm under her hand, though she couldn't fathom the reason for it. Only when her plate had been set to the left of his did he relax.

"There, that's better. Now we shall be able to talk without shouting at each other," he said.

"I always rather wanted to dine in state," she confessed, as he held her chair out for her.

"Did you? Perhaps you'll have your chance someday."

"I rather doubt it."

"Sir, the Christmas candle," Hooper said.

"I hadn't forgotten, Hooper." Simon took the lighted taper Hooper handed to him, and turned toward the large white candle set in a tall golden candle holder on the floor nearby. "A good, large candle," Simon said, as he lighted it. "It should burn through the rest of the day and the night, I should think. More good luck upon this house. Have you ever noticed," he went on to Rebecca as he sat down, "how many Christmas customs have to do with luck? Rather a pagan idea. I wonder what your father would say to it."

"I collect you are trying to provoke me, my lord," Rebecca said serenely. "It will not work."

Simon gave her a look. "No?"

230

"No. I have decided to be charitable, since it is Christmas."

"A setdown, indeed," he said, ruefully. "Ah. Here is the feast."

And a feast it was, a meal of such proportions Rebecca had heard of but never seen. There was a turkey, huge and golden brown and sending up a savory scent that made her mouth water. There was a baron of beef; there were potatoes and vegetables in sauces and bread, and more wine than she had ever drank at one time. And, of course, there was the Christmas pudding, brought in with great ceremony by Cook herself, the brandy that had been poured over it aflame and flickering blue and orange. Both Simon and Rebecca smiled like children at the sight, and eagerly tucked into the slices that were served them, though a moment before Rebecca had been convinced she would never be hungry again. She was savoring the pudding when her teeth crunched upon something hard and metallic.

"What in the world?" she said, bringing her napkin to her mouth to remove the object.

"You must have got one of the trinkets Cook put in," Simon said, leaning forward.

"I'd forgot about that. Let's see, there's a thimble for spinsterhood—"

"And a coin for a fortune."

"And . . . this." Her face suddenly serious, Rebecca held up a plain golden ring. Simon's eyes met hers, and she glanced quickly away, forcing laughter to her lips. "I shall be married within the year! Oh, how absurd."

"Why?" Simon sat back, frowning, though she could not imagine why. "I thought it was settled between you and Woodward."

"No." She shook her head sharply. "No, I'll not marry him."

"No? Why not?"

"Because I've changed my mind." *Because I could never*

231

*marry anyone else, loving you.* "I'm quite happy as I am."

"Taking care of everybody else, never having a home of your own, and someday being only a maiden aunt?"

"Mm-hm." She smiled brightly and nodded. "Far better that than an unhappy marriage. You see, Simon, I have foolish dreams. At least, my mother always told me they were foolish." She slipped the ring on her finger, held her hand out to admire it, and then slipped it off again. It was the wine making her act this way, she thought, remembering the lesson she had learned just last evening, but she didn't care. After today she would never be this close to Simon again, and if she made a fool of herself, who would be hurt? Only herself. And only she would regret it if she was not herself with him, instead of the girl everyone thought her to be. "I want to marry for love. Laugh at me if you wish, but it is what I want. And my mother is a fine one to talk, when she and Papa were so happy together. I want what they had. I don't think Mr. Woodward has quite enough imagination for that. Not a man who grows turnips."

Simon's lips twitched. "No, somehow I cannot see you with him, either. If you were the person you pretended to be, perhaps, but you're not. Tell me, Becky." He leaned forward. "Why is it no one ever sees this side of you? Why do you hide yourself?"

"What choice do I have?" she said, suddenly serious. "My family needs me. I do wish sometimes that life had been different, but it does no good to refine on such things, I think. I am happy, Simon, believe it or not." Or she had been. How she would feel when he left was something she didn't want to think about. "I like my life. But I do thank you for this Christmas." Her eyes softened as she gazed about the room. "It's been like nothing I've ever experienced."

"Mmm. It has been good, hasn't it?" Simon sat back, his face serious. "Everything has been just about perfect, except for one thing."

"What is that?"

"We did not exchange presents."

Rebecca laughed. "Of course we did not. I did not exactly come prepared for gift-giving, Simon, and even if I did, what would I give you? You already have everything."

"You've given me more than you know." His eyes burned into hers. "I want to give you a gift, Becky."

"Oh, no—"

"It isn't much," he went on, ignoring her protest, "but I want you to know how much these past days have meant to me. This was my mother's." From his pocket he withdrew a simple gold bracelet, studded with pearls. "I'd like you to have it."

Rebecca's chair scraped back as she jumped to her feet. "What do you think I am, Simon Westbridge?" she demanded. "One of your London flirts that you can buy off with a trinket?"

"Becky, for God's sake—"

"Devil Westover. Now I know how you got that name. You could charm the devil himself, couldn't you? But I haven't forgotten all that I've heard about you. I'm just another woman to you, am I not? Who I am, what I want, doesn't matter, so long as you can have your pleasure? Well, you've a sad letdown coming, my lord. I'm not like that. I'm not a green girl to believe you when you protest your love, like that poor Miss Phillips was! How could you ever have jilted her? And I'm not some doxy for you to seduce and then fight a duel over."

"Damn it, Rebecca, you have it all wrong!"

"No, you're the one who has it wrong, sir!" She threw the bracelet down onto the table. "I will not take your gift, and I will not be your mistress!"

"I didn't ask you," Simon snapped, at last goaded beyond endurance, and Rebecca drew back, stunned. Then, in the sudden silence, both heard clearly the sound of the knocker crashing on the door.

For a moment, no one moved, until the knocker sounded again. "See who it is, Hooper," Simon ordered, and Hooper, who had been a fascinated witness to this exchange, went slowly out, casting looks back at them.

They stood in frozen silence, Rebecca turned to look out the window, her arms crossed over her chest, both listening for the visitor. The road from the village must have been cleared.

"I say, Hooper," a man's voice said from the hall, and Rebecca spun around. "My sister never came home the day of the storm, and we've been looking for her. Is she here, by any chance?"

"Yes, Mr. Ware, in the dining room with his lordship."

"Is she, by God?" the man said, and walked into the room. "Oh, Rebecca. There you are."

Rebecca sank weakly into her chair. "Benjamin," she said, staring at her brother. His interruption was both opportune and unwelcome. Her mind whirled, memories of the days past mingling with things she had just said to Simon and with her worries about her family. Uppermost, however, was one thought, and one regret. Christmas was over.

# Eight

Rebecca rose from the table, drawing her normal self-possession about herself, though she felt anything but calm. "The roads from the village are clear, then?"

"Yes. I say, Rebecca, here we've been worrying about you, and you are enjoying a feast!"

"Westover was kind enough to take me in from the storm."

"Dashed good of you, Westover. Remarkably foolish of her to go out in the snow, wasn't it? You'd best come home now, though, Rebecca. Everything's all upset. Deborah tried to cook Christmas dinner, and lud, she made a mull of it. And no one wrapped any presents, and the twins decided they would do the decorating, and—"

"I'll get my cloak," Rebecca said hastily, before Benjamin could go on enumerating the problems that had arisen in just the few days of her absence. And here she had been, enjoying luxury such as she had never known. It made her feel quite guilty. "If you'll just wait, I'll be down in a moment and we can leave."

Simon followed her into the hall. "We have much yet to discuss, Rebecca."

"Do we?" She gave him a completely dazzling, and completely false, smile. "But I cannot imagine what. I must thank you again, Westover, for your hospitality, but I really must get home now. My family needs me."

"Rebecca," he protested, but she was already gone, flee-

235

ing up the steps. Running away from him. He stared after her for a moment and then turned, to see Benjamin regarding him with interest. All his anger and frustration suddenly crystallized into one thought. He could give Rebecca a gift, though not the one he had planned. "Come into the library, Ware," he said. "You look as if you could use a brandy."

"Dashed decent of you, Westover. Don't mind if I do," Benjamin said, and followed Simon into the room.


The red velvet gown had been exchanged for her blue merino, and she had on her serviceable gray cloak again. Rebecca was ready to leave. Casting one last glance around the room, she went out, her head held high. She would never forget these past days. Feel guilty about them, yes; regret some of the things she had said, yes. Never, though, would she forget them. Never again would she be the same.

The hall was empty when she walked downstairs, and so, she saw upon further investigation, was the dining room, save for the servants who were clearing the dinner away. "Oh, there you are, miss," Hooper said, as she was about to withdraw. "You forgot this."

He was holding the ring from the Christmas pudding out to her. "Thank you, Hooper," she said, and turned away, suppressing an almost hysterical desire to laugh. She would be married within a year? What nonsense! She would never marry now.

It wasn't until she was back in the hall, the ring carefully secreted in her pocket, that she realized she had forgotten to ask where her brother was. Perhaps the drawing room? She opened that door, and again quickly pulled back. Benjamin wasn't in there, but Simon was.

"Rebecca," Simon called, and she stopped, closing her eyes. She couldn't face him. She couldn't. "Please come in. I'd like to talk to you."

"I think we've said everything, my lord," she said, without turning her back.

"Becky. Please? I need to talk with you."

That did make her turn. There was no mockery in his voice, no teasing. And she supposed she did owe it to him, after what she had said at dinner. "My brother will be waiting," she said, coming into the room and closing the door behind her.

"Your brother is in the library, enjoying a brandy and doing some serious thinking."

"Benjamin?" She strove for a light note. "He's never thought seriously about anything in his life."

"Then it's about time, don't you think? I took the liberty of telling him some home truths."

"Excuse me?"

He crossed the room to her. "Well, it's high time he grew up, isn't it? He's the man of the family now and should take on some responsibilities."

"Yes, but—"

"I think it did your family good to be without you these few days. Yes, I can see you're feeling guilty about that, but it wasn't your fault, you know."

Rebecca turned away. "No, but I didn't have to enjoy it quite so much."

"Why not? There's nothing wrong with it."

"I'm not like you," she said, looking up at him earnestly. "You can take your enjoyment and then go on to something else. I'm not like that. I don't have that luxury."

He looked at her for a moment. "Becky, please sit down. There are some things I would tell you about myself."

"You needn't, sir."

"Oh, yes, I think I need to very much. I told you once that I didn't earn my nickname, but you chose not to believe me. Fair enough, with the stories you heard. I think it's time you knew the truth."

"You fought three duels."

Sitting beside her on the sofa, he smiled. "No. Only two."

"Only!"

"One was a nonsensical affair when I was still at university, an imagined slight by one of my friends. When we sobered up—yes, I admit I was somewhat the worse for drink at the time—we realized how silly it was, but we went through with it anyway for honor's sake. We both fired into the air, of course. The other was more serious." His face sobered. "I was still quite young, on the town for the first time. It doesn't excuse my actions, of course, but it makes them more understandable. To make a long story short, I fell in love with a woman I thought an absolute angel. When another man insulted her in my presence, I called him out. We dueled, and I wounded him slightly. When I told the woman what I had done, she laughed." His mouth set in a grim line. It had happened long ago, but he didn't like remembering his foolishness. "She was, it turned out, not only not in love with me but faithless, as well. She wasn't worth what I'd done. It was a hard-learned lesson, Becky."

"You were young," she said softly, responding to the self-contempt she had heard in his voice.

"Yes. But I haven't been a saint, Becky." He turned and looked at her. "There have been women, I'm not going to deny that. But they're all in the past."

"And Miss Phillips?" she said, after a moment.

"The most damaging story of all, because it's true."

"You did jilt her?"

"I cried off our engagement. There's a difference."

It was hard to ask, but she had to know. "Did you not love her?"

"No. But that isn't why. I should never have proposed in the first place, but my grandmother had just died, and—"

"You were lonely."

"Devil a bit. It simply seemed the time to set up my nursery."

"You were lonely," she repeated.

"Have it your way. What I didn't know was that Miss Phillips had a longstanding attachment to another man. Of course, her parents wouldn't hear of her choosing him over me, and she wasn't brave enough to confront them. So I bowed out. So, there." He spread his hands, smiling at her. "There you have the history of Devil Westover."

"I see." Rebecca looked down at her hands, feeling terribly guilty. She liked to think that she looked beyond appearances to the real person underneath, but she hadn't even tried to do so with this man. Instead, she had clung to the image his reputation had conjured up, to protect herself. For, if she thought him unworthy of her, she could dismiss what she felt for him as a passing fancy. Now she knew it was not. It was going to be very hard, leaving him. "Not such a terrible history."

"I don't think so." He turned to her. "So, you see, I am not quite the man you took me for. And you, Rebecca, are not the woman I thought you were, either."

Rebecca jerked back from the hand he reached out to her. "Thank you for telling me this, my lord. I assure you, people around here will learn the truth of the stories."

"That's not necessary, Becky."

"I must go." She rose, pulling on her mittens. "I can just imagine the shambles the cottage is in, if the twins tried to decorate! And I don't dare to think what Deborah's cooking is like, and—Why are you grinning at me like that?"

Simon had risen and was facing her. "You are standing under the Kissing Bough, Becky," he said, his voice grave, though his eyes twinkled.

Rebecca looked up. "Oh, no!" she exclaimed, and took a quick step back. Not again. She couldn't bear it again.

Simon walked purposefully toward her. "You cannot

239

run away, Becky."

"I—I must thank you for the last few days, my lord."

"I don't want gratitude from you."

"Oh, no." She looked up at him, so close, and knew there was no escaping. "What—what do you want?"

"This," he said, and swooped down upon her. It was not a brief kiss, nor was it particularly gentle. Instead his lips came down hard on hers, hard and firm and warm, branding her as his forevermore. And she responded. His arms were like iron bands around her, telling her without words that there was no escape, but she wished for none. She was spiraling out of control, pressing up against him, her fingers pushing into his hair, and she didn't care. In some deep part of her being she knew that this was real, this was right, and she wished it would go on forever.

Simon was breathing quite hard when he at last raised his head, and she looked up at him with dazed eyes. "Simon," she whispered.

"Shush." He tightened his hold upon her, if that were possible, and held her close, cherishing her. "I love you, Rebecca Ware. I love you."

Panic gave her strength. "You can't!" she exclaimed, pushing at his chest, and broke free. "You can't love me."

"Becky," he began, and then stopped, dropping the hand he held out to her. She looked charmingly befuddled, her lips pink from his kiss, and just a little frightened. "But I do, love." He kept his voice gentle. "I love everything about you. I love the way you care about people, the way you put others first. I love your sweetness. I love the woman you really are, Becky. I even," his voice was wry, "love the way you sing. Becky." He stepped forward, gripping her hands. "Dare I hope that you might love me someday?"

"You love the way I sing?"

"Yes."

"Oh, Simon!" she exclaimed, and cast herself into his

arms.

"Dare I take that as a yes?"

"Yes."

"Yes, you think you could love me?"

"Yes, I already do." She raised a shining face to his. "But I never thought that you—"

"You gave Christmas back to me, Becky. I was fooling myself, thinking it was the guests and the parties that made it special when I was a child, but it wasn't. It was the love. You showed me that. If you leave me, Becky, you'll take Christmas with you."

"I won't, Simon." She tightened her arms about his neck. "I promise you I won't."

"Then you'll marry me?"

"Oh, yes, Simon."

"This isn't the way I planned to do this." He held her a little away from him. "I meant to do it right, courting you first—I don't even have a ring for you."

"But I do." Laughing, she pulled away and fumbled in her pocket. "Look. From the pudding."

Simon joined in her laughter as he took the ring from her. "Somehow this seems appropriate," he said, slipping the golden band onto her finger. "You'll be married within a year after all, Becky."

"It's a lovely ring, Simon," she said, looking down at it.

"Yes."

The serious note in his voice made her look up. Oh, heavens! She knew what that look meant, though she hadn't seen it very often. And, since he had just given her a Christmas beyond compare, how could she refuse? Standing on tiptoe, she looped her arms around his neck and gave herself up to his kiss, knowing that they had been given the greatest gift of all. They had found love, under the Kissing Bough.

# Christmas at the Priory

by Meg-Lynn Roberts

A crow flying overhead cawed loudly, breaking into the gloomy thoughts of Lord Anthony Maitland as he sat huddled in his greatcoat under a gnarled old oak tree at the top of the rise that looked down on his ancestral home, Maitland Priory. The fifteenth-century house of mellow Cotswold stone caught a shaft of the fast fading afternoon sunlight as it nestled snugly between two hillocks. It looked quite cozy and serene from this distance, belying its rather decrepit and decidedly "uncozy" state. Tony shivered in the cold December air and considered what had best be done to put things right.

He thought of his cousin Clio—not his cousin, really, but a distant relation of his mother's—who had made her home with them forever. Damnation, but Clio had descended into an old maid while he was away. How was he to have known that financial matters had come to a rather desperate pass while he was with Wellington's army in Portugal, since neither Mama nor Clio had deemed fit to write and tell him.

"Now, Tiny," Clio had said when he'd come home last week, "you know I would never worry you with insignificant details of the estate management when you were away fighting Boney tooth and nail. And then, after we heard that you had been wounded and were recovering in hospital, we wouldn't have dreamed of bothering you with such petty matters as a leaking roof. Good heavens, it's not as though we've gone without food and shelter. You make much of nothing." She had said this lightly and dismissively when he had exploded at her about the state of the manor house and about why in the name of heaven she and his mother went about dressed in rags instead of having some new gowns made up.

"We can't be *that* far under the hatches, can we?" he had asked, disbelieving.

"Well, Tiny, we've been struggling to make ends meet for some time now. The crops have failed for two years in a row, and your tenants haven't had the money to pay the rent. Without the rents, the estate brings in little money on its own, as all your land is under cultivation to your tenant farmers. We've had a small portion of the interest from your mother's income and some cash from your own investments forwarded to us by Mr. Evans, your man of business in London. But that is to be used strictly to run the house, not to buy frivolous and quite unnecessary garments for your dependents."

"Devil take it, Clio. . . ." He had protested to no avail.

And why Clio continued to refer to him as "Tiny," his despised childhood nickname, he had no idea, since he was now more than half a foot taller than she. Here he was a man grown, no weak sapling but a strapping six-footer with shoulders that nearly spanned the doorway. He could surely encircle her waist with his two hands; yet she still called him Tiny just because he had been an undersized boy until he was in his late teens.

"And whatever am I to do with these strangers Mother has landed in on us for Christmas?" he had asked Clio, exasperated.

. When he had arrived home he had found two elderly ladies, the Cartwright sisters, and a mysterious little man called Clausen ensconced at his mother's whist table in the drawing room. Whist had ever been Lady Maitland's passion. It was a social outlet unsurpassed in her mind; she had used the card game to occupy and entertain herself ever since Tony could remember. And yet she wasn't an expert tactician despite all her years of practice; she talked too much to the other players to concentrate. Oh, well. He sighed. He knew his mother was an eccentric. She had taken up the game in earnest to console herself after his father had died.

"Now, Tiny, you shouldn't be surprised," Clio had answered patiently. "You know Auntie's penchant for whist. Miss Ellie and Miss Essie and Mr. Clausen make up her table. And if they have nowhere else to go at this holiday season, then in Christian charity we should share our home with them, or rather you should, for I know that I, too, am only one of Aunt Hermione's charity cases."

"Now, Clio, I won't have you talking like that. Maitland Priory is *your* home, too. You've lived here since you were a girl. And as you've done all the donkey work in the last few years since Mama abdicated her responsibilities to you, you should well be considered mistress of the place." Clio blushed at his words, for reasons Tony couldn't fathom. Yes, and now that he thought about it, she had blushed like that when he had given her a smacking kiss and a bear hug on his homecoming last week, too. Well, she had been the one who rushed out of the front door and down the steps to throw her arms about him just as he had descended from his carriage.

"Yes, well, that's nonsense, you know," she had said. "You say you've been in contact with Mr. Evans about releasing some of your funds from bonds to make a few repairs to the Priory. I must say, I think you are wise to do so, if you feel you can do without the interest the bonds would bring in future years. We don't want the place falling down about our ears." She smiled at him. "Especially now, with winter upon us." She shivered lightly under her old, heavy wool shawl that showed signs of having been darned in several places.

He reached down to place the strand of light brown hair that had escaped its bonds back behind her ear and saw her blush again as he said, "Yes, and I want you and Mama to do yourselves up, too. We'll refurbish the house and its occupants while we're about it." He looked down at the rather worn claret-colored jacket he wore. "I daresay I could do with a few smart new togs, myself." The left sleeve of his jacket hung loosely over his wounded left arm which had taken an indirect hit from a piece of burning shrapnel. It had required months to heal and had ended his army career abruptly.

The arm would never regain all the muscle that had been lost or be as strong as it once was, but Tony knew he was lucky to still have an arm at all. He had worked hard to restore some strength in the limb throughout his lengthy recuperation. He was proud that he could now drive a carriage again, holding the reins in both hands.

"Might I have a word, Lord Maitland?" his mother's friend Clausen had asked after dinner last night when the ladies had departed for the drawing room.

"The ladies would be a tad cozier if the chimneys could be swept and the fires built up higher in their rooms. I know that Miss Ingram does without a fire in her own bedroom. She's economizing, she tells me, and she's used to it; very poor excuses to keep oneself half-freezing, as I'm sure you'll agree, Lord Maitland. I know you wouldn't want her to make such an unnecessary sacrifice, my lord.

"And Lady Maitland would be very grateful if you could set in train the mending of the roof. With new slates in place, the rain won't get in and rot the attic floor and drip down on our heads. Such repairs will prove to be a good economy, I've no doubt, for they will save you more extensive replacement costs in the long run. I believe you're already out of pocket for a dozen new packs of cards as it is, my lord. The others succumbed to the mildew, you know." Clausen had laughed merrily.

"Anything else to recommend for the comfort of my family, Mr. Clausen?" Tony had asked ironically, raising one dark brow. Really the fellow took a lot upon himself to tell him how to go on, Tony thought irritably. He already had it in mind to instruct the servants to build the fires up in all the rooms, even the servants' quarters, for the infernal cold and wet was rotting the wood and furnishings of the house as well as imparting a most unpleasant smell of dampness everywhere.

Well, perhaps Clausen was right, damn him, Tony had to admit as he pulled himself upright from where he sat on the hard ground. He shivered again; it had grown even colder as the sun began to set behind the gray clouds in the late afternoon sky and he was ready to set off back home. Best get on with it, he thought as he rose to his feet and went to untie his horse's reins from the nearby hedge. He put his booted foot into the stirrup and mounted in a powerful but graceful movement, still thinking abstractedly about how to enliven this holiday.

He would contact the slater in town about the roof, hire some extra help to clean the place up, and enlist Clio's help in decking out the Priory for a proper Christmas, the kind he had enjoyed as a boy, with all the seasonal foods he loved and festive decorations and people to stay. Yes, it was an idea that pleased him enormously. He would invite a few friends to come and share the holidays with them and dispel the gloom that seemed to envelop the Priory as winter deepened. After all, he reasoned, his mother already had her cronies. He would invite some younger people for himself and Clio, just for that week or so before Christmas and for the day itself. He couldn't afford to be too extravagant and entertain a houseful for an extended time. Feeding such a crew would eat up his funds as fast as they ate up his food.

Clio. He grinned as he thought of the companion of his youth. It was time she was married, and with no one else to make a push to find her a suitable *parti,* as head of the family he supposed it was up to him to think about these things. It was clear his mother would never bestir herself in the matter.

Now who could he invite for Clio? . . . Hmm. John

Parker, a friend from the army, lived in the vicinity. He was turned thirty, a widower with two young children. Would such a fellow appeal to Clio? As Tony thought about it he supposed that John would be considered a handsome man, tall and slender with midnight black hair and striking green eyes. But more importantly, Major John Parker was an excellent fellow. He had been a caring leader of the men under his command, making sure that they always had food, clothing, shoes, and ammunition for their guns when these things were in short supply and some of the other regiments went without. Always careful of them in combat, seeing to it that every last man understood the battle plan and his role in it, the major never risked his men unnecessarily.

Tony knew that it had been a hard decision, but John had sold his commission after his wife died so that he could look after his two young children. During his convalescence Tony had learned that John had purchased a small estate not too far distant from Maitland Priory, and he looked forward to renewing his friendship with the major.

Clio would make an excellent mother, he felt sure. Would she take to John's two motherless children? It would be interesting to see how the two of them reacted to one another.

Clio would need new clothes if she were to stand a chance with John, though. She wouldn't attract a beggar in the patched and faded gowns she now wore. He was determined to make her see the necessity of ordering new gowns, and to hell with the expense.

Well, that would do for Clio's entertainment. Now what about himself? He grinned as he thought of the flirtatious Miss Marianne Milverton, daughter of the local squire, a sprightly blonde with big brown eyes that she knew how to use to good effect on the gentlemen. He had met her in town this morning when he had gone in to send off an express to Evans. Little Marianne had certainly matured from the underdeveloped girl of fifteen she had been when he had last been at home three years ago. She had grown into quite a beauty, in fact. Yes, he would invite Miss Milverton and the squire and his wife. And his cousin Serena and her husband, Nigel Amberton, lived not far away. Perhaps they would like to join him at the Priory for an old-fashioned Christmas celebration. He had always liked Serena. She was the daughter of his mother's sister and had often visited the Priory as a girl. She was a year or two older than himself and Clio. She and Nigel must have—what?—two or three children now.

Feeling considerably cheered by the plans he had made, Tony rode back to the Priory to tell Clio about his ideas and to enlist her help. Though, of course, he wouldn't reveal *one* of his reasons for inviting John Parker. She might scratch his eyes out. He laughed to himself, for she used to be a fierce little thing when they were children, though he had to admit that more often than not her fierceness was used in his defense against older and bigger boys rather than against him.

"A Christmas house party! Here? But, Tiny . . . have you considered the work involved? And can you afford it?"

"Clio, I've been looking forward to Christmas celebrations for months now. I thought about home all the time I was recuperating, and when I got back to the Priory and saw everything looking so dreary and gray, I felt pulled down. Let's do up the house like we used to when we were children and invite friends and relatives to visit. Let's have some fun around here for a change, celebrate in style. I don't mean to invite masses of people. It won't cost the earth. Come, my dear, won't you help me?"

"I'm sorry, Tiny dear. Of course, we must do as you say and have a proper celebration this year—to welcome you home. And I believe Aunt Hermione would enjoy it, too."

"What about you, Clio? Will you enjoy it, despite all the hard work you'll be called on to put in, working your fingers to the bone for my pleasure? I'll hire some girls from the village to come in and help out, shall I? And I'll do my

251

share, if you'll advise me how I would best be employed."

Clio smiled widely. "Yes, I can just see you mending the sheets, Tiny, and rolling out the pastry for the mince pies!" They both laughed at the picture her words conjured up.

When it was put to the dowager, Lady Maitland greeted her son's announcement of a house party for Christmas with her accustomed mildly abstracted tone. "Well, Maitland, if you and Clio can handle the arrangements, that will be fine. Be sure to inquire whether those coming can play whist, for it would be quite a treat to vary the table every now and again and play with different partners, would it not, Mr. Clausen?"

"As you say, my lady, the more the merrier. I think it's a capital notion of Lord Maitland's to celebrate Christmas in style, for it will cheer you all up. Just what this old house needs, a group of people in a festive mood and some excited children. Why, it will rejuvenate us all!" The jolly little man laughed in delight.

"Yes," the dowager said peevishly as she continued to regard the cards she held in her hand, her mind half on her next play, "but if we don't find that ring, the party will be a disaster just like all the other things that have gone wrong since it went missing. First, Maitland's dying so suddenly like that, then Tony nearly losing his arm—I *told* him if he went off with the army before we found that ring some disaster would befall him, but he took no notice. And now the roof falling down on us. I put it all down to the loss of that ring. And it wasn't my fault, for I put it carefully in my jewel case, just as I did every time I removed it from my finger—it was so heavy, you know, that I couldn't wear it for everyday; I saved it for best."

Tony rolled his eyes and caught Clio smiling absently at the oft-repeated claim of the dowager that the family luck had taken a turn for the worse since the Maitland engagement ring, a heavy gold affair filled with rubies and diamonds, had gone missing over a decade ago.

"All the Barons of Maitland have given that ring to their fiancées before they married."

"Mama! There have only been four barons altogether, three before me."

"The number makes no odds. That ring's always been the family's lucky charm."

"Oh dear, Lady Maitland, I hope your mentioning the missing ring doesn't mean that ill-luck will rub off on this hand we're playing," Miss Ellie Cartwright, partnering the dowager at the moment, said worriedly.

Mr. Clausen reached over and patted Lady Maitland's hand. "Never fear, dear lady, the ring will turn up one day. Probably when it's needed again. I'm certain of it."

"Oh, do you really think so, Mr. Clausen?" tittered Miss Essie Cartwright, his partner. "I'm sure Lady Maitland would feel ever so relieved if it could be found before she goes to her eternal rest."

The dowager actually looked up from her cards to stare crossly at Miss Essie for giving voice to such a gloomy thought. "I only hope you may be right, Mr. Clausen, for Anthony can't get married without it. Not that he's ever shown any sign of wanting to get married. But perhaps if the ring were to be found he would start thinking about it. Who knows? If the ring isn't found, he may predecease me, and then none of us would have a roof over our heads at all, leaking or otherwise, for that nitwit cousin of his, Cecil Pringle, would inherit the title *and* the Priory and toss us all out on our heads."

"Mama! What a preposterous thought!" Tony exclaimed.

"Now, Aunt Hermione, give over such dismal thoughts, do," Clio said practically. "You know you are in fine fettle, and here we have Tiny back among us, safe and sound." She smiled over at Tony.

"Well, almost sound." He grinned ruefully, looking down at his wounded arm.

"And such plans as Tiny has made for Christmas. We will all be as merry as grigs! Speaking of which, I had better see Cook about the Christmas cake and mince pies. She will want to make a start on her cooking if we are to have guests and celebrate in a grand fashion." So saying, Clio took herself out of the room with her accustomed energy, the housekeeping keys jangling at her waist as she went.

"An excellent woman, there, Maitland. One in a million," Clausen remarked to Tony. "Will make some lucky man a superb wife one day."

"Yes, indeed," Tony said repressively. He didn't need a stranger to tell him about Clio's good qualities. She had been almost as a sister to him since they were both nine, when she had come to live at the Priory after her parents had died in an influenza epidemic. Her mother had been a favorite cousin of his mama's. Tony felt protective of her and knew his responsibility to see to her future — and that would inevitably involve finding her a husband.

"She's an exceptionally good-looking woman, too. Odd that she hasn't married yet. She'll look fine as fivepence in the new rigs you are buying the ladies for Christmas," Clausen predicted.

"Yes, Clio could do with some smartening up," Lady Maitland said, proving that her mind was not wholly given over to her cards. "It's been years since she's had a new frock. She's not interested in clothes, though, you know. You might have a hard time convincing her to rig herself out in the latest fashion."

Clio returned to her chores, thinking that this notion of Tiny's to have a house party would certainly involve a lot of work and put some extra burdens on her shoulders in the next few weeks. But she would gladly shoulder them if it would help to cheer him up after his ghastly experiences in the Peninsular campaign. He was still not completely recovered from his wound, she knew, though his sunny nature seemed to have survived intact. Perhaps that was what had seen him through the horror of his war experiences in the first place. A lively Christmas celebration might be just what he needed.

She would do anything for Tiny. She had loved him since they were children growing up together at the Priory.

She knew that Tiny looked on her more or less as a sister, and took her affection for granted. Well, she had no right and no hope to expect anything else, she scolded herself sternly.

Clio was five and twenty, just six months younger than Tony. She was a competent young woman with no illusions about her chances of contracting a suitable marriage at her advanced age and with her lack of dowry. And she had no illusions about her appearance, either. She was of average height with light gray eyes, a dusting of freckles across her nose, and light brown hair that went slightly fairer in the summer. She had a nicely proportioned figure, neither too slender nor too well fleshed. What she didn't know was that she had a smile that lit up her whole face and lent a sparkle to her gray eyes, making them shine brightly and transforming her regular features into something approaching true beauty.

But now was not the time to worry about her appearance, for she had to sort through the linen closet to check if they had enough good bedsheets and table linen to accommodate Tiny's guests. There was certain to be a fair amount of mending to be done as well as all the washing and ironing. Then she would have to make up the menus and see about getting in the extra provisions they would need. She would also have to speak to the staff about cleaning the Priory from top to bottom and see to the hiring of extra help from the village. It was fortunate most of their small staff were local people and often had relatives who would welcome a few extra shillings, especially at this time of the year. Clio began to hum happily as she went about her tasks.

A few evenings later Mr. Clausen approached Clio in the drawing room after dinner as she sorted through the sheets of music on the pianoforte, putting aside the Christmas carols and hymns that someone—not her, though—would undoubtedly play during the holiday.

"My dear Miss Ingram, that was a most excellent dinner. I don't know when I've had pork roasted to such a turn. And the apple tart was almost heavenly!"

"Thank you, sir. I shall convey your compliments to Cook. Mrs. Hyssop will be pleased to hear them. She's quite masterly with a joint and her pastry is light as air, but she's getting a little fidgety with so much company due to arrive so soon. Mrs. Hyssop is a good cook, but she fears that all the extra dishes and fancy foods Tiny has it in mind to serve up to his guests will defeat her. I encourage her and tell her otherwise, that there's nothing but a little more decorating of the sweets, a few extra sauces to make, and a bit of dressing up of the fish and fowl to be done."

"Yes, yes, Miss Ingram, I quite agree. You just keep encouraging her. She has fed us so well while I've been with Lady Maitland that I fear I may have put on a few extra pounds." Mr. Clausen chuckled and patted his ample girth, which shook at his laughter. "The house is looking quite attractive, if I may say so, under your excellent ministrations, Miss Ingram. I take it Lord Maitland means to provide you ladies with a new frock or two—an excellent idea, if I may make so bold. A little sprucing up improves us all. I plan to go into town tomorrow and get these white locks and beard of mine trimmed and buy a new jacket for the occasion; I thought I might splash out and buy a jacket cut in this new style I see Lord Maitland to be sporting. Perhaps in dark red superfine. What do you think?"

"An excellent choice, sir," Clio said brightly, her eyes sparkling in the candlelight.

"And what have you in mind for your new gowns, my dear?"

"Why, I haven't given it much thought. I've been busy with all the plans. . . ."

"You must do so, my dear Miss Ingram! Why, just think what pleasure it will give all of us men to see you looking your best in new finery and with hair coiffed to set off your delicate features. Lord Maitland will want us all looking presentable, and we wouldn't want to let him down in front

256

of his guests. We must do what we can to look our best."

Tony was pleased. His plans were progressing nicely. The weather had been gray and dull, but no rain had fallen within the last two weeks so the slater had been able to get on with the roof repairs, mending and pinning down those slates that could be saved and replacing those that had crumbled. He and his team of craftsmen were almost finished.

"Clio, you've done wonders, my girl," Tony exclaimed as he stood back and viewed the effect her labors had had on the inside of the Priory. She had taken on several girls from the village to help turn the whole house inside out. And now, even if the fittings weren't of the newest, the whole place gleamed from the effects of washing and cleaning, dusting and polishing.

"Yes, it was a splendid notion of yours—or was it Mr. Clausen's—to turn everything out and do up the house," Clio said. "I daresay the Priory hasn't looked this well in years. And Mr. Clausen's made several suggestions that have helped."

"Yes, he always seems to be on hand to hint us in the right direction, doesn't he? Quite uncanny, I would say," Tony mused. "He's even persuaded Mama to abandon the card table and take the air for half an hour after luncheon every day. Quite improves the digestion, he's told her, and I daresay he's in the right of it."

As Tony stood surveying the hall, he sniffed the air and smiled in delight. Now that the chimneys had been swept and the fires were drawing properly once again, the sweet odor of wood burning permeated the rooms without the unpleasantness of smoke swirling about. The wood scent mingled with the smell of beeswax polish that had been used on all the woodwork and with the fresh scent of outdoors emanating from the berries and fruits of the season and the holly and ivy he and Clio had been collecting. The tantalizing aroma of pies and cakes baking and of spiced apple cider boiling over the kitchen hearth made Tony's mouth water and led him to accompany Clio down to the nether regions to see what Mrs. Hyssop was up to.

He followed her to the kitchen and watched as she began to sort through a motley collection of hand-written recipes she was using to make out the menus. He then sat on a stool and interrupted her, making sure she planned to include all his favorite foods—partridge and bread sauce and plum pudding and stuffed goose. "Did I tell you that everyone has accepted my invitation? They should start arriving the day after tomorrow."

"You must be pleased, Tiny," Clio commented as she glanced at yet another receipt for molded jellies and absently reached over and took her menu back from his hands.

He grabbed her hand to recall her attention before relinquishing the paper to her. "Clio, we must start collecting evergreen boughs for decorating the house. We'll want to put them in the hall and drawing room, and thread them through the railings of the staircase, at the least. Do you think we should put a few over the mantel in everyone's bedroom, too?"

She smiled up at him as he reminded her of their activities in younger years. "Ah, yes. It was always our job as children to raid the hedges and copses and to collect as many boughs as we could without denuding every tree in sight, wasn't it?"

The day before his friends were due to arrive Tony and Clio were on their way to find suitable boughs of greenery to cut and bring indoors. There was a touch of frost in the air, and the clouds hung low overhead, heavy with unshed snow.

"Do you think it will snow before tomorrow and delay some of our guests?" Tony asked worriedly as he gazed upward.

"It's hard to say." Clio's eyes followed the direction of

Tony's. "I've seen the sky look like this without a flake falling. At other times there will hardly be a cloud; then suddenly the wind whips up and a blizzard sets in. We'll just have to trust that everyone will arrive safely. After all, no one lives that far away. You could have the old sleigh repaired and send it for them if it does snow enough to make the roads impassable."

"Mama will blame any ill weather on that deuced ring, you know," he said, a smile tugging at his lips.

"Yes, and Mr. Clausen keeps assuring her that the ring will turn up this holiday. I don't know how he can make such a rash promise, for it will lead to Auntie's hopes being cruelly dashed when it doesn't. Where does he get his information, do you think? Perhaps he talks to spirits."

"Well, I find he's made some inroads into my wine cellar since he's been here. Perhaps those are the 'spirits' he's been communicating with," Tony said dryly, as he looked somewhat askance at the new way Clio had styled her hair.

He still couldn't get used to the change, not after seeing her with long, light brown locks pulled back smoothly from her face and forehead since she had been a young girl. Now she had had her hair cut short, and surprisingly, without the heaviness of those long tresses, natural bouncy curls had been revealed. The curls framed her face, making her look younger and far more frivolous than her usually serious, no-nonsense nature warranted. Tony frowned as he watched her select a likely looking bough of evergreen.

"What's the matter, Tiny? Surely this tree can spare us a few of its branches."

"It's not that. The tree will be fine. Here, let me cut those branches for you, Clio. I don't want you to scratch your hands. I've brought heavy gloves."

"Well, why are you looking like a thundercloud, then? I thought everything was going smoothly," she said, stepping back so that he could get at the low-growing tree with the shears. "Your arm doesn't hurt, does it?"

"No, no. Nothing like that."

"Well, what's disturbing you then?"

259

"Well, Clio, it's your hair," he said with a pained look on his face.

"My hair!" Her hand went up to the few short tendrils becomingly framing her face and curling up around the outside of her new fur hat. "Don't you like it cut this way? Mr. Clausen said it was very becoming."

"It's not that I don't like it. It's just . . . it's just that it's not *you*."

Clio laughed. "You mean it's far too youthful a style for an old maid like me."

"No, no. Not at all. That wasn't my meaning. It makes you look quite different, and I don't feel I know you as I used to do. You don't seem my same comfortable Clio somehow, my companion in so many youthful larks."

"You mean to remind me of the days when I was a hoyden. And now you're afraid I might take some freakish start into my head and begin acting like a giddy girl. Well, never fear, Tiny," she patted his good arm that now held the cut boughs, "it's not my nature to act so."

In an exasperated tone, Tony asked, "Clio, how many times have I asked you to stop calling me 'Tiny?' " Now that I'm a grown man, and a tall one, there is no reason to continue calling me by such a preposterous nickname."

"Oh." She looked at him, surprised. "You're right. It's just been habit, I suppose. I didn't mean to insult you, you know; it was done out of affection. I'll try to remember in future, Ti — Tony. Or should I more properly call you Lord Maitland? We're so distantly related that —"

"Don't be foolish, my girl," he cut in. "We're closer than some brothers and sisters. Why, I think I would be more offended if you were to call me by my title than if you were to continue calling me 'Tiny,' " he teased.

And they gathered up the evergreen boughs he had cut, piled them in the small gardener's wagon they had brought for the purpose, and took them back to the house, on the way indulging in companionable conversation.

* * *

"Oh, Lord Maitland, your house looks so lovely! All the evergreen boughs tied with those red ribbons and the candlesticks entwined with holly and ivy! And even the table. The white cloth looks like the snowy ground outside," Marianne Milverton gushed over the soup course the following evening. The seasonal decorations and the loveliness of the house were refrains the girl had resorted to at least ten times that day already, Tony thought with amusement.

"Not half as lovely as you, Miss Milverton," he said to the blushing girl. She sat to his right, where he had asked Clio to place her when she had determined the seating arrangements. It was going to be an entertaining few days with this little minx to dally with. Tony smiled in satisfaction. The girl had wasted no time in setting up a flirtation with him. She had been up to her tricks since she had entered the house early that afternoon with her parents. Though the Milvertons lived only fifteen miles the other side of town, they had welcomed the chance to stay at the Priory and give their daughter a chance to drop her handkerchief in front of a peer of the realm while saving a quid or two of their own expenses at the same time.

All the guests had arrived safely, despite the fact that it had, indeed, started snowing the evening before. All during the day it had been but a light fall, adding a glitter and sparkle to the landscape but causing no problems for the travelers. However, the last time Tony had looked out the window, he could see that the snow was accumulating quite rapidly now and showed no sign of stopping.

He turned his attention back to his dinner companions. Really, this idea of his to invite the little Milverton minx was proving quite a delightful inspiration. He didn't know when he had enjoyed the game more. It was all sugary and light, nothing serious in their dalliance at all. Still, the exchange was boosting his spirits, that's what it was doing.

And he could see as he glanced down the table, as he frequently did, that John and Clio were getting on famously as well, if the number of times their heads were together and their frequent laughter were anything to go by.

What did they find to laugh about so often? he wondered. Clio was usually the most prosaic of females and only spoke with him about mundane items of family and household interest.

She looked very well tonight, in her new gown of light blue velvet with creamy lace at the neck and cuffs and with her hair curling round her face. He wished he hadn't ripped up at her about having had it cut, for it really was most attractive.

He looked at her more closely. Why, he really did believe that she was *flirting* with Parker as much as Marianne was flirting with him! What a surprise! He didn't know she had it in her. Perhaps she was tired of her spinsterish existence and had decided to set her cap at the major. Well, why did he suddenly feel qualms, since the whole idea behind inviting John had been for just such a purpose?

He remembered how Clio had greeted the Parker family that afternoon.

"How do you do, Sam." Clio had smiled gently as she had knelt down to shake the hand of John's five-year-old son, after Tony had introduced her to Major Parker. "I bid you welcome to Maitland Priory. We hope you will have a very happy Christmas here this year." And then she had turned her most special smile on three-year-old Carrie Parker, saying, "Ah, Miss Parker, you do look lovely and warm in that beautiful red coat. Is it new? How I envy you," she had added on a theatrical sigh. "I wish I had something half as fashionable to keep me warm." Carrie had giggled and had come forward shyly to take Clio by the hand and then had begun chatting about the journey to the Priory in her papa's coach through the gently falling snow.

"Well, I must say, Miss Ingram, that is the first time I've known Carrie to talk with anyone other than her nurse or myself. Even her grandmother has trouble getting more than two words at a time out of her," John Parker said, turning the charm of his bright smile full upon Clio.

Both children had seemed more at ease after the warmth

of Clio's welcome, Tony thought, impressed. He wished he had done as well with the young Parkers. He would have to let Clio show him the way to make friends with them.

After his cousin Serena had arrived with her husband and their three children, the five young ones had had a noisy game of spillikins with Miss Milverton. John had expressed his amazement to Tony that both Sam and Carrie seemed to take to Miss Milverton as well as Miss Ingram. Miss Milverton had almost seemed one of the children as she sat on the floor and laughed merrily, looking bright-eyed and pretty and deliciously cuddly all at the same time, Tony observed. Well, after all, she is only eighteen, he reminded himself.

John had sat on the floor, too, holding his daughter Carrie on his lap until she felt comfortable enough to leave the security of her father's knee and join in the noisy game with her brother and Serena's three children: seven-year-old Sophie, five-year-old Tom, and four-year-old Phyllis. Tony had felt like an old man, looking on from his chair while everyone else sprawled on the carpet. Clio had not been present; as the *de facto* hostess of the house she had been seeing to some matter or other for his guests' comfort.

His mama was happy as a clam with the Misses Essie and Ellie Cartwright and Mr. Clausen to entertain her. When she found that the senior Milvertons played whist, too, her joy was almost complete. The old girl looked almost regal on this night in her new silver satin gown, her hair becomingly styled. Even the frivolous red feathers stuck in her coiffure didn't look silly, but rather added to the festive atmosphere.

Yesterday he had convinced Clio to hang some mistletoe tied with red bows in the center of the arched hallway, and this afternoon Tony had been very amused to see Clausen take his mother by surprise and give her a chaste salute on the lips under the green plant with its polished white berries. His mother had almost blushed as she tapped Clausen on the arm of his new red jacket and called him a "naughty boy."

263

"Oh, but you're not attending, Lord Maitland." Marianne tapped him on the arm with her spoon, recalling his attention to the table. "How vexatious that you should find my company dull so soon!" She laughed up at him.

"Not a bit of it, my dear! I was thinking about how to best entertain you after dinner and remembered the mistletoe we've hung in the hallway." He was delighted to see a charming blush rise in her cheeks as she lowered her lashes over dark eyes.

The gentlemen did not spend too long over their brandy after dinner, but made haste to join the ladies in the drawing room where Serena was already seated at the piano, lightly running her fingers over the keys. Tony walked over to her. Clio had draped an old piece of white silk shot through with gold threads over the piano, and on it stood two silver candelabra decorated round their bases with shiny green holly sprigs heavy with red berries.

"I'm glad you and Nigel could come with the children this year, Serena. It adds to the gaiety to have the little ones about."

"I hope you still think so after a week of their rather boisterous company, my dear." She smiled up at him. "It quite takes me back, Tony, to when you and Clio and I were children. Remember how we used to run back and forth to one another's rooms in our excitement after the grown-ups thought we were fast asleep in our beds. . . . I hope my three aren't upstairs right now teaching those darling children of Major Parker's all our old tricks."

Tony grinned. "Well, let them have their fun. Are you planning to play something we can all sing?"

"Yes, indeed. And I shall refuse to play unless *everyone* joins in. What is the fun of Christmas unless one can sing carols at the top of one's lungs!" They laughed together. "I must say, Clio has done a marvelous job of decorating the Priory this year, Tony. She must have worked nonstop for weeks! I hope you provided sufficient help, my dear." She glanced up to see his reaction.

"Oh, she enjoyed it, you know. Clio's always had a talent

for organizing the household and seeing that things run smoothly. And, yes, I did my best to help her, but she's not happy unless she's in charge." His eyes crinkled as he grinned and Serena laughed.

"It's kind of you, Tony, to allow Aunt Hermione to invite her whist-playing friends. I believe that's the very best present you could devise, unless you could somehow magically discover that blasted ring after all these years!"

He shrugged his shoulders. "You know Mama, she'll invite any riff and raff to make my home theirs so long as they can play whist."

"Fiddlesticks! You're a kind man. . . . I must say, Mr. Clausen seems an enigmatic sort of character for Auntie to take up with—jolly, though. Where did he come from? Do you know anything about him?"

"From the north is all he's told me. Not very helpful, I'd agree, but he seems harmless enough, unless you count the number of times he's convinced me to spend more money on this place or to buy new clothes for Mama and Clio."

"Well, good for him, then! Clio looks better than she has in years with her new frock and her hair cut so becomingly. I daresay having you home all in one piece has something to do with her glowing looks, too," Serena said as they both glanced to where Clio was laughing with John Parker.

Tony scowled at the picture they made. "Yes, well, I hope she's not planning to throw herself at John's head."

"You sound jealous, Tony dear. *I* think they are a well-matched couple, he so dark and Clio so fair, both mature and level-headed people. He seems a thoroughly decent chap. Clio could do a lot worse, even if he already has two children."

"Do you think so, Serena? Would he really suit her? She and I have always been close, you know, growing up together as we did. I care for her too much to see her made unhappy in any way." Tony felt disturbed and didn't know why, when his plan seemed to be working so perfectly.

"I think it's too soon to tell, my dear. Clio is sensible, though. If he's not the man for her, she won't accept him, even if it means she'll remain on the shelf."

Tony frowned as he heard Serena's words and glanced at Clio and John once more.

Marianne came giggling up to him just then and took him by the arm, distracting him.

"Are we to sing carols, Mrs. Amberton? I just love to sing, don't you, Lord Maitland?" she asked, as she gazed into his dark blue eyes, her brown ones opened to their fullest extent.

Tony winked at her and patted her hand where it rested on his sleeve.

Clio looked over to where Tony and Serena were chatting by the pianoforte only to see Marianne Milverton join them and attach herself to Tony's arm without so much as a by-your-leave. Clio had noticed all day how the girl flirted with Tony—and Tony hadn't been slow to flirt back either, she allowed. Well, that was why he had invited the girl, she supposed. Why else had he taken such an interest in the seating arrangements for dinner when he usually left such mundane chores to her, not giving a be-damn about such things. And why it should annoy her so, she didn't know. She had realized long ago that Tony was susceptible to attractive women and that he would marry one day—but Miss Milverton was still a child. . . . Anyway, he would certainly never look at *her* the way he was at that young girl. And she didn't really expect him to; she had known forever that he looked on her as one of his family.

But if he could play at that game then so could she, she decided as she looked up at John Parker again. "Your children seem to have settled in comfortably enough," she said, smiling brightly.

"Yes. I must say that I was surprised. They are usually slow to take to strangers, especially Carrie. But they like you, Miss Ingram. And Mrs. Amberton's children seem a lively trio who have made it easier for Carrie and Sam to feel at home. I was surprised to see that they responded to young Miss Milverton so well, too. And with Tony making us all so welcome, this will be a happy Christmas indeed for all three of us."

Nigel Amberton joined them. "Will you both join us at the instrument? Serena has her heart set on singing carols. Do you think we dare disturb Lady Maitland?" he asked with a humorous glint in his eye.

"I don't know if she will join in, but she will enjoy hearing the rest of us sing," Clio told him. "I believe the others may wish to join us, though. Mr. Clausen, in particular, is always humming Christmas songs and hymns. He assured me that this is his favorite time of year."

Marianne, meanwhile, enjoyed batting her long lashes at Lord Maitland for a time, but when he began to turn the pages of music for his cousin, she dropped his arm and wandered over to where John Parker stood looking through some periodicals on a raised mahogany table at the side of the room.

"Mr. Parker, or should I say, Major Parker, is this not a splendid idea of Lord Maitland's to have us all to stay? I've never been to a Christmas house party before. Indeed, I've never been to a house party of any kind, because I'm just out, you see." She giggled, then blushed at her schoolgirlish behavior with this handsome man. Why, she really believed he was better looking than Lord Maitland, who was well enough with his teasing blue eyes and his dark brown hair already sprinkled with a distinguished gray.

"I was pleased that Tony invited me and my children, and I'm certainly enjoying the company of you and your family and the others, Miss Milverton. It will be a happier Christmas for me and my children than we've known for the past few years." Parker looked slightly disconcerted at his own words, not knowing what made him refer to the past sadness of his wife's death.

She didn't seem disturbed as she smiled up at him. "You do have sweet children, Major Parker."

"I think so, I'm glad you agree. Thank you for playing with them this afternoon. It's not often an adult will indulge them so generously and so wholeheartedly." There was a warm glint in his eye as he teased her.

Marianne blushed. She had forgotten she was an adult as she had enthusiastically joined in the childish game earlier. "Oh, I didn't mind. I must confess that I enjoyed myself! I hope you didn't think it too childlike of me," she said somewhat hesitantly.

"Not at all! I've been known to join in a lively game of spillikins with them myself, ere now," he teased lightly. "Now that the snow has started to settle, I was hoping to take them out sledding tomorrow. Would you care to join our expedition? I know that Carrie, for one, would be inordinately pleased. But perhaps you have other plans and wouldn't care to subject yourself to all the cold and wet. It can be a messy business, sledding."

"Why, I would enjoy a sledding party above all things, Major Parker! May I indeed come with you? Are any of the others coming?"

He smiled at her frank enthusiasm. "I shall have to put my head together with Mrs. Amberton to see if we should join forces, but I will be sure to tell you of our plans." He had seen her flirting with Tony and had assumed a mutual attraction existed in that quarter. But now she seemed quite happy to go off with him and his children. No doubt the lovely young girl looked on him as a fatherly figure, a kind uncle; for he was five or six years Maitland's senior.

They joined the others around the piano and everyone sang a rousing "Deck the Halls with Boughs of Holly" and then the "Wassail Song" before Serena began to play the softer melody of the traditional "Sussex Carol," the women and men singing alto and bass.

"On Christmas night all Christians sing
To hear the news the angels bring.
News of great joy
News of great mirth
News of our merciful King's birth."

Though he himself stood shoulder to shoulder with Miss Milverton, Tony didn't quite like the way John had a hand on Clio's shoulder as he stood slightly behind her, nor did he care for the way Clio smiled up at John from time to time and let their voices blend together in song. He was happy to see her move away from his friend afterward as she dashed off to see about supper being served in the drawing room.

Tony was chatting with Clausen and watching his guests. He saw that John was making Marianne laugh at something he was saying. And his mother, who had been seen tapping her fingers on her knee in time to the music, had resumed her game. This time Squire and Mrs. Milverton had joined in and Miss Essie Cartwright was given a break while her sister Ellie played staunchly on. The Milvertons were teaching the others the new craze, five-point whist, a shorter, more exciting variant on the Long Whist they were used to.

"Well, Lord Maitland, you are to be congratulated. The celebrations have commenced happily this evening. I feel myself more in a Christmas mood after all the seasonal music Mrs. Amberton so graciously played for us."

Tony murmured his thanks for Clausen's commendation.

"I thought Miss Ingram was in particularly good looks tonight. Nothing like the admiration of a gentleman to set a lady to looking even more beautiful than usual, is there?" He laughed.

Tony's eyes narrowed. He was disturbed to find that someone besides himself had noticed how Clio glowed in John Parker's company. "Yes, she certainly looked in fine fettle tonight."

"It was an admirable notion of yours to order new gowns for the ladies. Was quite a generous early Christmas present for them. Your mother looks as fine as fivepence in her silver and red. Looks regal, almost, does Lady Maitland. She's even left off play to chat with your guests, you see." Clausen laughed again as he directed Tony's eyes toward his mother, who had indeed put down her cards and was accepting a cup of tea from Clio while she chatted with the Milvertons.

"You must excuse me, Lord Maitland. I just have to check on my team. They were restless earlier today," Clausen said as he set down his cup of warm mulled cider on a silver tray on the sideboard.

Tony was puzzled as he watched the little man disappear out the door. He had mildly objected to housing Clausen's team of four gray horses, eating their heads off at his expense for the last month. What the devil did the fellow want with such a team when he didn't even seem to have a home of his own to go to? At least his having a team of horses meant that Clausen used his own animals and not Tony's for his frequent, unexplained trips to town. And since he had his own means of conveyance, perhaps he would leave soon, Tony thought hopefully.

After the dowager and most of the guests had gone to bed, Tony and Clio met under the mistletoe in the Priory's large, Gothic-arched hallway. It bespoke the original use of the building as a monastery before Bluff King Hal had disbanded its inhabitants, confiscated most of its contents, and handed the building over to one of his favorites. The Maitlands were comparative newcomers. They had acquired the house and land relatively recently, through marriage to one of the descendants of its original roguish Tudor owners.

"What's on the agenda for tomorrow, Clio?" Tony asked with a smile, after trying unsuccessfully to conceal a large yawn behind his fist.

"I take care of the menus, you take care of the agenda, Anthony," she said somewhat shortly. "With all this snow, I don't think you will be short of things to do outside, if your guests don't mind getting themselves a little cold and wet."

"Hey, puss, don't heap coals on my head. What's gotten you so upset? . . . Is it all the extra work this party has heaped on your shoulders? I'm sorry if so, but I thought we would all enjoy it." He reached out to rub his hand along her upper arm, then began to gently knead her tense shoulder muscles with his long fingers.

His action brought a tightening to Clio's throat. She looked away from him and said, "I'm just tired, Tony."

"I'll promise to help you more tomorrow, I shall. Did I tell you that several people — gentlemen — commented on how well you looked tonight? The new gown suits you. And the admiration of *one* gentleman, in particular, has lent a glow to your cheeks and put a sparkle in your eye."

"Oh, and which gentleman would that be?" She smiled up at him, ready to engage in one of their teasing matches.

"Why, John, of course. I believe he admires you, Clio. He's a fine man, you know . . . and his children are well behaved. Nice little mites, in fact."

"Did you perhaps invite him with me in mind, Tony?" she questioned as this suspicion dawned.

"Alas, you're too perceptive for me, wench," he said, grinning at her.

"Well, I'll do my best to attach him, then. Best get on with my beauty sleep," she said with a tightening of her smile. But then she relaxed and added banteringly, "I had best practice my flirting technique." She fluttered her lashes at Tony playfully. "Is this how Miss Milverton does it? I shall have to take lessons from her. What does she do that you find most appealing, Tony?"

"You'll have to practice pouting with your lips," he quipped.

"You mean like this." She formed her mouth into a perfect pout and Tony, not slow off the mark, leaned down and kissed her tenderly on those invitingly soft, warm lips. His hand, which had been resting on her shoulder, accidentally brushed against her breast as he lowered it to clasp her around the waist. She jerked back slightly at the touch.

"Oh, Tiny, you didn't need to do that. I was only joking."

"I know, but look where we're standing." He grinned again and pointed over their heads, where a large bunch of mistletoe tied with red ribbon was dangling from one of the beams of the arched ceiling.

Clio stuck her tongue out at him and proceeded upstairs,

her cheeks a bit heated and her heart beating just a little faster than was its custom.

Tony watched her climb the steps musingly. Since when had Clio had such feminine curves? She used to be quite lacking in that department as a girl, he remembered. And that lighthearted kiss had given him quite a jolt. He was surprised that he had actually wanted to reach out and pull her tightly against him and kiss her properly. And it was his cousin *Clio* he was having these thoughts about, he reminded himself severely, shaking his head in stupefaction. Now if it had been Miss Marianne Milverton, that little bundle of femininity, cuddly as a kitten . . . but Clio— more like a tiger with sharp claws. Must be the spirit of the season infecting him so giddily, he grinned to himself, not to mention the spiked mulled cider he had just drunk.

The following day was snowy and cold, but the spirits of all were uplifted when they awoke and looked out of their bedroom windows to see the bright, sparkling picture that met their eyes. The snow of last evening now lay like a shimmering white blanket covering the Priory lawns, stretching as far as one could see.

In the nursery the children were occupied in drawing finger pictures on the frosty window panes. "I'm afraid if you don't finish dressing soon, there will be no time for sledding today," Serena said to convince her three to pull their outdoor clothing on, while John Parker was helping Carrie put her arms through the sleeves of her new fur-trimmed coat. Sam sat on the floor at his father's feet struggling to pull on his outdoor boots.

Above the peals of laughter and squeals of excitement, Serena heard the knock on the open nursery door.

"Can you use any help?" Marianne Milverton asked brightly as she tripped into the room, already decked out in a forest green, hooded cloak and black boots with green and red tassels.

"Ah, Marianne, come in, my dear," Serena said. "An ex-

272

tra pair of hands would be most welcome, don't you agree, Major Parker?"

"Yes, indeed. If Miss Milverton would be so kind as to button Carrie into her coat, I could help this young gentleman of mine pull on his new boots." John smiled up at Marianne from where he knelt in front of his daughter. Marianne's breath caught in her throat as she saw him looking up at her. A lock of his black hair had fallen forward over his eyes, and he brushed it back impatiently, missing the look of tenderness that came over Miss Milverton's face at the picture he and his daughter presented.

"Would you let Miss Milverton help you, sweetheart?" he asked Carrie.

Carrie nodded shyly and walked over to Marianne and smiled up at her, her bright green eyes wide. Marianne knelt down beside the child. "This is such a pretty coat. Is it new?"

Another nod of shining black locks, so like her papa's. "Papa got it for me for Christmas, but he said I was to have it early."

"Well, what a nice papa you have. It was very thoughtful of him to give it to you early, for you will need it today."

"Papa, Mr. Clausen came in earlier to read us a story about a jolly snowman who came to life and played with all the children. May we build a snowman of our very own?" Sam asked excitedly. The Amberton children had broached this idea with their mother moments earlier and all five children now began to jump up and down in their enthusiasm.

"Well, what do you think, Mrs. Amberton? Shall we organize these children into teams and build a family of snowmen?" John asked.

"Yes, yes!" chorused Sophie, Tom, and Sam. The two younger girls, Carrie and Phyllis, looked hopefully at their parents for the decision.

Serena laughed. "Well, I think that's an excellent idea. You shall have to use your organizational skills to marshal the troops, Major Parker. Everyone must agree to keep their mittens on and to let us know if they become too cold or if their fingers or feet feel like they're going to fall off from the freezing snow."

Marianne clapped her hands. "Oh! May I join in? I haven't built a snowman since I was a little girl."

"You're welcome to help, Marianne, if you're willing to get your beautiful coat wet through and through. The more adult hands, the better, don't you think, Major Parker?" Serena laughed.

"Miss Milverton, are you sure you want to risk yourself with this group of wild savages?" John teased.

"Please, Papa." Carrie pulled at his jacket. "May Miss Milverton be on my team?"

"Well, Miss Milverton, what do you say? Would you like to help this little imp, here?"

"Oh, yes. It will be such fun. What kind of snowman or snowlady shall we make, Carrie?"

John's smile was a bit crooked as he looked down to see Marianne Milverton stoop down and put her arm around the waist of his shy little daughter. He had thought the girl a rather flirtatious little minx the night before, but today he saw that she had a kind heart to go with her beautiful face.

Tony greeted the party as it trooped out to the south lawn, where extra snow had accumulated at the bottom of a gentle slope. The children were chattering loudly in their impatience to be outside.

When he asked about the state of their sledding party, the children informed him of the change in plans. "Ah, you're all going to build snowmen, instead," he responded.

Clio, passing by on one of her many errands, overheard the slight disappointment in Tony's voice. Why, he had been looking forward to the sledding, much as a child would! She smiled to herself. "Tony, perhaps you can go sledding in the afternoon," she suggested.

"Yes, let's do that, Lord Maitland," Marianne said with a bubbling laugh as she looked up at him. She was holding tightly to Carrie Parker's mittened hand. "Why don't you join us now and help. You could be on a team, too."

"Well . . ." He hesitated and looked at Clio.

"Yes, go on, Tony," Clio said. She could tell that he very much wanted to join in. "I can very well see that the best china for our Christmas Day meal is taken out of storage and carefully unpacked."

"I promised to help you, Clio. Come, let's do it together."

"No, no. It won't take me long, and one of the footmen will help lift the boxes. You go on with your guests. It will be fun."

"I'll go only if you promise to join us when you've finished. If you don't come out in half an hour, I'll come and get you and carry you outside, kicking and screaming, and dump you in a snowbank." Clio laughed and resisted the temptation to stick her tongue out at him as she had the night before.

"Do come out and join us, Clio, as soon as you can. And if Nigel gets back from town with the last-minute provisions you decided we needed, send him out, too," Serena called to her as she led her troop down the stairs of the back terrace, reminding them all to take care on the slippery steps.

Clio had an amused smile on her face as she watched Tony run after the party of children.

"Snow makes children of us all, doesn't it, Miss Ingram?" Mr. Clausen came up behind her and looked out at the happy group.

"Yes, there's something about its purity and beauty, especially when it first falls, that tempts us all to go out and play in it. That is, if it doesn't fall on us when we're in the middle of a journey somewhere or other and leave us stranded far from home and friends."

"I shall be making a long journey in the snow soon."

"Will you? Where will you go?"

"Ah," he said, laying his finger beside his nose, "I'm afraid that's a secret for now, my dear Miss Ingram."

Clio listened to him with a distracted air. She was watching the group from the long window beside the door and

275

saw Tony catch up to Marianne and link his arm through hers. She turned away abruptly, preparing to get on with her work.

"I must say, Miss Ingram, you looked quite lovely last night. Lady Maitland tells me you have a special new gown you're saving for Christmas Eve. It will be a treat for us all to see you decked out for the festive occasion."

"You seem to have quite an interest in ladies' fashions, Mr. Clausen."

He chuckled. "I like to see the ladies make the most of their assets, and you, Miss Ingram, have been hiding your light under a bushel long enough. It quite lifts a gentleman's spirits to see a pretty woman well dressed. . . . But I'm keeping you from your work. Best make haste so that you'll be able to join them. Take the children a few things to decorate their creations, a few carrots for noses and some pieces of coal for eyes. Perhaps one of the footmen can dig out some old coats and hats and scarves. It's amazing how a little decoration seems to transform a heaped mound of snow and bring a snowman to life, just as the right dress can highlight a woman's assets to best advantage," he called after her as Clio strode away in businesslike fashion.

His words made an impression on her, though, and not just those about decorating and transforming frozen bits of ice and snow.


At the great age of seven Sophie, the oldest Amberton child, insisted she wanted to make her snowman on her own, while each of the other children had the help of an adult: Marianne with Carrie, Serena with Phyllis, John with Sam, and Tony with Tom. Serena kept a close eye on her older daughter and lent a surreptitious hand now and again. There was much laughter and teasing as the adults competed with one another as much as they helped the children. John and Tony, in particular, were determined to build the biggest snowman.

When Clio came out, followed by a footman with a box full of old clothes and oddments, she was greeted with shouts from all sides, asking her to give her opinion on which was the best, the tallest, the roundest, snowman of them all. She laughingly declined to be made to judge as she handed round carrots and pieces of coal and funny pieces of old clothing, and then helped Sophie decorate her snowman, a lopsided but friendly-looking figure. They decided to give him a crooked grin and a winking eye. Sophie loudly claimed hers was the most human-looking of them all, for cousin Clio had given him a proper face.

Friendly arguments and shouting and laughter ensued. Who threw the first snowball, no one afterward could say. Clio could have sworn it was Tony, while Serena pinned the blame on her irrepressible five-year-old son, Tommy.

Within minutes the children were happily pelting each other with fistfuls of snow, while among the adults a fierce competition was also taking place. John hit Marianne on the shoulder and when she turned in surprise, he held up his hands, saying, "I'm sorry Miss Milverton. My aim must be off. I was trying to knock the hat off your snowman."

"Oh, really, Major Parker. Do you expect me to believe that? I'm not so easily fobbed off." She picked up a handful of snow and held it between her two green mittens as she advanced on him.

As she came up to him, John grabbed her hands when she tried to throw the snow into his face. She twisted and turned, her hands caught between his. "Oh, Major Parker, unfair, unfair!" She laughed breathlessly.

He held her still, his green eyes glinting down at her. At the sight of soft pink lips and snow melting on her lashes, John's heart skipped a beat.

"Why, Miss Milverton, if you want to play the game, you must pay the forfeit." He leaned down and claimed her lips in a swift kiss. Marianne surprised herself exceedingly by kissing him back.

On the far side of the slope Clio hit Tony full in the back

of the head with a large lump of cold, wet snow for daring to laugh at her efforts to make Sophie's snowman look human.

"I was modeling him after you, Tiny," she said sweetly as he turned to look at her, determination writ large on his face. "Uh-oh," she exclaimed and turned to run, for she knew from their childhood fracases that he was likely to take his revenge with a little something extra added for good measure—to remember him by, he would say.

She ran down around the slope of the south lawn to the row of hedges at the west side of the Priory. He followed her, knowing that she couldn't escape him for long. Clio ducked in and out of the privet hedge, laughing like a girl.

"You may as well give up, Clio. It's going to be tit for tat, my girl, for daring to land me such a flush hit when I was off guard." He was almost upon her when Clio dodged him, ducking under his arm. Unfortunately she tripped on the hem of her skirt and fell forward into the soft snow.

"Ha! Got you now," Tony said, advancing on her with a large grin on his face.

She lifted her foot and caught his ankle, tripping him up. As he fell she tried to scramble out of the way, but he reached out an arm and brought her sprawling again. Rolling her over on top of himself, he pinned her arms above her head with his hands.

"Clio Ingram when will you learn that you can't get away with assaulting me without some punishment in return?"

She looked into those familiar dancing blue eyes only inches away and gave in to her childish impulse to stick her tongue out at him. "You were ever a bully, for all you were so undersized as a boy."

"Clio . . . your tongue is bringing you into as much danger as it always used to."

She struggled to get away, laughing, while he transferred her two hands to his right one and used his weaker left hand to unbutton her thick outer garment. He planned to tickle her mercilessly.

"Stop, stop! Tiny . . ." She laughed and moved her head

back and forth as she struggled to free her hands.

"This will teach you, Clio." Tony was trying to tickle her under her arms, but she was flailing about so with her legs that he abruptly flipped her beneath him.

Neither knew when their play changed tenor, but suddenly they were looking into one another's eyes, each breathing shallowly. Tony became aware of a tremor in his thighs where Clio lay against him.

Her gray eyes widened as she saw him looking purposefully at her parted lips. She couldn't help but moisten them with the tip of her tongue. . . .

"Clio, Tony, where are you?" Serena called. "Oh, shameful," she said, coming upon them as they were struggling to get up. Both of them were covered with snow, and Clio's cloak was hanging open. "Rolling about on the ground like children! What an example you have set for the youngsters." She grinned at them and helped Clio brush herself off.

Clio was blushing, not daring to look at Tony. What in the world had been about to happen? she wondered in acute embarrassment.


The children had straggled back to the house, happy and tired, and had agreed to a quiet rest in the nursery after luncheon before undertaking any more activity that afternoon. Truth to tell, the adults were as tired as the youngsters and welcomed the respite, and several of them were trying to sort out confused thoughts.

Marianne had taken refuge in the nursery with the children, while John Parker was pacing from the morning room to the library and back again.

Tony stood in the privacy of his study, looking out the double French windows at the snow-covered lawn beyond where he had tumbled Clio to the ground and wondering what in the devil's name had gotten into him to behave in such a way. He had suddenly been seized with the desire to kiss his old playfellow until she begged for mercy. Surely *that* hadn't been the punishment he had had in mind when he began to tickle her!

He berated himself for his lack of control. It was true that he had been a long time without a woman; since before he was wounded, in fact. But that was no excuse for having *that* kind of urge where Clio was concerned. My God! Clio was as good as his sister, wasn't she? Instead he should concentrate on the little Milverton. Nodding his head in sudden decision he determined to steal a kiss from her under the mistletoe this very night.

Clio busied herself upstairs, preparing some of the baskets to be presented to the servants on Boxing Day. She deliberately tried to banish thoughts of Tony by blanking her mind to the episode in the snow—she succeeded for all of half a minute. Her treacherous response had almost betrayed her emotions to him, she felt sure. Blushing, she remembered the feel of his body covering hers. He had only been playing—just as he had when he'd kissed her last night. But loving him as desperately as she did, it was awfully hard not to let her love show when he held her so and looked at her with desire in his eyes. Everything had been perfectly comfortable between them since he had come home from the war until he had kissed her last night, she thought, sighing deeply. She was going to have to conquer this ridiculous response she had to his every touch, every glance, or she would soon make a complete fool of herself for all to see.

John found Marianne in the nursery, sitting on the floor and reading a children's version of the Christmas story to Sophie, Tom, and Sam. The younger ones, Phyllis and Carrie, were yet napping.

"Might I have a word with you, Miss Milverton," he said at the door to the nursery.

Oh dear, he looks quite serious. I hope he's not going to scold, Marianne thought, biting her lip as she got to her feet to follow him out into the hallway.

"I'm sorry for what happened outside earlier, and I beg that you will accept my apology, Miss Milverton," he said without preamble. "My conduct was entirely uncalled for."

He looked over her left shoulder as he spoke, Marianne noted. Her shoulders drooped in dejection at his tone.

"Major Parker, there's no need. . . ." She blushed. She wanted to raise her hand and touch his arm, but she couldn't seem to let go of the folds of her skirt, which she clutched nervously in both hands.

"No. There's every need. What I did was not the act of a gentleman. It won't happen again. I pray you will excuse me, please," he said as he bowed stiffly. Then he turned and walked away.

Marianne looked after him sadly, nibbling on her lower lip. She had come to the Priory fully intending to do her best to attract the attentions of Anthony Maitland, but when she had met Major John Parker her plans had been scattered to the four winds. Once she had looked upon his handsome face and gazed into his melancholy green eyes, she had felt an irresistible attraction to the man. Though she was trying, the pull was too strong to be suppressed.

Yes, and his children were little darlings, she thought. She had never known she was the motherly type, but to have little Carrie, who looked so much like her father with those shining black curls and deep green eyes, clinging to her hand and looking up at her so trustingly, had tugged at her heartstrings. Whenever she was near the major she had a queer feeling in the pit of her stomach that was quite new to her. And when he looked into her eyes she became quite breathless. The light touch of his lips against hers when he had kissed her that morning had sent a warm glow tingling all the way down to her toes. She sighed and went back into the nursery to the children. She would just have to console herself by redoubling her efforts to attract Lord Maitland, she told herself resignedly.

John walked away from Miss Milverton with his jaw

clamped shut and his fists clenched tightly at his side. His thoughts were confused. She was a lovely young girl, but he was far too old for her. And, burdened as he was with two young children, any inclination to court her—and he admitted it was a strong one—would have to be sternly suppressed. Miss Ingram was the lady he should seek to know better. His children responded well to her, too. She was a little older, more mature, more sensible than the vivacious Miss Milverton. If her rather understated appearance and calm manner and common sense didn't stir his senses, then so be it. He was not about to become a cradle robber at his age!

To Serena's relief, Nigel returned from town in the early afternoon. "It's started to snow again," he reported, "and it's getting quite deep out there. Beginning to look like we might even be snowbound for a few days. It's lucky Tony has that old sleigh, should we need it; for I saw several wagons bogged down on the way to and from town."

"I wonder if I might borrow the sleigh myself, Lord Maitland, to go into town this afternoon?" Clausen asked.

"Are you sure you feel up to undertaking such a journey? It's pretty damn, pardon me, it's devilish treacherous out there," Nigel said.

"Oh, my stars, don't think of risking yourself, Mr. Clausen!" Miss Ellie exclaimed anxiously.

"Now, now. Don't disturb yourself, ma'am," Clausen said, taking up Miss Ellie's hand and patting it kindly. "I find that I still haven't completed my shopping. Afraid I'm a bit of a slowtop at these things." He laughed at himself. "I will use my own team, of course. They are quite used to long, cold journeys and are quite steady in the snow. I must finish before tomorrow night—wouldn't want any disappointed faces on Christmas morning."

"He's a funny man," Serena stated to the room at large as Clausen took himself off to the stables after securing Tony's permission to borrow the sleigh yet again. "Always off on some secretive shopping expedition or other. He must be quite plump in the pocket to afford all the gifts he seems to be buying."

"Yes, I don't know quite what to make of him—or even why he turned up here in the first place. Clio doesn't seem to know, either. He arrived at the door one day, just as Mama had bid her last whist-playing guest farewell, asking if he could rack up here for the night. When Mama discovered he could play her favorite game, well, he was persuaded to stay on," Tony responded in a bemused tone.

"Still, he's made Aunt Hermione very happy, Tony. You should be grateful to the man," Serena commented.

"Should I? I don't know that, Serena," Tony said with a gleam in his eye. "To be always playing cards to the exclusion of all else seems a dreadful waste of one's time, not to mention boring one to flinders."

Serena laughed. "Everyone to his own taste, my dear."

Clio delayed her return to the drawing room for as long as she could, but it was time for the tea tray to arrive. Aunt Hermione would expect her to pour, and she was never one to shirk her duty. She descended the stairs, took a deep breath as she put her hand on the doorhandle to the drawing room where everyone was congregated, and walked in to actually hear her aunt bestir herself to suggest some entertainment for the guests.

"If you're all going to stay indoors this afternoon," Lady Maitland called from her place at the card table, "I suggest you organize a search through the house and attics. As a gel, we always had treasure hunts at Christmas time. Perhaps if all of you look hard enough, someone can turn up that dratted ring!"

Clio blinked in surprise, then said, "I think that an excellent notion, Auntie. We could look for more decorations, and the children can help as well."

Tony moved his shoulders away from the mantel on which he had been leaning to exclaim, "What! We're not to have our sledding party this afternoon?"

"I'm afraid the light has already grown so dim that there

just isn't time today, Tony dear," Serena pointed out to him.

"Yes, it's a deuced pity that the sun sets so early in December. I was in Portugal so long I'd forgotten how much further north England is," Tony said as he moved to look out the window. "I believe the wind has gotten up, too, to judge by all the snow swirling about."

"Perhaps when we are all fresh and rested in the morning, we can take the children out to sled on the hill below the summerhouse. You remember, Tony, how you and Clio and I used to slide down on our homemade wooden sleds."

Tony laughed at the memories Serena had called forth. "Yes, indeed. And I remember being the fastest down in all our races."

This smug comment provoked a heated rejoinder from Serena, and even Clio voiced a disclaimer. "What a bouncer, Tony! I would say that of the three of us, Serena won more often than you or I did. Besides, you were so reckless and intent on proving your bravery in getting up the highest speed, more often than not you overturned into a snowbank before you reached the bottom." Everyone laughed, and Tony smiled directly into Clio's eyes for the first time that afternoon. She looked away in confusion.

"As you suggested, Serena, we will have to take the children out early tomorrow morning, if you're still of a mind to take them all sledding, for Nigel, John, and I will have to cut the Yule log and cart it to the house in the afternoon. Clio and I found a likely looking specimen in the copse when we were out collecting evergreen boughs. We can't bring it inside until Christmas Eve, you know. Wouldn't want to violate tradition and bring any ill luck down on our heads during the new year," Tony winked at Serena.

"Of course, we remember, old boy," Nigel said. "And you must use the remains of last year's log to light this one. I would wager that Clio has the matter in hand." He looked with raised blond brows to Clio as the person likely to know if this part of the tradition had been preserved while Tony was away.

"Auntie and I *did* have a log last year while Tony was in Portugal, as he had written expressly reminding us to do so. And I do have the pieces to use for kindling this year's. It would be unlucky if we had not, wouldn't it, Aunt Hermione?" Clio looked at the dowager.

"Makes no odds about some dratted pieces of half-burned wood. Won't change the fortunes of this house. We'll have nothing but ill luck until the Maitland ring is found," Lady Maitland insisted. "Are you going to stand about all afternoon, all of you, or are you going to organize a hunt for that ring?" she prodded.

"Let us all just have our tea first, to fortify ourselves, Auntie," Clio answered as a servant entered the room at that moment, bearing the good silver teapot along with a selection of Mrs. Hyssop's Christmas baking. Bite-sized sugar-topped mince pies, currant cakes, and little sweetmeats covered in sweet dough filled the tray, as well as apple tarts and jam pastries and Cook's best bread cut into star shapes and buttered lavishly.

Clio was glad to busy herself over the tea tray, helping everyone to refreshments while Tony acted the jovial host with his guests. Both were taking care to avoid one another until their memories of the morning's incident had somewhat dimmed.

Stationed behind the pot as she was, Clio greeted John Parker with relief when she handed him his cup and, with his ready cooperation, was able to engage him in a sustained conversation. Parker was more than willing to let Miss Ingram distract him as Miss Milverton had just come into the room.

Marianne had been abovestairs since luncheon, but she knew she would be missed at tea time, and her mama would likely come in search of her and ask some awkward questions if she didn't join them. Quietly entering the room, she immediately looked for Major Parker, and when she saw that he turned his back on her without a greeting she flushed and bit her lip. It was evident that he was at pains to ignore her. She fixed a bright smile on her face and made her way to a seat near Anthony Maitland who greeted her effusively.

With one eye on Clio, who chatted intimately with Parker, Tony proceeded to engage Marianne in a light flirtation, accompanied by much laughing and complimenting. Some half an hour later, everyone claimed to be invigorated by the extravagant holiday tea and ready to act on Lady Maitland's suggestion to search at least the attics, if not the whole house.

"Serena, my love, are the children not joining us?" Nigel questioned as his spouse appeared at the top of the attic stairs somewhat later to meet the other adults already assembled there.

"I think not, my dear. I've left them all happily drawing with charcoal and paper in the nursery," she told him. She had decided that the children would be better employed creating pictures of the baby Jesus in the manger rather than getting themselves thoroughly dirty by searching through debris in the attic.

"Look, Tony, remember these?" Clio called over to him spontaneously before she remembered to be embarrassed.

He came to her side to look at the set of four little silver houses she had unwrapped from crumbling old pieces of tissue paper. She had unearthed them from the bottom of the large trunk from which Marianne Milverton was yet pulling things out.

Clio held up the largest house for his inspection. Sitting on his haunches beside her, he took the object from her hands and blew off the dust. He opened the set of small doors at the front of the house and peered inside.

"Yes, of course I remember. Papa used to put something special inside for me to find on Christmas morning when I was a boy. And later, after Papa died, you and I used to hide special gifts for each other inside one or the other of the houses."

"Yes, I remember." She laughed, looking away. She was

all too aware of his shoulder pressing against hers as he remained beside her. "I once worked an atrocious pair of house slippers for you, and another time I gave you an egg from my most treasured bird's nest. You weren't particularly appreciative at the time, Tony!"

"Yes, and I gave you a whole succession of my cast-off or worn-out treasures. I remember the rudimentary fly I made for fishing in the stream, thinking that you'd like to try your luck with it as I'd never had a single nibble when I used it, and an old pair of my driving gloves. Now those were a rare prize, you must admit. And when I was more sophisticated, I realized you'd like something feminine and pretty, and so I gave you a bright pink ribbon snipped from one of Mama's gowns," he said, his eyes brimful of laughter.

"Yes, nothing was too good for me. I prized all your gifts, however absurd or useless," she said lightly, hoping he wouldn't realize how near the truth that was.

Tony held up the largest box. "This is the one we thought was a miniature model of the Priory. Remember."

"Yes, I do, Tony. We saw it with the eyes of children, I suppose, because now I can see that the resemblance is only slight."

"Only slight! Why it's the very picture of this house!" Tony exclaimed, his lips quirked in a half-smile as he turned his head and looked into her eyes. "Where's your romantic imagination, Clio?"

"All gone, now that I'm grown up, I'm afraid," she said, rising to her feet. She could not bear to stay in this disturbing proximity to him a second longer. As it was, her breathing was disordered and she felt sure her color was heightened. Thank goodness the gloom of the attic hid her complexion from the others, she thought on a small sigh.

"Let's put them near the hearth for the children to find on Christmas morning, shall we?" Serena said brightly as she keenly watched this byplay. "Perhaps each family could use one house to hide small gifts or messages in—one for Major Parker's family, one for us, the large one for you and

Tony and Aunt Hermione, Clio, and one for the Milvertons. We will have to find something else for Mr. Clausen and the Misses Cartwright."

"What about this for Miss Ellie and Miss Essie?" From her place on the floor next to the trunk Marianne held up an old music box lined with gold cloth. The outside had been covered in multicolored paper and coated with several layers of enamel giving it a most pleasing mosaic effect. When Marianne had dusted it off, everyone could see that it was in perfect condition. She handed it to Tony, who stood up and came around the trunk to assist her to her feet.

"It's kind of you to think of them, Marianne," Serena said, noticing how John was gazing at the girl with a softened expression on his face. Marianne made a very pretty picture standing amid the dusty old furniture and artifacts of several generations of Maitlands, clad as she was in a bright pink woolen gown trimmed with blond lace, her long, gleaming curls catching a bit of light and looking lustrous even in the dimness of the attic. It was clear to Serena that the major was smitten. So much for a match between him and Clio, she thought before she turned to the group at large. "I think this old card case of Uncle Randolph's would do for Mr. Clausen, don't you, Tony? After all, it is made of gold," she said.

"Yes, that will do nicely," Tony agreed. "Well, Mama will be disappointed. We've gone through piles and piles of old rubbish and no sign of the Maitland ring!" he said as they prepared to abandon their search and take their few treasures downstairs.


After dinner, Tony opened the infrequently used ballroom, rolled back the carpet, and asked Serena to play some country dances on the large pianoforte kept there. "Do you trust me not to damage this magnificent instrument? I do tend to pound the keys rather forcefully, you know," she said.

Tony laughed down her protestations. "Give over, Serena, do. You've played on this instrument since you used to visit us as a girl."

Despite persistent quizzing by Nigel and Tony during dinner, Mr. Clausen had been quite taciturn about his latest journey to the small market town five miles distant from the Priory. He was now at his jovial best as he persuaded Lady Maitland to abandon her whist and join them in the ballroom, even to dance with him.

"Lady Maitland, I believe the spirit of the season is moving me to a bit of jollification this evening. Let us abandon the cards for once, dear lady, and show these young folks how to shake a leg, shall we?" he said, cajoling that good lady to take the floor with him. After his dance with the dowager he used his charm to encourage Miss Ellie and then Miss Essie to partner him in turn. Squire and Mrs. Milverton were induced to take to the floor, as well, and they danced energetically, evidently enjoying themselves.

Miss Ellie Cartwright came to relieve Serena at the pianoforte so that she, too, could join the dancers, which she did, radiating high good spirits as she was the partner of John Parker, then her cousin Tony, and finally her own Nigel. Then Marianne asked her mother to play some of the new waltz tunes she had recently learned.

"My dear Marianne, you wouldn't want me to embarrass myself in front of Lord and Lady Maitland and their guests, now would you, dearie?" Mrs. Milverton laughingly protested, afraid that her modest musical talents would not show to advantage.

"Please, Mama," Marianne begged, and Mrs. Milverton's protestations were at last overcome as Lady Maitland, tired of the argument, said, "Oh, go on Martha."

Sitting down at the instrument, Mrs. Milverton began to play one of the scandalous new waltzes for any couple brave enough to try the steps.

John attempted to guide Clio in the unfamiliar movements of the new dance. She was quite light on her feet and soon mastered the steps even though she found it somewhat disconcerting to be held so closely in a gentleman's arms while dancing. She noticed the look of longing on John's face as he gazed over at Marianne, who was waltzing with Tony, then heard his sigh.

"She's a very beautiful girl, is she not, Major Parker?" Clio remarked, glancing over and seeing Marianne laugh gaily up at Tony as the pair executed the steps of the dance with somewhat more verve than she and her partner were exhibiting.

"Alas, am I so transparent, then?" He smiled ruefully.

"I would imagine it would be hard for a gentleman not to be captivated by such beauty, but in this case, I believe Miss Milverton's temperament is as warm as her smile."

"Is it not foolish, Miss Ingram, for an old fellow like me to allow himself to believe he has lost his heart to such a spirited young girl." John laughed self-consciously as he guided Clio down the room, gaining confidence as she easily followed his lead.

"She does have a high spirit, but I believe her heart to be gentle and unselfish despite the tenderness of her years," Clio reassured him.

"The tenderness of her years, indeed," he said on another sigh. "Never fear. I shall not act on my feelings. I wouldn't make such a cake of myself."

"Why, Major Parker, I think you do yourself an injustice. It would be wrong *not* to give yourself a chance at happiness. I must tell you that I, and my cousin Serena, too, have observed that Miss Milverton seems to favor you. Before I came down for tea this afternoon I found her crying in her room, and when I knocked on her door and asked her what had upset her so, she said she feared that she had offended you."

He looked amazed at this information.

"At least give yourself, and her, time to see if the attraction is mutual." Clio continued to encourage him, but he looked skeptical.

Tony glanced over to where John waltzed with Clio, thinking his friend held her much too tightly and that her new gown of shimmering gray-blue watered silk, while extremely fetching, enhanced her newly revealed curves entirely too well. Why, he hadn't realized before Clio had donned her new finery that she had such a shapely form. He clamped his jaw shut as he quelled an angry desire to snatch her from John's arms.

As the dance came to an end, Marianne pleaded, "Play once more for us, Mama, please."

As Mrs. Milverton complied, John bowed to temptation as he stood before Marianne and begged for the honor of her company. "Will you favor me with your hand for this dance, Miss Milverton?"

"Oh, yes, Major," she said on a catch of breath. Blushingly she put her hand in his, and they took the floor.

"Well, Clio, do you think you can trust me not to tread too heavily on your toes if we give it a go," Tony asked her good-humoredly as he extended his right arm to her. "I'm not too experienced at this new dance."

"As for experience, you seemed to be performing like a born caper merchant just now with Miss Milverton. And I've never known you to be ungraceful, Anthony Maitland. Just remember, it will be tit for tat for you, sir, if you so much as *think* about stepping on my feet." She laughed up into his eyes and saw that they were crinkled in amusement. She glanced away again immediately, feeling a distinct jolt in her midsection.

"Ah, you mean to pay me back for this morning, I can see," he said before realizing that this was a most unwise comment. It was a mistake to refer to the snowball fight. Clio was blushing, and he could feel the heat rise in his own cheeks. Yes, and as he held her about the waist with one of her hands in his and the other resting lightly along his shoulder, he could feel again that traitorous response of his body to hers. He hadn't felt like this a minute ago as he'd held little Marianne in a similar embrace. No, he had only felt the fun and exhilaration of the dance and the pleasure of her company. The girl was much more beautiful than Clio, but somehow she didn't provoke this worrying physical reaction.

"Have I told you you look bang up to the nines tonight, Clio. Indeed, I don't believe I've ever seen you looking more beautiful."

"Th-thank you, Tony." Clio faltered, not daring to look at him.

"Is this new come-out having the desired effect on Parker?" he heard himself ask, dismayed to be sounding so irritable.

Clio looked up, hurt and bewildered by his tone.

"I'm sorry, my dear. That was a deuced ill-natured thing to say. Please don't take any notice. I don't know why I'm ripping up at you for looking so lovely. I must be out of sorts, I suppose."

"Never mind. Is your wound bothering you? All the extra activity of this house party must have put quite a strain on you."

"Devil a bit of it!" He grinned. "Oh, there's the odd twinge now and then in my arm, but nothing to signify," he assured her, wanting to remove the look of anxiety on her face. He tightened his arm around her waist and drew her against himself, saw her flush, and immediately loosened his hold.

Why couldn't he act naturally with Clio as he always had? Tony wondered. After all, he had known her most of his life. Why had this heightened awareness of her eyes, her lips, her body arisen so suddenly during this holiday to disturb him so? He swallowed uneasily and looked over Clio's shoulder to where Marianne was dancing with John Parker. He frowned in puzzlement. They were dancing stiffly, and the high-spirited Marianne was blushing and looking at the floor like a witless little ninnyhammer—quite unlike the way she had looked and behaved with him. Had John done or said something to embarrass the girl? He couldn't believe it of his friend. Anyway, he was resolved to rescue her from John's company, as soon as this uncomfortable dance with Clio was over—and claim that kiss under the mistletoe he had promised himself. Maybe then he would forget the feel of Clio in his arms and the strange desire he had to kiss her rather than the winsome Marianne under that bough of greenery.

Tony easily maneuvered Miss Milverton out the ballroom door and had his kiss under the mistletoe. She puckered her lips quite willingly as he bent down to her. But her lips were cold, and he felt no response as he briefly touched her mouth with his own—so different from the feel of Clio's warm, yielding lips last night.

Clio had seen Tony steer Marianne out the door, and she had known with a heart-sinking certainty that he was kissing her. When Tony and Marianne came back in, laughing and joking, she saw the grim lines around Major Parker's mouth, noticed the way his fists were clenched at his sides, and knew that he was upset, too.

Clio walked over to him, took his arm, and led him to the door. "Do not let it upset you so, my dear Major," she said in a low voice, trying to calm him and distract herself, too.

"I'm sorry to show so little control. It's stupid of me, I know."

"We can't help our feelings, Major, and yours are nothing to be ashamed of," Clio said gently.

"Thank you, Miss Ingram. You are very kind," he said even as he spied the gay red ribbon of the very object that had sent his spirits plummeting. "Shall we?" he asked as he led Clio through the door and gestured above their heads. Clio smiled at him as he lowered his head. His lips found her soft ones and lingered there for some little while, seeking and receiving comfort even as he gave comfort in return. The kiss was not as brief as either party had intended, both needing and taking solace for their heartaches. They did not purposely make a spectacle of themselves, but neither had thought to close the partially open door.

Marianne's lips quivered as she saw John kiss Clio, and

she had a hard time not bursting into tears then and there. She wanted to flee to her bedchamber, but that would have meant walking past the couple in the hallway. She turned away and tried to bring herself under control.

Tony stood watching them, a thunderstruck look on his face and a clenching in his stomach. He was furiously jealous. It was all he could do to stop himself from stepping forward, pulling Clio out of Parker's arms, and landing his friend a stinging facer.

"The children all snug in their beds, my love?" Nigel asked as Serena joined him in their bedchamber after she had been to the nursery for a last-minute check. She nodded in her husband's direction. "Yes, I think they will be well rested and ready for more devilment tomorrow, just like their father."

He smiled. "Are you implying that I will be getting up to 'devilment' tomorrow?" he quizzed her. He was lounging against the mantelpiece, his arms folded across his chest as he regarded her lazily. He was wearing a midnight blue silk dressing gown and very little else and the gleam in his eyes was definitely anticipatory she saw, with a heightening of her own senses.

She ignored his taunt as she went to the dressing table to brush out her long hair and instead asked, "Did you see John Parker kissing Clio under the mistletoe?"

"Yes. And I also saw Tony enthusiastically performing the same ritual with Miss Milverton." His sapphire blue eyes twinkled wickedly.

"Somehow I think the two couples are mismatched. Don't you?" Serena asked. "I wish there were some way to get them to change partners."

"Matchmaking, Serena?" Nigel raised his blond brows and grinned at his spouse as he pushed his broad shoulders away from their resting place and came toward her.

"Oh, you!" She picked up a cushion and threw it at him. "You know that Clio has been in love with Tony forever. If only the nodcock would realize the treasure he has right under his own nose! How he can be unaware of it when they would be perfect for one another is beyond me!" she exclaimed. "Instead, he may lose her to John Parker. And it's clear that the handsome major has a *tendre* for little Miss Milverton—but he thinks himself too old for her. . . . What fools you men are sometimes."

"Acquit me of being one of your fools, my love. When I met you, I knew right away I had met my match," Nigel said as he put his hands at Serena's waist and pulled her up against his lean strength. He kissed her soundly, then grinned devilishly. "It's perfectly proper, you see." He raised one hand and held it over her head. She glanced up to see that he held a sprig of mistletoe.

"What foolishness!" She laughed. "If you hadn't been so handsome, I doubt I could have forgiven you your propensity to tease me so unmercifully." She sighed dramatically.

"Ah, thank God I am 'so handsome,' then." He kissed her again lingeringly as he untied her dressing gown and slipped it from her shoulders. "I don't think we have further need of this pagan plant with its reputed magical powers, do you?" he asked huskily, putting one arm under her shoulders and the other under her knees and then picking her up.

"Nigel! Put me down this instant."

"I fully intend to, my love. But first I must tell you what that fellow Clausen has been hinting to me," he said as he carried her the few steps to the bed.

"What?" Serena asked, trying not to let her husband see how breathless he could still make her and what desire he could still arouse in her after nine years of marriage.

"That a brother would be good for Tommy. What do you think of that!" he grinned as he put her down on the sheets. For answer Serena tightened her arms about his neck and brought his head down to hers, showing him her opinion in actions rather than words.

The children awoke in a boisterous mood on Christmas Eve. They hurried to the windows to peer out and make sure their snowmen were still standing. The weather remained frosty and even as they looked about they could see that snow was still drifting lightly onto the rolling lawn.

An hour later the youngsters spilled out of the house, ready for the promised sledding expedition. Tom and Sam were running ahead with Sophie while little Phyllis was being carried in her father's arms. Serena walked behind the children with John Parker, trying valiantly to keep up with them. Marianne walked beside Tony, one arm linked through his, while little Carrie Parker held to her other hand. The child had refused to let go, even when her father had said he would carry her to the small hill Tony had chosen for the sledding.

Although he had been looking forward to the sledding as much as the children, Tony was distracted. Much to his exasperation, Clio had refused to accompany them, saying that she had too much to do at the house. Was he some slave driver that he forced her to work like a drudge in his home while he went off to enjoy himself? he fumed. He didn't want to see Clio acting like some upper servant, and this morning she had infuriated him even further by donning an ugly mobcap to cover her hair.

Carrie decided to run forward and catch hold of her father's hand with her free one, forcing Marianne to go along with her. Serena, despairing of keeping up with the three older children, fell back to walk with Tony. "What ails you, coz, that you should have such a Friday face on this beautiful day?" she asked.

"Oh, nothing. Well . . . it's Clio, I suppose. Why the devil does she insist on acting the drudge? We've hired plenty of extra help for the holiday. She should be out here enjoying herself instead of exhausting herself at the house . . . It's really not necessary. Mama could very well break off her game now and again to lend a hand, too, you know."

"She does it for love of you, Tony, dear," Serena said

boldly. At his startled look, she laughed and said, "She's the sweetest and hardest-working woman I know. She feels obliged to you and Aunt Hermione for providing her with a home all these years."

He gave an inarticulate exclamation. "That's rubbish, you know. We don't expect her to pay back any assistance we've provided with hard labor. We love Clio for herself—"

"Do you, Tony?" She looked at him intently and Tony felt himself flush.

He cleared his throat, then said, "Well, you know, Serena, that she and I have been as brother and sister for many years. Why hasn't she married, do you think?" he asked, changing the subject abruptly.

"Why, I assume she hasn't yet met the right man—or the man she loves is unaware of the fact," she prodded.

"Well, Miss Milverton, Carrie has certainly found a friend in you." John looked at her as his daughter walked between them. "I hope you don't mind her monopolizing you this way."

"Oh, not at all, Major Parker," she said, not quite meeting his eyes. "She is a sweet little girl. I . . . I like both your children. You're lucky to have them!" she added emphatically, angry with herself for always appearing so missish in his company.

"Marianne's coming down with me in the sled." Carrie laughed up at her father.

"No, Carrie. I think you had better let Papa take you down. It wouldn't be fair to ask Miss Milverton, sweetheart."

"Oh, Major Parker, I don't mind in the least. As a matter of fact, I think it would be great fun . . . if you'll allow me to take her, that is."

"I see that I had better consent," he said with a smile. "Else I'll have two ladies berating me for spoiling their fun."

There was much squealing and laughing as groups of

two took turns sliding down the gentle slope Tony led them to. Tom and Sam insisted on going together, paying no heed to Serena's warning that they would overturn if they didn't wait for one of the adults to take them. When they inevitably did turn sideways and tilt over into the soft snow, Nigel teased his wife. "Well, little mother hen, how does it feel to always be in the right of it?"

"Oh, you! They're not in the least hurt. I think they enjoyed rolling in the snow as much as Tony enjoyed taking Phyllis down between his knees. Have you ever seen a grown man get so much enjoyment out of a childish pastime?"

"Well," he said, his eyes twinkling, "I don't know about that. But, if you'll give me your permission, I intend to have a go myself and see if the exercise is as enjoyable as Tony's laughter would indicate."

"Nigel! I never thought I'd see the day when you would risk your dignity!" She laughed at him as he went over to persuade his daughter Sophie to let him sit behind her on her next turn.

Marianne went down once with Carrie, then Carrie's father took her down a second time. Anxious to tell her friend all about her second ride, Carrie tried to get up from her seat too quickly at the bottom of the hill and bumped her knee against the side of the sled in her haste. John picked her up to comfort her, telling her it was only a scratch, but she insisted that she couldn't stop crying until her friend Miss Marianne gave her a hug to console her.

"I'm afraid that nothing will do for Carrie but to tell you all about her injury, Miss Milverton," John said on an embarrassed laugh as he carried his daughter up to where Marianne stood chatting with Tony at the top of the hill.

With a smile, Marianne took Carrie from her father's arms and allowed the child to clasp her about the neck. "It's quite all right, Major Parker. I remember as a little girl wanting my nurse to the exclusion of anyone else—doting parents, grandparents, and any number of aunts and uncles notwithstanding. We ladies have these whims, you

298

know," she teased, and was relieved when he smiled at her more naturally.

When they got home the children were dispatched to the kitchen to make gingerbread men after they shed their wet outdoor clothes. "Mama," Sophie said when she saw the dough Mrs. Hyssop had prepared for them, "I want to make my gingerbread man look just like my snowman!"

"Oh, my," Serena exclaimed with a rueful grin on her face as all the other children digested this idea and then clamored to do the same. Carrie had not released Marianne's hand all the way home, and Marianne had been forced to accompany the child to the kitchen, although she had done so quite willingly. "I think we should make *your* gingerbread man look just like your father! What do you think, Carrie, love?" she said, giving the major a saucy smile when he would have prevented Carrie from dragging her along.

The afternoon flew by in a frenzy of last-minute activities. The men brought in the huge oak Yule log after dinner, and Tony ceremoniously lit it with the charred remains of last year's log. The children were allowed to join the adults while everyone sang a few carols around the hearth as the log began to burn lazily, and Tony assured them it would be properly ablaze when they returned from the midnight church services that were a Maitland family custom. With great difficulty the parents persuaded their excited little ones to go up to their beds and at least *try* to sleep.

"I'll bid you all a happy Christmas now, as I regret I won't be accompanying you to the service," Mr. Clausen said to them as they gathered in the great hallway in preparation for walking the short distance along the snowy path Tony had cleared to the Priory chapel.

"And a happy Christmas to you, Mr. Clausen. We'll see you tomorrow, then," replied the dowager, muffled in her best furs. She did not quite like this desertion as she had counted on his arm for support.

He winked at her and said enigmatically, "Never fear, my dear Lady Maitland, tomorrow there will certainly be a gentleman eager to sit at your card table and partner you." And he gave them all a cheery wave as they set out.


Walking home from the candlelit service, Marianne found herself holding onto the arm of Major Parker without quite knowing how it had come about. She had planned to attach herself firmly to Lord Maitland. She didn't want to embarrass herself more than she felt she had already by revealing her emotions to a man like John Parker, an experienced man of the world who undoubtedly looked on her as a naive schoolgirl.

She could feel the tension in his supporting arm even as her fingers, jumping with nerves, rested along its coat-clad length.

"Miss Milverton, I have been wanting to speak to you privately all day, but somehow we—I—never had the opportunity."

Without looking up at him, Marianne spoke breathlessly, "What was it you wanted to say to me, Major Parker?"

"My dear, I've known you such a short time, but I've come to feel for you . . . you've been so kind to my children, especially Carrie. . . . You're so lovely! May I call on you—get to know you better?" His military forthrightness came to the fore as he decided it was time to quit shilly-shallying and come straight to the point. "Damn it all, Marianne, I want to know whether or not there is any hope for an old codger like me?"

"An old codger?" Marianne said on a spurt of laughter. "Oh, John . . ." She looked up at him finally, her eyes shining. "Do you love me?"

"Love you? I adore you! Is there any hope you could come to view my suit favorably?" he asked anxiously, confused by the teasing way she was looking at him.

"Oh, John! I fell in love with you, too—the minute I met

you! But I thought you would think me an empty-headed ninnyhammer, never sophisticated enough for a handsome man of the world like you."

"Do you mean to tell me all my agonizing and holding back has been for nought?"

"Don't look so surprised, my love. I've been doing my best to keep away from you, afraid that you would see me languishing after you and laugh at me for being silly."

"*Laugh* at you?" He stopped walking abruptly and pulled her into his arms beneath the leafless lime trees lining the walk back to the Priory. "I would never laugh at you. *This* is what I've wanted to do to you for ages," he said as he took her face between his gloved hands and bent to kiss her properly. Marianne sighed and threw her arms around his neck, giving herself up to his kiss and his care for a lifetime.

"Tony dear, is your arm paining you?" Clio asked, seeing the frown on his face as he stood before the now blazing Yule log, holding a glass of brandy between his slender fingers. She was surprised to see him still up and wondered what was keeping him from his bed. Everyone else had retired after returning from the midnight service. Clio was just checking out a few last-minute details.

Tony turned at her entrance and set his empty glass on the high mantelpiece among the evergreen boughs entwined with red ribbons that Clio had used to decorate the room.

"No more than one could expect from the workout it's had in the last few days," he replied, flexing his arm slightly as he gave her a somewhat lopsided smile. "Don't look so concerned, my dear, it's been worth it. I admit that I'm tired this evening, but I've enjoyed our party, haven't you?"

"Indeed, I have, Tony. And it's given your mother a great deal of pleasure, too. Though she's worried about where Mr. Clausen has disappeared to this evening. . . . What a surprise about John and Marianne, though! You're not upset about it, are you?"

"Surprised? No." He waved a hand in dismissal of such a thought. "Clausen tipped me the wink that the wind was blowing in that direction. I daresay he gave the lovebirds a nudge or two in the right direction as well." He grinned widely.

"Yes, he always seems to be nudging and winking everyone into doing what's best for them, whether they will or not. Almost as though he knows something the rest of us aren't aware of."

"So, it's not to be John for you or Marianne for me, it seems. Are you very disappointed, Clio? John's not the man for you, you know."

"No, I never supposed he was." She shrugged indifferently, but Tony heard the tiny sigh she could not suppress.

"Have you been hard at work since we returned from church, seeing that all is in readiness for tomorrow — or should I say today?"

"There were one or two last-minute things I had to see to, but all should be to your satisfaction now, my lord," she said, perking up slightly. Her eyes, reflecting the firelight, gleamed brightly at him.

He smiled at her teasingly. "Have I thanked you enough for all the hard work you've put in these past weeks?" he said, thinking again how beautiful she looked in her new silk gown with her curls, now charmingly ruffled, framing her delicate face. "You're remarkable, Clio, do you know that?" he said on an exhalation of breath he didn't know he'd been holding.

She blushed rosily but didn't drop her eyes from his. "Trying to turn me up sweet, are you? And what next will you ask of me to serve your pleasure, sir?" she said lightly, thinking to tease him further. Was he thinking to pour the sauce over her because he wanted her to help oversee his next house party? she wondered uneasily, thinking she could not bear to see him flirting with any more eligible young beauties.

"My pleasure?" He lifted a brow. "Come over here and

I'll show you."

"Don't be so silly," she scoffed, a bit disconcerted that her own words had given him such an opening.

"Afraid, Clio?" He grinned and beckoned her over to his side. She stood her ground. Tony pushed his shoulders away from the mantelpiece and walked over to her, a light twinkling in his eyes as he did so.

"You're standing in a *most* opportune place for my pleasure, you know." His blue eyes glinted down at her as he put his hands on her shoulders and drew her nearer. "How fortunate that Nigel reminded Serena to hang a fresh bunch of mistletoe before the Yule fire on Christmas Eve. It's traditional, you know. . . ."

"Tony, don't be mad! Have you lost your senses!" she said, but she didn't struggle when he raised his hands and caressed her face with gentle fingers.

"John's had a turn. Surely you can give your favorite cousin as many privileges as you do a mere acquaintance. Best wishes of the season, my dear," he whispered, then lowered his head and kissed her warmly.

He looked up again almost immediately. "I haven't *lost* my senses, my dear; I've just come to them," he said huskily as he kissed her again, setting his arms at her waist and pulling her firmly against him. This time his lips were not gentle nor did he lift them after a brief moment. Instead, he increased the pressure and opened his mouth over hers, demanding a response that Clio was helpless to deny him.

"Oh, Tony, I do love you so," she murmured against his lips as she wound her arms around his neck and pressed herself against his warm length. She had been waiting for this, wanting this to happen for years, ever since she had become aware that she didn't love Tony at all as one did a brother. And if it were only a special Christmas Eve gift, then she would accept it and give him back kiss for kiss, using these few enchanted minutes to show him all the love she was capable of giving. She loved him totally, and the last few days when he had touched her and kissed her, in a way no mere friend and relative should, would be the most

303

precious memories of her life. A Christmas gift to remember, to take out and examine in the privacy of her thoughts, to warm her heart in the lonely years ahead.

His arms were as bands of steel forging them together, he hugged her so tightly, trying to draw her into his very soul. The embrace, along with his breathing and heartbeats, spun out of control as he kissed her with a longing he could no longer suppress. He kissed her lips, her face, her eyes, her neck, murmuring endearments against her soft skin, even as he moved his hands over her body, willing her to feel as deeply as he did the strength of the emotion between them.

One of the faggots used to light this year's Yule log hissed amid the flames and fell to the hearth, splintering into pieces and startling the two lost in an embrace that had rendered them both shaky and breathless. Tony looked up, and Clio jumped back from his arms, her breast heaving as she looked at him out of passion-glazed eyes.

Without her there to support him Tony felt as though his knees would give way. He put a hand up to his face and began to laugh at how shaky he felt and at the wonder and joy of finding that the love of his life had been under his nose all these years without him recognizing it until now. "Well, how do you like that, Clio!" He grinned, extending a hand to her that was not quite steady. But at his laughter all her newly fledged hope died, and she turned and fled without seeing his gesture.

"Damnation! Come back here, Clio. Clio . . ." But the door had closed behind her. She was gone. Tony was left to get himself under control and wonder what to do next.


Christmas morning dawned bright but cold. The children were to open their presents in the nursery with their parents, and no one else had come downstairs yet when Tony entered the drawing room. He walked forward and drew the curtains back from the long windows that looked out over the southeastern side of the house to see that the sun was beginning to brighten the eastern sky. Its light just touched the blanket of white spread across the Priory lawns, making the icy snow crystals sparkle like a thousand winking diamonds as far as his eyes could see. He was almost blinded by the prospect; he turned away, blinking wearily. He had been quite unable to sleep due to wondering how on earth he was going to pin Clio down long enough to ask her to marry him when she kept scurrying away from him every time he touched her. Yet he was convinced that she had responded to his heated embraces with an ardor equal to his. Take last night, for instance — especially last night. . . .

As he looked toward the hearth to see that the Yule log still burned brightly, he heard the door open behind him. He turned quickly to see Clio standing across the room, her complexion turning fiery red at the sight of him.

"Happy Christmas, my dear!" he said, looking at her apprehensively. "Don't go!" he said as she made to leave. He knew he must convince her that he loved her and that she must marry him without delay. While he debated how best this would be accomplished, she moved across the room, avoiding his gaze.

To escape Tony's scrutiny Clio walked over to the hearth, bent down, and picked up the silver house she was to share with him and her aunt, hoping madly all the while that someone else would come into the room soon. He followed her over and watched as she opened the double front doors of the little house and removed a small package wrapped in gold cloth.

"Clio —" he began to say.

"Whatever is this, I wonder?" she asked to forestall him. She could feel his eyes on her, like a caress, and her fingers began to tremble nervously.

"You open it, Clio," Tony said. A small smile played about his mouth as he watched her and thought how utterly lovely she looked this morning, with her curls looking quite tumbled and her complexion still tinged pink from her confusion in his presence.

Still not daring to look at him, Clio fumbled with the wrapping and uncovered a small box. Lifting the lid she beheld an ornate gold ring set with an overabundance of diamonds and rubies. "Oh!" she exclaimed in astonishment.

"What is it, Clio?"

"Why, this must be the Maitland ring—the ring that Aunt Hermione has moaned about all these years!"

"So it is." Tony reached over and took the ring from her nerveless fingers. "I remember Mama wearing it when I was a lad," he said, holding it up to the light.

"But . . . Who can have put it in here? Was it you, Tony?"

"Not I, my sweet. Look, there's a note," Tony said as they saw a bit of white paper flutter to the floor when he lifted the box and shook it. Clio stooped and picked it up.

"Why, it's from Mr. Clausen," she said as she spread open the small sheet and read the message. " 'To the happy couple on this Christmas morning. May every Christmas you have together be as joyous as this one.' What in the world can he mean?"

"Oh, I think I know what he means, Clio," Tony said, a wide smile lighting his face. "He means this." He picked up her left hand and slid the ring onto her third finger.

"Tiny!" Aghast, she looked down at her hand resting in his, reverting to his nickname in her agitation. "But, no. . . ."

" 'No?' You mean 'yes,' don't you, my love?" He grinned.

Clio looked up at him, not daring to believe what she was hearing just yet, but he was looking at her with such love shining in his eyes that her heart began to somersault in her breast.

"Will you marry me, my sweet darling? As soon as possible?"

"You *can't* want me!"

"Oh, can't I just! Why do you think I've been unable to keep my hands off you and my mind from thinking about you every aching hour of the day until I thought I would

306

go mad. I've realized, at long last, my love, that you are the only woman for me. Forgive me for being such a slow-top all these years. It was that fellow Clausen who finally opened my eyes to what a gem you are, Clio, my love!" He reached out and drew first one of her arms, then the other, round his waist, before placing his fingers along either side of her jaw to tilt her face up to his.

Seeing her still looking dubious, he said, "Ah, you still doubt me, do you, love? Well, if my honeyed words won't persuade you that I speak the truth, then I'll have to resort to physical coercion to make you believe me." He lowered his head and touched her lips with his. Meeting with no re-sistance, he began to prove by actions more eloquent than mere words that he did, indeed, mean what he had said. When she was on the way to being thoroughly convinced, as evidenced by her arms tightening about his neck and her yielding body arching into his, he looked up from his task and asked in an uneven voice, "Convinced yet, my darling love?"

She smiled up at him. "Umm. Not just yet, my love. I think I would like a little more inducement to accept you."

"Take a lot of convincing, do you? That suits my purpose admirably, my girl. I've hardly begun yet!" As Tony was willing to devote the rest of his life to convincing her of his love, and Clio seemed to enjoy his methods, they spent a blissful Christmas morning enthusiastically demonstrating their mutual affection.


"It's all very well for the six of you to engage in such bill-ing and cooing. But it's enough to drive the rest of us loony," Lady Maitland remarked as a Christmas twilight fell outside the Priory windows. She looked over in turn to where Tony and Clio sat side by side on the settee, holding hands, and to where John bent down next to Marianne, who knelt on the floor, helping Carrie dress her doll for the tenth time that day. Sam played nearby, and Nigel and Serena sat in wing chairs smiling across at one another over the heads of their children.

Everyone was sitting around, too full to move after a huge Christmas dinner of stuffed goose with all the trimmings, capped off by a flaming Christmas pudding with rum sauce. And now even the children were playing quietly on the floor near the fireplace after the excitements of the morning.

"Yes, Serena—no need to look at me like that, my girl. I include you and Nigel, too."

"You're just jealous because your cicisbeo has deserted you, Mama." Tony laughed after referring to the absence of Clausen who had not returned to the Priory.

"Pish-tish. Cicisbeo indeed! But where in blue blazes could Clausen have got to, answer me that?"

"No one knows, Aunt Hermione," Serena said. "He just disappeared."

"Apparently he went to the stables and harnessed his team to Tony's old sleigh just after we left for church and set off for God-knows-where in the middle of the night," Nigel told them. "Your groom said the sleigh was weighed down with large bundles of Christmas gifts wrapped in bright paper. Didn't Clausen leave you a note, Tony, saying he would see that your sleigh was replaced with a new one as soon as he reached his home and could make the arrangements? Pretty fair exchange, if you ask me. That sleigh of yours was falling apart, old man," Nigel laughed.

"Well, why didn't he leave anything for me, or at least a note telling *me* his plans," the dowager asked querulously. "He just up and vanished, leaving me without a partner. Just when I'm learning to play this new version of whist the Milvertons are teaching me," she said, nodding to Marianne's parents. "Ellie and Essie can't seem to get the hang of it at all, drat them."

As if on cue, the Maitland butler appeared in the drawing room with the news that a visitor had arrived.

An elderly, rather stout man walked into the room. "Brewster Hawthorne! Fancy you turning up after all these years!" Lady Maitland exclaimed, holding her hands out to

308

the newcomer in greeting. The plump but impeccably garbed gentleman walked into the room and came forward to take the dowager's hands and place a flourishing kiss on each one.

"It was most extraordinary, Hermione, but a fellow named Clausen called on me last week, asking if I could recall anything about the Maitland engagement ring and extracting my promise that I leave my cozy fireside and visit you here on Christmas Day," Hawthorne said.

Tony recognized the man as a distant connection of his mother's. "It's the deuced fellow who first taught Mama to play whist," he whispered to Clio, his lips against her ear. "The man has a lot to answer for."

"Clausen called on you?" the dowager asked, puzzled. "But how did he know you? And *did* you know anything about the ring?"

"Of course I did. Don't you remember, Hermione, you gave it to me for safekeeping more than a dozen years ago?"

"No! I don't recall I did that."

"Well, you did, my dear. It was shortly before poor Maitland died, and perhaps you were so distracted after the tragedy that you forgot. I never recalled the ring until that Clausen fellow mentioned it. In any event, I gave it to him and he assured me he would return it to you. Has he done so?"

"He certainly did. Just in time, too," Tony said as he lifted Clio's left hand to show Hawthorne that the ring was being put to its proper use in proclaiming the engagement of the lord of Maitland Priory to his chosen lady. Tony then brought the hand he held to his lips and smiled into Clio's eyes.

"Well, now that *that* mystery is solved, what do you say to a hand of whist, Brewster?" the dowager asked happily. "You taught me Long Whist so many years ago, and now I'll return the favor by teaching you this new version—only five points to win instead of ten. Goes much faster. You don't know the game yet, do you, Brewster?" she peered closely at him.

On Hawthorne's negative shake of the head, Lady Maitland took him over to the table, gestured for the Milvertons to join them, and they were off, Miss Essie and Miss Ellie looking over their shoulders and trying to get used to the new game.

"It seems Clausen arranged the best Christmas present he could possibly devise for Mama. I dare swear she finds a new companion at her card table even more gratifying than the return of the ring!" Tony said dryly to the family gathered cozily around him.

"Yes, he's certainly brought the spirit of the holidays to the Priory this year," Clio added with a laugh. "A real Father Christmas!"

# Winter Enchantment

## by Olivia Sumner

# *One*

After dismissing Jacob, his valet, for the night, Robert Gregory, Earl of Malden, strode to one of the narrow windows in his bedchamber and pulled back the burgundy draperies to stare into the darkness. Earlier he had glimpsed the evening star through the scudding clouds, but now the clouds had thickened and he heard the whisper of snow being driven against the window panes.

Lord Malden's mood was as dark as the stormy night. December had once been a month of joyousness in Malden Hall, but there would be scant joy this year. He had no spirit left for the trappings of Christmas, no one to wish him well and, God knows, enough enemies to wish him ill.

The winter wind swept round the great house like the avenging hawk on the Gregory family crest. A hawk in flight was the symbol of the family motto: *Vindex iniuriae*. An avenger of wrong.

Lord Malden smiled grimly. Most of his thirty years had been dedicated to being faithful to that motto. He would never have been able to return to this, his home, otherwise. In the end he had triumphed, crushing those who had paupered his father, a disgrace that led to the early deaths of both his parents and of his ailing elder brother as well. He had been the last of the Gregorys, a friendless, penniless orphan of thirteen, wanted by nobody.

Today he was one of the wealthiest men in England, and even more important to him, he had forced the usurpers from his family's estate and had thus returned in triumph to the place of his birth. More than once Malden Hall had been described as "a gloomy pile of stones situated at the end of nowhere." Still, this was his home, and by the grace of God, a lifetime of damn hard work, and a bit of luck, it was now his for good and all.

He derived satisfaction from knowing that he had achieved his revenge completely on his own; he had never once asked for assistance, nor would he. To Lord Malden, seeking help was a sign of weakness, besides being an invitation for someone to betray him.

Now, at last, it was over; everything he had vowed to accomplish was done. What did he care if everyone he knew and, quite likely, many who were complete strangers thought him a curmudgeon or worse? He nodded emphatically. He had no need for friends. No need at all.

As he allowed the draperies to fall back into place and turned from the window to warm himself at the fire, he was startled by the despairing yowl followed by a thudding crash coming from the next room. More accustomed to acting on his own than ringing for servants, he threw open the connecting door to the unused sitting room.

A bedraggled cat crouched in the unlit grate of the fireplace, its fur damp and streaked with soot. The animal's green eyes stared warily at him; obviously it considered him a threat.

"How the devil did you get in here?" he muttered even as suspicion flared in his mind. One of the servants had placed the cat in the room with the intent of bedeviling him. No, they would never dare! Incredible though it seemed, the cat must have fallen down the chimney.

His harsh words had alarmed the cat into flattening its ears and growling. Lord Malden's annoyance fled; he found himself shaken by a sudden sweep of sympathy for the forlorn animal. How well he knew the feeling of being cornered by an implacable enemy! Besides, you could trust an animal to be true to its nature. Unlike a human being it would never seek to deceive or betray you.

He pondered what he should do for a moment before finally sitting on the floor, hoping to look smaller and less threatening to the frightened cat. Recalling the way his father's old groom had once calmed a panicked horse that had badly injured one of the stableboys, Lord Malden began to speak in a low soothing voice.

"There now, puss, you have a friend; yes, you do. No one will hurt you as long as you have me to protect you. No one will dare hurt you. Come, puss, come to me."

The cat's ears perked up and the growling stopped. Pleased by the response, Lord Malden went on crooning to it, scarcely aware of what he was saying, intent on winning the cat's confidence. When the animal finally crept cautiously from the fireplace and inched toward him, he slowly offered his hand for the cat to sniff.

Very carefully he smoothed the matted fur behind the cat's ears until, reassured, the cat crawled onto his lap and began to purr. Eventually he was able to carry it into his bedchamber and lay it on his bed while he gently brushed off the worst of the soot with a towel.

"What shall I call you?" he wondered aloud. "Since you appeared from heaven as if by magic, you shall be Merlin, the magician."

Under the dirt, the cat's fur seemed to be a pale buff, but possibly it was white. "Merlin," he said, sitting on the bed next to the cat, "I daresay we may have to give you a bath to discover your true color."

Merlin looked at him and meowed piteously. Was the poor animal in pain? It had no obvious injuries.

There came a light tap at the door. "Milord?" Jacob said. "I thought I heard you call."

He bade Jacob enter. The valet, a handsome young man, stopped short, his mouth gaping open when his gaze fell on the cat. It was the first time Lord Malden had ever seen the usually impassive servant at a loss.

"As you can see I have a visitor," Lord Malden said. "What do you know about cats, Jacob? My friend Merlin here seems to be in some distress. Perhaps from his fall down the chimney."

Jacob closed his mouth and then the door. Coming to the bedside, he peered at the cat, being careful not to touch it.

"Well?" Malden asked after a time.

"Milord, I don't believe, uh—Merlin, did you say?—is a tomcat. Toms, to my knowledge, are unable to bear kittens, and I fear this one is about to birth a litter."

"Kittens?" Lord Malden stared at Merlin, who was now crouched on the bed and grunting. He watched in amazement as the unmistakable head of a kitten emerged from the cat's hindquarters.

"Sir, allow me to have one of the maids remove the animal to a more suitable place—I fear she's ruining your bedclothes."

Lord Malden shook his head. "My bedclothes be damned. She stays here; I refuse to have her disturbed. Since she chose me as her foster father, the least I can do is support Merlin in her travails."

Jacob frowned, his brow clouded, and his face took on an almost pained expression. "If you say so, sir."

"Since I expect her to be hungry once her family has arrived, you might bring Merlin some food—milk and a bit of the fish served at dinner ought to do nicely."

"Certainly, milord." As Jacob left, Lord Malden asked himself whether what he heard in the valet's voice had been disapproval or amazement or something else entirely. By God, he thought, Jacob had finally shown some emotion.

Jacob and every other servant in the house treated their new employer with stiff propriety. When he had returned the month before as master of Malden Hall, he had kept on all of the servants who wished to remain, which was everyone but Mrs. Avery's abigail and her housekeeper. He realized the servants were afraid to displease him and thus risk dismissal.

At least some of them, those dating back seventeen and more years to his father's time, had cause to fear him. Renfrew, the butler, Emma, the cook, and Lewis, in the stables, had worked for his father, then had stayed on after the Averys had forced his parents from their family home. His upper lip twisted in scorn. Such was human loyalty.

As soon as Merlin had cleaned her three kittens, two of them rooted blindly at her stomach, found teats, and began nursing. The third, smaller than the others, failed even to find its mother. Malden gingerly picked up the tiny kitten and carefully positioned it in the proper place. He was worriedly watching its struggles to locate milk when someone knocked on his door.

"Come in, Jacob," he muttered, his attention fixed on the kitten.

The door opened. "Beg pardon, sir, 'tis Renfrew, not Jacob," the elderly butler said as he entered the room. He gazed down his nose at the domestic scene on the bed. "Sorry to disturb you, milord, but there seems to be an awkward situation downstairs."

Malden glanced at him. Whatever had happened below must be completely out of the ordinary. "A situation *you* find yourself unable to cope with, Renfrew? That surprises me."

"Sorry, sir, this is quite beyond my experience. As you may know, the snow is falling heavily."

"And what is difficult about snow, pray tell?"

"In this sort of foul weather, I hardly felt we could leave the child on the doorstep, milord."

Renfrew's words succeeded in capturing Malden's entire attention. "Child? Child? What the devil are you talking about?"

"There came a knocking at the front door, sir."

"I heard nothing."

"Since I was on my way to retire for the night," Renfrew went on, "it took me some time to reach the door and open it. No one was there. That is, no one old enough to be able to reach the knocker. Whoever had plied it was gone, milord, but I regret to say whoever the person was, he or she left a baby on the doorstep. Unfortunately, I had little choice except to bring the child inside. Because of the snow."

Lord Malden rose from the bed, leaving Merlin to deal with her brood. "Where is this baby?" he demanded.

"Cook has taken her into the kitchen, it being the warmest room in the house."

"Her?"

"The child gives every evidence of being a female, sir."

The sooner he cleared up this ridiculous muddle the better. There was bound to be an explanation, and he meant to do all in his power to force it into the open without delay. With a last glance at Merlin and her kittens, Lord Malden let Renfrew lead the way down the back stairs.

317

Not only were Emma and Lewis in the kitchen, but at least half the household staff was gathered near the chopping table, where Malden found the cook in the process of fastening a clean linen towel around the baby's nether regions. Renfrew was correct—the child was undoubtedly a girl.

"I take her to be some five or six months old, milord," Emma said without being asked. "And lucky it is for us, her being big enough to learn to drink milk from a cup."

Lucky? How could Emma use the word in connection with a forlorn, unwanted baby abandoned on a stranger's doorstep in the midst of a snow storm?

Finishing with the improvised napkin, the cook lifted the baby and held her out to Lord Malden. Too surprised to refuse, he took her and held her at arm's length. The baby stared wide-eyed at him as she clutched at the sleeve of his dressing robe. Her chin quivered, and she began to wail. He didn't like *that* above half.

Without thinking, he shifted the baby against his shoulder and began to pat her back, trying to soothe her much as he had soothed the cat. "Hush, hush, little girl," he said softly. "You're safe in my house—no one will hurt you."

The baby's crying gradually lessened and then stopped completely as he continued to speak gently and pat her. Intent on the baby, he only gradually became aware of the gawking servants. "Do any of you know whose baby this is?" he demanded.

His question was met with averted eyes and shrugs but no answers. They might not know who the mother is, he thought, but they give every evidence of having their suspicions. He looked over the assembled servants. "Do any of you have experience in baby care?" he asked.

Again no one replied.

Gazing at the now-drowsy baby, he noticed for the first time that she had a tiny rose-colored ribbon tied in her dark hair. "Listen, little Rosie," he murmured to her, "my house is open to you. But as far as nursemaiding goes, you must make do with someone else."

"Pardon, milord." The timid voice came from a plump, red-cheeked girl standing at his elbow. "Me name's Hilda and I ain't never been no nursemaid, but I got six wee sisters at home I helped Ma with."

Lord Malden promptly handed the baby to her. "Your only duty henceforth will be to care for Rosie. I expect you to feed her and to sleep in the nursery with her. Do you understand, Hilda?"

"Yes, sir. I'll do me best."

He looked up as he heard the repeated banging of the great, bronze, front-door knocker reverberating through the house. *Damn, what now?* "I believe I shall answer that myself," he said.

Lord Malden marched through the corridors and rooms to the massive double doors in the entry hall, with Renfrew trailing behind. He grasped the right-hand knob and flung the door open.

"Oh, thank God!" a young woman cried as, covered with snow, she stumbled inside, half-falling over the threshold.

Lord Malden caught her, leaving the butler to wrestle the door shut against the cold blast of the wind. "Steady," Lord Malden said to the woman. "You're safe now."

"No, no!" she cried, drawing away from Malden. "I must not abandon poor Owens." Her green eyes gazed imploringly into his. "Please send someone to rescue my coachman before he freezes to death. He fell just inside your gate, and, unable to urge him to his feet, I was forced to leave him to go and seek help."

Lord Malden dispatched Renfrew to the kitchen to send two of the footmen to the coachman's rescue. Keeping an arm around the slight young woman, he led her into the drawing room where the remnants of the evening fire still burned in the hearth. He lit both of the wall lamps above the mantel.

"Owens is no longer young," she said distractedly, ignoring his attempts to remove her hooded cloak so she might better warm herself before the glowing coals. "I do hope they find him quickly, for his health is less than robust." She bit her lip. "I should never have allowed him to attempt this journey, but who else was there to drive the carriage?"

Lord Malden nodded, not wishing to distress her further by indicating that he had no idea what she meant. At last he managed to induce her to part with her now-dripping cloak, and as the hood slipped from her head, his eyes widened. This was no poor storm-tossed waif; rather, she was one of the loveliest young women he had ever seen, slightly bedraggled though she might be. Auburn curls cascaded over her shoulders, accentuating the vivid green of her eyes. Her long-sleeved, high-necked wool traveling gown, though drab in color, covered a far from drab form.

All in all, she was quite fetching.

"I must make certain Owens is all right," she said as she stripped off her gloves. "Will they bring him in through the front door?"

"More than likely by the kitchen entrance. In the meantime, allow me to introduce—"

"Please take me to the kitchen at once," she pleaded.

A niggle of doubt wormed its way into Lord Malden's mind. Did she intend to make a cat's paw of him? To bamboozle him? Many men had accused him of being hard hearted so perhaps he was wandering off course with his suspicions, but this worry about an old coachman seemed too much of a good thing.

Was he allowing his appreciation of her beauty to blind him to what might well be the truth? Did his snow maiden wish to be taken to the kitchen because she was searching for what she herself had left on his doorstep scant minutes before?

In short, was she no maiden at all but the mother of the abandoned baby? That must be the long and short of it; she had left the baby and now had returned to be certain her child had been found and was being cared for. Or perhaps she had suffered second thoughts about the wisdom of her actions.

"I am Lord Malden," he said curtly, "and this is Malden Hall." He offered her his arm. "Allow me to show you to the kitchen."

"Miss Julia Frost," she said, laying a tentative hand on his arm. "I fear I owe you an explanation."

"Just so." He clipped the words short and made no further conversation as he escorted her from the drawing room.

He sensed she was glancing at him curiously, no doubt noting his changed attitude and wondering if he had caught out her deception. Did she take him for a fool? Little did she realize that no one had taken advantage of Robert Gregory for

320

many a year. Trust no one was a lesson he had been forced to learn early in life.

He thought it unlikely her story of the coachman had been fashioned from whole cloth. Her speech, manner, and clothing labeled her as well bred, and Malden Hall was so distant from any other estate of any size that she must have arrived at his gates in a conveyance of some sort and that meant she'd had a driver. Whether the coachman was sickly and old remained to be seen.

"After Owens has been properly taken care of," Miss Frost said, "I intend—" She broke off abruptly, and he became aware that the baby had begun to cry again.

"Oh, dear," she said. "I trust your family will excuse any inconvenience I might have caused."

"I have no family." Bitterness edged his words.

"A servant's child, then?"

"No." She is an excellent actress, he admitted to himself. Anyone less easily cozened might very well be taken in by her. He wondered if, once faced with her baby, she would have the gall and the heartlessness to maintain her innocence.

He pushed through the swinging door to the kitchen, finding the room even more crowded than before; practically every servant on the staff was now here watching Hilda, who sat on a stool, trying to coax the fretting child to swallow milk from a mug. Only Jacob seemed to be missing.

"As you can observe," Lord Malden said caustically, "your child is quite well."

"My child?" She looked from him to the baby.

"Yes, the baby you abandoned on my front steps not more than thirty minutes ago. Do you take me for a fool, Miss Frost? I saw through your scheme at once."

"Surely you—"

The outside kitchen door opened and the two footmen entered, carrying an old man. "He's fair done in," one said as they laid him on the floor.

Julia Frost cried, "Oh!" and rushed to him, flinging herself down at his side and grasping his gnarled hand. "Owens," she said gently, bending over him, "this is Miss Julia."

Lord Malden frowned at the grizzled coachman, hearing

his attempt to speak to Julia end in a fit of coughing. Owens was indeed a sick old man, but fortunately, his was not a churchyard cough; with rest and proper care he should recover.

Could I possibly be mistaken about Miss Frost being the mother of the child? Malden wondered.

"Renfrew, have Owens taken to one of the guest rooms," he ordered. "See that a fire is lit, and see to it that someone tends him." He looked at the cook. "Emma, do you know any remedies for lung fever?"

Emma, a well-padded woman of a certain age, struggled to her feet. "I do, sir. 'Tis what I plan to dose him with, soon as I put the concoction together." She turned away and began setting the kitchen girls to various tasks.

"Pray, tell me Owens will recover," Julia said, still on her knees beside the old man.

"Emma is an excellent nurse, so I have every hope he will."

Tears brightened her eyes. "This is all my fault. If only I had had the sense not to attempt so much."

He reached down to help her up, but she shook her head and pushed herself to her feet without his assistance. She drew in a deep breath, her distress replaced by anger. "So you believe this baby to be mine," she said, nodding at the infant cradled in Hilda's arms.

Lord Malden was nothing if not stubborn. Even though he now doubted his original surmise, like a good soldier he refused to retreat under fire. "That seems the logical assumption, madam," he told her.

"If that is what you think of me," she said, "then I prefer to chance the storm rather than accept the so-called hospitality of Malden Hall."

She whirled away from him and ran from the kitchen. Taken aback, he hesitated before following, reaching the entry in time to see her open the front door and disappear into the swirling snow.

# *Two*

As soon as the wind-driven snow struck her face, Julia regretted her rash flight from the shelter of Malden Hall. Her anger at Lord Malden had caused her to forget the ferocity of the storm. How insufferable he was! How dare he accuse her of being the mother of that poor abandoned child? It was bad enough for him to believe she was a woman who would have a child out of wedlock, but to also reproach her for abandoning the baby was intolerable.

She refused to remain under his roof another moment. She would never go back!

Julia pulled the hood of her cloak over her head and, leaning forward into the chill wind, plodded ahead without any notion of where she was bound or what she intended to do when she arrived there. If she arrived anywhere in this storm. Without meaning to, she glanced back over her shoulder at the front door and, despite herself, gave a sigh of relief when she saw a dark figure appear in the yellow rectangle of light.

"Miss Frost!" Lord Malden called after her.

She turned angrily away from him to struggle once more through the deepening snow. She heard his muttered imprecations; then a hand gripped her arm, adding fuel to her anger. She swung around to tell him precisely what she thought of him.

Before she could speak, he growled, "Come back to the Hall."

So Lord Malden saw fit to command rather than request. "To be insulted by you again, sir?" she asked.

His hand dropped from her arm. "I meant no insult."

He had not the slightest intention of apologizing for his unseemly behavior, she decided. What manner of gentleman was this? If he expected her to be all meek compliance, he was sadly mistaken. Without a word, she whirled from him, preferring the fury of the storm to his overweening arrogance.

Again he gripped her arm. Without another word he spun her around and, putting his hand beneath her knees, swept her up into his arms. She gasped, surprised by his strength as, pinioned against his body, she struggled to free herself. To no avail.

"Are you demented?" he demanded as he carried her back toward the Hall. "Has all the world gone mad? First Merlin and then the kittens and then the abandoned baby and now you." Shaking his head, he looked up into the whirling snow. "Have I so displeased the gods that they see fit to punish me?"

Merlin? Kittens? *He* must be the demented one.

Lord Malden strode through the open door into the Hall, crossed the entry, and entered the drawing room where he deposited her full-length on a sofa. Looking up at him towering over her, the melting snow whitening his black hair and leaving beads of moisture on his face, she shivered. Not from fear; his gruffness failed to frighten her. From the chill of the night, then? Or could there be another reason entirely?

"Do I have your promise to behave sensibly?" he asked. "Or must I have you locked away for your own well-being?"

She sat up. "I give you my word not to bolt again," she said, "*if* you in turn apologize for your baseless accusations."

She could have taken an oath that his glowering face reddened. He started to speak, only to hesitate as his gaze remained fixed on her. As she saw his glare soften, her annoyance melted like the snow and she felt something pass between them, an acknowledgment, an understanding. Nothing like it had ever happened to her in all her nineteen years.

"You have my humblest apology," he said. "The baby girl is certainly not yours. How could I ever have believed it might be? I only wish I knew who the mother was. And the father as well."

"Could the father be Merlin?" she asked.

"Merlin? No, absolutely impossible." His lips twitched, and she thought he was about to smile, but he did not. "Merlin happens to be a cat who fell down my chimney tonight," he said, "and a she-cat at that, the mother of three kittens whose father also happens to be unknown."

He drew in a deep breath. "Enough of this maddening mull of babies and kittens; you must be exhausted. Margaret, one of our upstairs maids, will show you to your bedchamber, and my footmen will bring your belongings to your room. Perhaps the morrow will provide answers to our questions."

When Julia woke early to see motes of dust dancing in a ray of sunlight slanting across her bedchamber, she blinked as she sought to recall where she was. Of course, she reminded herself, she had found refuge in Malden Hall, home of the dour but intriguing Lord Malden. She had quite forgiven him for his behavior of the night before, realizing how overwrought he must have been after finding a baby on his doorstep.

Throwing back the bedcovers, she hurried to the window, her gaze roaming from the pristine whiteness of the snow-covered grounds of the Hall to the branches of evergreens drooping beneath their ermine mantles under the cloudless blue of the sky.

As she hurriedly dressed in a simple though, she hoped, flattering white muslin frock, she experienced an unexpected but vivid sense of anticipation. The reason, she admitted to herself, was that very soon she would see Lord Malden again.

He seemed so different from other men; proud, with a natural air of command. Yet able to readily admit error. And, of course, though dour he was quite handsome.

She first sought out Owens, finding the old coachman resting comfortably in the servants' quarters on the floor above hers.

"And what day is this?" he asked her.

"The twenty-second of December."

"Thank God, there still be three days till Christmas; I thought I might of lost a day or two. God willing, I'll be on me feet afore the holiday. I know your heart's set on getting to your uncle's by the twenty-fifth, Miss Julia."

After assuring him that his health was infinitely more important to her than her mission, she left Owens to make her way down the sweeping staircase to the breakfast room, where Emma came in from the kitchen to inform her that Lord Malden never ate this early; in fact, the master of Malden Hall rarely took a morning meal at all.

"How surprised I am to see no preparations in the Hall to celebrate Christmas," Julia said when Emma lingered, seemingly eager to talk.

"Nary a one. Not like the old days, with the sleigh rides and the feasting and a bit extra in the pockets of us that worked here. 'Twas when the master was a boy, that was, a time of joy and laughter in this house, not like nowadays when all is dark and drear. 'Twere happy days for us all then, make no mistake, miss, though little did we appreciate our good fortune at the time."

As Julia finished her meal of tongue, cold beef, bread, butter, jam, and coffee, Emma described in vivid and lengthy detail the overthrow of the Gregorys and the subsequent coldhearted reign of the off-putting Averys, followed by the recent triumphant return of the only surviving Gregory, the present Lord Malden.

"His heart was fair hardened by his adversities," she said and then, lowering her voice, added, "and there's some, mostly them what never knew him in the old days, that say he's past redemption."

"No one is beyond saving," Julia said emphatically, "especially not in this season of hope and joy, of birth and new beginnings for all the world. Perhaps it can be for Lord Malden as well."

"Kindness itself he is, underneath his rant and his scowl. Lord ha' mercy, look at how he took to them kittens and then agreed to care for that poor wee tyke out of the goodness of his heart."

"I feel so sorry for that dear little baby with no mother and no father."

Emma again lowered her voice. "Just between you, me, and the gatepost, there ain't much doubt in my mind who the bairn's mother is." Almost a year before, she told Julia, one of the upstairs maids, a certain Nellie Carson, had been dismissed by Mrs. Avery when it became obvious she was in the family way. Nellie had dropped from sight after that. "But I hear she's been seen in these parts lately," Emma added. "Her people live in Northbury, you know."

"Northbury!" Julia gave every evidence of being startled at the mention of the name of the village. "Is it possible that Malden Hall is near Northbury?" she asked.

" 'Tis no distance at all; less than three miles as the crow flies, a mite farther by the road through the forest. Most of Lord Malden's tenants live round about Northbury. 'Tis a bit of a surprise you've heard of our wee village."

"Northbury," Julia repeated. Shaking her head, she thought quickly, unwilling to fabricate but not wanting to reveal the complete truth either. "Northbury was mentioned in a letter from my uncle," she said. "I thought it much farther to the west."

Emma waited expectantly, but when Julia offered no more information she said, "As for the father of the babe, like as not he's one of the servants here at the Hall. As to which one, I got my suspicions but—" Emma stopped abruptly, glancing toward the door.

When Julia turned to follow her gaze, she saw Lord Malden in the doorway, holding a large wicker basket. "Suspicions are not enough," he said, speaking to Emma but with his eyes either unwilling or unable to leave Julia, "if the man refuses to acknowledge his daughter."

"Sad but true, sir," Emma acknowledged.

Lord Malden bowed as best he could to Julia. "This is Merlin—and her kittens," he said with a nod at the basket. "My room is draughty so I decided to bring them to live in Emma's domain."

At his invitation, Julia accompanied him and the cook into the kitchen. When Lord Malden placed the basket near the hearth, she knelt and peered down at Merlin and her litter.

"How tiny they are," she said.

Lord Malden knelt beside her, his sleeve brushing against her arm and making her acutely aware of his presence. "Last night," he told her, "Merlin plummeted down my chimney as though by magic."

"His—that is, her—appearance must have been an omen," she said, smiling up at Lord Malden.

"You actually believe in omens?"

"Of course. Everything that happens to us has a meaning; nothing occurs merely by chance. And usually omens come in threes. Could it be happenstance that Merlin fell down your chimney and a baby was left on your doorstep on one and the same day? The very same day the sun ended its southward journey and stopped to prepare to return north?"

He raised his eyebrows. "And your arrival was the third fateful event? Yes, you do believe that to be the case; I can read it in your eyes. Yet what do these omens portend, Miss Frost? Do they bode good or ill for Malden Hall?" He sighed. "If our history over the last twenty years is any guide, they bode ill."

"We may never learn precisely what the omens mean, but I prefer to believe they are favorable. Change is coming to the Hall, I suspect, and change for the better, not the worse."

"All life is change," he pointed out. "A prognosticator who merely foresees change is never in error, and if he at the same time foresees a downturn in fortune he assures himself of being right more often than not."

"What a gloomy man you are! For my part, I always expect the best. When you look for good fortune you usually find it."

He shook his head as though saddened by this new evidence of the mistaken optimism of youth. Then he stood and, as he helped her to her feet, said, "I had your carriage taken into the stables. Unfortunately one of the boxes in the boot broke open when the equipage left the road in last night's storm."

Although the gifts in the boxes were probably quite safe in the stables, Julia immediately expressed a desire to see the damage for herself. While the snow-spangled day was too beautiful for her to ignore, she had another reason for proposing an excursion to the stables. If she could but entice Lord Malden away from the dark confines of Malden Hall, perhaps she could work a miracle and brighten his bleak outlook on life.

As she expected, they found that the beribboned packages had escaped the mishap unharmed. "These are Christmas gifts I was taking to my uncle," she told him.

"Your uncle must be very dear to you to warrant this generosity."

"He is." She realized he expected to hear more of this uncle of hers, but she refused to be drawn, hoping he was too much of a gentleman to press her. Fortunately, peering into the dark recesses of the stable, she spied a means to divert his attention.

"Is that a sleigh?" she asked, knowing full well it was even though its red and black paint was faded, chipped, and covered with a thick coat of dust.

Nodding, Lord Malden said, "That must be the same sleigh I rode in when I was a boy. I never expected to see it again after all these years."

"With a little soap and water and a coat of wax for the runners, it would be as good as new."

He looked from the sleigh to her. "Do you want to . . . ? Would you like to . . . ?"

She nodded eagerly. He frowned and for a moment she thought he was about to have second thoughts, but then he said, "Miss Frost, may I have the pleasure of your company on a sleigh ride?"

When she said "Oh, yes, I'd like nothing better," he smiled at her for the first time, a rather captivating smile, she decided.

If only she could find a way to make him smile more often.

# Three

As they drove between the stone pillars and onto the high road, Julia exulted in the bite of the wintry wind on her face. They had left the somberness of Malden Hall and had entered a silent, magical world of white where the sun reflecting from the snow dazzled her and the only sounds were the snow-muffled beat of the horse's hooves and the faint hiss of the runners.

"At home at this time of year," she told Lord Malden, "we always burn a Yule log, we decorate the house with pine boughs and with holly, we organize tableaus, and we walk from house to house, singing carols." Caught up in happy memories, she sang, " 'God rest you merry, gentlemen, let nothing you dismay. . . .' "

"You have a lovely voice," Lord Malden said. When he glanced at her, his gaze lingering, she felt her face redden.

"I recall singing carols when I was a boy," he confessed, his voice becoming softer and sadder, "and listening to stories on Christmas Eve as we gathered around the hearth — my mother, father, and brother — not only the Bible story of the Christ child in the manger but fairy tales and ancient Celtic myths as well."

When he spoke of those long-ago days, she noticed that his look gentled and he seemed to become younger, almost boyish. "Though Christmas Eve is still two days distant," she said, "would you tell me one of those tales?"

He frowned and she thought he meant to refuse, but then he shrugged. "Your singing did remind me of one story my mother loved to tell," he admitted. "I never considered it a true Christmas story, though now I believe it might have been after all. You decide whether it is or not, Miss Frost.

"Once upon a time," he began, "in a land far to the east, there was a small kingdom by the sea. The old king had only one child, a young and beautiful princess, and this princess had three suitors, each of them a handsome prince.

" 'The time has come for you to marry,' the king told his daughter, 'for I am old and have no son.' When she agreed, the king summoned the three princes to his palace and said to them, 'You are all good and honorable men. If you will each offer my daughter a wedding gift, she will marry the one whose gift most pleases her.'

"So each prince visited the princess in turn. The first offered her great riches, promising her gold and silver and precious stones. The second offered her power, the opportunity to be the queen of a great kingdom.

" 'I have no riches to offer you,' the third prince told her, 'and, since I am the second son, I possess no kingdom.' And then he played his lyre and sang to her, the words of the song offering her his love and nothing more."

"And so she chose the third prince," Julia said.

"No, this princess happened to be neither romantic nor sentimental. She selected the first prince, not so much for his riches but because she admired the color of his eyes and the curl of his hair."

She stared at him and, seeing him smile, realized he was funning her.

"Of course she married the third prince," he said, "the one who offered her love."

"Just as I would have done," she said, "since love is so much more important than riches or pride of place."

When he said nothing, she looked at him from the corner of her eye and saw that he was deep in contemplation, but what thoughts occupied him he did not say, nor could she hazard a guess.

While he'd told the story they had been riding through a forest in which the trunks and branches of the leafless trees on either side of the road were etched in black against the white snow and the blue sky, but now the road left the forest and crossed fields divided by hedgerows. When Lord Malden stopped the sleigh at the crest of a low hill, they looked down at a cluster of houses and a steepled church.

"This is Northbury," he told her, feeling a twinge of guilt at the sight of the village, for he realized he had shamefully neglected his tenants during the last few months. He had not even taken the time to call on the new clergyman, a Mr. Davies. "Shall we drive into the village?" he asked.

His question was less than innocent, for earlier that morning, when he had paused in the doorway of the breakfast room, his curiosity had been piqued when he'd chanced to hear Julia exclaim at Emma's mention of Northbury. How would she reply to his suggestion to visit the village? he wondered.

Julia glanced quickly from the village to Lord Malden, much like an animal might when caught in a snare, he thought. "I have a better notion," she said. "Would you think me presumptuous if I suggested you bring a Yule log to Malden House? Instead of driving to the village, we could return to the forest, select a log, and you could send men with a team of horses to drag it to the Hall."

What was she concealing from him? he asked himself as a snake of suspicion slithered into his mind. He decided to approach the matter obliquely, and so he agreed to her suggestion and swung the sleigh in a circle and drove back toward the trees.

"I suspect Emma told you much of my family history," he said, "yet I know nothing about yours."

"My family is very ordinary," she said, going on to describe a happy childhood in Surrey as the youngest of five children of a country squire whose life centered around his family and his shooting, hunting, and fishing. Her two brothers and two sisters had married, leaving her the only child remaining at home.

"Now I know something of where you come from," he said, "but nothing of where you might have been going when you arrived so unexpectedly at Malden Hall last night."

"Do you prefer seasoned food or plain?" she asked.

He cocked a surprised eyebrow at her before answering, "Seasoned."

"I believe," she said, "that a woman without at least one small secret is akin to food served with no seasoning. For the moment, at least, allow me to keep my secret."

He scowled at this seeming confirmation of his suspicions. Miss Frost might be amiable; she was certainly sprightly and charming, and quite fetching in appearance; yet she also gave every evidence of being exceedingly devious. The Devil, he reminded himself, had made use of a woman, Eve, to bring about the fall of man and his expulsion from the Garden of Eden.

"Are you, perchance, acquainted with the Averys?" he asked.

"The family that wrested Malden Hall from its rightful owners? No, certainly not. I never heard of them until Emma told me the history of Malden Hall this morning."

Should he believe her? She looked so fresh of face, so very innocent, and yet innocence could well be the guise of the practiced deceiver. God knows, though, he wanted to believe her.

"Would you force me to reveal every secret of my heart?" she asked him. "I was on my way to my uncle when I arrived by misadventure at Malden Hall. You must be satisfied with that, my lord."

Perhaps a lover awaited her at her uncle's, Lord Malden told himself. If so, what possible concern was it of his? None at all. Then why had he felt a sudden pang of jealousy when she had hinted at an affair of the heart? Enough, Malden, he admonished himself, her romantic intrigues mean nothing to you. She would leave Malden Hall in a day or two, and that would be the end of it.

"We might drive in that direction," she said, nodding ahead of them to a track leading deeper into the forest.

He guided the sleigh from the road onto a pathway so narrow the branches of the trees met overhead. The snow had not been trampled here and in places the drifts forced their horse to slow.

"There," she said, "that fallen tree might be the very thing."

He stopped the sleigh in a small glade, and she sprang to the ground without waiting for him to help her, trudging through the snow to the deadfall. "A portion of this log will do," she said. "You will have it brought to the Hall?"

Vexed with her, both for harboring secrets and being unduly forward, Lord Malden refused to smile at her enthusiasm. Since he had had considerable practice in not smiling during the course of his life, he had little difficulty in accomplishing the

333

feat. He did, in fact, manage to scowl most convincingly.

"You look so frightfully serious and out of humor," she said. "What a stern taskmaster you must be."

Lord Malden started to protest that he was not in the least an overbearing master, that she misunderstood his character completely. Before he could utter a word, however, she reached down, packed snow into a ball, and threw it at him. He ducked, the snowball narrowly missing its mark.

He walked toward her, his hand held in front of him to ward off further missiles, and again, laughing, her face flushed, she packed a snowball and hurled it at him, the ball grazing his shoulder. When he was a few feet from her, he stopped to lean over and scoop up snow in both hands. Then he advanced on her as she backed away, shaking her head, still laughing, teasing him as she dared him to do his worst.

All at once she stumbled over a root hidden by the snow and fell backward. He rushed to her, letting the snow fall to the ground as he knelt at her side. "Are you all right?" he asked, concern evident in his voice.

Looking up at him looming over her, she drew in her breath, then nodded. He picked up more snow, raising his hand threateningly above her as though to wash her face, and she gasped. His gaze held hers, his brown eyes mesmerizing in their glittering intensity. All at once his face softened, and when he leaned down to her, she found herself unable to speak, unable to move, not knowing what to expect. The only sound she heard in the forest was the rapid beating of her own heart.

Leaning still closer, his cold lips touched hers in a tender, fleeting caress. She turned her head away, not because she wanted to but because she realized she should. His hands cradled her head, the snow on them cold on her cheeks as he turned her face so she looked up at him. Before she could protest, he kissed her slightly parted lips, this time with passion rather than tenderness, his kiss seeking, demanding. An answering passion swept through her, and before she could prevent herself she responded ardently. A belated prudence finally made her pull away, but she feared it was far too late. What must he think of her!

For a time neither of them spoke, neither of them moved,

and then Lord Malden pushed himself to his feet and reached down to help her to hers. She hesitated before allowing him to clasp her hand and pull her up beside him.

"Allow me," he said, reaching out to brush the snow from her coat.

She shook her head, not trusting how she might respond if she allowed him to touch her, and stepped away from him, brushing off the snow herself. Suddenly awkward with one another, they walked to the sleigh without speaking and soon were on their way back to Malden Hall.

Lord Malden was shaken. Never had a woman, much less one of such short acquaintance and one he distrusted, had such a devastating effect on him. He desperately wanted to prolong her visit to the Hall, and he vowed he would. Somehow. He could never ask her outright to stay, for Gregorys refused to beg and as a result were beholden to no one. No matter how charming he thought her to be, no matter how enticing, that was the way he was and that was the way he would remain. And yet he longed to do whatever else he could to keep her with him.

Julia soon became uncomfortable with the silence. Why was he so reluctant to talk to her? He must still distrust her, but there was no way to tell him what her destination had been and remain at Malden Hall. And she intended to remain as long as she could, since, from the very first, she had realized that this proud and prickly man, with heaven only knew what other faults still unrevealed, touched something within her that no man had ever touched before.

"That fallen tree we found in the forest would make a fine Yule log," she said at last, breaking the uneasy silence.

"I intend to have it hauled to the Hall later today."

When she glanced at him, she saw him staring straight ahead as though handling the reins required all of his attention.

"Besides lighting the log, we could sing carols on Christmas Eve and present a tableau of the Nativity as well as have a grand dinner for all of the servants." She smiled wryly. "You must consider me terribly presumptuous to be so free with Malden Hall."

I behave almost as though I were mistress there, she chastised herself.

"If we did all you suggest," he mused, as much to himself as to her, "the Hall might seem as it did years ago when I was a boy."

"I never attempt to relive the past," she told him. "When and if I reach the age of three score and ten, perhaps I may see fit to sit before the fire and reminisce, but not before then."

"I must seem ancient to you." Again, he almost smiled. "No, say nothing. I suspect I might not want to hear your opinion on the matter of my age." After a pause, he said, "Do whatever you wish for Christmas; consider Malden Hall to be yours to do with as you will until the clock strikes twelve on Christmas night when, I expect, you will disappear, leaving me with Merlin, her kittens, and the abandoned baby."

As he spoke an idea occurred to her, an improbable and unlikely scheme. Yet, she reminded herself, if she ventured nothing she could gain nothing. And, she was coming to realize, she had much to gain. "Before my coach turns into a pumpkin," she said, "I might very well be able to discover the identities of both the mother and the father of the baby, thus solving one of your problems."

"If you do," he said as they drove between the pillars at the entrance to Malden Hall, "you will have convinced me that miracles are still possible."

## Four

Julia realized she had a great deal to do and very little time in which to do it, but she was eager to begin for she had never been able to resist a challenge.

As soon as she returned from the sleigh ride with Lord Malden, she set to work, first enlisting the aid of Emma, Renfrew, and Jacob.

"The master wants to celebrate the Yule?" an astonished Emma asked. When Julia assured her he did, the cook said, "Lord love us, 'tis a miracle," while casting a speculative and admiring look at Julia as though wondering what sort of spell she had succeeded in casting on Lord Malden.

Did they have a supply of Christmas candles in the Hall? Julia wanted to know. They did not, but as many as needed could be purchased in Northbury. Could holly and evergreen boughs be brought from the forest? They could. Did mistletoe grow nearby? Yes, on some of the hawthorns in a nearby grove. What of a fatted pig and other delicacies for Christmas dinner? There was just such a pig. Were there materials in the Hall to fashion clothes for the tableau of the Nativity scene? If not, they could easily be obtained.

There had always been guised dancers in Northbury, Renfrew recalled, but these disguised pranksters had long avoided Malden Hall. Could they be encouraged to reconsider? Julia asked. Renfrew expressed doubts, but he would make inquiries.

At last satisfied that all her desired preparations were understood and well under way, Julia climbed the great staircase to her chamber, where she wrote two letters, one directed to a resident of Northbury, the other to her father in Surrey assuring him of her safety. As soon as she sealed the letters with wax, she sent a stableboy to Northbury to personally deliver one letter and to post the other.

Early the next morning, before Lord Malden was up and about, Edmund, the coachman, was surprised to find himself driving the young Miss Frost to Northbury in the Malden landau and was astonished when he discovered the cottage that was her destination. He noted with interest that, as they drove through the village, Miss Frost drew her cashmere shawl up about her face even though the day was not at all windy and, in fact, was quite mild for the end of December.

When she returned to Malden Hall, Julia discovered Lord Malden waiting for her on the front steps. "The Yule log is in the stable yard," he told her as he helped her from the carriage, "ready to be brought to the hearth."

She shook her head. "The log must remain outside the house until tomorrow," she told him, "until the twenty-fourth." When he gave her a questioning look, she explained. "A Yule log in the house before Christmas Eve," she said, "brings bad luck. And, once lit, the log should be kept burning for the entire twelve days of Christmas as a sign of the hospitality visitors will receive at Malden Hall."

Although he raised his eyebrows, he said, "As you wish." Escorting her into the Hall, at first he watched her preparations for the holiday with amusement, as a parent might observe a favorite child at play, then with some slight degree of consternation as the servants, preoccupied with Miss Frost and Christmas, seemed to forget that *he* was the master of Malden Hall; but finally, when she asked for his suggestions and advice, he little by little began to help her and, wonder of wonders, found himself enjoying the task.

As for Julia, are there any young ladies who never imagine themselves the mistress of a great house? She realized she risked having him think her presumptuous, but she was unable to resist seizing this opportunity to celebrate Christmas as she felt it should be celebrated while at the same time attempting to rescue Lord Malden from his self-imposed misanthropy. And she had another objective, one she only half-admitted to herself; that was to be with him for as long a time as possible.

At her coaxing, he climbed onto a stool in the entry while she handed him branches of holly, the "Holy Tree," to place atop a portrait of his great-great-grandfather.

"I often wonder when the custom of decorating with evergreens began," she said.

"Perhaps in Biblical times," he said, climbing down. "If I remember aright, it was Isaiah who said, 'The glory of Lebanon shall come unto thee, the fir tree, the pine tree, and the box, to beautify the place of my sanctuary.' "

"I never heard that verse before," she admitted, surprised that he had.

"When I was in search of furs in Canada," he told her, "I spent a winter in the wilderness with only the Bible as a companion."

She knew so little about him, she realized. And wanted to know so much. When she questioned him, he told her, at first reluctantly but then with fervor, of his years in America, of his success in the fur trade, of his grudging admiration for the savage Indians, and of his return to England to become master of Malden Hall.

"If there were a mistress at Malden Hall," she said, "she would be the one in command during the next twelve months."

He blinked in confused surprise. "And how did you ascertain that?"

"By seeing how smooth the leaves of these holly branches are."

"I suppose if they were prickly the opposite is true."

She smiled. "Exactly, my mother always said that would mean the master would rule until the following Christmas."

"Do you actually believe these superstitions?" he asked with a skeptic's smile.

"Oh, yes." She smiled up at him as, on the stool once again, he placed holly over another of his ancestor's portraits. "At least I do for the most part," she added, teasing him a bit because he seemed so serious and because he obviously did not believe, and yet she was truthful in her answer. "There are others. I also believe the Yule log should be lit by a brand from last year's log. And if an unmarried young lady happens to see an eligible man in a looking glass on Christmas day, that will be the man she marries."

His look said, "What nonsense," but he held his tongue as he stepped down from his perch and carried the stool to the archway between the entry and the great hall.

"No, no," she said when he started to mount the stool again, "this is one decoration that must be set into place by a woman, else no good fortune will ensue."

He helped her climb onto the stool, then handed her the Kissing Nough, a large and elaborate arrangement of holly, ivy, and other greens; of colored ribbons and paper roses; of apples and oranges; and three small dolls representing Jesus, Mary, and Joseph.

"All these odd notions of what represents good and bad fortune and what brings bad luck must have passed me by unawares," he said. "Are there still more?"

"Many more. When I visited my Aunt Pamela in Derbyshire two Christmases ago, we played an intriguing game. On Christmas Eve, my aunt brewed a posset of boiling milk and ale, bread, ginger, sugar, and nutmeg. My uncle placed the bowl in the center of the table, and all the single ladies and gentlemen gathered round.

"My aunt dropped a wedding ring, a bone button, and a coin into the bowl, and each of us began to drink by using a long-handled spoon to dip into the very bottom of the bowl. Whoever brought up the ring would be the first to marry; whoever dipped up the bone was fated to be an old maid or an old bachelor; and the one who retrieved the coin would become the richest."

As she spoke, Julia attached the Kissing Bough to a hook in the archway, tied a sprig of mistletoe to the bottom of it and started to climb down from the stool.

"Allow me," he said, reaching up and grasping her about the waist. "And which prize was yours?" he asked, his hands almost girdling her waist, his brown eyes holding her in thrall.

She seemed unable to speak; he felt her tremble. "Which was yours?" he asked again.

In a voice so low it was almost a whisper, she said, "The bone button."

He lifted her from the stool and swung her to the floor so she stood facing him. Forgetting where he was, oblivious to everything but Julia Frost, his arms enfolded her, drawing her to him. "Allow me to prove how misguided these notions are," he said, leaning over to kiss her.

For a moment she was drawn toward him; then, shaking her head, she pushed him away, turned, and ran from the hall.

Lord Malden stared after her in dismay, angered at himself. She was a guest in his house, after all, and he had thrown propriety to the winds by attempting to kiss her. Not only had he tried to kiss her, he had done it in a place where anyone might witness his transgression.

Yet, he reasoned, she had enticed him by having him help her hang the Kissing Bough. She was a temptress, not only a temptress but a young lady with a penchant for deceiving him. Why had she refused to reveal her reason for arriving at Malden Hall in the midst of a snow storm? Without a doubt she had used her wiles on some other man and had been on her way to keep a rendezvous with him when fate brought her here.

If only he possessed more experience where young ladies were concerned, he might know how to cope with Miss Frost. He had, however, been so determined to avenge himself and his family that he had had no time to learn the ways of fashionable young women. But did it really matter? In a few days, he told himself, she would leave Malden Hall and that would put an end to his dilemma.

He should, he knew, find the thought of her departure comforting. Instead, he was devastated by the idea that he would never see her again or talk to her again or, yes, he admitted with a rueful sigh, kiss her again.

Lord Malden was still entangled in this web of confused conjecture late the following day, Christmas Eve, when he joined the servants and their families in a great hall aglow with the light from a multitude of candles. Outside, the night was clear and cold, a half-moon throwing pale shadows across the snow. The wind soughed in the bare branches of the trees and moaned around the eaves and chimneys of the Hall.

Julia led Owens, now almost completely recovered from his

malaise, into the great hall and escorted him to a straight-backed chair near its center. Her coachman, she explained as she sat on a hassock beside him, wanted to contribute to the festivities and so had agreed to relate Christmas tales he had heard many years before when he was a lad in Cornwall.

He told them stories replete with portents and wonders, of cocks crowing all night on Christmas Eve and of angels visiting the earth. He told them of a village in Cornwall where the people's wickedness rivaled that of Sodom and Gomorrah, a village more evil than any other in all of England. The Lord, greatly displeased, visited the village in the guise of a beggar, but wherever he sought help he was turned away with oaths and blows.

In his anger, the Lord caused a great earthquake to destroy the village, burying all the houses beneath many feet of rocks and soil. To this day, Owens affirmed, if on Christmas Eve you go to the place where the village once stood and, on the stroke of midnight, kneel and place your ear to the ground, you can hear the village church bells toll far beneath the earth.

He told of cattle kneeling at the stroke of midnight on Christmas Eve to pay homage to the Christ child, and of birds and animals briefly gaining the power of speech. One farmer, he averred, a wicked young man who had betrayed a woman who loved him by abandoning her after she gave birth to his child, scoffed at this notion and, to prove himself right, hid in his stable on the night before Christmas.

"A few minutes later," Owens went on, "the wicked young man was amazed to hear his oxen speak. 'We are going to have a hard and heavy task to do later this week,' one said. 'How is that,' a second answered, 'since the harvest is in and we have drawn home all the winter fuel from the forest?' 'That may be so,' the first replied, 'but we shall have to drag a coffin to the village churchyard, for our master will most certainly die before the week is out.'

"On hearing this dire prophecy," Owens told them, "the farmer cried out and fell to the stable floor where he was discovered the next morning, having come to a most untimely end."

The great hall was silent when Owens finished, the assembled servants and guests obviously struck with a sense of awe and wonderment. Emma sat staring wide-eyed at Owens, Lord Malden noticed, Renfrew rocked slowly back and forth with his arms folded and his eyes closed as he mumbled silent prayers, while Jacob was hunched in upon himself with one hand concealing his face. Even Lord Malden, who deemed himself a modern, rational man, felt his skin prickle when the restless wind came up, moaning around the house as though in frustration while it sought entry through every crack and cranny.

Julia, wearing a white sarcenet gown with lace-trimmed puffed sleeves, an ermine band trimmed with seed pearls encircling hair dressed high on her head, walked slowly forward carrying the abandoned baby in her arms. At the same time Lord Malden saw young boys carrying shepherd's crooks begin to gather at one end of the hall near a group of girls garbed in white and wearing angel wings.

"We intended," Julia said, "to present a series of tableaus tonight while we listened to the Christmas story as told in the gospel of St. Luke. As you see, we have the child for the scene in the manger" — she nodded at the baby in her arms — "and we have the mother of the child."

Julia held out one hand, and when a young woman, a stranger to Lord Malden, stepped hesitantly forward, the spectators murmured one to another. She curtsied to Julia and then took the baby from her. This young woman, dark and pretty, wore a plain gown of royal blue and a white cloak with the hood covering her black hair.

"Who is she?" Lord Malden whispered to Lewis who stood next to him.

" 'Tis Nellie Carson, milord," Lewis said.

Lord Malden frowned as he searched his memory. Finally he recalled who Nellie Carson was. "The upstairs maid who was sent packing?"

"One and the same, sir. Increasing by leaps and bounds she was."

Of course, Nellie Carson was the maid who found herself in a family way. *She* must be the mother of the baby. He shook his head. How on earth had Miss Frost discovered her identity and her whereabouts?

"We do not, however," Julia said, "have anyone to portray

343

Joseph."

Lord Malden could hardly credit this statement. To have selected actors to portray the shepherds, the angels, Mary, and the child, as well as the three wise men he had noted off to one side, and not to have anyone to portray Joseph was not like Miss Frost at all. She was too clever by half to omit such a leading character in her tableaus unless she had done so on purpose.

"Will someone pray favor me," Julia said, "by stepping forward to take the part of Joseph?"

The assembled servants looked at each other, the men uneasily shuffling their feet while the women whispered to one another behind their hands. The pause lengthened. Did she want *him* to play the role? Lord Malden wondered. Had she chosen to portray Mary herself, he would have offered his services in an instant but as it was . . .

Hearing a rustle of excitement, he glanced over the heads of those standing to his right and saw Jacob walking hesitantly toward Miss Frost. Without looking at her or at Nellie Carson or at the baby, Jacob mumbled, "I will, ma'am."

Julia took the baby from Nellie's arms and offered it to Jacob. For an instant he made no move; then he reached out and, taking the infant, cradled it awkwardly in his arms. A sigh swept the assemblage, a sigh accompanied by the sage nodding of heads. Realization dawned on Lord Malden: Jacob was the baby's father!

Julia, who had walked over to stand at one side, began to read the familiar words of St. Luke, " 'And it came to pass in those days, that there went out a decree from Caesar Augustus, that all the world should be taxed. . . .' "

As she read, Lord Malden watched her, full of admiration, not merely for her beauty but for her cleverness as well. Was it possible that Jacob had been led to reveal himself merely by the solemnity surrounding Christmas Eve heightened by the spell cast by the tales of the old coachman? No, not likely. Not after keeping his secret all these months. There must be more to what had just transpired.

While Lord Malden had no notion of what it was, he certainly meant to find out.

## *Five*

Christmas dinner was served at two on the following afternoon and when, after almost three hours, the festivities ended, there was naught but praise for Emma and her kitchen helpers, who had prepared and served the roast pork, the Christmas goose, the minced meat pies, the Christmas cakes of molasses and spices, the plum pudding, and all the other meats, fish, vegetables, puddings, cakes, and assorted delicacies.

At the conclusion of the meal, glasses of Madeira were raised in toasts to Lord Malden and in praise of his generosity, the more welcome because so unexpected, and to Miss Julia Frost who, besides providing the inspiration for the celebration and the spirit to make it a success, had also contributed the small gifts that she had brought in her carriage; these consisting mainly of oranges, sweetmeats, dolls, and toys for the children of the servants.

After the last gift had been unwrapped and the last toast proposed, Lord Malden turned to Julia, intending to praise the success of her efforts, but she had left his side and was nowhere to be seen.

Renfrew approached. Clearing his throat, the butler announced, "Miss Frost awaits you in the drawing room, milord."

Lord Malden strode across the entry hall, stopping abruptly in the doorway of the drawing room, taken aback. Julia, facing away from him as she looked down at the leaping flames of the fire, was dressed as she had been on the night of her arrival — was it possible she had come to Malden Hall only four days ago? — in a long, hooded gray cloak.

Feeling inordinately out of sorts, he walked slowly toward her. She turned to greet him with a joyless half-smile; he stopped, unsure of himself and once again awkward in her presence.

"Owens is quite recovered," she said, "and so we must be on our way. I can never thank you enough, Lord Malden, for extending the hospitality of Malden Hall to me as well as to Owens in our time of need."

He bowed a stiff acknowledgment. "I must thank you," he said almost shyly, "for encouraging us to celebrate the Christmas season."

She sighed. "If only the guised dancers had come from Northbury, the festivities would have been complete. Perhaps after they learn of the gracious reception they would have received, they will reconsider and visit Malden Hall next year."

What did he care if the guised dancers came another year? Or ever? Her presence was what mattered. He started to tell her so and barely caught himself in time. Obviously she cared nothing for his feelings; otherwise why would she be in such a hurry to leave?

Her mention of Northbury recalled her reluctance to drive into the village with him and brought back all of his questions about the possible reasons behind Miss Frost's precipitous arrival. Had she driven through the storm-tossed night to keep a rendezvous? Whatever her mission might have been, he, for one, did not intend to detain her at Malden Hall. Not only did he have no excuse to do so, it appeared evident to him that she had no inclination to linger. Why then, with all his doubts about her, did he feel in his heart that when she left his only hope for happiness would leave with her?

She had succeeded in bewitching him, that could be the only logical explanation for his strange urge to take her in his arms and plead with her to remain at Malden Hall. No! Gregorys had always been self-sufficient. They need rely on no one but themselves; they begged no favors from young ladies no matter how enticing their green eyes, how lovely their auburn curls, or how beguiling their smiles. Though it was not merely her pretty face that attracted him but her inner beauty as well. She had filled Malden Hall with light and warmth.